CHARACTERS

ADAM KANE	OWNER OF LO GARRANTRAA COUSIN OF ZEO NEPHEW OF ELLANNA/APRILIS
ZEO	YOUNGER SON OF CONSUL PRIMUS AND APRILIS
JOHNNY PRENDERVILLE	LIFELONG FRIEND OF ADAM BROTHER OF ADAM'S …
'PRAVUS' SORUS	GOVERNOR OF …
PUTO POLLUX	DEPUTY
REPTUS REPTUM	HERPET…
SUGA CAZO	COMMA…
ZEOR	CONSUL
APRILIS	WIFE OF …
ZEOR JNR	ELDER SO…
LIVIA	ONLY DAU…
EUANDER	NEW RECR… … *OPTIO* TO ZEO, ADAM AND JOHNNY
CAMILLA	ZEOR JNR'S FIANCÉE
BALLIO MAXIMUS	GOVERNOR OF *ORIENS* ABDUCTER OF ELLANNA DIDO'S BIOLOGICAL FATHER
DIDO	DAUGHTER OF BALLIO MAXIMUS FIANCÉE OF 'PRAVUS' SORUS
PORCIA	FORMER HOUSEKEEPER TO OTHO NOW HOUSEKEEPER TO ZEO'S FAMILY
GENERAL ELECTRA	FOUNDER OF SITANTAL'S FIRST ALL FEMALE CAVALRY CORPS, *VIRAGO*
SEMELE	ABANDONED WIFE OF 'PRAVUS' SORUS *VIPERA DOMINA*
BELVIA	FIRST WIFE OF BALLIO MAXIMUS DAUGHTER OF URSUS
URSUS	PREVIOUS GOVERNOR OF *ORIENS* FATHER OF BELVIA
COMMANDER OTHO	FORMER WARDEN OF TABO PRISON NOW IN CONSUL PRIMUS ZEOR'S FORCES
MAI PRENDERVILLE	JOHNNY'S MOTHER
TERRY PRENDERVILLE	JOHNNY'S FATHER
PIPPA PRENDERVILLE	JOHNNY'S SISTER
AMBER DE VINE	JOHNNY'S GIRLFRIEND
MRS MOUNSEY	ADAM'S NEIGHBOUR IN TRIDENT VALE
DON BALDWIN	ADAM'S LAWYER
PHILLIP BALDWIN	DON BALDWIN'S FATHER
GINO COSTANTINO	RESTAURATEUR *'GINO'S RISTORANTE ITALIANO'*
FRIDAY	ADAM'S GOLDEN LABRADOR
CANDEO	EUANDER'S WHITE COLT

BELOW MOUNTAIN AND SEA©

VOLUME THREE

THE TEMPLE OF THE GODS©

JAMES A. CRANEY

TO MY SISTER MAUREEN

CHAPTER ONE

Early morning. March Sixth.
What should have started off as a well deserved and triumphant journey home for the two conquering heroes of Sitantal was anything but that. No sooner had the honour escort to the two *Praecipuum* become a departing convoy, a deep gloom descended on the pair. They both remembered the first time they'd entered *Secundus* from *Tertius* and how elated and exhilarated they'd been then but there was no exuberance now.

The suddenness of the parting was by far the hardest thing to bear; even Adam who'd recognised all along that their mission would be over when they'd freed Zeo's family now felt that it had ended a tad too soon. But having to stand idly by as the Consul Primus and his men had overrun the enemy camp the previous night had made him feel as though he and Johnny were intruders in a private affair. Even though the leader had explained that the exclusion was for their protection, it had riled him slightly at the time. He was now positive that his friend Johnny had reached a similar conclusion when he'd announced that it was time for them to go home. Johnny's silence on the way to *Extremus* during the night spoke volumes for how he'd felt, Adam deduced. Even now as he briefly reflected on the events of last evening he felt that they should have had an input into the plans regarding their departure from the place where they'd freed Zeo's family and the other political prisoners and had given them an opportunity to free their country from the despot 'Pravus' Sorus. The other thing which had made these events unpalatable for him was when his dog had declined to leave with him, even though he'd put a brave face on it at the time to hide his disappointment. But inwardly it had been disheartening and galling!

Feeling uncomfortable on where his musings were taking him Adam deliberately abandoned his querulous thoughts by turning to his uncharacteristically silent friend.

'I think we should hit the road straight away Johnny. I also think we should wait until we reach home before having a chinwag about everything! Is that okay with you?'

'Absolutely! I'd prefer not to think about it right now Adam so I'm definitely not in the mood to talk about it!'

These laudable intentions suffered an onslaught of mental anguish from word go when each of their brain's Limbic System's bombarded their psyche with destructive emotional diktats and ideas with all of them potentially soul-destroying if allowed to flourish. Luckily their Primary Motor Cortex's exercised motivational control and spurred them onwards at quite a pace. By mid-afternoon they'd reached the area where the Spit-fire buzzards had experienced the ground-to-air fiery counter-attack almost six weeks ago.

The propelling urge to reach the outside world gained further momentum and by late evening they'd traversed over half the distance through *Secundus*. Though their thoughts were miles away they were aware that the few Spit-fire buzzards they spotted overhead showed no interest in them. They noticed too that the white rabbit population in the western sector appeared to have multiplied since their previous trek and when they entered the eastern sector they witnessed a similar increase in the volume of white rats scuttling about, almost carefree.

At nine o'clock they agreed to take a six hour rest period and unpacked the old Moka pot and their meagre ration of ground coffee and had their first fix of the day. Oddly for them the desire to have one sooner had never crossed their minds such was the urge to get out of here. They dined on just a portion of the saliva inducing food packed for them by the plump little housekeeper Porcia, who'd become almost inconsolable when she'd been told that her *'paulus puer'*, little boy, Johnny was leaving. Touched deeply by this reaction he'd given her a big hug and almost swept her off her feet. This had made matters worse and she blabbed noisily into her apron. Johnny hastily searched through the odds and ends in his belt pouch and fished out a smiley-face key fob and presented it to the sweet-natured lady. She'd become so enamoured with the little token that she completely forgot to cry anymore.

On the previous evening when Adam and Johnny had prepared for the journey home they'd retained just the basics of equipment that they thought they'd need for their protection in *Extremus*. They'd given the remainder of the stuff to Zeo and Adam suggested he try find someone mechanically and technically minded who might be able to replicate some of the weapons and equipment they'd brought with them to Sitantal. They'd been invaluable to them in the past and he was sure that 'Pravus' Sorus would throw everything he had at the Consul Primus when they met in battle which was bound to happen in the not-too distant future he predicted.

Their friend was almost overwhelmed when they'd given him the unused spare Moka pot and virtually the entire coffee supply in their possession but when Adam handed him a small sachet of green Arabica coffee beans and suggested he try and cultivate them here; that he believed the climate would be ideal, he was thrilled.

    At three o'clock on Sunday morning the pair trekked eastwards again and like the previous day, most of the conversation between them was about their surroundings and the occasional recognition of previous landmarks they'd encountered in *Secundus*. Just after nine o'clock they reached the gaping entrance to *Tertius*. They brewed up and sat back gazing into the bright and airy landscape they'd covered in record time and knew that what they'd have to face over the next few days would be much more perilous and unpleasant for them.

It took them the best part of an hour to get used to the dreary sogginess and the dismal blackness of *Tertius* but though they had tumbles after stumbles on the slippery uneven ground they resisted the temptation to use the only torch they now had, having gifted the other two together with the last remaining unused batteries to Zeo. They craned their necks looking out for any signs of Three-fanged snake-rats, One-horned boring-bats or Two-mouthed gigantic speed-worms but so far their presence in their habitat hadn't stirred these voracious carnivores into action. Besides having to remain vigilant for these creatures they also had to try to pinpoint familiar features in the surrounding landscape to make sure they kept to the right track to the exit which they found to be a difficult and near impossible task having viewed the gloomy place from a totally different perspective on their inbound journey. They trudged forward and used instinct as their guide for most of the time. The dank depressing atmosphere compelled them to rest more that once and before four in the afternoon they stopped and had their second helping of Porcia's appetising fare.

They carried onwards into the late evening until they found a narrow ledge wide enough for two sleeping bags where they settled for the second six hour rest.

On Adam's watch it had just gone four o'clock on Monday morning when they finished their coffee and continued the journey through the environs of the third region in *Extremus*. Just like the two previous days the conversation was limited and the coffee breaks were even less frequent.

Four hours into the trek they spotted a Three-fanged snake-rat dash behind a cluster of slimy rocks about a hundred feet to their right but they were able to relax and re-upholster their weapons when they saw it move quickly downhill in the opposite direction. Here they finished their last portion of real food and from here-on-in they would have to survive on the few remaining bars of misshapen chocolate in Johnny's backpack.

It was almost nine o'clock when they reached the windy section they'd experienced when they'd first entered the underground world with Zeo and knew that they were now mere miles away from the outside world. Though their weary muscles ached and pleaded for some respite their emotions told them otherwise and they opted not to bed down for the night. But they did have one last coffee break before making the final push forward. It was almost six o'clock on Tuesday morning on the ninth of March when they reached the exit chamber below the high plateau on Garrantraa Mountain.

Johnny crossed the damp floor and pulled on the iron and lead counterbalanced lever.

The rock door closed silently behind them as soon as they'd stepped outside into the bracing but nevertheless embracing mountain breeze.

They both felt a surge of relief but also a shock to their systems when they stood there just as dawn was breaking on Garrantraa Mountain. Even though Adam reckoned that spring was technically about two weeks away he felt that it was already in the air. The snow had totally cleared at ground level but when he tilted his head and gazed skywards he could see the white rugged peaks where it held fast. He and Johnny paused for a few moments to take it all in before moving downhill through the sodden mountain forest. They crossed over the fast flowing tributary river and into Wildwood and weaved their way into Texas where they paused again to view the welcoming landmarks of home in the far distance.

As soon as they passed behind the large barn they were able to get a clear view of the house and both friends uttered an involuntary cheer of satisfaction together.

'It's great to be back home again, Johnny!'

'Yeah, Adam! Oddly enough I agree with you about that, though I never thought I would!'

He went upstairs to shower as Adam set about stoking the Rayburn and raiding the freezer for breakfast but spotting Friday's empty basket beside the cooker brought a lump to his throat and without finishing what he was doing he carried it out of sight into the pantry.

Within a quarter hour the smell of sausage, bacon and hash browns sizzling on the pan filled the kitchen. When Johnny returned he was dressed in the clothes more in keeping and contemporary with their present surroundings and it was at this point it became more obvious to Adam that his friend had shed quite a few pounds since he'd taken part in their joint adventure.

When Johnny took charge of the culinary task at the cooker Adam hurried off to the shower and like his friend discarded the clothing worn in the world below mountain and sea and in the process he realised that he too had become much leaner.

The only things they discussed over breakfast was what they'd do later, all mention of Sitantal was deliberately avoided again. Adam suggested they have a short rest and then return to Trident Vale and if Johnny had no objections he'd like to call with Don Baldwin and Tom Reagan at Gallendon on the way.

Johnny wakened Adam at one o'clock and told him the kettle was on the boil and added that he was going to get the Range Rover from the shed.

When Don Baldwin's secretary told Adam that her boss would be in the High Court in the Capital until Friday he arranged to meet on the following Monday and fifteen minutes later when a visibly nervous Mrs Reagan saw Adam on her drive he reassured her straight away that Friday was fine and that he was with his cousin. He told her he'd call again on Monday afternoon when she said that Tom was playing football after school and wouldn't be home until late evening. He was more than pleased when she told him that Sally was expecting pups in about three or four weeks from now.

Mai Prenderville whooped with pleasure when she received the telephone call from her only son as the Rover sped along the dual-carriageway to Trident Vale. She caused ear-rasping distortion on the cell phone's speaker with her high-pitched squeals when he told her that he and Adam would be home before five o'clock. She insisted that Adam have dinner with them later and that he stay overnight.

Mai, Terry and Pippa were waiting at the front door when they arrived at Johnny's home and they could barely control themselves. Before the car had stopped fully on the drive they wrenched the doors open to greet them, literally dragging both of them from the Range Rover. They were kissed, squeezed and embraced with so much pizzazz it was breathtaking for both of the returnees and left them reeling and exhausted. Eventually everyone ran out of steam and separated, laughing and giggling at the manner they'd welcomed home two of the most important and special people in their lives.

But it was a great thing to be able to do and they'd enjoyed every minute of it!

CHAPTER TWO

Antemeridianus, Martius VI.

When Zeo, together with his brother and the returning mounted escort raced across the open plains of *Oriens* before dawn and reached the freed prisoners temporary base, he'd found his father inspecting a group of soldiers who were about to board the fleet of *naviculae* moored on the Trans-*Medius* canal and a troop of mounted men were waiting restlessly on the dirt track running parallel with the wide channel. The Consul explained that they were going to attempt to take Esta City in northern *Medius* before word got out about their escape from Nox or about the rout of the new outpost in northern *Oriens* last night. They had to act immediately before the city's defences could be strengthened by forces loyal to Sorus and Maximus. He was pretty certain the city's population had remained true to him during the putsch. If successful they could then establish a more permanent base where there would be suitable accommodation for the women and younger people and easy access to a more reliable food supply; the city being close to the province's agriculture heartland. From here they could despatch messengers to the various regions for their allies and supporters to join them he averred. He insisted that his sons and the escort remain at the temporary camp as protection but also to have a rest before joining him because everyone needed to be alert and fighting fit from now on.

Zeo's mother Aprilis fussed around her two weary boys insisting they have food and drink following their overnight dash. Zeor junior accepted eagerly but Zeo explained that he first had to pray to the Gods for his friends' safe journey home through *Extremus* among other things. With so much happening recently he'd neglected speaking with Them for far too long he explained.

He left his mother and brother and took the short journey to a small annexe nearby and on the way he paused and waved to Livia and Camilla as they meandered through the camp in the little painted carriage being drawn by a happy looking Felix.

Friday cavorted alongside the tittering pair.

The pleasing sight made him think afresh of how much this nation owed his two friends and the pangs of doubts which had troubled him on the ride back to base now resurfaced once more.

When he'd said farewell to his friends he'd begun to think more clearly about his father's decision that Adam and Johnny should leave Sitantal for their own safety but he'd wondered if their leaving had been premature. Though he always knew that sooner or later this would happen he hadn't expected it to come about quite so soon. The decision had been vexing him all along and he'd felt uneasy and uncertain, even more so when his father had bestowed *Praecipuus* status on them. The honour was more than well deserved he knew but he wasn't sure that his father should have arranged their departure at that stage without having sought their opinions first. Some days ago when the Consul had first proposed their leaving he'd considered speaking with him later and querying his decision but then his respect for his fathers' sagacity and his office prompted him to acquiesce. He was well aware that Johnny was reluctant to leave then but he remembered that Adam had intimated all along that their mission was to assist freeing his extended family from imprisonment and confirming that the infant taken from Garrantraa Mountain so long ago was in fact his father's sister and once these things had been resolved they would go home.

But somehow it just didn't feel right. He hoped that the Gods would put his mind at ease.

He dropped to his knees and lay spread-eagled in obeisance on the hard floor.

It was almost an hour later when he rejoined his mother looking strained and contemplative. His face was so white she thought he was about to faint and she rose to support him but he shook his head. He slumped in dejection to the couch.

'*Quia per errorem Mater, Oportet ut meus amicitia*

Adam et Johnny redeo iam vel nos et fatum!'
When Zeo told his mother that it had been a mistake to insist that Adam and Johnny leave Sitantal at this time and that the God's had told him that he must proceed to ask both of them to return immediately because Sitantal was still in great danger, she gasped and asked him how could this be so. He told her that the Gods were displeased because They had never indicated at any time that his two friends should return to *Terra Ferusum* before the enemy had been totally defeated. That he, Zeo, had allowed this to happen was a betrayal of their trust; that he should have been loyal to his friends the way they'd been steadfast for him from the very beginning. The Consul should know that when he'd bestowed the status *Praecipuus* on Zeo's friends only those two heroes or the God's could determine their future from here-on-in; absolutely no one in Sitantal could tell them what to do, ever again. Adam's and Johnny's unconventional, unrestrained, imaginative and objective approach was what was needed right now to defeat the *Anti-God* 'Pravus' Sorus. For too long the Consul and the Governors had ignored the looming threat and they had appeased the vile creatures who threatened this idyll instead of facing the problem head on. By their actions and inaction they'd allowed the centuries-old customs and culture of Sitantal to be subjugated and diminished by a demonic godless tyrant who cared nothing for this tranquil nation. The first duty of the Consul Primus should

be simply to free the political prisoners in Vili City when he had established a permanent base for his growing rank of followers. Only when he'd achieved these goals should he attempt to engage with 'Pravus' Sorus and then only when he was certain that he had sufficient manpower to defeat him. If he attempted to overthrow the *usurpator* before this had been achieved the Consul would be defeated and the country would suffer a reign of terror which would spiral into anarchy, never to recover. But what Zeo revealed next caused his mother to sway and sink slowly onto the couch beside him, her face now whiter than her son's.

      The news which came from Esta City in the late afternoon was good! The Consul Primus and his forces had occupied the northern city without any resistance.
Sorus's *custodis* based in the city had fled or had been placed under guard though some had switched sides. The runner from the Consul instructed those in the temporary camp to proceed to the city without delay in the *naviculae* now waiting for them on the canal.
Zeo harnessed Felix to the painted wagon and loaded all his possessions into the rear and kept pace with the fast moving convoy and mounted men. Friday had leapt onto the wagon and now sat beside him on the front bench, panting excitedly and staring directly ahead.

      He and his family and all their fellow travellers arrived in their new and what they hoped would be their permanent refuge just when the city was gearing up for the night. The outer walls and civic buildings were festooned with the colours of the Consul Primus and the city's population appeared to be still galvanised by the earlier arrival of their ousted leader and his band of supporters and a steady line of young and older people stretched around the corner of the forum preparing to sign up for military service in the Consul's forces. The citizens understood that their city would now become the main target if the dictator decided to unleash his forces against his sworn enemy and they were determined to defend it at all costs.

Aprilis and her family were directed to the house vacated by the city's *Praefectus* who'd fled when he'd heard that the Consul Primus and his supporters had entered the city unopposed.

Porcia dashed round the kitchen like a headless chicken trying to prevent the evening meal from spoiling as the rest of the family waited for the Consul to return home when he and his elder son, together with the provincial Governors and the *Praefecti* had spent most of the day in the forum organising the city defences where they'd dispatched clandestine couriers to all corners of Sitantal seeking assistance from the people loyal to the old regime.

Zeo remained at the house and attempted to rest but so much was churning through his brain that eventually he gave up and he rose from the *lectus* and itemised what things he needed to do before his departure.

Shortly after the Consul and his elder son arrived home they joined the others in the large comfortable room. When they'd dined and the Consul prepared to rise his wife indicated that Zeo had something important to tell them.

He related what had transpired in his discourse with the Gods that morning and no one in the family was surprised to hear their son and sibling utter something so profound.

They'd known for years that Zeo was as one with their Gods but it was a startling piece of news to Porcia as she cleared the tables. She listened agog to what he told his captivated listeners but when he recounted what he'd been commanded to do by the Gods she lost concentration and dropped a salver noisily to the floor. Only at this point were the others aware that she was still in the room and listening.

The Consul waited for the little housekeeper to leave before he nodded in agreement and rose from the *torus* and stood behind his younger son where he rested his hands on his shoulders and spoke softly.

'Filiolus es rectus per panton aiunt. Vestri officium est ut Filiolus!'

When his father told him that the Gods were correct in everything and that it was their duty to follow those wishes it relieved Zeo enormously whereupon he rose and hugged his father affectionately.

He believed that a large part of his inability to rest earlier had been due to the fact that he was worried how his father would react to the reproof by the Gods for his actions both recently and in the past. To hear him accept the censure was a tremendous relief for him.

Aprilis, Zeor junior and Livia joined them in a combined family embrace.

Porcia wiped the tears from her eyes as she peeked through the teeniest space between the door and its frame which she'd deliberately aligned to achieve this advantage when she'd exited the room.

But before Zeo was ready to fulfil the command from the Gods he told his family that he had a mission for his brother to do which might give them the edge over 'Pravus' Sorus in any future engagement. He led them to his bedroom where most of the weaponry and equipment they'd acquired in *Terra Ferusum* was piled on the middle of the floor. He selected the skeleton-frame crossbows and quarrels together with the blow guns and darts and asked him to check if there were any craftsmen in the city who were capable of reproducing them in large numbers; that having used them in the past he knew that they were more effective long range than their native weapons were. He concluded by promising his brother that he'd give him lessons early the next day on how to use the different arms. His brother took up the challenge enthusiastically but then his father insisted that he too would like to learn how to use them. At this point Livia spoke up and said that she should be included also; that she'd heard all about Camilla's escapades and she now wanted to be a warrior, just like her.

The Consul Primus called his elder son to one side when they left the room and gave him a second commission which he insisted must be completed before his brother left for *Terra Ferusum* even if it meant the artisan working overnight.

It was later than usual when the Consul and his wife adjourned to their apartment and though they were both exhausted from the hectic day they spent some time in intense whispered conversation about their younger son and the demands imposed on him by the Gods believing that there was a strong possibility that they might never see him again. They'd endured months of uncertainty when they'd been separated from him when they'd been confined to the prison in Nox, not knowing if he was dead or alive and the very thought of having to go through more torment just when they were celebrating his being with them again was unbearable.

Neither parent wished to contemplate ever losing their son Zeo who symbolised the completeness and strength of their family unit.

When Zeo was born almost eighteen years ago they knew from that very first instant that their second child was uniquely special. Just looking at their little boy gave them a sense of serenity and of being in the presence of someone supernal. When family and friends had visited to see the new-born boy they'd fallen silent as they'd gazed with admiration on the wide-awake little occupant of the cradle. Their emotions would change to quiet wonderment as the infant's bright blue eyes made intensely focused contact with each of them in turn. It had become slightly unnerving for most of them and they'd felt a little queasy and even a bit silly when they imagined that he was peering deep into their souls. Without exception all of them had left the nursery thinking that they'd been the one's who'd been appraised and this by a baby who was barely two days old rather than the other way round. Some even believed that their foibles and idiosyncrasies had been exposed and had been duly noted by him. The customary salutations to the proud parents afterwards had been done with a degree of distracted thoughtfulness by quite a few of the visitors.

Over the years of his infancy and onwards his uniqueness was felt time after time but no one could really define what this was, only that they were happy and at ease in his presence. Had someone asked them to elaborate further on their feelings they would have replied that they felt *'tutis'*, protected, when he was with them. His older brother Zeor and sometime later, his new sister had idolised their sibling from first contact with him. The new baby Livia had gurgled with pleasure every time he came close to her cradle.

During his formative years Zeo had surprised and impressed his *magister* on numerous occasions with his uptake and understanding of things temporal and spiritual and before long both tutor and pupil would take lessons almost as equals, with both learning from each other.

When he attended the temples in the Capitol the *augures,* the temple priests, began treating the young boy with a degree of respect normally reserved for the elders. On the one occasion when he was introduced to the *Pater Antistes,* the high priest conciliator, the holy man had spent more time speaking and listening to him than to all the others in toto in the room.

With Zeo, every day was an adventure and by the time he'd reached his twelfth year he knew virtually everyone within the spreading metropolis. And when he'd been gifted Felix with the little four-wheel wagon on his thirteenth anniversary he'd been able to spread his wings even wider.

No one communicated with the Gods more than Zeo and yet nobody, young or old, felt uncomfortable with this or ever tired of his company. Everyone who'd ever met him believed that the second son of the Consul Primus was their friend and they were proud that this was so.

CHAPTER THREE

Shortly after dusk on Monday evening Zeo secured the saddle-bag on the black pony then turned to face his family who were lined up at the bottom of the steps leading to the front porch of the villa. He embraced them all individually and before turning away he patted Friday between his ears.

With one voice his family chorused 'Nos totus diligo vos'

Hearing them shout that they loved him he saluted them and bowed deeply and when he caught sight of Porcia dabbing her eyes in the shadows of the porch he waved to her and then turned away and mounted the dark steed. With a final farewell gesture to his family he urged the mount towards the city's postern gate.

He raced eastwards and it was only when the city lights had well faded he became aware that he and the pony weren't alone on the plain. He unsheathed his sword and adjusted his night vision goggles and reined in the horse. He peered into the blackness behind and for a few seconds he thought that he was being followed by a wolf but then suddenly realised that it was Friday.

He dismounted and waited for the dog and bade

him to return to the city but the animal was having none of it. He defiantly stood his ground and refused to budge no matter what tone of voice Zeo used to order him to go back. When he remounted and moved forward Friday trotted alongside. It slowly dawned on him that perhaps this was why the dog had refused to go with Adam; that he knew that at some stage they would have to follow him to Lo Garrantraa. As he dismounted again his thoughts drifted back to when all three friends had realised that the dog would do his own thing, regardless. Who would have thought that when Friday had been left behind in Gallendon that he'd turn up at Gaius's camp just in time to save his life and later on he'd been instrumental in saving Johnny in Tabo City too he mused.

He undid the rolled up sleeping-bag and placed it forward of the saddle and lifted Friday and settled him astride the padded bundle and if the horse objected to having a second passenger he didn't show it as they cantered off into the night. Zeo kept to the same route they'd taken a few nights ago when escorting Adam and Johnny through *Oriens* on their way home. It was the least populated area with much of the countryside consisting of grassland and moorland and most of the few dwellings he came closest to were in darkness but Zeo was well aware that by daylight this scene could change and with that, the danger would increase one hundred fold. By now word would have reached Governor Maximus in Ciro City he was sure and probably to all the smaller towns in the region. He'd bet his every coin that come morning the countryside would be teeming with *custodis* on the move to reinforce the numbers already stationed in the towns and hamlets throughout the province.

He maintained a steady even pace not wanting to over exert the horse, allowing for the extra weight he now had to carry; he'd noticed that Friday had been indulged with *'bit-tits'* from everyone including him since he'd arrived in Sitantal and it now showed, big time!
Friday was a fatty!

He crossed several roads and canals and some three hours into the journey he passed over the bridge spanning the west channel tributary river south-east of Oppida where it branched off and headed south from the Raging River deep in *Primoris.* An hour later he reached the paved road connecting Ciro City with *Extremus* without having seen any form of humankind whatsoever on the overland trek.

He continued into *Primoris* and breathed a loud sigh of relief when they reached the familiar rickety wooden bridge in the middle of the dead jungle. Here he and Friday dismounted where he removed the saddle, bag and harness and then fed and watered the black steed.

He faced the pony west and patted his nose in thanks and then slapped him firmly on the haunch and sent him galloping back down the road towards *Oriens*.

He and Friday watched until the animal was out of sight and then they shared some of the tasty food prepared for him by Porcia. She'd had it prepared and packed when his mother had gone to the kitchen last evening to request it and when she returned she espoused the belief that the little housekeeper was a *hariolus,* a gifted seer, because she seemed to know of things in advance.

Zeo hid the gear well out of sight in the dead jungle and packed the stuff he thought he'd need in his backpack for the journey through *Secundus* and *Tertius.* Shortly he and Friday set forth along the cobbled road as his body clock informed him that it was just after one o'clock in the morning. He remained vigilant to what was happening both in front and behind him, well aware that the last thing he needed would be an encounter with *custodis* here in *Primoris*. He didn't fancy the idea of having to take cover in the dense foliage with the added peril of Rootless creeping thorn-vines to contend with.

He and the dog were nearing the opening into *Secundus* when the animal veered across his path and went south along the sheer cliff face separating sector one's dead jungle from the second sector.

He called on the dog to rejoin him but he was ignored and the animal continued further into the narrow space between the rock divide and jungle. Here the dog paused and faced Zeo panting and yelping with his head angled almost in a pleading manner. Friday refused to respond to Zeo's continued demands to return despite him raising his voice to an irate pitch and when he advanced towards the dog the animal turned and went forward again going even deeper into the shadowy depths of the tight space. Zeo became more annoyed by the dog's behaviour and was about to turn away to see if the dog would follow him when it dawned on him that the dog wanted to go this way for a reason. When the message registered fully with him he called out 'Okay Friday, you win! With you I'm coming!'

Friday allowed him to catch up and they continued going south and Zeo wondered if this was the route that the dog had used to enter Sitantal from *Terra Ferusum* when he'd joined up with them in Nox several weeks ago and if it meant avoiding the perils of the other two sectors in *Extremus* then it was a plus and hopefully it would be a shortcut and less time consuming. But it would mean he now had to remain alert for Rootless creeping thorn-vines.

   Friday navigated through the tight space with relative ease where the vegetation was less dense at floor level whereas Zeo had to bend and squeeze between the solid rock on his left and the greasy entangled scrub to his right and his backpack added to his problems continually. After an hour of putting his body through so many distortions and contortions he began to have misgivings about allowing the dog to convince him to take this exasperating route.

But just as he was planning to leash the dog and return to complete their journey along the established route the space in front almost doubled in width. Here he relaxed and removed his backpack and sat down and leaned back against the cragged precipice and took a few swigs from his coffee bottle. Though the beverage was cold it was still nectar as far as he was concerned and he wasn't tempted to share his limited supply with the dog but he did give him some water.

They made good use of the wider space and two hours later the gap ended abruptly at a jagged outcrop of rocks. He pondered for a few seconds but when he saw Friday go round to the other side he followed and saw the dog go straight into a cleft in the rock face barely three feet high and about two feet wide. Without further hesitation he undid his backpack and followed him through the claustrophobically narrow gap which weaved awkwardly for about fifteen feet until the fissure led to a tunnel which was very spacious in comparison. The shaft was close to seven feet high and about three feet wide he observed when he swept the torchlight ahead and he could tell straightaway that it had formed naturally and wasn't man-made. Compared to the caves and caverns in *Tertius* this place was stone dry with no drips or signs of water anywhere. He scanned the walls and floor for graffiti or discarded detritus which would show if anyone had ever passed through here in the past but there was nothing. The lack of droppings, dried vegetation or bones convinced him that even the wildlife had given the place a miss. The fact that the only way to this place was through the dead jungle could explain this, he surmised. But the one thing that totally convinced him that the tunnel had been completely isolated and unused by any living thing ever was the fact that Friday never sniffed at the walls or floor, not even once. As far as he was concerned the place was virgin territory.

His inner clock told him it was four in the morning and because of all the ducking and diving he'd done getting here he hadn't a clue how far he'd trekked. He removed his backpack and shared his meal with Friday. Luckily for them Porcia had prepared more food than what Zeo had thought was necessary for the journey even though she hadn't known then that the dog would be sharing it with him…
But then again perhaps she had!
A half hour later they were on the move again and Zeo used his night visions continually to save his torch for more needy examinations along the way. He'd noticed almost from the beginning that the tunnel was gradually ascending and he was perplexed and at a loss as to where it might take him but the more he tried to figure it out the more he became confused. He and Friday kept going until fatigue forced him to rest. He used the floor incline to his advantage when he spread out the sleeping

bag where he and Friday sprawled on top.

Four hours later they rose in tandem and had another portion of the rations and set off through the tunnel again and continued nonstop for a further six hours when he had a cold coffee and Friday lapped up his water ration with relish.
The floor gradient continued as before and the width of the channel rarely deviated from what it had been at the beginning but three hours later he noticed a difference from the previous configurations. The passage was becoming more convoluted, with more twists and bends than before and he also felt that it was becoming chillier and he was sure that the air was getting fresher by the minute. His instincts told him that they were nearing the end of the channel and he wondered with a little apprehension at where on earth its terminal might be.

The end of the tunnel hadn't been as near as he'd anticipated when near midnight on Tuesday they were still moving upwards and onwards. Weariness was beginning to overcome him and just as he was about to tell Friday that they'd rest he detected a weird rumbling sound in the distance. He continued with some trepidation and called on the dog to stay close. The tunnel took several acute turns both to the right and left and the noise increased with each step he took forward. When he rounded a bend on his right and emerged into a massive cavern he was confronted with an unexpected sight. Ahead of him was the largest sloping symmetrical boulder he'd ever seen and it looked so smooth that for a moment he thought the thing was man-made but as he drew closer he knew otherwise. The boulder filled the south side of the vast cavern and sloped upwards ramp-like from the floor to where it ended about six feet from the cragged roof and he reckoned that the amazing slab was about forty foot high. From behind the upper space came the thunderous roar that filled the cave and echoed down the tunnel. He shone the torch searching for a way out of the chamber but there wasn't another openings save the one he'd just come through with the exception of the gap at the top of the stone ramp.

He calculated then that he had only two options; one was to return to *Primoris* and continue through the other sectors and lose valuable time in the process or assume that this was an alternative way in and out of the mountain. He had to take a gamble whether to go back or go forward and he quickly decided on the latter option. Knowing that it was now well past midnight and he was jaded he decided to wait until daylight to attempt to reach the outside world from here, that is, if the outside world was actually on the other side. For all he knew this place could be miles away from Lo Garrantraa or from anyplace else that he was familiar with.

Spreading out the sleeping bag in the channel behind one of the bends where it was fractionally quieter than in the chamber he and Friday finished off the remainder of the packed food and settled down together for the night.

When Zeo wakened before seven o'clock on *Martius X,* faint light was filtering into the passageway from the large chamber and when Friday saw him rise he followed suit. Both went through to the outer cavern where everything had changed or so Zeo thought but nothing really had, it was just that he was seeing it naturally and not with the aid of night visions or torchlight. A dull grey light streamed in from the space between the top of the ramp and the vaulted roof. The new perspective added a glimmer of hope and gave him renewed confidence to attempt to scale the smooth slope. Then he'd discover what was on the other side where he'd find out what was causing the deafening din but more importantly he'd see if this was the way out of here. He stood at the base and examined the smooth rock and realised that he'd have to scale it in his socks, the ridges on his boots wouldn't be able to sustain a grip on the flat surface. He returned to his backpack and selected only the items which might be useful to him from this point onwards and he stashed the remainder together with his crossbow and sword in the passageway behind. He joined Friday at the bottom of the ramp and removed his boots and tied them together and hung them round his neck. He called 'let's go, pal!' and watched as the dog shot up at speed on the left side of the gradient and he didn't stop until he reached the top. Zeo reckoned that

Friday's padded feet allowed him better traction and he decided to remove his socks hoping that his bare feet would have a similar effect. He moved back several feet from the base and raced forward and up the slope and near the top he felt that he was losing it but he used his fingers to grip the rough side wall and managed to lever himself up to the edge. He straddled the narrow summit of the boulder and peered down the other side and gaped wide-eyed at what he saw.

About twenty foot below the reverse side of the wedged-shaped boulder was the most violent pool of water he'd ever seen.

His thoughts were that this was *aqua pura* gone crazy!

It reminded him briefly of that day at Lo Garrantraa when he'd seen for the first time the washing machine in action when Adam had insisted that if he was going to wear the uniform taken from the dead *custodis* it would need more than one wash. He'd gazed into that machine and had watched it churn and turn until it almost hypnotised him. But this frenzy was enormous in comparison to that and so much more vicious and agitated. Just below him he could see the source of this water's mania where from an opening in the rock wall on his left a mass of pressurised water exploded and hit the pool with such force it sent waves of liquid and spray high up on the other side walls which then splashed back and caused more upheaval and churning froth in the basin. The overflow burst

from the basin through a wide deeply serrated gash in the wall below and opposite to him. Here it escaped to the outside world because it was through this gap the faint grey daylight entered the massive chamber. He gazed directly below and experienced a feeling of nervousness deep in his stomach when he guessed that anybody going into that pool would be shredded to bits in seconds and he wondered briefly how the dog had managed to cross the water pool unscathed. Then he speculated if the dog had come this way before or perhaps the water pressure wasn't so intense at that time. He turned to the dog more in bemusement than expectation and saw that Friday was now showing him the answer to the conundrum. Friday had moved further to the left where he now stood on a narrow ledge which was shrouded by the mist-like spray rising from the pulverising crash of water below. The near-nine inch wide ridge on the rocky wall sloped steeply down to the other side of the chamber and passed about eight feet above the inrush of water into the whirlpool. The ledge continued down to the opposite corner of the chamber where it then took a short sharp turn to the right and ended at a narrow slit near the edge of the giant escape hole. Rather than being relieved at seeing the freedom route Zeo was deflated at the thought of having to sidle down the narrow strip of damp rock knowing that with just one slip he'd be macerated in minutes.
But immediately he got annoyed with himself for

having defeatist thoughts and he edged across the crest of the smooth boulder until he was behind the dog. He stood upright and slipped into his socks and raised his voice above the thunderous din 'Over with it let's get, Friday!'

But he hesitated for a second to decide how he'd approach the new challenge, whether to face the wall or the turbulent chasm and opted to move forward with his back to the rock face. When he took his first step onto the ledge the dog was already half way down the narrow ridge. He eased along feeling every step tentatively and resisted the temptation to look down and he kept his eyes peeled sideways staring at the ledge to make sure that his left foot was firmly anchored before he slid his other foot alongside. After what felt like forever he guessed he was above the water spout and he'd swear that here the wall behind him and the ledge underfoot vibrated from the force of the discharge into the pool. At this stage he didn't have a clue where the dog was and just hoped that he'd already made it to the end without mishap. The acute angle at the corner wall brought his heart to his mouth as he manoeuvred his body to the right and onto the short protuberance that would get him to the slim breach near the gagged hole and hopefully release into the outside world. He gripped the edge of the opening and pulled himself through the tight space near the voluminous mouth and found that he was mere inches away from the heaving outrush of escaping water before it cascaded and crashed into the ragged channel gauged into the steep mountainside.

His heart was returning to its rightful place as he removed his helmet and shook the shiny droplets from the surface of his clothing and slumped to the ground beside Friday who'd been waiting patiently for him on the shale and rock strewn slope. He hugged him round his neck and croaked 'did it we, my friend! But I wonder how know you of this way to Sitantal'

When his breathing returned to near normal and his hearing had readjusted to the distinctly different sound of the water churning on his right he relaxed and finished off the last of the bottled coffee. He gazed out at the landscape beyond and then at the forest canopy below with a feeling of relief which quickly turned to exhilarating pleasure.

It was just great to be back in *Terra Ferusum* again!

He could see where the destructive water cut through the mountain forest at the base and where it veered off to the left. He used his mini binoculars and scanned from right to left over the tree tops and then jumped to his feet in jubilation when he saw in the far distance a cluster of outbuildings and a collection of trees surrounding a house. He yelled out in delight because he was absolutely certain it was Lo Garrantraa.

He quickly slipped into his boots and proceeded steadily down the steep rocky slope until he reached the tree line at the base where he turned to view the mountain behind. As he scanned the solid majestic mass his eyes were drawn back to the silvery sparkling water cascading from the grey granite and judging by the waters course his instincts told him that this was probably the source of the Dancinaire River. Convinced of this he and Friday followed the river through the mountain forest and almost an hour later they came to the point where the main confluence was joined by the tributary stream coming from the east. He and the dog crossed at the shallowest point into Wildwood and continued until they reached Texas. They hurried across the large expanse and arrived at the house just after eleven o'clock. His excitement turned to disappointment when he failed to see smoke coming from the tall chimneys and then after getting no response to banging on the front and rear doors he became worried that his friends might not have made it safely through *Extremus*. He returned to the yard and checked the tractor shed through the cracks in the door and saw that the Range Rover was missing which virtually confirmed that his friends had already returned to the house but had moved on. More in hope than expectation he searched the spot where they'd hidden the keys in the past and was surprised and elated to find a key to the house and he wondered if his friends had expected him to follow. Friday appeared to understand Zeo's transition from dysphoria to euphoria as they hurried to the back door. The faint smell of fried sausage and bacon still lingered in the kitchen as Zeo went upstairs to his old bedroom to find that his gear was still there and then rushed to the shower. He heard the grandfather clock in the front hall strike noon but he already knew that anyway.

Friday vainly searched the kitchen for his basket.

CHAPTER FOUR

Adam was in something like a fugue when he wakened late on Wednesday morning and it took him a few seconds to figure out who or where he was when he gazed around his late fiancées bedroom. He lay in the large double bed and reflected on how things might have been had Sue not died. So much had happened since that fateful time he wondered if things would have been any different for him if she was still alive. He'd planned to go to Lo Garrantraa with his grandfather some weeks before Christmas so more than likely she would have joined them there too. But whether he'd have made the momentous visit to the high plateau on Garrantraa Mountain or not, there was no logical answer to this *what if* question he reckoned. But just then he remembered how he'd thought of Samantha Conlon since that dark time and quickly jumped from the bed feeling mean and guilty.

    Mai Prenderville was preparing lunch when he joined her in the kitchen where she told him that Johnny had still not surfaced.

When Adam announced that he'd head for home Mai would have none of it and insisted that he stay for lunch, that from what she'd seen of him and

Johnny they both needed some motherly care and attention and a good dose of home cooking. She suggested that he remain with them for a few days or even longer and much to his surprise he heard himself saying 'Okay Mai, I'll take you up on your offer, but only for one more day'

He could see that she was equally surprised but visibly delighted as she went into overdrive and literally floated across the kitchen floor. She cheerfully told him there was a blazing fire in the living room where the morning's newspaper was waiting for him and that the coffee pot was coming to the boil. Though he protested that he'd wait in the kitchen she ushered him down the hallway and into the front room.

He'd just turned to the sports section in the paper when Johnny entered carrying two mugs of coffee and declared cheerfully *'Ave amicus'*

It never ceased to amuse and surprise Adam how Johnny could recite so many foreign greetings and expressions at the drop of a hat and, as far as he knew; they always sounded apt and linguistically near perfect too.

He allowed mother and son to manipulate the early afternoon for him and following lunch when Johnny suggested they visit the cemetery Adam dutifully followed him to the Range Rover.

Later on he directed Johnny to drive to his home in east Trident Vale on the way back from the cemetery, saying they'd have a coffee there and give his mother a break, plus he wanted to pick up his cell phone and charger.

They were accosted on his drive by his next door neighbour, the ever-blooming Mrs Mounsey who'd just exited his house where she squealed in delight on seeing them and waited patiently until Adam had alighted from the car where she landed a suction-like kiss on him leaving a near-perfect lust-coloured facsimile of her voluminous botoxed lips on his cheek. The normally dexterous Johnny thought he'd sidestepped and evaded her advance but on this occasion she was wilier than he when she cornered him and landed a noisy well-aimed smacker which was visibly just a fraction off the bull's eye. Following her conquests she smiled with satisfaction and called out *'toodle-oo boys'* as she skipped to her house with a girlish spring in her step.

They spent the next few hours drinking coffee so much so that the large Moka pot rarely had a chance to cool down. They debated every aspect of their adventure underground in Zeo's homeland and the dangers they'd encountered there but also the great fun and camaraderie they'd enjoyed in each other's company. It was something they would never forget. Nor would they ever want to!

The only disappointment they both shared was with the early departure from Sitantal. That it had been a bit of an anticlimax was an understatement because they both believed that there was so much more to see in that weird and wonderful country. They'd hoped to see all the regions of Sitantal, *Me-*

dius, Occidens and *Australis* but in fact they'd seen only a very small fraction of northern *Oriens* and a vague shadowy image of *Septentrio* and most of that was while they were under pressure of one kind or another.

All they could do now was wistfully ponder *if only?* Johnny freely admitted that his wish to stay there forever had been a bit selfish, silly and totally unrealistic. And it was only last night when he was at home with his family that he fully appreciated being with them and realised he'd never wanted to be parted from them permanently, no matter what.

Adam urged him to recall the time they'd watched Zeo and Friday in the kayak on the Dancinaire River where they'd both discussed the planned trip to Zeo's homeland and the possibility that the whole thing might be just a dream and that if it turned out to be a dream they'd hoped they wouldn't wake up until after they'd been there?

Johnny replied in a whisper, 'Adam, you and I have lived that dream and I wish that more people could have witnessed what we've seen. Sitantal is more than just a pleasant fantasy...it is blessed! It is Heaven on Earth exemplified! And just like Heaven had to deal with a nasty problem a long time ago, now Sitantal has to do battle with evil too! It is good versus evil all over again, Adam!'

He paused and added emphatically 'Good *must* win!'

Adam eyed his friend suspiciously and wondered

what was on his mind.

As far as he was concerned Sitantal was now history and they had done their bit.

He'd uncovered the truth about the disappearance on the mountain of his father's sister and had helped save her and her family from almost certain death.

There was nothing more to be done other than every now and then he and Johnny having a good old trip down memory lane. The saga was over now, plain and simple, and that was that!

Life had returned to normal for them and they had to forgo that part of the past.

He glanced at his watch and realised that he'd have to put his other plan for today on hold until tomorrow. He'd been looking forward to getting something for Johnny that might help get him back on track for university but accepting the invitation from Mai had scuppered the idea for the time being. He knew exactly what he himself was going to do in the future and in no way would it be linked with what they'd recently experienced.

He and Johnny were about to return to south Trident Vale just before five o'clock when the house phone stopped them in their tracks.

Johnny remarked 'Adam, if that's Mom, tell her we're on our way'

Adam pressed the speaker button for his friend's benefit.

The voice on the other end was nothing like Mai Prenderville; it was male, husky, wheezy and smoke-laden and Adam was surprised to hear the familiar voice say;

'Adam, is that you? It's Phillip Baldwin here!'

'Yes Phillip, It's me! How are you?'

'I'm fine thanks, Adam! I have someone here who's looking for you!'

Adam raised an eyebrow to Johnny who returned the look with a quizzical gaze.

'Your cousin Zeo is here at my home and he would like to speak with you. By the way, he also has your dog Friday, Adam!'

'You cannot be serious, Phillip!

'Trust me Adam, I am! Here he is!'

'Adam? Zeo son of Zeor this is!'

Johnny moved closer to the phone with a look of amazement on his face.

'Zeo, this *is* a surprise! I presume you've come from Lo Garrantraa but tell me, how did you get to Phillip Baldwin's home?'

'On the mountain bike very slowly because of Friday, Adam'

'Okay! Say no more, Zeo! I'll pick you up in less than two hours. By the way, Johnny is here and he'll come with me, I'm sure'

'Hey! Zeo, you can bet your bottom dollar I'm coming with Adam and I'll drive so we should be there even sooner!'

Adam asked Zeo to put Phillip back on the phone.

He told him briefly of their plans and said he'd speak with him on arrival.

Before they left the house Johnny called his

mother to say they were going to Gallendon to meet Zeo so they'd be a little late getting home. She insisted that Zeo come to dinner too when they reached Trident Vale.

Adam was still in a state of puzzlement and his thoughts rumbled around inside his brain on the reasons why Zeo had left Sitantal. Could it be that he'd decided that he wanted to get away from it all and settle down in *Terra Ferusum* and have a different lifestyle to what he would have at home? Was it something to do with Pippa? He hoped that it wasn't about her because last night she'd made it quite clear that she'd found a new boyfriend who was absolutely the *'bees knees'* and that Zeo had been just puppy love.

Though it wasn't exactly what Adam had wanted to hear from her he was pleased to know that she'd taken his advice to forget about Zeo and find someone local who'd be there for her always.

When Johnny reached the dual-carriageway going north from Trident Vale he increased his speed and interrupted Adam's jumbled thoughts.

'What do you think is happening with Zeo, Adam?'

'I've been trying to figure that one out for the last fifteen minutes and I still haven't got a clue, I'm baffled!'

'I can't imagine that he's deserted his family to come and live here, can you?'

'That would be totally anathema to the Zeo I know and I just can't see him ever doing something like that, Johnny'

'Me either!'

The conversation continued in this vein with neither of them able to think of what could cause Zeo to leave his homeland but they agreed that he must have followed behind them not long after they'd left *Primoris*.

Just over ninety minutes after receiving the startling phone call they came to a grinding halt on the gravelled driveway at Phillip Baldwin's home in Gallendon where Zeo's mountain bike rested against a pillar at the lighted front porch.

The door to the house opened before Adam and Johnny had exited the Rover and Zeo and Friday burst forward and they were followed at a much slower pace by Phillip Baldwin and a rather elderly grey-haired woman who they presumed was his wife.

When Zeo was about six feet away from his friends he stopped abruptly and bowed deeply to both of them in turn. Adam and Johnny were taken aback and rushed forward in case he might salute them too in his unique way. But they knew that it was too late, both onlookers had observed the display of respect and were obviously bemused why a young man would greet his peers in this way.

Friday raced to Adam first and all the disappointment that he'd felt when the dog had refused to come with him dissipated when the animal launched himself at him, barking and yelping excitedly. Friday licked his hand as if he hadn't seen him in a month of Sundays and Zeo embraced

Johnny and Adam as if he'd also not seen them for a similar amount of time.

When they separated Adam was introduced to his wife by Phillip Baldwin and he in turn presented Johnny to both of them and he thanked them for taking care of Zeo and the dog.

Adam moved to the porch to collect Zeo's bike and when he turned Mrs Baldwin was waiting to speak with him, alone.

'Mr Kane, I'm so delighted to meet you at long last. My husband and my son speak very highly of you and it's nice to meet the person responsible for capturing their attention and imagination so completely. But were you aware that I knew your grandfather Benjamin, Mr Kane?'

When Adam shook his head in the negative the lady continued.

'Yes, I met him many times at the office a long time ago; you see I'm the Corbally part of the firm, Mr Kane. It was my maiden name.

But that's enough of ancient memories; I have something more current to say to you. In all my life I've never met anyone quite like your cousin Zeo and I only wish that the time he spent in my home hadn't passed so quickly. I can tell that the young man is very worried and carries a great responsibility. I suspect that he needs your assistance and I pray that you will help him if you can. I believe that your cousin is unique and is very special, Mr Kane! And I also believe that you won't let him down'.

Though he was taken aback at the intensity of her request Adam nodded in agreement.
They all shook hands on parting and the lady stood beside her husband at the front porch as Adam joined the others and helped load the mountain bike into the back of the Range Rover where he accepted Johnny's offer to drive the return journey to Trident Vale.
Johnny tooted the horn in a parting farewell gesture as they drove towards the gates.

Zeo was the first to speak inside the car when he asked Adam and Johnny if they could wait until later when he'd tell them why he was here, that he was tired and the lights from the oncoming traffic were distracting him and he couldn't concentrate properly. What he had to tell them was complex and everyone needed to be totally focused and attentive.
Johnny wide-eyed Adam in the front passenger seat but they replied in unison.
'No worries, Zeo!'
Zeo closed his eyes and nestled against Friday on the rear seat and appeared to be asleep already. When Adam sneaked a quick look at the two rear seat passengers he thought that his cousin looked more strained than he'd ever seen him in the past, even when Zeo's confidence had been at its lowest on his traumatic arrival in last December in *Terra Ferusum*. He wondered afresh what had happened since he and Johnny had left him and his family less than a week ago.

He mused briefly over the words spoken by Phillip Baldwin's wife a short time ago. She was the second person to tell him that Zeo was very special; Mai Prenderville had been the first.

Zeo slept for most of the journey and only stirred when they reached the flashing neon lights in Trident Vale after eight in the evening. When Adam told him that they'd been invited to dine at Johnny's home he didn't exhibit the degree of excitement that any previous invite had evoked and Adam was sure that it had nothing to do with the probable presence of Pippa.

*

Zeo's melancholia and doubts had occurred as he'd ridden the mountain bike along the deserted road from Lo Garrantraa to Gallendon that afternoon. He'd dismounted and walked every hill to allow Friday some relief and had rested at the roadside several times along the way but it was during one of these breaks that he'd recalled the discourse with the Gods and the reason why he was here. They'd questioned the treatment meted out to the heroes of Sitantal and his failure to intervene on their behalf and the more he thought of what he'd done or had failed to do the more depressed he became. What had started off as a relatively carefree jaunt on his mountain bike had now descended into a journey filled with foreboding and with doubt. He was now convinced that his friends would refuse to help him again and who would blame them he'd asked himself again and again. He'd failed them abysmally and now he was here because the Gods wished his friends to do something which almost everyone in Sitantal feared more than anything else. He had to prepare for defeat and rejection and he could only guess what the ramifications of what his failure might mean for him, his family and the people of Sitantal. Had he been able to beat himself black and blue he'd have done it there and then.

By the time he reached Gallendon he was totally dispirited and a virtual wreck and he felt nothing like the wonderment he'd experienced when he'd first entered this town several months ago.

The Prenderville's greeted him with open arms, even Pippa welcomed him with a tight embrace but during dinner it was obvious to all of them that he wasn't partaking in or responding to the lively family conversation. At one time or another Adam made eye contact with each of the family separately at the table and was met with an enquiring look and a nod in Zeo's direction but all he could do was give a *'I haven't got a clue!'* shoulder shrug in response.

As dinner ended Adam asked Johnny if he'd like to stay overnight with him and Zeo at his house and his friend jumped at the chance.

Though it was well after ten o'clock Adam filled the kettle when he'd turned the central heating up and allowed Friday a run in the back garden. He suggested to Johnny that it might be a long night when he brought the mugs and coffee pot to the table and when they were all seated he enquired;

'Now then Zeo, when did you and Friday arrive in Lo Garrantraa?'

'At noon today, Adam'

'But when did you leave Esta City; did you follow right behind us on the same day?'

'After dusk on Monday I left'

'What? You're joking! Are you saying that it took you less than two days to reach Lo Garrantraa, Zeo?'

'Yes Adam, came I another way!'

'How come? You said that the only way into or out of your homeland was the route through *Extremus*!

'Believes everyone that but Friday another way showed me'

Just then the dog scratched at the back door and Johnny let him in.

'The *dog* knew another way! Are you serious? Is it through *Extremus* Zeo?'

'Only *Primoris*, then through tunnel and out came I on Garrantraa Mountain at place where begins the Dancinaire River, think I'

Both Adam and Johnny whistled in tandem and Johnny muttered 'I'll be a Dalmatian!'

As Adam filled their mugs again he told Zeo he could tell them all about the tunnel later then he changed tack and asked him what his reasons for returning were.

Neither he nor Johnny were expecting what happened next.

Zeo slumped forward with his head cradled in his hands and begged them to forgive him for not being a true and loyal friend.

Johnny was the nearest and was the first to reach him where he guided him from the table to the only armchair in the kitchen. Zeo continued to groan and mutter into his hands and neither Johnny nor Adam could understand what he was babbling on about. It took them the best part of three minutes to calm him down. Adam and Johnny lowered themselves onto each of the amply stuffed arms of the chair and every now and then they gave their friend a reassuring pat on the shoulders, not sure what else they should do.

'Zeo you've got to tell us what happened since we last saw you on Saturday morning. We thought that you'd be helping your father and your brother prepare for the showdown with Sorus which is bound to happen in the near future. But here you are, right out of the blue and large as life in Trident Vale! Before you explain anything else you've got to tell us why you think you've been disloyal to us!'

Zeo related what had happened when he'd spoken with his Gods and how he'd been chided for not reminding his father that as *Praecipuum* only the God's or Adam and Johnny themselves could decide when they'd leave Sitantal but he'd been reluctant to disrespect any decisions made by his father in his role as Consul Primus.

Adam interrupted 'You didn't betray us by accepting your father's decision that we must leave at that time. In my view, your father is your father who is also the Consul Primus so therefore his decisions are final and should be respected. This applies to you, to us and to everyone else in Sitantal otherwise its dog-eat-dog where no one is in control anymore.
Your loyalty must always be to your father both as your parent and as Consul Primus. Neither Johnny nor I would want it any other way. So Zeo, you weren't being disloyal to us at all, you were doing your duty to your father! Period! Forget it! We might have been a bit peeved at the time but now we're happy to be home. I hope you didn't come here just to apologise for that. Enough said about it! What other news have you for us?'

Zeo related that because his father had them leave prematurely the future of the nation was now in greater danger without them, the God's had told him so and that he must now rectify this. They'd bestowed some advice for the Consul on what he likewise must do before confronting the dictator. They'd also intimated that both of them might decline to return.
'Hold on, Zeo! Are you saying that you want me and Johnny to go back to your homeland to help you? Are you? Well, I only speak for myself on this but I can tell you straight away that I'm not sure about going back and I'll need some time to figure out if I want to do that'.

'Adam is spot on with what he said and like him I'll also need to think about it too, Zeo'.

As Adam rose to make fresh coffee Zeo stopped him in his tracks.

'There more is I have to tell but don't know how'

Johnny was about to move over to the table but he remained where he was and waited until Adam was seated again.

'Just get on with it Zeo. We won't bite you!' he prompted.

'We to *Templum Filiolus* must first go if to Sitantal return you with me!'

'What or where is that?'

'Sorry! Named it is The Temple of the Gods and in *Australis* is it'

'Hold on a minute! You want us to return to Sitantal to help defeat 'Pravus' Sorus but now you say that if we do go back to help we must first go to this Temple of the Gods, have I got that right?'

'Yes! Right is that Adam'

'But what on earth is this temple and why must we go there? Who or what is there?'

*

No living person in Sitantal had ever received a command to enter the Temple of the Gods and nobody who was still *compos mentis* had ever expressed a wish to get one either according to Zeo.

It was a really big No-No!

Down the centuries accounts of people who'd gone there of their own volition but had never returned was well documented and the last official record of someone being summoned there almost a century ago hadn't chronicled her coming back.

It was customary for all parents to escort each of their children on their seventh birthday to within sight of the Temple of the Gods but absolutely no further.

The unimaginable crystal-glass edifice was located on a steep rocky expanse in the eastern region of *Provincia Australis*. Even from the regulatory one mile distance stop-point it was an incredibly stupendous sight to see. Pilgrims would spend hours and some would even linger for days as they gazed in awe at the revered site.

Sited around the perimeter of the exclusion zone were groups of established and some wannabe artists endeavouring to capture on canvas the memorable phenomena of the fabulous wonder. Here a myriad of mesmerising colours soared up and out, fan-like, and bathed the surrounding landscape in brilliant hues like a recumbent rainbow.

The dizzyingly perpendicular triangular entity appeared to reach the very heavens and no one at ground level could see to where it soared with the naked eye. Each side of the three-sided prism was thousands of yards wide and was encircled by a swathe of lava-like multicoloured crystal boulders and projections on the elevation. The shifting, drifting colours emanating from this rugged patchwork surrounding the Temple of the Gods gave the appearance that the awesome structure on its peak had ascended from within a turbulent bed of simmering volcanic fire.

The only entrance into the Temple of the Gods was located at the northern elevation and was accessed from ground level by a steep stairway winding up between the luminous boulders but only an exceptionally long-sighted person might see sections of the steps from the viewing point. When darkness descended, the Temple of the Gods and the colourful strata it domineered changed to turquoise blue and even then quite a few of the pilgrims, artists and spectators remained on vigil near the exclusion zone throughout the night still enthralled by the monumental edifice.

When Adam and Johnny heard this narrative describing the Temple of the Gods their curiosity buds were whetted anew but they didn't declare this to the eager narrator.

It was almost two o'clock in the morning when they adjourned the thought-provoking conversation and they all agreed that they needed some sleep. Adam and Johnny felt that their brain cells needed a break too and then they could look further into what Zeo had proposed with a clearer perspective.

Though Adam was jaded he struggled to sleep because what Zeo had told them kept swirling round inside his head but the one thing which had baffled him was the news that there was another way to

Zeo's homeland which no one had been aware of until now except Friday. And this threw up more questions than he had answers for.

He remembered asking his grandfather where he'd gotten the dog when he'd asked him to care for him when he was in hospital and he'd said that he'd arrived at his house from God knows where almost two years ago and when nobody came looking for him he'd been more than happy to keep him. Because he didn't have a name-collar or other identity marks he'd named the dog after the day on which he'd arrived at Lo Garrantraa!

As he drifted to sleep Adam concluded that Friday had probably come from Sitantal and he wondered if there'd been a particular reason why the dog should leave there and come to Lo Garrantraa!

CHAPTER FIVE

It was well after nine o'clock on Thursday morning when Zeo joined the others in the kitchen and he still looked tired and apprehensive. Unlike his two friends he'd suffered a nightmarish restless night and again unlike them he had little appetite for the scrambled egg, baked beans and toast prepared by Johnny who'd been the first to arrive downstairs. Friday was still curled up in his basket and had yet to show a desire to go into the back garden. His reluctance may have been caused by the torrential rain noisily lashing the window panes but there was a strong possibility that he'd had an unsettled night like the returning guest.

Zeo's persisting anxieties together with the miserable weather were the perfect ingredients needed to complete what might be a deeply depressing day ahead he deduced with an ever sinking heart.

Earlier Adam and Johnny had had a brief debate in Zeo's absence about the proposals he'd revealed last night and hadn't yet decided on what they'd do. Adam in particular was finding it almost impossible to accept that they were being asked to return to Sitantal to help in the defeat of the usurper 'Pravus' Sorus. That Zeo's Gods were displeased that they'd been allowed to go home before the enemy had been defeated; that what they had to offer in this war was what was needed for success, though they took this as being complimentary and flattering Adam found it improbable that the fate of Sitantal could depend on two ordinary guys like them and them being two outsiders, to boot! The whole scenario was incomprehensible and totally bizarre in his opinion. And as for the proviso that they must go to the Temple of the God's if and when they would return there, well, that little addendum had tickled their curiosity buds, big-time, but it had also caused Adam some unease.

When they'd heard Zeo on the stairs they agreed to return to the subject later when they'd fleshed out the pro's and con's of the proposals a little bit more. Johnny was sprawled out in the armchair sipping his second coffee when he casually enquired of Zeo where his family were right now and what their reaction had been when he'd told them that the God's had advised him to go and seek their help once more to defeat the usurper.

Zeo had been wrecking his brain on how he could approach the subject again and he was super grateful to Johnny for giving him the opportunity to test the water afresh. He was well aware how his friends had taken the news which he'd brought them but he hadn't had an outright refusal though it had been difficult not to be pessimistic up to this point. The revelation about the imposition from the Gods that they must go with him to the Temple of the God's if they returned to Sitantal had reduced what little hope he'd had then to less than zero, especially with his cousin. When he'd ascended the stairs to his old bedroom last night his heart had been as leaden as his feet.

Images of his family being imprisoned again or even worse had kept flitting into his mind every time he closed his eyes. He'd turned and tossed so much so that eventually Friday had sprung up from the rug beside his bed and had scarpered downstairs to his basket, probably to get some peace and quiet Zeo had surmised.

Adam kept the noise to a minimum as he cleared the table and listened to his cousin discuss what had happened since their departure from Sitantal on the previous Saturday.

Zeo told Johnny of the Consul's occupation of Esta City without resistance from its defenders and that it was now home to the prisoners from Nox and was the new headquarters of the counter coup movement led by his father. From there they'd sent messengers nationwide to summon support from people who'd steadfastly refused to recognise the usurper as the new Consul Primus. Zeo now anticipated that it would probably be several months before his father would attempt to dislodge 'Pravus' Sorus and in the meantime they planned to free the political prisoners in Vili City. During the intervening time it was crucial that they prepare to rid Sitantal of the vile dictator for good.

He enthused that his father, brother and even his sister had practiced with the new weapons and equipment from *Terra Ferusum* and that Zeor junior was attempting to find an engineering deviser to replicate the crossbows and equipment and then he'd train their best men and women on how to use them. He mentioned that his mother and the rest of the family had now got a permanent place to live and were happy once more and how Porcia was spoiling them daily with her succulent cuisine. He remarked gleefully that she continually wore his smiley-face key fob round her neck with tremendous pride, like a badge of honour.

Adam had listened in silence as Zeo wistfully told Johnny about the recent events and what was being planned for the future in his homeland. He'd observed the intimate conversational and almost seductive tone and couldn't help but feel that Johnny was being subtly lured into a pretty little web. Not for a moment did he think that Zeo was doing it in a deliberately Machiavellian way but he'd noticed the little nuances about his mother being happy in her new home, his brother and *even* his sister doing weapons training to bravely defend their country, his crusading father preparing to free the political prisoners in Vili City, the final battle to cleanse Sitantal of the evil 'Pravus' Sorus and even Porcia cooking scrumptious food and showing off of Johnny's little parting gift.

But his cousin was selling his own romantic visions of how he wanted Johnny to view his beloved, once idyllic country after all. It was definitely how Zeo yearned to see Sitantal again and how he hoped it would be and really, there was nothing wrong with that.

He was tugging at Johnny's heartstrings, big time, and this was quite acceptable in these circumstances as far as Adam was concerned.

It had been obvious to him for a long time that his cousin would do whatever was necessary for his family, his country and for his God's and Adam was totally convinced that he would one day make a great leader of men.

Johnny glanced at the clock on the kitchen wall and sprung from the armchair and asked Adam if he'd drive him home, that he'd promised his mother that morning that he'd be home for lunch.

Adam threw him the keys to the Range Rover and told him to use it, that he'd call a cab because he intended to have lunch in the Grumpy Old Beggar if Zeo didn't mind.

Zeo gave the thumbs up at the prospect of going to the pub and also to have another opportunity to find out if Adam was still less than enthusiastic to return to Sitantal. The conversation he'd just had with Johnny had lifted his spirits out of the gloom. And when his friend had shown interest in what he was saying he was certain that Johnny was more than halfway to offering his support to him. He wondered momentarily if his cousin would choose to remain here yet allow Johnny to go it alone.

When they sat down to lunch in the Grumpy Old Beggar Adam fixed his gaze on his cousin.

'Zeo I have a question for you which needs a definitive answer and it's to do with the demand that if we return to Sitantal with you we must first go to the Temple of the God's, right?

'Yes Adam!'

'From the history you've given to us of this place, no one wants to go there and anybody who did go, it appears, has never come back! So what guarantees are there that this won't happen to us?

'I the God's do not question, I only the messenger am, Adam'

'That's all fine and dandy but could it be a trap set by your Gods, Zeo?'

'Adam!' He was horrified at the question and almost choked on his roast potato.

'Well, Zeo, funnier things have happened on the way to the forum and this could be one of them, for all I know'

Zeo was lost; he hadn't a clue what Adam was talking about. He just sat and stared at him, still confounded by the question he'd been asked previously.

'Anyway, just so that there are no hidden agendas in store for us and before I'd even contemplate going back to Sitantal or to the Temple of the God's I want a solemn guarantee from your God's that nothing duplicitous is being planned against me or

Johnny. After all Zeo, they are your God's only and are neither mine nor Johnny's!'

Zeo gasped again and dropped his knife and fork on the table with a clatter as if they'd become too hot to handle.

Adam also noticed that his cousin hadn't touched his food since he'd mentioned the word *trap* a few minutes ago.

'They everyone's God's are, Adam, thought I that you knew!'

'Sorry mate, but I never heard of them until you came along'

'But knew They of you and Johnny before met I you!'

'Whatever! Anyway don't forget to mention the guarantee when you speak with them again otherwise Johnny and I stay put! And that doesn't mean that I'm agreeing to anything either. Now eat your lunch before it goes cold!

    The doggy bag contained more of Zeo's food than what he'd eaten from his plate but Friday didn't show any sign of a guilt complex when he finished it off when they arrived back at the house. Adam spent the rest of the afternoon sorting through the stack of post which the bountiful Mrs Mounsey had piled high on the hall table and then booted up his computer and checked the abundant emails in his inbox. When that was done he went to his studio and checked through the few remaining works he'd done in *plein air* that he was satisfied with and parcelled them up for shipment to the gallery in the capital who handled his sales and as he did so he wondered when he'd be able to get back to doing the job he loved. But the great satisfaction and knowledge he'd gained from having had the enforced sabbatical in Sitantal and the marvellous sights and things he'd witnessed over the past few months had made it more than worthwhile in so many ways. He couldn't wait to depict his stored memories onto canvas with the aid of oil paints and recently inspired brush strokes.

He made a memo that this future work would be titled *"Illusions can be real!"*

While Adam was bringing some order to his affairs Zeo remained cosseted in his room.

Johnny phoned at six o'clock saying that they were invited to dinner and that Amber De Vine and Pippa's new boyfriend James would also be there.

Adam accepted the invite even though he was unsure what Zeo's response might be when he heard but he was determined that his cousin should shake off the mantle of gloom he'd been displaying on and off, but mostly on, since he'd arrived here. It was time for him to question his God's and not just accept directives willy-nilly; blind faith had to be open to scrutiny too, as far as he was concerned. He had to get him to realise that he and Johnny were entitled to know everything, what was in store for them and what they were likely to encounter if they were to put themselves in danger again on his behalf. It was a total no-brainer to him and deserved a straight answer.

When Zeo entered the kitchen thirty minutes later he caught Adam by surprise with the change in his demeanour. Every line which had furrowed his brow earlier had vanished. He now had a glint in his eyes as he greeted Adam cheerfully with a broad grin.
'Adam, you right so often are!'
'Yeah? Tell me about it Zeo'
'The God's agree you with that before take you actions think through consequences must you first. Safe will be Johnny and you in Temple of the God's and learn we will of things which will our future decide. Protect us they will but if foolish risk by anyone is taken they cannot undo. We must aware always be that some to kill us will try!'
Adam pondered about what his cousin had just said before he replied 'Tomorrow we'll all get together and discuss everything, and then Johnny and I will give you an answer. In the meantime we've got to prepare for dinner at Johnny's'
He glanced at the clock and said 'He's probably on the way to pick us up right now!'
Zeo ascended the stairs two steps at a time. He fought hard to keep a lid on his optimism but failed.

CHAPTER SIX

Dinner at Johnny's had been a cheerful affair but Mai's disapproval of Amber De Vine hadn't completely dissipated though she was able to mask it for most of the time. She was thoroughly charming with Zeo and with Pippa's boyfriend James and fawned and fussed over them for most of the evening.

When Adam was preparing to leave she waylaid him in the hallway and directed him into the now vacant dining room.

She crossed to the fireplace and picked up the golden statuette which Zeo had presented to her and Terry in January when he was offering what was supposed to be his last goodbye to them before returning to his homeland. She caressed it in silence for a moment and then gazed fixedly at Adam.

'When are you and Johnny leaving with Zeo again, Adam?'

'Who said anything about us going anywhere with Zeo, Mai?'

'This sculpture did, Adam!'

'What?'

'Yes, Adam! It tells me everything I need to know!'

Mai went on to tell Adam that before they'd left Lo Garrantraa to go to Zeo's homeland the statuette had remained warm to the touch but on at least ten occasions whilst they were away the temperature had risen, sometimes only briefly but on several days it had become warmer or even hot to the touch for some time and on one occasion the raised temperature had lasted almost twenty-four hours. She told him that she'd kept the golden image close to her at all times when he and Johnny were away and she'd even taken it to the bedroom at night. And to prove her point about the temperature changes she withdrew a tiny notebook from her pocket and showed Adam page after page of entries she'd made daily, dated from late January onwards.

The notations had recommenced two days ago.

Adam turned the pages over one by one. Most of the entry dates read *warm* but about six had *'warmer'* and four had *'hot'*. He realised that on the date he'd been captured by the Pirates of the Dark she had listed the ornament as *'very hot'* as was the day when Zeo and Camilla had been taken captive by Gaius. And on the day that Johnny had been injured on the canal and then again at the rear of the barracks in Nox the temperature was described as *'Exceedingly hot'* And from the day Zeo had arrived here from Sitantal, Mai had noted the ornament was *'warm!'*

Adam was dumbfounded but he tried to remain relaxed and noncommittal about the significance of

the temperature variation of the object. The only sensible reply he could think of was 'Very interesting, Mai!'
'Yes, I think so too, Adam!
As they joined the others in the hallway Mai whispered in Adam's ear which increased his pre-occupation two-fold 'Oh! By the way, Adam, I've already told Terry and Pippa to be prepared for Johnny's departure with you and Zeo sometime very soon!'

When Zeo tried to engage his cousin in light conversation on the drive home all he got for his troubles was a distracted grunt or humph in response. But when they reached the house Adam asked him if the golden statuette he'd used in the *voveo* rite which he had presented to Mai and Terry, had any supernatural powers?
Zeo replied that it was an explicit scaled miniature of the great sculpture surrounding the entrance to the Temple of the Gods but that it only worked wonders for true believers.
That last bit left Adam stumped.

'We need to talk ASAP, Johnny! Are you free today?' Adam enquired into the phone shortly after nine o'clock on Friday morning. Johnny replied that Pippa was still using his car whereupon Adam left the house and hopped into the Rover. As he'd exited the front door he told Friday to wait for Zeo and keep him entertained until he returned.
When Johnny had belted up the first thing Adam mentioned was the conversation he'd had with his mother the previous evening about the different

temperature signals coming from the statuette Zeo had given to his parents and also her prediction that they would return with Zeo to his homeland.
Johnny laughed loudly 'That's Mom! She just loves all the mystery and intrigue with Zeo but I'm glad that she feels that she's in the loop. Do you remember, Adam, when Zeo gave that thing to her and Dad he did say that it might bring them some comfort? So there you are, it must be working! Anyway mate, let's pull over there and figure out what we're going to do about him!
They stopped off at a CoCo coffee bar and spent the next half hour discussing Zeo's appeal to return with him to Sitantal. Adam told Johnny of the solemn commitment which Zeo had extracted from his God's but they'd been warned that there were no guarantees for their safety before or after their visit to the Temple of the Gods; in fact, by the sound of it, the safest place in Sitantal for them would be when they were in the Temple.
By the time they'd each finished their second fix they'd decided that they'd return to Sitantal to help Zeo again but they both admitted that they'd known all along that they'd never let their friend down and they confessed that they did want to see more of Sitantal, especially the Temple of the Gods.
    They found him arm-wrestling with a zealous Mrs Mounsey at Adam's front door and it was only when the amorous lady turned to see who'd driven in behind her that Zeo was able to wrench

free from her clutches. She shifted her attentions to the new arrivals and invited them for tea to her house and was clearly disappointed when they declined and explained that they'd just had several coffees up-town.

Zeo was sprawled in the armchair in the kitchen still recovering from his close encounter with the vamp and he only managed a weak hand wave when they entered.

'I asked Friday to entertain you while I was away but I can see that it wasn't sufficient for you Zeo, you had to have more! We'll keep an eye on you in the future!'

He flushed and stuttered but whatever he yelled out was drowned out by Johnny and Adam's raucous laughter.

When they stopped guffawing and teasing him Adam made a fresh pot of coffee and placed three mugs on the table and signalled to the others to gather round.

'Zeo, Johnny and I have agreed to go to Lo Garrantraa to see the source of the Dancinaire River and check out the newly discovered entrance to your homeland, if that's okay with you?'

Zeo sprang from the chair in delight, forgetting about the recent close encounter and shouted 'Really? Today? Decided have you to Sitantal go and again help me, guys?

'Yeah! Yeah! Yeah! Does that answer all your questions?'

'Guys! Wait! Something have I for you from my

father. Must I to my room go'

Johnny turned to Adam and asked what was going on but all he got was a blank look and a shoulder shrug in return.

In less than a minute Zeo returned carrying two exquisitely formed gold medallions with interlocking 'PS' characters prominently emblazoned on red and green enamelled insets with a white lozenge shaped inlay between the two vibrant colours. Each had an equally superb gold linked chain attached to it though this could be removed and the medallion alone could be worn as a badge. He explained that the 'PS' initials depicted their unique *Praecipuus of Sitantal* status and would be recognised and acknowledged by all and sundry wherever they went in his homeland. The two recipients gazed with admiration at the emblems and even though they had previously been derisory about the honour bestowed on them they now felt proud of the award though a little humbled. They both genuinely thanked him.

Johnny made good progress on the dual-carriageway to Gallendon and from there to Lo Garrantraa where they arrived just before noon. At the house they offloaded Zeo's mountain bike from the Rover and changed into the clothing they'd worn in Sitantal but slipped on Wellington boots rather than the boots worn with the outfit. They crossed Texas in the four-by-four and parked at the western corner of Wildwood. Zeo led the way close to the riverbank on the edge of the woodlands and over the tributary and then through the mountain forest. Friday was well ahead of them for most of the trek and obviously guessed where they were going and when they reached the base of the mountain below the cascade of gushing water Adam and Johnny stood and gazed at the sight which was now sparkling in the transient rays of sunlight breaking through the fast-moving silvery clouds overhead.

The rush of water was an awesome sight and was, for sure, how the Dancinaire River had got its name Adam concluded silently. He remembered promising Sue on the first weekend they'd spent together at Lo Garrantraa that they'd visit this place in the summer, but now that would never be.

     It took them almost an hour to climb to where the water escaped the sheer rock wall and to where it cascaded over the serrated rock below the opening. It was virtually impossible to define where this opening was behind the bursting spurts and spray. Some of the surges soared way above the top of the crevice and plunged steeply down again. Zeo had to guide his friends to the very edge of the deluge to pinpoint the narrow crevice which gave access into the inner chamber.

He led the way through the tight opening between the gushing water and the mountainside through the vapourising spray where Adam and Johnny crouched and peered over his shoulder into the dim interior of the vast space where the churning froth heaved and exploded within the great basin just a few feet below them. He pointed out the slim sloping ledge which they would have to navigate upwards to get to the other side of the frenzied ruckus and into the tunnel beyond.

They edged back to the outside when the others tapped Zeo's shoulders when they'd seen enough to allow them to plan what to do before they'd attempt to go any further.

They zigzagged down the steep rock and shale strewn incline bordering the gauged-out channel which amplified the turbulent sounds of the labour strains and birth of the Dancinaire River.

On the drive home to Trident Vale Adam pointed to the red sunset on his right and revealed that he intended to return to Lo Garrantraa the following day and unwind for the rest of the weekend and take the opportunity to think things through and also to reacquaint himself with nature again now that the weather looked promising. He reminded Johnny that he'd arranged to meet his lawyer and also Tom Reagan on Monday which he could now do on his way back to Trident Vale. He was quite surprised and rather pleased when both Johnny and Zeo volunteered to join him and when Johnny asked to use the Rover for his date with Amber later Adam secured a promise that he'd return with the car early in the morning to help compile a list of the tackle and weapons they'd take with them on their return to Sitantal.

    Zeo prepared dinner while Adam booted up the computer where he searched several mountaineering and rappelling equipment sites and placed orders for ropes, crampons, carabiners, pulleys, bugaboo and knifeblade pitons, hammer picks, harness and other bits and pieces which he thought would make easier access to the hidden tunnel, guessing that they'd have more kit this time round.

True to his promise Johnny breezily arrived proclaiming *'Buon'giorno ragazzi!'* just after nine o'clock on Saturday morning and carried his laptop under his arm.
Adam and Zeo had finished breakfast where the kitchen table was still littered with the print-offs of the climbing gear ordered the previous day but before Johnny sat down he announced that he'd had a brainwave as he'd showered that morning which he wanted to run across them straightaway. His unfettered enthusiasm got their attention and he quickly explained that he believed they should up the ante on the methods they'd used in the past with a change to their psychological strategy and to the gear they'd wear in Zeo's homeland. He was certain that by now the enemy would have heard about how they'd operated previously and would be better prepared for them this time round. He was also convinced that they'd know that Zeo had left Esta City to ask them back so they'd know what to expect and there'd be no need for them to blend in with the locals anymore. He believed because of this that it would be better if they stood out from the crowd but in a more menacing way.

Their opponents would also know that there was nothing supernatural or invincible about them, just two ordinary blokes from *Terra Ferusum* and Zeo but with different weaponry than theirs.

Johnny paused here and looked expectantly at each of his friends.

Adam and Zeo nodded their heads impatiently and waited for him to reveal the brainwave he'd mentioned to get their full attention.

With a theatrical *"Ta-Dah!"* he tapped the screen on his notebook and displayed the image of a figure dressed in black combat gear with the acronym s.w.a.t. emblazoned on the badge.

Johnny deciphered the acronym for Zeo as meaning "Special Weapons And Tactics" and went on to explain in more detail the methodology and tactics which were now quite commonplace in areas where law enforcers were under serious threat from dangerous individuals or terrorist groups.

Meanwhile Adam rose from the table and searched the internet on his desktop until he found a site where everything needed for this type of operation could be found.

The trio consumed unquantifiable pots of coffee as they mulled over the online catalogue and finally settled on an array of new additions to the already expanding inventory. But the common denominator which united them all was that their new combat uniforms would be entirely black as would be all their gear if possible.

Within two hours of Johnny's arrival at the house

Adam had placed express delivery orders for crossbows, blowpipes, ammunition, smoke grenades, tear gas, torches, binoculars and night vision goggles along with three s.w.a.t style uniforms and supplementary paraphernalia together with a multitude of various lithium batteries and other odds and ends. When he'd completed the list they went uptown to the plumbing and hardware suppliers and literally cleared the store of blowtorches and Propane gas refills, a miniature diesel light tower and micro torches. They crossed town to the marine warehouse on the waterfront on the Great Trident River where they purchased dozens of red, orange and white night flares and several hand-held launchers.

They crossed town again and stocked up on supplementary and survival meals, water-proof holdalls and three sturdy collapsible two wheeled trolleys. The Range Rover was packed solid when Adam filled the tank on the outskirts of the city and headed north. Johnny passed the time initialling each holdall on the journey and wrestling with Friday over the limited space in the rear.

   They arrived at Lo Garrantraa in the early afternoon where Zeo volunteered to cook while the others unloaded most of the gear into the barn while Friday stayed close to the more promising savoury action in the kitchen.

After the meal they returned to the barn and arranged a bench and vice where Adam went to work with a hacksaw and screwdriver together with some copper piping, flux and solder and modified the blowtorches into his unique but successful unpatented version of a flamethrower. As each remodelled piece was finished the others tested and placed the finished article in the bag marked '*F*'.

Later they returned to the house where Zeo sketched from memory the route from *Primoris* to the Temple of the Gods in *Australis*. He did his best to recall and map the villages and towns which they'd need to avoid though he believed that the greater danger was further inland. He still hoped that only his family knew of the quest he'd been given by the God's and that no one would expect anything to happen so far south. Even though his onetime grandfather Maximus was bound to be on heightened alert following the breakout from Nox he was sure he'd concentrate his efforts on his own personal stronghold in Ciro City and further north of there. He reckoned that they could reach the Temple of the God's within four or five days when they'd exited *Extremus*.

After dinner Adam lit the sitting room fire and as the others sprawled out on the sofas with a bottle of *Prosecco spumante* he settled in an armchair with a generous measure of whiskey. As he relaxed he made a note of all the things which needed repairing around his house including the windows and shutters damaged by Zeo's pursuers last Christmas and it was during this exercise that Johnny interrupted his thoughts.

'Adam, I meant to say earlier that I'm sorry for

lumbering you with the extra expense of the s.w.a.t uniforms today. This whole thing must be costing you a fortune, mate'

'Hey! Don't worry pal. I'm glad you had the brainwave; I think it's a brilliant idea and I'm not one bit bothered about the cost. Let me put it this way my friend; had Ellanna not been kidnapped and taken away to Sitantal both she and my father would probably have inherited everything between them, including Lo Garrantraa. And had she had children in this part of the world they too would've been in line to benefit from it just as much as me. I honestly don't care one iota about the expense; I'm doing it for all my family, both living and dead. And by the way Johnny, I've got more money than I'll ever need. I'm not boasting about it, I'm just stating a fact. What I've spent is just a drop in the ocean. Trust me, everything is fine!'

The sun was a perfect sphere in a spring blue sky when Adam joined Johnny and Zeo in the kitchen on Sunday morning. He announced over breakfast that he was going to tour Lo Garrantraa with Friday and invited them to join him too if they were up for it.

They were, and when they saw Adam pick up his grandfather's blackthorn stick from the hall they followed suit and rummaged through the collection in the hallstand and almost came to a tug-o-war over one which they both fancied.

They strolled along the lane at a leisurely pace

as the dog scampered ahead and explored both side verges and undergrowth. They reminisced and recounted events they'd experienced in Sitantal but only spoke of the amusing episodes and steered well clear of the not-so-funny gory incidents which they'd encountered there. When they crossed over the gate into Southpark, Adam surprised them when he pulled a hip flask of whiskey from his pocket and said that they had some business to do at Grampa's Wall.

When they reached the top of the incline Johnny gazed through his binoculars and whistled and turned a full circle to take it all in. It was the first time he'd ever seen Lo Garrantraa in panorama and he exclaimed 'Adam, I already realised from what I saw on the Dancinaire River and from Texas that this place was idyllic but from up here it's truly awesome. When we return from Sitantal I want to come here with my camera and spend some time shooting, if you don't mind. Hey guys! Just look at Garrantraa Mountain with sun-rays lighting it up in segments and over there, if you look further to the left, I swear that's near to where we were the other day at the Dancinaire River's source. Am I right? You know something, Adam Kane; you're really one lucky guy!'

When Johnny had finished his eulogising monologue Adam opened the flask and asked his cousin to fulfil his mother's wishes and to rename the wall in memory of her brother and without hesitating Zeo took the flask.

'*Avus* Benjamin Kane, your grandson Zeo am I. My mother, your daughter, asked that this wall *commemoramus* your son Joshua, her brother to honour. *Vale!*'
Zeo saluted with his clenched right fist to his chest then splashed most of the spirit on the mossy stones. The trio shared the little that was left and celebrated the inauguration of the Joshua Wall.

They wandered down Nightingale Hill behind the dog and weaved from field to field where Adam gave a running commentary of what he'd learned about each of the areas when he was only a boy. But they spent more time in Wildwood than anywhere else on the farm and the dog would have remained there for keeps had he had his way.
It was three in the afternoon when they arrived back at the house and collapsed around the kitchen table and waited impatiently for the black cast-iron kettle to boil which as usual seemed to take forever.
They lounged around for most of the late afternoon and into the evening drinking coffee but at six o'clock hunger forced them back to the kitchen. All of them mucked in preparing dinner but they drank oodles of *Prosecco* in the process which made the task less stressful and more enjoyable. The chilled sparkling north eastern Italian wine was like nectar and it helped whet their appetite no end. After dinner they returned to the sitting room and continued the carefree bonhomie until they eventually called it a day after nine o'clock.

Adam was first to arrive downstairs just after seven on Monday morning and moved the Rover to the rear yard and gave the car a much needed detailing, both inside and out and when he'd almost finished the task Johnny waved a frying pan in the air at the back door and got a positive thumbs-up in reply.

He was ushered into Don Baldwin's office at two o'clock and he was greeted cheerfully by the lawyer and his father Phillip. Following the opening formalities he changed quite substantially the terms of his last will and testament and then dealt with the aftermath of the Raising Kane and Co termination. Later he was shown his new licence for his grandfather's two shotguns but when Don rose to fetch the weapons from a cabinet Adam asked him to hold onto them until he returned in the future. He gave Don the list of the repairs which needed doing to the house in the country when the lawyer confirmed that he knew a father and son carpentry team personally who'd worked on his home and were top rate at this type of vintage woodwork and craftsmanship. Adam handed him the keys to the house and to the main gates but asked him to wait at least a month before handing them over if and when they agreed a contract.
Phillip Baldwin had sat silently near the open window puffing his pipe patiently but when he saw that the meeting was coming to an end he interjected with the good news that Zeo's family were covered by the *Convention on the Reduction of State-*

lessness which related to people who had to flee their homeland without documentation.

Adam thanked him and added that he hoped that the situation had been resolved.

When he was leaving the lawyer's office he casually asked Don if he'd heard from Miss Samantha Conlon recently and was told that she was attending the annual Horse Show and sales in the capital and wouldn't be returning to Gallendon for at least another two weeks; that springtime was usually the busiest period on her calendar.

When the door closed behind his client Don Baldwin grinned and nodded his head in satisfaction having just detected a fleeting trace of disappointment in Adam's eyes.

On the way to join up with his friends in the park Adam took his time and mulled over what he'd just learned. Since he'd returned from Sitantal he'd passed the entrance to Sam Conlon's stud farm at least five times and on each occasion he'd been tempted to call at her home but he just couldn't muster up the courage in case she still had the hump with him about the faux adventure park at Lo Garrantraa. But more importantly for him he wanted to be alone when they met again. He'd just have to wait until he returned from Sitantal, that is, *if* he ever returned!

Young Tom Reagan ran down the drive and gave Friday a big hug and the dog returned the greeting with a face wash with his tongue. The young lad noticed the Labrador's cut back right ear and Adam answered that it happened when Friday had taken part in a brave fight for a friend. The heavily pregnant Sally shyly greeted her prodigal mate with some tentative sniffing and a feeble little whimper and Adam apologised to Tom for his dog's inconsiderate behaviour in going AWOL and joked that he was thinking of enrolling him in a parental guidance class. He explained that he and Friday were going away for a while but that he'd call when they returned. In the meantime if Sally had two or more pups he'd like to have one, preferably a male and to name him whichever day of the week it was born providing it wasn't on a Friday.

The three friends had dinner at the Crazy Horse Inn and then returned to Trident Vale.

CHAPTER SEVEN

'Pravus' Sorus sat in bristling silence at the large ornate table where the evening meal prepared by his personal chef and taster remained untouched. The foul mood which both yesterday's and today's messengers from the north had inflicted on him still festered inside his brain. It had oozed out and had now corrupted the entire building and was palpable to those who toiled nervously within the imposing decorated walls. He regretted not summoning his Commanders for new orders before he'd allowed his aides, *factotum* and his pageboy to leave earlier to go watch a game of *Trigon* in the city arena but from now on he'd make sure there was someone on hand to do his bidding night and day; there was far too much at stake here and it didn't make sense to allow people time off to watch or compete in silly games.

Just a few days ago he'd learned of the death of Erebus which had happened several weeks ago and of the expulsion of the Pirates of the Dark from Nox by three alien warriors together with the assistance of the young woman he'd promised in marriage to his ally. It was only when the ramshackle convoy of small craft laden with the deportees had arrived in *Occidens* after more than two weeks afloat on the east-west canal in the dark province did it become known what had happened there. From all accounts that journey had been beset with calamity after catastrophe when the only horse towing the flotilla had collapsed and died. This was followed by the nervous breakdown of an old aunt of Erebus who had to be restrained and strapped tightly to a plank when she'd attacked and killed all the chickens in transit during a prolonged bout of *delirium tremens*. Though Sorus regretted the death of his crony it was mainly because it had put an end to the supply of stolen booty coming his way in the future.

But today's messages were considerably worse and had inflicted serious damage to his master plan.

The first had told of the defeat of the prison guards in Tabo City and the release of the captive Consul Primus and of all the political prisoners in Nox about four days ago. This event had been followed shortly by the rout of the temporary army camp in northern *Oriens* which was supposed to control access along the canals since the massacre at the garrison at the entrance to Nox. But more bad news had come from the later runner who'd informed him that Esta City had capitulated to Zeor on the previous morning without resistance and was now under the freed Consul's control.

The reports had sent the rigged senate into a deep panic and it had taken Sorus all his cajoling powers and ingenuity to quell their fears. He'd finally restored calm when he pointed out that regardless of the people who were loyal to the former Consul they still had twenty *custodis* for every one of his men and the retributions he planned around the country would send fear and terror into the hearts of those who didn't support their cause. He assured the assembly that *Urbis Capitolium* was impregnable and furthermore that several hundred freshly trained men would arrive within the next few days from *Occidens* to bolster the existing forces and that even more would follow in the very near future.

Governor Maximus had also been alerted to the ongoing developments and was now reinforcing the cities and towns throughout *Oriens*.

But the one vital piece of information which he hadn't expanded on with the senators was that all of these incidents had come about because of the intervention of the brat Zeo with the help of two young men from *Terra Ferusum*. He still had great difficulty believing that all the chaos besetting northern Sitantal during the past month was the work of three young men only. So far he'd managed to deflect the probing questions and he was certain if the truth came out it would send his supporters scuttling for cover. The only comfort he got from learning about this was that the two strangers had now returned home and were no longer helping in the uprising against him. He directed the bulk of his smouldering rage on what he'd do with the little *merda* Zeo when he got his hands on him and he mentally promised that the rat would welcome the pain on offer in *Tartarus* right now rather than the punishment he'd get from him!

When he'd left the senate building earlier he was ready to explode with pent-up anger and he mentally promised that before the week was out he would prorogue the house and get rid of the few meddlesome troublemakers and doubters who were still there. He would bring forward the agenda which he'd intended to enact following *Dies Exsecutio* but he'd been hamstrung by the Statutes of Sitantal for far too long already. From here-on-in the swords were unsheathed and as far as he was concerned the ancient Charter would be annulled, repudiated and invalidated at the next and last meeting of the senate and be consigned to *oblivio* with all the other detritus of old history.

The nonchalant-sounding knock on the great door increased his smouldering ire but he exercised all his willpower and refrained from charging across the room, instead he aggressively bade the disturber of his thoughts to enter.

His pent-up fury eased somewhat when he saw the visitor was his most trusted confidant and collaborator, Commander Puto Pollux, his Deputy Governor of *Occidens*.

Sorus knew that his deputy was extremely proud of what had been achieved so far and that he'd stop at nothing to help his mentor to realise his dreams to the full.

Pollux took his job as Deputy Governor very seriously and when Governor Sorus had appointed him to his new post almost a year ago he was the only one inside or outside their province who hadn't been surprised by the move and he was also the only one who knew of the Governor's master plan which he'd named *"Plaerique et Eradamus"* Infiltrate and Eradicate, which would in time facilitate him taking over the whole country. In fact Pollux had known for almost five years, from the time he'd been appointed *Praefectus* of the *custodis* in *Occidens* and had been given responsibility for enlarging and re-training the ragtag army of men into a more efficient force. It had been a much tougher task than even he had envisaged. Having being born in *Occidens* Puto Pollux was well aware that almost everyone there, men, women and children, were intrinsically laid back and lackadaisical and invariably thought that tomorrow would be a much better day to do something that actually needed doing straight away. And it was this persistent national perception of the people from *Occidens* which had made it that much easier for Sorus to achieve his goal so smoothly and quickly. The status quo in the Capitol had consented to the shake-up of the forces in the backward province but neither they nor the fledgling officers within the revitalised army were aware of the existence in the far west of the province of the clandestine troop of cavalrymen *Mors Manipulus;* The Death Squad, though they'd soon acquired the soubri-

quet *"Homines Tollo"*, the *"Removal Men"*
They'd been the personal brainchild of 'Pravus' Sorus and were answerable only to him. When he'd achieved his ultimate goal of being the new undisputed Consul Primus they would then become his personal guard. The squad consisted of one hundred and fifty troopers and were men of the most brutal and barbarous disposition that could be found in the country. Only felons convicted of a heinous crime were considered suitable and most had been enlisted into the unit directly from the prisons.
The group leader, now elevated to the rank of commander, was Suga Cazo, a despicable serial killer pardoned by Sorus as he was being dragged to the gallows. Within hours of his reprieve he'd dispatched, as a *quid pro quo* to his saviour, a *Iudex*, a judge who'd become a thorn in the side of Sorus who now regretted that he hadn't used his covert death squad on the Consul Primus' family and others instead of sending them to the prisons in Tabo and Vili City.
While all this intrigue was fomenting in *Occidens* Consul Primus Zeor, just like most of the population, thought that nothing would ever change and life would cruise on serenely forever and ever and that the God's would protect them always, no matter what!
That belief, they'd found out four months ago, had been a big, big mistake!
    Now that his deputy had arrived earlier than

he'd expected was all the more reassuring for him and his mood shifted significantly to a more rational equilibrium.

Though the self proclaimed Consul Primus was anxious to discuss the latest situation in the north with Pollux he was well aware of the commander's appetite for good food which was now patently obvious from the size of his expanding waistline. He'd noticed that since he'd come into the room his eyes had been focused entirely on the untouched meal on the table. Sorus slid the laden platter across the polished surface towards the nearest chair and indicated that he should help himself.

The bon vivant chomped his way through the food on the plate and quaffed quite liberal helpings of red wine to facilitate its passage through his bulging gut. He was glowing with satisfaction when he laid the cutlery to rest on the empty dish and concentrated his full attention on his leader.

The pair drank late into the night formulating what they would do to contain the freed Consul Primus in northern Sitantal and prevent support for him gaining momentum nationwide. It was a long and varied discussion but Zeo's name popped up more often than any other but eventually the wine won the day and the pair staggered to their respective quarters at midnight vowing to meet the senators and the city's *Praefectae* in the morning to announce what they'd decided to do to defeat the counter insurgency. They stretched out on their comfortable couches, contentedly believing that their problems were mere irritants and would be neutered in no time at all.

Pollux dreamt of being the principal guest at the most sumptuous banquet thrown in his honour when he'd defeated the enemies of his hero, Consul Sorus and even though he was sleeping blissfully he unconsciously smacked his lips and loudly belched twice.

The imaginary feast was truly *magnificus*!

In the meantime Sorus drifted in and out of a fuzzy slumber where his brain was filled with repugnant images of what he was going to do with Zeo, the *faex* of Zeor, when he captured him. No sooner had he conjured up one grisly method of torment and gross defilement something even more macabre and gut-churning popped into his warped mind but the one thing he was totally clear about during his hazy reverie was that the misery and death of the *nothus* would be witnessed by a vast crowd in the Capitol and would extend slowly and torturously over a two day period...at least! Anyone and everyone in Sitantal would be invited or if necessary commanded to attend and witness the agony and execution of the *merda*. Those dates would become public holidays with free wine and food in celebration annually for all time.

This would send out a clear message to everyone; something they'd remember forever!

*

Meanwhile, the sole subject of 'Pravus' Sorus's delirious and gruesome fantasy was many miles away astride a black pony accompanied by a dog named Friday.

*

Commander Pollux was halfway through *ientaculum* when 'Pravus' Sorus entered the room suffering the worst headache he'd had for years. The sight of his pot-bellied colleague stuffing himself made him want to throw up but he quickly averted his eyes and he tried to concentrate on what they'd planned last evening. He was about to call the *factotum* when the aide cheekily popped his head around the door and announced that there was a messenger from the north waiting to see him.
The dictator bade him to let him enter and as he waited Pollux joined him at the desk.
Sorus recognised the courier as being the one who'd brought the first message yesterday but this time he didn't recite the news verbally but instead handed him a sealed pouch.
Sorus told the courier to get refreshments and wait for a possible reply as he impatiently broke the seal.
  The news was from his undercover agent in Esta City and informed him that the former Consul Primus had strengthened the city's defences and was now stockpiling equipment and provi-

sions in preparation possibly for an attack. He'd commissioned all the smithies and metallurgists in the city to produce large quantities of arms and ammunition. He'd also dispatched riders all over the nation to garner support and was also preparing a force to free the prisoners in Vili City two weeks from now.

The final portion of information in the top secret note told of Zeor's son Zeo returning to *Terra Ferusum* to get his two friends to return and assist them in defeating the new regime but before they'd join with Zeor they were going to the Temple of the Gods.

The news caused the dictator to utter a tirade of profanity and depravity directed at the piece of *stercus* which caused Pollux to cringe with embarrassment, though he'd be the first to admit to it that he was no shrinking violet, but what he'd just heard coming from his superior had been just mind-blowing, disgusting and obscene!

The plan to update the senate was put on hold as the two collaborators plotted well into the late afternoon and at five o'clock Sorus ordered two fresh horses be saddled and brought to the mansion straight away.

They left the Capitol at speed with their helmet visors pulled low over their faces and raced across the open grassland away from the Capitol. They kept to little-used tracks and avoided all towns and villages on the way to the south eastern corner of *Medius*.

Before Sorus had set off with Pollux he'd given instructions to his *factotum* for immediate dispatch to Commander Cazo which instructed him to have his *"Removal Men"* increase the action on the town and city temples immediately and not to delay a day longer and when the campaign of destruction in *Australis* was complete they should move on to *Oriens* but to avoid the Temple of the Gods until all the regional temples had been rendered defunct.

He'd messaged Dido, his bride-to-be, to ensure her father followed his orders to seal off the only entry point from *Extremus* and prevent the rat Zeo and his two conspirators from escaping from there when they returned to Sitantal and opening up another front in the south so that he could concentrate his efforts on beating the enemy in the north. Had he not thought it essential to bring forward this plan he'd have had Cazo's unit wait at the Temple of the Gods for the brat and anyone with him from *Terra Ferusum* and destroy the edifice whilst they were inside but he reckoned the alternative arrangement he was going to put in place for them that evening would be more effective in driving them away from the area and prevent them reaching their goal. He had to force them to abandon the attempt because he believed that if they were successful in entering and then exiting the Temple of the Gods they would be lauded as special and heroes across the whole country and could jeopardise all of his plans. They had to be frightened away from *Australis* with their tails between their legs and made to come north and right into his hands and he was sure he had the solution on how to achieve this. The mere thought of what he intended to do to them when this was achieved appealed to his perverted mind all over again and he began to conjure up more loathsome scenarios to enact. He swore that if the two interlopers from *Terra Ferusum* did come to help the rat they would get similar treatment. He personally would deliver the final blows to the three *bastardus* in the Capitol before the whole population.

The two horsemen continued south at great speed, hell-bent on meeting with the person who, without doubt, was as obnoxious as them and who'd come to the tyrant's assistance a long time ago and well before he'd taken control of Sitantal.

*

No one knew for certain the true identity of the herpetologist who lived in the rancid sprawling compound in the middle of the tropical-like swamp in *Inferus Medius*, near the *Australis* border. He'd been there for as long as the people in the surrounding countryside could remember and some even believed he'd been there forever, in one form or another. Without exception everyone locally gave the noxious zone and its occupant a very wide berth even though this added substantially to the journey-time between the small villages adjacent to the forest's perimeter. There were numerous

potholed trails intersecting the loathsome sector but the locals never ventured to take advantage of them, regardless of the urgency of their errand. If a local boy or girl was naughty or recalcitrant they'd be threatened that they'd be given away to Reptus Reptum and this warning always had a chastening effect on the brattish delinquent. It was now recognised far and wide that the children from the surrounding regions were paragons of virtue.
Some were even nice!
But despite his repellent appearance and the perceived isolation from human contact, Reptus Reptum did have occasional visitors. They invariably arrived during the dark hours and were usually accompanied by a covered carriage, but tonight his two visitors arrived on horseback only.
One of the riders was 'Pravus' Sorus, the other was his henchman, Puto Pollux.

They found Reptus Reptum in one of the smaller cabins close to his shack where he was transferring some hatchling snakes from a shallow tank filled with a fetid liquid into a straw bedded container. Nearby was an array of different shaped glass fronted terrariums with a collection of juvenile snakes slithering about inside. When Commander Pollux enquired what he was doing he explained that when the hatchlings were born he weaned them in a strong acidic mixture to prepare them for their future role in life. At this point his gummy mouth contorted viciously.
'Pravus' Sorus brought the conversation to an

abrupt end by indicating that they had business to discuss and it would be better to do it outside; that the stench here was intolerable. During the negotiations the herpetologist brought his visitors to the largest building within the compound and indicated the number of stalls that were occupied. He told them that the most operatives he would have available for their assignment was fifty-one, possibly fifty-three but unfortunately two inmates were pregnant and he wasn't sure when they'd be delivered. Neither 'Pravus' Sorus nor his deputy inquired if they'd been pregnant before they'd arrived or if their confinement had happened since. They were well aware that the snake breeder's fees were flexible and proportionate with the age of his new guest, the younger and prettier she was, the less expensive the tariff became.

No one had ever enquired of him what happened to the babies born at his facility but then nobody had ever seen a child within the confines of the place either. The entrepreneur extraordinaire believed that he'd established a successful and a wholly essential private enterprise here because business was booming and none of his clients, who he knew to be connected to some of the most powerful families in the country, had ever complained. He had accumulated a sizeable hoard of gold and silver for his endeavours and without a shadow of a doubt he'd experienced great job satisfaction on a regular basis too!

It was a labour of love in more ways than one he

professed!

CHAPTER EIGHT

Her features were etched with a combination of sadness, pain and fear, but beneath the wretchedness she bore the hallmarks of having once been a very beautiful woman. The dried animal skins which hung loosely over her emaciated body were her only defence in protecting her modesty. Now, even though every movement caused her unspeakable torment, she dragged herself out of sight into a dark corner. She thought again of death and prayed to the Gods that it would come swiftly. No sooner had she thought these thoughts new spasms of pain wreaked through her frail frame forcing her to curl up on the ground, convulsed in agony.

Her name was Semele…the betrayed, violated and abandoned wife of 'Pravus' Sorus!

She thought that nothing could make her feel worse than she already did but the sight of her treacherous husband and his fat friend together with her vile tormentor standing at the door to the compound had. She instinctively knew that they were here to cause her more anguish but how that was possible was beyond her imagination.

*

She'd lost track of how long she'd been here but she knew that it had to be at least six years. But she could remember with vivid clarity the last evening she'd spent with her husband and his reaction when she'd told him earlier that day that she intended to leave him and move away to the country where she'd be immune from the sniggering and malicious rumours of his numerous affairs. She should have known better when he'd begged for her forgiveness and pleaded with her to dine with him that evening where he would confess to all of his transgressions and he'd promised to make amends. The beautiful gold and sapphire necklace he'd given her then had blurred her senses and she had agreed. He'd fawned over her and told her how he'd be lost without her and as she sipped the wine he'd fussed and encouraged her to have more. Just as she'd thought that perhaps their marriage could be saved after all she felt herself strangely drifting and then slipping from the seat to the floor. Before she lost consciousness she felt the necklace being roughly removed from her neck. When she wakened she realised that she was in a curtained, careering coach and she was bound hand and foot and unable to move. The torturous journey seemed to be interminably long but eventually the speeding, squeaking carriage stopped and the rear door was jerked open.
Her husband was with a young officer, *Optio* Pol-

lux and another most obnoxious and filthy looking being and she knew there and then that she'd arrived in *Tartarus*.

Together they'd manhandled her from the carriage and carried her to a putrid smelling shack and dumped her on a foul mattress in a corner. Her husband threw a small bag of coins to the floor beside her and he and Pollux quickly left the room. Her new captor forced her to swallow what appeared to be wine but she'd hoped it might be poison but inwardly she knew her degradation was only just beginning. As she felt the effects of the potion take hold she prayed to the God's to save her from this gross indignity.

When she awoke her worst fears had been validated. Her bonds had been removed as had all of her clothing. She was lying on a bed of straw in what looked like an animal stall in a large dilapidated building. Her throat ached and burned the whole way down to her abdomen which was churning and heaving, causing her to wretch involuntarily. When she touched her midriff to try to ease the pain she felt something move inside her. She cried out and then screamed in terror as she sprung to her feet and ran from the enclosure into the centre of the barnlike building. Her fear intensified when she saw a long row of similar stalls along both sides of the barn and inside most of the booths she was certain that there were other humans crouched low or lying down. Then she heard the other stifled moans and cries which up to now

had been drowned out by her own terrified wails. She edged slowly to the nearest occupied box and peered at the naked blonde woman who was curled up inside. Without warning the woman shot upright and stared at her through glaring bloodshot eyes.
Semele was about to ask who she was and what was this place when the woman's mouth bulged and puckered as if she was about to vomit but instead her lips split apart to reveal a green viper's head forcing its way to the outside with its forked tongue flicking from side to side.
Semele recoiled and screamed even louder than before though her throat felt as if it had been shredded. She wondered if she'd become insane or could it be that she really had gone to Hell after all though she couldn't remember having done anything quite so bad that she deserved a punishment such as this.
She staggered back to the empty pen and pondered on what had happened to her and all the while she tried to ignore the moving sensation inside her. She'd almost convinced herself that what she'd just witnessed in the other stall had been a figment of her silly imagination and that it had nothing to do with her predicament.
Suddenly the filthy beast that had drugged and stripped her bare was standing at the entry to her space. He smirked and began to whisper with a hissing tone and she wondered what he was trying to say to her when suddenly her chest felt that it

was being torn apart and she could barely breathe. She thought that her tongue was about to explode inside her mouth when beyond her control her mandible was forced down from inside and below her nose there appeared the head of a green snake. It was just like the one she'd seen earlier and like the other viper its forked tongue flicked back and forth. Instinctively she reached up to wrench it from her mouth but it was faster than her and retreated back inside. Her airway was now blocked and she collapsed to the floor unable to breathe. After what seemed ages the reptile inside her relaxed and she was able to gasp small amounts of air but she knew that it was waiting within. The repellent representation of humankind whispered once more and her mouth was forced open again. But before she had time to grab the reptile he'd pulled a live mouse from a deep pocket and dangled the writhing animal by its tail in front of her nose. She was so petrified she was paralysed and was unable to move any part of her body and in seconds the reptile snapped the wriggling rodent from his dirty fingers and was gone. She fell to the floor again, gasping as the green creature and its victim slid down her oesophagus and into her stomach. The feculent specimen of mankind was still smirking as he trudged away and out of sight. It finally dawned on her that her body had cruelly metamorphosed. No longer was she a free-spirited human being;

She'd mutated into a *Vipera Domina*…a Mistress to

a Viper!

CHAPTER NINE

On Tuesday morning Zeo stunned Adam when he arrived downstairs at eight o'clock by asking him if he'd drive him to the cemetery after he had breakfast. Adam was about to enquire why he wanted to go there but instead he cracked the boiled egg for the second time with his spoon and replied 'Okay!' At the memorial park Adam deliberately took his time to exit the car and allowed Zeo to move ahead at a faster pace and he was at least ten yards behind when his cousin reached the graveside. He watched him bow his head and then stand erect and salute with his clenched fist to his chest. Then in a loud purposeful tone he delivered a message from his mother to her dead brother, his father Joshua.

He related that she and her family had been heroically rescued by his son Adam and their great friend Johnny and that he should be proud to have had such a brave and honourable son. His mother believed that Adam had inherited these qualities from her brother and having met and spoken with her nephew she felt that she'd been reunited once more with her long lost family and her sibling. She promised Joshua that she'd search for him in *para-*

disus when her time in this world was over.

Zeo took one pace back from the graveside and bowed his head briefly and saluted once more and then uttered '*Vale!*'

Adam had stood riveted to the ground as he'd listened to the moving message to the dead and though it hadn't been his intention to eavesdrop on such a personal assignment from his father's sister, when he heard the intro he'd been unable to turn away.

Though his mind was elsewhere he crossed the pathway and he too bowed his head in respect at Sue's grave but he found it impossible to concentrate because the poignant intimate sentiments he'd just heard kept reverberating in his brain.

If Zeo was aware that his cousin had listened in to what he'd said he didn't mention it as they crossed town.

They arrived at Prenderville's twenty minutes later where Mai met them on the drive where she'd been seeding a flower bed beside the kerb.

'Hello Adam, Hello Zeo! Johnny's waiting inside for you. He's like a cat on a hot tin roof and drinking so much coffee one would think that he'd become addicted to the stuff. Zeo would you like to go and join him while I have a word with Adam?

Zeo looked nonplussed when he heard this suggestion but then he hurried away.

'It's fortunate that we didn't have a wager when we spoke the other night Adam, isn't it? You would have lost, wouldn't you?'

'Honestly, Mai. Neither Johnny nor I had made our minds up to go with Zeo at that time!'

'It's okay Adam, I appreciate you didn't know that you would go but I did. From the evening Zeo arrived here I realised that he needed your help again and I knew that you or Johnny couldn't or wouldn't let him down; you're like three peas in a pod! Do you know that we're all very proud of you both for helping him and his family? When you and Johnny returned home we felt that you'd both accomplished something honourable whilst you were in Zeo's homeland. Terry and I could sense it when you both walked through the door; there was a distinctive aura of certainty and fulfilment surrounding the pair of you and it was good. Anyway, I've said enough for now, let's have a coffee with Johnny and Zeo otherwise they'll feel neglected'

'Thanks Mai, has anyone ever told you that you're very observant and erudite?'

She laughed heartily 'All the time, Adam! Believe me! All the time!'

The dauntless Mrs Mounsey arrived right behind them when they parked on the drive and she managed to corner Adam before he'd seen her when he alighted from the Rover. Her markswomanship excelled on this occasion when she hit the target spot-on and she stepped back to admire the proof of her expertise and giggled like a coquettish little girl 'Adam sweetie, I have a package for you from New York and it's quite bulky and heavy. One of your friends will have to help you, or better still, both of them!'

Johnny and Zeo had been chasing Friday around the front lawn using it as a cover to laugh and smirk when they'd catch sight of Adam's Lust-tinted mouth.

'Come along boys and help Adam with the package!'

The sybaritic next-door neighbour marched them to her front door and from there straight into her kitchen, a rather circuitous route to the garage which temporarily baffled them all. They were surprised even more so when they saw the considerable number of enlarged framed photos hanging on every wall in the kitchen and all of the images were gender male. Her picture gallery could have been mistaken for the mugshot display in the local slammer because all the subjects depicted were unsmiling and shifty-eyed and they all looked as guilty as sin, Adam speculated as he gazed at the exhibits.

He was taken aback to see so many faces he recognised; clergymen, policemen, milkmen, deliverymen, postmen, meter readers, gardeners, window cleaners and even the young paper boy was up there with the others. The posers varied in age from sixteen to sixty.

Johnny and Zeo were just as startled as Adam was when she stopped them in their tracks before they could enter the garage. She quickly extracted a digital camera from her apron pouch and made them stand still while she took a snapshot of each of them in turn. But they got a further eye-opener when they saw the size of the package they'd come to collect. It was anything but bulky and heavy and to prove that point Adam left the garage with it tucked under his arm.

'Make the coffee extra strong, guys!' he called out as he placed the package on the hall table and went to the bathroom to check that he'd erased all the lipstick from his mouth with the tissue.

The certainty that their randy neighbour would now add them to her conquest display was a topic over coffee and raised a few laughs but they soon went on to discuss more serious business. The package they'd just received contained smoke grenades and tear gas but they were without the uniforms, the rest of the weapons and the rappelling equipment and they agreed that someone should remain at the house until all the stuff had arrived. Adam feared that the couriers were about to refuse to deliver to his neighbour and if he was being honest, he too was fed up trying to avoid her constant advances.

Over lunch as they planned what to do in the meantime Adam told Johnny that he wanted his parents, Pippa with her boyfriend James and Amber to have dinner at Gino's on this Friday evening so that they'd be ready to leave immediately.

Johnny leapt from the table exclaiming 'What Ho!

What a spiffing idea, my good fellow! Bravo!' He paraded around the room making calls on his cell and gave the thumbs up after each one and when he returned to the table he remarked 'It's too bad that you two will be playing gooseberry at Gino's, that is unless we can find a couple of old biddies for both of you in the meantime!'

'Old biddies? Gooseberry? What talking are you about?'

When Zeo was told what the expressions meant he spluttered and peppered the table with a mouthful of garden peas.

Later Adam went online and tracked the remaining orders and was about to log off when the doorbell rang.

'Am I glad to find you in, mate? Now I don't have to go to that ogre next door!'

Adam assured the driver that he or one of his mates would be at the house in future if there was a delivery to his address and arranged to phone his depot early every day to check. He gave the distressed guy a very generous tip and a friendly pat on the back to placate him but added wickedly as he departed that he looked cool in the photograph on the ogre's kitchen wall.

The courier was still mouthing expletives as he drove erratically from the drive.

    They spent the afternoon browsing the instructions and rereading downloaded information about rappelling and how the gear should be properly used and anything that befuddled them they went online and searched until they discovered the answer.

At six o'clock they called it a day and Adam asked Johnny what he wanted to do; take the Rover and go home or remain for dinner with them and when he opted to go to his family Adam threw him the keys to the car.

When Adam heard that there was nothing at the parcels depot for him rather than wait for Johnny to arrive, both cousins and the dog left the house after nine o'clock and walked up town. While they were both in the barbers and Friday was secured to the lamppost opposite the window Johnny phoned and agreed to meet them outside Ricky Bloom's on the High Street in twenty minutes. He found a parking space nearby and they went together to the outfitters leaving the dog to look sadly through the windscreen. Outside Blooms Adam insisted that he was treating himself and both of them to new gear and footwear saying that they'd all become leaner and perhaps even taller over the past few months and right now they looked as if they'd been shopping in *XL-stores* specialising for gluttons and the obscenely fat in denial.

Johnny resisted the offer until Adam said he'd choose whatever he thought would suit him anyway and the threat made him change his mind pretty sharply and he reluctantly followed them into the outfitters.

An hour later they deposited several bags and

boxes into the Rover.

Zeo still couldn't get his head round the chip and pin method of payment and he was still convinced it was some kind of fraud. He'd felt nervous and guilty when leaving the shop and was expecting the alarm to be raised at any moment and it had taken every ounce of his resolve and self control not to drop everything in the doorway and make a run for it.

They collected Friday from the car and crossed the street to a CoCo coffee bar and were served three large Cappuccinos and also a cup cake for the dog. They relaxed al fresco on the terrace at one side where they observed urban life in Trident Vale go shuffling by.

Later on Adam handed the car keys to Johnny when he suggested that he spend the next day with his family and Amber De Vine and reiterated that as soon as all the gear had arrived at the house they'd go to the country.

Adam spent part of Thursday morning browsing the internet while his kinsman flicked from one rolling news channel to the other on the television. Then in the early afternoon he took Friday for a walk in the park and later on he and Zeo had dinner at the Grumpy Old Beggar.

'*Guten Morgen, Herren!*' Johnny announced when he joined his friends on Friday morning in the kitchen and without breaking his step he filled the Moka pot before he sat down.

He gave them a brief rundown on the things he did

the previous day as he waited for the pot to splutter and gurgle and signal that its contents were ready.

They passed the morning and afternoon at the kitchen table drinking volumes of coffee and debating things past and possible future scenarios and at five o'clock they prepared to meet with Johnny's family and the others up-town.

Gino Costantino was in an ebullient mood as he greeted the three friends when they exited the taxi at the impressive entrance to his glitzy upmarket establishment. He whimpered and gesticulated in despair because it had been such a long time since Adam had dined in his humble little *ristorante*. Adam stifled a grin by biting his lower lip when he heard this woeful lament and gazed round the chic and opulent restaurant which could seat up to eighty diners easily and was busy every day. Everybody in the city knew that Gino was a millionaire, probably several times over.

He asked Adam if he'd found a new love since his terrible tragedy and when he shook his head the restaurateur's eyes lit up. He informed him that his niece Graziella from *Napoli* was arriving next week and that she was *una bella donna. Perfetto!* Gino insisted that Adam must meet with her then.

Adam nodded enthusiastically and smartly moved inside.

    The family group and their friends dined on *Insalata Caprese, Cotoletta alla Milanese, cubetti di patates arrosto in olio d'oliva con rosmarino* and double helpings of *Gran Treviso Tiramisu*. They also enjoyed several bottles of *Brunello di Montalcino* and *Caronelli Conegliano-Valdobbiadene* Prosecco during the three hour bash.

Though everyone was aware that this was a goodbye occasion Adam and his surrogate family and friends did their utmost to remain cheerful and positive and steered well clear of any reference as to the *what-for* or the *where-to* they were going.

Adam was disappointed on Saturday morning when he phoned the parcels depot to be told that there was nothing for him and he realised they would now have to stay in Trident Vale until Monday at the least. He phoned Johnny and told him the position and told him that he would stay put and chill-out at home over the weekend but he and Zeo were going to the pub later on.

The Grumpy Old Beggar was bulging at the seams and pulsating to the sound of music as usual when Zeo and Adam alighted from the cab after eight o'clock. They were zigzagging their way to the crowded bar when Johnny's voice challenged the in-house sound system as he called out and waved crazily from a far corner table.

They were surprised to find Mai, Terry, Amber De Vine and at least eight other people Adam was acquainted with, most of whom had been friends of both Sue and him. He felt slightly awkward on meeting them again due to the fact that he'd failed to respond to numerous emails and text messages they'd sent following Sue's death and some which were more recent than that, but if they were aggrieved they didn't show it now. Within minutes he was able to relax and enjoy the lively banter and the music though it was more *discordant* than disco!

Just before the last orders bell and as the DJ was winding down the evening with mushy ballads, Mai leaned over and whispered in Adam's ear; 'Adam, don't you think it's time for you to find another girlfriend. Terry and I don't expect you to stay single forever on account of Susan. Everyone has to move on and the same applies to you. You know you can't exist on memories alone!'

Adam hoped the flashing lights from the stage would camouflage his blush as he raised his glass and drained it as casually as possible to give him time to respond.

Little did anyone know how rarely he thought of his dead fiancé anymore and the stark realisation made him feel like a louse. For a start, no one knew of his interest in Samantha Conlon or for what it was worth, Camilla either! And his thoughts about them couldn't be described as purely platonic. He faced Mai with the most sombre and dead-pan look he could muster.

'I know, Mai, I know! Maybe when we return from this task for Zeo I'll be able to work things out but at the moment I've got too much on my plate to even think about romance'

'Good, Adam. Good! I knew I was right to ignore Johnny's protestations when I told him that I was going to mention it to you!'

Adam stifled a groan and stared into his empty glass despondently as the last bell tolled but his spiritlessness wasn't drink related!

Sunday was another day spent chilling out and conceptualising but Adam broke the monotony by taking Friday to the park, not once but twice, in the morning and again in the afternoon. Zeo took a rain check on joining them and not just because it lashed down all day but because he was glued to the box and as usual to the news channels. In the afternoon Pippa dropped Johnny at the front door but refused coffee saying she was off to the flicks with James.

Adam declined to have dinner at Prenderville's saying that he intended to have an early night but the real reason was that he was afraid that he'd have to endure more toe-curling sentimental advice from the well meaning Mai.

Before Johnny drove off in the Rover to pick up Amber he promised the guys that he'd see them in the morning and as soon as the car left the drive Adam phoned the pizza shop.

Before he had time to check with the courier company on Monday morning the driver was at the door with several large packages but Adam was disappointed to find that they were still missing the crossbows but his regret was lessened a little when he saw that one of the packages contained the kilo of coffee seed he'd secretly ordered for Zeo to take home to Sitantal. He pleaded with the driver to deliver any packages that arrived in the depot overnight and he now regretted the tease he'd made at the guy's expense on Saturday's delivery.

When Johnny arrived shortly afterwards he was equally gutted with the news and Adam went back online to verify the tracker status and reconfirmed that the crossbows had been dispatched over a week ago.

There were glum faces and not a lot of small talk or raillery between the friends during the morning as they concentrated on sorting out the stuff which had arrived. The dejected mood prevailed during the take-away lunch and Friday reaped the benefit, big time!

At three o'clock they were startled by the doorbell and none of them was prepared to answer in case it was their feisty next door neighbour and none of them was in the mood for another session of ducking and diving right now. When the bell sounded again, but this time more stridently, Adam waved his fist threateningly at the others as he left the kitchen.

He almost hugged the deliveryman when he told him the packages he was waiting for had arrived just as he was clocking off and he'd decided to get it to him right away.

The bonus he gave the chap exceeded all the previous tips put together and the guy's smile broadened further when Adam told him that it was the final piece of gear he was expecting and that from tomorrow he'd be gone for some time but on the off chance that something else might arrive afterwards to hold it at the depot until he returned.

When he closed the front door he yelled 'Hey guys, all the stuff's here now so get ready to roll!'

Just after eight o'clock on Tuesday morning Adam faced the never-ending hazard of the salacious Mrs Mounsey when he called with her to say that he'd be away from Trident Vale indefinitely. He presented her with a bottle of Krug Grande Cuvee Champagne and his libidinous but nonetheless ever useful and accommodating neighbour was visibly overwhelmed with emotion as she gazed tenderly at the gift. He was able to beat a hasty retreat to his car as she fondled and caressed the present with delicate affection. She waved at his retreating figure with genuine tears which were causing untold destruction as they streamed down her rouge painted cheeks.

He and Zeo were surprised to find that the complete guest-list from the dinner party on Friday evening were waiting at Prenderville's to wish them bon voyage. In contrast to the previous departure this one was a more light-hearted affair and within minutes Johnny joined Friday on the rear seat and the Range Rover set off at speed for Lo Garrantraa.

They arrived in the country just before twelve noon having stopped off briefly at the supermarket and take-away in Gallendon. They offloaded most of the gear into the barn and quickly changed clothing and in fifteen minutes they'd reached the north-western corner of Texas. Between them they hauled the climbing equipment to the base of the slope below the water cascade and slipped from the wellington boots and strapped on the crampons. They scaled the mountain side with greater ease than they'd thought possible. Here they buckled the belt and leg loop harness and attached the knotted safety rope to Adam's belt who'd won the argument on who'd spearhead the team in the risky internal chamber. Taking Zeo's advice he and Johnny removed their boots and hugged the rock surface as they manoeuvred between the surging water and the edge of the vast opening.

Johnny fed the link rope behind Adam whilst Zeo held onto the slack from both safety ropes. Adam searched for a suitable spot for the first piton and hammered it firmly into place and proceeded further round the bluff and into the corner beside the narrow ascending ledge and there he located the second anchor point. He proceeded slowly up the ledge whilst Johnny attached a carabiner to the ropes and corner piton behind. Over three hours later he'd reached the top and was able to view the cavern behind the massive wedge-shaped divide which Zeo had told him about. Here he hammered home a larger piton and attached a pulley and fed the large coil of rope hanging from his belt through the wheel and slowly inched his way back down the ledge to where Johnny was waiting in the corner of the chamber. Zeo was at the edge of the opening and the worry lines didn't vanish until Adam had linked the haul rope to the pulley at the entrance.

It had begun to rain heavily on the mountain while they'd been inside the chamber but nonetheless they sat down beside the dog on top of the rocky gradient beside the birth canal of the Dancinaire River and were almost oblivious to the downpour. All of them were drenched through to the skin and the rain was a mere rinsing compared to the permeating spray within the chamber.

Both Johnny and Zeo congratulated Adam profusely on his stellar feat and if he were to admit to it he was quite pleased with his handiwork too.

Daylight was on the wane when they got back to the house but the excitement from the experience didn't lessen and they decided to leave for Sitantal in the morning. Any thought of celebrating the afternoon success on the mountain with wine at dinner was dismissed and immediately after they'd dined they did a further inventory check on the holdalls and then, one by one they showered and each of them was sound asleep before nine o'clock.

They dressed in the more simplistic body-hugging clothing customary to Sitantal for the initial entry phase into the watery chamber to give them more flexibility and preserve their new multi-pocketed uniforms from becoming waterlogged before they'd even started the journey underground. They set off across Texas in the Range Rover before eight o'clock on Wednesday morning with Johnny at the wheel and parked close to the tributary at Wildwood near to where it coalesced with its big unruly neighbour, the Dancinaire River and offloaded the gear. When he rejoined the others almost an hour later after garaging the car, all the equipment bags was piled up at the foot of the steep slope.

They made numerous trips up and down the mountain side and when all the gear was in place at the top they removed their rappelling gear and edged into the hydro chamber in bare feet. Adam attached his safety rope and eased along the ledge and in ten minutes he'd reached the top and signalled to Johnny to attach the first bag to the haul rope. It was almost ten o'clock when the last bag was delivered to the summit and here Johnny untied the rope at the opening and allowed Adam to reel it in. Zeo was next on the ridge and then Friday. The guys had thought of harnessing the dog but had quickly dismissed the idea when they figured that the animal had crossed the ridge before without assistance and as if to prove that he required no help he crossed the ledge surefooted and seemed totally unfazed by the spray and noise surrounding him.

Johnny checked to ensure that they'd taken everything with them and had left no evidence behind and took a deep breath and sidled up the wet ridge and no sooner had he reached the top they turned their backs on the churning basin below and descended the steep ramp into the parallel chamber below. This was the first opportunity they'd had to talk casually for almost two hours and the first words spoken were 'How about some coffee, guys?' Johnny had already been rummaging through their provisions bag to retrieve the brand new Moka pot and gas stove when he'd asked the salient question and as he prepared the brew Adam explored the threshold of the tunnel and saw that the stuff which Zeo had abandoned on the journey here was undisturbed. He shone his torch over the surface walls and floor and came to the same conclusion as his cousin had done; that up to the present time the passageway appeared to have remained undiscovered by mankind for millennia and was practically virgin territory.

As they waited on the pot to boil they changed into their s.w.a.t. gear and each of them immediately felt the impact it had, not only to their psyche but also the persona they visually projected which was threatening and aggressive looking. Even though they'd checked that the gear fitted them comfortably when it had arrived in Trident Vale and they'd thought it formidable then but here in this austere place, away from the homely ambiance at the severe stone portal into Zeo's homeland, it depicted a sharper purpose and a more sinister intent.

For the second time Adam told Johnny that he'd got it spot on when he'd called his idea a brainwave but Johnny already knew that anyway.

CHAPTER TEN

A week after his younger son had left for *Terra Ferusum* the Consul Primus and his men followed the upper east-west canal connecting Esta City in *Medius* to Vili City in *Occidens.* His compact army consisted of a *turma* of thirty cavalry and a *century* of infantry on board ten *naviculae*. The muffled steady drumbeat came from one of the central craft and was just sufficient to reach the forward and rear boat crew.

A pair of four-wheeled wagons each pulled by two robust cart horses trundled behind the mounted troop and were laden with provisions, extra weapons and equipment. The mounted troop and wagons kept to the paved road which ran parallel with the canal.

They'd left Esta City shortly after eight o'clock that evening on what they estimated would be a seven hour journey and hoped to arrive at Vili City well before the *Tempus Dico* announced daybreak to the urban population. The Consul had decided to hit the iron while it was hot when he'd got news from a senate *factotum* earlier that morning who'd fled from *Urbis Capitolium*, that Deputy Governor Pollux from *Occidens* was still with 'Pravus' Sorus in the Capitol and would remain there for another few days. Word had it that Sorus had learned of Zeo's departure to *Terra Ferusum* to persuade his two friends to return and he was also aware of where they'd been commanded to go when they returned. He was able to tell the Consul that Governor Maximus had been ordered to seal off the exit at *Extremus* and to apprehend and capture or if necessary kill them when they re-entered *Oriens* but the dictator wanted their bodies kept intact. But he'd also planned another ambush should they manage to evade Maximus and reach the Temple of the Gods. The Consul had immediately sent for Commander Otho and had entrusted him with responsibility for the safety of Esta City while he was away but also to select his most reliable and brightest recruit to prepare to cross country during darkness and to bypass any guards posted at the entry into *Extremus*. This man must wait in *Primoris* to warn Zeo and his friends of the dangers awaiting them there and also at the Temple of the Gods.

The discovery that the enemy had a well informed spy in Esta City with intimate knowledge of what was happening there and even what had happened within Consul Zeor's own household had come as a shock to the leader and he'd called on his elder son to summon the freed Governors, the Commanders and the city's *Praefecti* to join him instantly where he informed them of the breach and cautioned them to be on the alert and not to leave a stone unturned until they'd found the secret agent in their midst. Earlier the defecting *factotum* had also told him that Pollux would take charge of several hundred newly trained men to bolster the Capitol's defences when he returned to *Occidens*.

Besides the plan to free the political prisoners in Vili City prison while the Deputy Governor was absent the Consul now intended to do his utmost to prevent these newly trained reinforcements from ever reaching the Capitol if he could.

 The advancing mounted troops moved forward through the darkness and were guided by the Consul's commands as they kept pace with the steadily moving flotilla on the canal and with minimum light. He wore the night-vision goggles gifted to Zeo by Adam before they'd departed for home and even now he was still enthralled with the optical gadget and couldn't resist slipping them from his eyes a fraction every now and then just to see again the magical difference they made. He was delighted when his elder son had told him that he'd found a *vitrearius*, a glassmaker and a metallurgist who'd assured him that they would try copy and reproduce them but the Consul doubted that they had the capability or expertise to pull it off. The same metallurgist had also found his son two artisan brothers who could copy the alloy skeleton crossbows and bolts and Zeor junior had instructed the craftsmen to hire extra apprentices and to work night and day to maximise their production.

 Before midnight the flotilla and cavalry

crossed from upper *Medius* into *Occidens* province without encountering any difficulty on the journey allowing the Consul Primus an opportunity to reminisce on developments further afield but his thoughts were soon disturbed by the returning *explorator* who'd scouted ahead of the convoy to reconnoitre the route and was informed that the column was about a mile away from a major three-way canal and road intersection alongside a village which had four night sentries posted at the junction who were wearing Sorus insignia. He'd been unable to verify if there was a larger force billeted in the settlement but he'd be surprised if there wasn't.

The Consul picked ten men from the mounted troop and ordered the remaining cavalry and flotilla to continue forward but at a much slower pace. He and his small unit followed the scout west.

They dismounted and tethered their horses in one of the many copses encircling the hamlet and stealthily continued on foot.

From the time the Consul had been freed from the prison in Nox he'd listened avidly to the adventures and exploits narrated by his son Zeo which he and his two friends from *Terra Ferusum* had engaged in and how they'd managed to outwit and defeat a vastly larger enemy network; starting with the inferno at the five man camp in *Primoris* where they'd freed Felix and later there'd been the pursuit and despatch of the men who'd overpowered Zeo on watch when they'd exited the Raging River and then the attack on the *custodis* manned *naviculae* on the west canal near Oppida. He recalled the gruesome execution at the garrison beside the entryway to Nox, then their encounter with Erebus with his wolves and the Pirates of the Dark and freeing Adam from the caged enclosure and also Camilla from a dishonourable forced wedding. They'd eliminated the outlaw leader in his own compound and at the same time crushed his Pirates of the Dark and banished them from Nox. Following all that they'd then wreaked havoc on the canal convoy sent to relieve the prison and execute him and his family there. After Zeo and Camilla had been captured by the traitor Gaius his son's two friends had saved the pair with the help of the dog from the jaws of certain death and had sent Gaius off to answer for his treachery to the God's. And finally, they'd taken on the prison guards in Tabo City and had brought them to their knees by sowing fear and terrorising the whole garrison until they capitulated. And all of this had been achieved by three young men and latterly with the help of a young maiden and a dog and not one of them had had combat training.

The sheer scope of their daring achievements had filled him with awe and admiration and if he lived to see peace restored to his nation these accomplishments would be forever memorialized and archived for future generations. They'd become compulsory reading at each academy and library in every village, town and city in Sitantal where it would help inspire and encourage young people what they could do when they had right on their side and were determined to succeed against the odds. The discourse with his younger son had taught him a valuable lesson which was simply; you don't have to be the stronger or the bigger to overcome your opponent. But you must use every subterfuge available and explore every possibility before engaging with them. When you inject confusion and fear within their ranks and they become convinced that something abominable is happening or is about to happen to them then you have triumphed over them. Zeo had called it Guerrilla and Psychological Warfare and acknowledged that it was his friends who'd taught him these tenets and tactics. Since he'd become Consul Primus on the death of his father more than twenty years ago he, just like almost everybody else had become complacent and had given very little attention to the art of warfare or even political subterfuge and power-play manoeuvres because the country had prospered and was at peace with itself, or so he'd thought. He'd known that Governor Sorus of *Occidens* had begun to bolster the number of *custodis* in his domain but he, like the other Governors and senators had been assured it was only to attempt to mend the seemingly genetic malaise which had beset the province for centuries and one had only to visit the area to see the widespread neglect and how depressing the place

had become to accept the reason without question. They'd heartily agreed to the secondment of a large number of Sorus' *custodis* into the ranks of the local guard in the other provinces to complete their training. He now accepted that this was part of their master plan from which they'd conspired to oust him and subjugate Sitantal.
He now fully accepted that he should have been more diligent in the past and silently vowed that never again would he allow evil to gain a foothold in his country.

The Consul Primus and his men spread out and crept silently through the undergrowth in a pincer-like formation and approached the patrolling sentries who were now less than thirty feet away and while he was lying flat out he subjected himself to a blunt appraisal and reality check and he was unimpressed with his findings.
Since he'd been freed from the prison in Tabo City there were times when he wondered if he was still living in the real world or stuck in some crazy otherworld. Though now in mid life he was being forced to face situations that were totally alien to him and as if to amplify that ghastly position, he now found himself crawling on his belly to do something foul that he'd never imagined himself doing before.

CHAPTER ELEVEN

When Adam drained his mug he glanced at his watch and saw that it was ten forty-four he announced 'Right guys, it's time to hit the tunnel!'

They packed away the coffee kit and loaded the equipment bags onto the collapsible trolleys and donned their new helmets and night visions before they entered the dark tunnel which would take them directly into *Primoris*.

Friday occupied the vanguard of the three-man single file column.

Johnny and Adam experienced a frisson of euphoria rush through their systems now that they were actually on the way to revisit the beautiful secret underworld which they, both were convinced, were the only humans on the surface of the planet to have ever entered with the exception of Zeo's mother at the time she'd been kidnapped from Garrantraa Mountain when she was a mere infant. Though Johnny had romanticised that Sitantal was archetypical of a Heaven on Earth both he and Adam were sufficiently pragmatic to realise that they were now committed to a more dangerous and diverse objective than on their previous mission below mountain and sea.

There was bound to be heightened tension along with increased security all round now that the deposed Consul Primus and the other prisoners had been freed from the tower in Nox and since the rescuees had departed the dark province they'd taken control of Esta City in northern *Medius*. The usurper 'Pravus' Sorus would know all of this by now they were certain and they fully expected that he and his cohorts would respond immediately and brutally to protect their powerbase and also their skins in anticipation of a possible gory day of reckoning for them in the future if the country reverted to the status quo. Both Adam and Johnny knew from past experience that their friend Zeo was merciless and took no prisoners when dealing with those who'd brought conflict to his beloved country and concern to his Gods.

    They made good progress down the gently sloping tunnel and continued apace without having a break until two in the afternoon when Johnny called a halt for a quick energy fix of coffee and cookies.

Because of the sameness of the featureless tunnel Zeo was unable to tell them how far they'd travelled in the passage but he was pretty sure they'd exceeded his progress on the outbound trek and would probably complete the return stage in less time than the two days it had taken him then even allowing for the extra heavy gear they were now hauling.

It was close to seven in the evening when they finally put the trolleys to one side and prepared the first proper meal since breakfast that morning at Lo Garrantraa.

Though they felt comparatively safe in the underground shaft they agreed to continue the routine they'd established on the previous trek through *Extremus* and always stay on alert.

Adam volunteered for the first watch of the night.

Because the surrounding lightless geography offered nothing visual to occupy his thoughts as he sat with his back against the wall Adam's considerations became focused on their pending mandatory visit to the Temple of the Gods and he wondered afresh about what awaited them there. Zeo's depiction of how it appeared from the exclusion zone had been exciting and tantalising and had electrified his artistic juices almost to frenzy. And though he tried to imagine what they might discover inside the temple he gave up the futile exercise after a few minutes. But he was positive about one thing and that was that although it was called the Temple of the Gods his innate instincts told him that Zeo's Gods wouldn't be found there and that the place was just a focal point for the faithful throughout Sitantal, much like the basilica he'd visited in Rome with his parents quite a few years ago. But nevertheless he couldn't help wondering if they'd find somebody or something mysterious or inspiring inside the forbidden temple, otherwise what was the point of it being there, or of them having to go there he mused?

He allowed his mind to drift away from these images and he wondered if he and Johnny were tempting providence by returning here when on the previous trip they'd both had had very close calls and taking everything into consideration they'd been lucky to get out of the place alive. The fact of the matter was that after the initial irritation and disappointment of being dismissed by the Consul Primus from any further involvement in the war against 'Pravus' Sorus he'd been looking forward to putting down some roots at Lo Garrantraa and had intended to seek expert advice on how he'd juggle the running of the farm commercially and still be able to continue his craft as an artist. He wanted both elements of his world to be successful and felt sure that with some professional guidance the farm could become a viable entity and still reflect and even enhance its stunning beauty which he wanted, altruistically, to share with a wider universal audience. He was confident he could achieve this and still have the time to gratify his creative streak which over the past three years had become increasingly favoured in the arty world and he wasn't ashamed to admit it, even lucrative. Long before he'd gained so much from his grandfather's legacy he'd been in a very comfortable position financially which Sue used to tease him about, saying that at least she wouldn't have to wait until he died like *Vincent Van Gogh* before his work became valuable.

Thinking of Sue diverted his thoughts back to her brother; his great friend Johnny and he became more despondent. He recalled the conversation they'd had on the day after their return to Trident Vale from Sitantal about three weeks ago when his friend had tried to convince him that everything was now fine with him and that his wish to stay in Sitantal forever had been selfish and silly and totally unrealistic and that he'd realised that he could never be parted from his family permanently. But only minutes later he'd exclaimed that Sitantal was *blessed* and that it *must* win this conflict with such passion that it was clear to him that his friend was in denial about his real feelings and longed to be back in this country again. And, more than likely, he still carried a torch for Zeo's sister Livia, he'd wager.

And later that same day when Zeo had confirmed in the phone call that he'd arrived at Phillip Baldwin's home by mountain bike had clinched it for him. He was certain that his cousin hadn't broken into the house to get the bike but it was only when he'd handed the keys to Johnny to drive to Gallendon he'd noticed that the spare house-key was missing from the bunch. At that point he knew for sure that Johnny had deliberately left a key in the hiding place but for whatever reason he just didn't know. On the journey home from there he'd been tempted to ask Zeo how he'd managed to enter the house and get the bike but decided then to let it go. Johnny had become more than just a great friend; he was his surrogate brother and he didn't want to see him hurt either physically or psychologically, ever. And he fervently hoped that his friend's future was trouble-free and happy because the guy was simply the best!

Johnny sipped his coffee on the second watch where he was surrounded by the same dark nothingness of the underground passageway as Adam had been earlier and he also allowed his contemplative mood to leapfrog onto a different plane. But the vision which appeared in his reverie was anything but inanimate, perplexing or vague.
It was vivaciously very real and tangible and she was stunningly beautiful too!
Livia!
Though he'd projected the impression that he'd gotten over the pain of having lost contact with her forever, somewhere deep within his heart the ember of love still flickered and smouldered where all it needed was a conductive waft of oxygen to reignite it. He recalled with some discomfort assuring Adam that his previous emotions had been a silly aberration and that since he'd returned from Sitantal he'd realised that he'd never think of leaving his family again. But this assertion had been just smoke and mirrors and even as he'd uttered this assurance to his friend he'd felt uneasy when he remembered how he'd secretly left a spare key to Adam's house in the faint hope that perhaps Zeo

and his family might be forced to abandon their troubled homeland and flee to Lo Garrantraa and if that happened then he'd be reunited with the girl who'd enchanted him the instant he'd laid eyes on her.

On the evening when Phillip Baldwin had phoned to say that Zeo was in Gallendon he'd fantasised for a moment that his boat had come in and during the journey there he'd fervently hoped to find that the entire family were in exile at Lo Garrantraa. But unfortunately Zeo's singular arrival had only restored a tenuous link between him and Sitantal and to Livia but it was the next best thing and that was surely better than nothing, in his book. Then when the reason for Zeo's arrival was revealed to him and Adam and he'd realised the great opportunity it offered him a return ticket to Sitantal it had taken all of his forbearance and guile to hide his true emotions and keep the cat in the bag.

He then thought of the other difficult spot he'd created for himself, the one which now made him feel like a beastly cad.

Amber De Vine!

She was a sweet, sensitive and intelligent girl regardless of what his mother might say about her but he was sufficiently clued-up to know that all mothers think the same when it comes to their sons girlfriends; they just don't like it when a visiting hen attempts to trespass in their nest and they have a tendency to get into a fit or a flutter about it. He knew Amber loved him mainly because she'd told him so before he'd left for Sitantal on the first occasion but he'd danced around the subject light-footedly and had avoided any reciprocity chiefly because he couldn't be certain that he'd live to see her again but he'd also needed time to think about it too, after all it was a consequential thing to submit to. But during that first journey through the underworld he'd thought of her more and more and pretty soon he'd realised that her absence was certainly making his heart grow fonder by the day until eventually he was convinced that this could only mean that he was actually in love with her after all.

But then he saw Livia and with that everything changed!

Though the prospect of seeing the Temple of the Gods was something which he didn't want to miss his real desire was for the day when he'd see the beautiful girl whose spirit had lain dormant in his heart.

But then again he recalled when he'd arrived back from Sitantal he was so far down in the dumps he believed that he'd stay home forever and when he met Amber his passion was rekindled again. It soared to a much higher level when he discovered that she was loved up with him even more than before.

He sighed audibly in the underground tunnel knowing full well that he was trapped between a rock and a hard place both literally and metaphorically!

Zeo's deliberations on his watch were focused mainly on how they could get to the Temple of the Gods in the quickest possible time to find out what was the purpose of the unprecedented decree that he must attend there and especially with Adam and Johnny. The latter part of the edict had baffled and worried him every bit as much as it had his two friends though he'd tried not to show it. Not for an instant could he question the wisdom or motives of the Gods but no matter how much he'd quietly deliberated on this puzzle the answer still eluded him. And how the detour to the deep south of the country would assist in the war against 'Pravus' Sorus, a journey which would take them hundreds of miles away from where he expected the action would be, equally mystified him. It just didn't make sense!
Eventually, and just as he was about to consciously direct his musings to less cerebral conundrums the solution burst into his brain:
Templum enim Dei in periculum!
The Temple of the Gods is in danger!
As they ate breakfast Zeo told his friends of the conclusion he'd come to about why they'd been summoned to the Temple of the Gods and when Adam and Johnny pressed him for answers on how this nationally revered place could be in danger Zeo threw his hands in the air and admitted that he didn't have the faintest idea but he was convinced nevertheless that he was right. But he reckoned that whatever it was it had something to do

with 'Pravus' Sorus. When Adam pushed him further and got a shoulder shrug response from his cousin he suggested that he speak with his Gods and find out what was going on and if the Temple of the Gods really was in danger. Zeo promised he'd confer with Them later that evening.

In the early afternoon of the second day underground the trio came to the end of the tunnel and onto the narrow track between the cliff and the dense silent jungle of *Primoris*.

They took advantage of the relative openness and lightness of the space compared to the claustrophobic tunnel to have the usual brew-up and prepare for the tighter and more difficult section along the cliff face which would take them onto the cobbled road leading to *Oriens*.

With the trolleys now dismantled and packed in a spare holdall they picked out the three heavier bags and squeezed between the rock face and the gnarled and twisted branches on the left but not before Zeo reminded them again to be on alert for Rootless creeping thorn-vines especially when they passed through the tighter section further on. When they'd reached the end of the narrow track they concealed the holdalls and left Friday to guard the spot and returned again and again until all the gear was at the holding point.

Adam and his dog squeezed through the final stretch and furtively edged onto the long road heading due west to Ciro City. He then crept up to the cleft in the sheer cliff dividing *Secundus* and

Primoris and checked to see if the sector was safe. The others joined him when he signalled that the coast was clear and loaded up the trolleys and continued along the cobblestoned road with Friday, as usual, leading the way until they reached the rickety wooden bridge. They agreed to remain here overnight which they'd done on the last occasion where they had a clear view in both directions and a fresh water supply below the bridge.

As he'd promised to do earlier Zeo climbed down the green embankment below the bridge following the evening meal. He sat motionlessly at the riverside and sought enlightenment from his Gods. And when he re-joined his friends later he looked edgy and perplexed and told them he'd learned nothing only that the reasons for their mission to the Temple of the Gods would become clearer in time.

At eight o'clock the sleeping bags were rolled out and neither Adam nor Johnny needed the soothing sounds of the rippling river to lull them to sleep.

Nearing the end of Johnny's stint on the last watch and just as he was about to brew up a sudden commotion followed by stifled cries of pain came from the jungle further west along the road which caused him to wake Zeo and Adam although he reckoned that by then the noise would probably have awakened them anyway. Friday had already sprung to his feet where he pranced around impatiently and growled and could barely wait for them to join him in the hunt.

They readied their weapons and donned helmets and moved quickly but cautiously along the road in the direction of the disturbance.

Several hundred feet from the bridge they were startled to find a bloodied young blond haired soldier attempting to crawl on all fours from the undergrowth where the dog waited expectantly for the command to attack the stranger. His uniform was torn and tattered and several nasty looking wounds to his arms and legs oozed blood.

His bulging blue eyes displayed the fear of death.

'*O Sanctissima! Da auxilium mihi!*'

Zeo studiously removed his visor when he heard the prayer and the plea for help from the injured youth and fixed a disdainful glare on the begging bleeder. But as their unperturbed friend coldly considered his options Adam and Johnny reacted instantly and without waiting for Zeo's response they pushed through into the brushwood and dragged the terrified young man clear of the trees and groundcover and onto the roadside.

He gasped audibly when the blind terror cleared from his eyes and he recognised that the man in black who appeared the least concerned about his plight was Zeo.

'*Gratias ago tibi! Consul Primus filius Zeo exspecto!*'

The remarks added an extra furrow to Zeo's frown and spurred him to move closer where he bent and spoke directly to the victim and sharply demanded to know why he'd been waiting for him.

When the injured youth stated that he'd been sent by his father the Consul Primus to warn him that 'Pravus' Sorus knew of his itinerary when he returned from *Terra Ferusum,* Zeo sprung into action and asked Adam to get him the first-aid kit right away and he began to remove the clothing and backpack from the heavily perspiring teenager. He called on Johnny to fetch clean water, a towel and a bottle of energy drink. He painstakingly bathed and cleansed the wounds and used plasters or where needed, bandages on the deeper lacerations while Johnny continually plied the shivering casualty with liquid.

Meanwhile Adam used his torch to penetrate the shadowy area of the jungle where they'd discovered the injured youth and found several purple **v-**shaped severed thorns in the scrub and it confirmed what they'd all suspected when they'd seen the nature of the injuries sustained in the attack; that the guy had disturbed a Rootless creeping thorn-vine and a brace of observations came to his mind.

Plucky Guy! Lucky Guy!

When Zeo had finished rendering medical aid his patient was exhausted and barely conscious and was unable to give coherent answers to the many questions which Zeo lobbed at him until eventually he conceded that he was getting nowhere. They quickly realised the unexpected event had thrown a spanner in the works but they also knew that they couldn't abandon the injured youth in

Primoris nor could they bring him with them either. They agreed to wait here for the rest of the day and find out everything he knew but also to see what the true nature of his physical condition was and only then would they decide what they'd do.

They placed him in one of the sleeping bags and carried him to the lay-by at the bridge but the youth was unaware of this.

The others breakfasted and debated in more detail the predicament they'd been lumbered with but the information that Zeo had gleaned from the young soldier that he'd been sent to warn them that the dictator was aware of their movements was invaluable even though it introduced another hurdle on their journey to the Temple of the Gods.

They'd never expected that this venture would be easy-peasy but they'd reckoned that whatever they'd encounter on the way would be totally random and haphazard but now they'd just learnt that they'd face an organised attempt to thwart them on the mission.

     They remained vigilant throughout the day on the off chance that their sleeping patient might not be travelling alone nor be a genuine messenger from the Consul Primus after all. In the late evening when Zeo was checking his wound dressings for the second time since morning the youth stirred and sat up and asked for water. The glucose drink appeared to revive and energise him even more than it claimed it could do on the label and in a very short time he and Zeo were engaged in an intense question and answer session.

While Johnny prepared food for four people and a hungry dog, Adam kept lookout along the cobbled road and into the jungle.

Zeo told them that the young man's name was Euander and that he'd enlisted in the embryonic army of the Consul Primus in Esta City just three weeks ago. Commander Otho had selected him to ride to *Extremus* mainly because his family had no political connection with any of the factions in the conflict but also for his prowess on horseback and his ability to use a *dirigo* or sabre effectively when on the move.

He told Zeo of the major troop movements taking place in *Oriens* which he'd managed to avoid by riding mostly during the hours of darkness. When he'd traversed the province and arrived at *Extremus* he'd found the new security camp was being built outside the opening. He'd been lucky to find a trooper's tunic badge issued to the men in the Maximus unit and he'd used the insignia to enter the encampment. Eventually and after a fraught two weeks pretending to being one of the camp company he'd surreptitiously slipped away and into *Primoris* three nights ago. The reason he gave for being caught unawares by the Rootless creeping thorn-vine was simply that he'd forgotten all about the hidden danger in the jungle. Last evening when he'd heard strange voices and had seen three black-clothed people and a dog approaching he'd immediately taken cover and hid in the brush. It was only when he was preparing to move closer to investigate this morning that he'd stumbled upon the deadly creeper. He stressed that he would be proud to die in battle for his country but the very thought of being slain by a length of vegetation would be a shameful dishonour and for that reason he was forever indebted to Zeo's two friends for helping him escape the blade-like scales of the weed.

Before they dined Zeo dutifully introduced Adam and Johnny to the injured youth and as they ate he and Zeo discussed how the exit from *Extremus* to *Oriens* was guarded and controlled. Every now and then Zeo paused the debate and explained to his friends what he'd learned from the newcomer.

Sometime later he informed Euander that they'd help him to return to the camp before daylight where he could receive the medical care he needed for his injuries. But it was those same lacerations and wounds which prevented the injured youth from jumping to his feet in protest. It was obvious to everyone there that this was the last thing he wanted them to do and he turned back to Zeo and angrily told him that he'd prefer if they left him to die here rather than abandon him with a group of conspirators who were bringing turmoil and death to his country. And furthermore, he angrily spluttered, on the day prior to him sneaking away from the camp he'd heard that the temples all over the country were being attacked and desecrated by unknown factions sanctioned by the powers that be and he wanted no part of it.

When Zeo heard this he almost lost track of his argument with the young man and wondered if the guy was exaggerating things just to strengthen his position. The premonition that he'd experienced a few nights ago fleetingly entered his thoughts but this only made him doubly determined to unload the encumbrance which this injured youth had now burdened them with; he'd served his purpose but would now slow them down and he couldn't allow that, regardless.

Johnny and Adam watched from the sidelines with mixed feelings. They understood the gist of Euander's protest when they sensed the intensity and passion in his voice and though they were marginalised and excluded by the language barrier and were unable to have an input in the personal exchange their gut feeling was that the new arrival in their camp had pluck and determination and would never capitulate to Zeo's proposition.

The heated conversation between the compatriots continued for the next fifteen minutes and at one stage Zeo jumped to his feet in frustration and paced back and forth irritably gesticulating in the air and shouting *'insania, insania!' insania!* until eventually he sat down exasperated when he recognised that the obstinate youth was no pushover and that he'd have to rethink his strategy. He turned in desperation to his friends.

When they both suggested that the decision be deferred until the morning when the position could be re-evaluated Euander fixed his gaze directly on Zeo's companions and he bowed his head to each of them in turn as if he'd figured out what they'd suggested. But the real reason was that he'd just realised that they were the two warriors from *Terra Ferusum* who'd been declared *Praecipuum* of Sitantal and he'd been merely doing his duty by acknowledging that fact.

The three watchmen took turns sharing the two remaining sleeping bags as the not-so-welcome guest slept soundly in Zeo's personal sleeping bag.

As Zeo prepared breakfast Euander eased carefully to his feet and approached him and enquired if he'd reached a decision about his future. When Zeo responded that if he was able to keep up with them and not delay them in any way then he was prepared to let him remain until they'd exited *Primoris*. But after that they'd try to find him a safe house to recover from his injuries.

The young man nodded his head and limped away. When Johnny and Adam finished bathing in the river Zeo told them of his promise to the injured youth and they agreed but both reminded their friend that Euander had taken considerable risks to warn them of the danger ahead and deserved consideration and a helping hand in return.

When breakfast was over Zeo cleansed and dressed the patient's wounds and unpacked his old uniform and substituted the youth's tattered gear with his own though the recipient was at least one size larger than him. The youth had gritted his teeth when all of this was being done and was doubly determined not to show any further signs of weakness or fear and silently prayed to the Gods to help him make a quick recovery and not be a burden or liability on the role models he'd hoped to emulate when he'd joined the forces of the ousted Consul Primus.

They left the rickety bridge camp site just after eight o'clock on Saturday morning and moved at a steady pace along the cobbled road though they were ever mindful of the hobbling newcomer to the group. When they agreed to a coffee break after eleven, oddly enough it was more out of sympathy for Euander than a sudden craving for the vital brew.

Both the patient and Friday made do with bottled water and as the group relaxed with their beverages Euander suggested that when they reach the *custodis* camp on the other side he would try and get one of the smaller, fast moving wagons to help transport the baggage. He had an idea on how it could be done but it would mean that they'd have to wait until dark when the camp was *dormiens* and there would only be four patrolling night sentries to contend with.

They all fancied and agreed with the scenario but they realised they still had to break through the heavily manned checkpoint unscathed before they could plan a wish list with such tempting accessories.

It was early afternoon when they saw the gaping gap into *Oriens* in the distance and took cover behind a thick wayward branch which jutted out almost to the centre of the cobbled road and here they waited for nightfall.

CHAPTER TWELVE

The newly built security checkpoint was arranged in an encompassing crescent shape on a four-step high wooden platform and had the appearance of a mini amphitheatre from a distance. It blockaded the only escape route into Sitantal proper from the extreme regions. The cobbled road leading to Ciro City dissected the central protractor-shaped space and was illuminated by six large lanterns which had their beams fixed towards the gaping split in the rock which left the perimeter of the camp shaded and in relative darkness. Diagonally crisscrossing the otherwise empty area and always precisely converging on the centre of the roadway were four silent patrolling sentries carrying long shields and lances.

The other four men, those with the golden Labrador, edged nearer to the wide breach in the rocky division separating both regions close to midnight, or the "Witchin Houah" as Johnny had put it when they'd been developing their escape strategy earlier.

Adam had timed the patrolling sentries outside and confirmed that it took exactly two minutes for each guard to traverse from one corner of the imaginary saltire to the opposite end and the trajectory of the route afforded two guards to have the opening continually in sight. Euander had mentioned that during daylight hours the inward facing canvas flaps on the bank of tents were flung open and virtually all activity within the garrison was conducted in the half circle giving a clear view of the target and making an escape from *Extremus* near impossible when the camp was active, underpinning his earlier suggestion that they make the attempt when the camp was *dormio*.

    A few seconds before midnight Adam raised his hand when the guards met again in the centre spot. Johnny darted to the middle of the rock fissure and launched the first white flare over the campsite. As it dazzled brightly in the night sky and lit up the entire area Adam and Zeo rushed forward with loaded crossbows and closed in on the distracted guardsmen. They brought two men down as their colleagues gaped with open mouths in wonderment at the glowing showering sphere overhead before they too hit the ground in quick succession. Contrary to their raisons d'être and obligations none of the sentries raised the alarm or even uttered a cry before dying.

The cousins each grabbed a shield from where they now lay unused on the cobbled road and spun round and raced in opposite directions to the extremes of the arc-shaped enclosure unhooking their flamethrowers as they ran.

But somewhere in the garrison somebody had been alerted by the startling illumination overhead and now screeched a frenetic stream of warnings into the night as Euander followed Johnny and hobbled along the cobbled road. They disabled each of the lanterns on the way with Johnny using crossbow and bolts while Euander employed a *dirigo* and *iaculum*. The entire camp had now erupted with a cacophony of conflicting orders ringing out as men scrambled from the *cubicula* uncertain what was happening. Some gawped upwards as the remnants of the first flare cascaded to the ground while others glanced to their left or right to both ends of the complex at the flames sweeping skywards where Zeo and Adam had attacked the canvas walls and wooden platforms with the flamethrowers.

The second flare was a bright orange burst which cast an eerie sepia-like shade over the scene and brought fresh shrieks and roars from the scuttling soldiers and several loud incantations to the Gods were plainly audible to Euander as he shuffled as fast as his patched-up wounds would allow him to in the direction of the garrisons' stables and paddocks. Though he'd been warned by Zeo what to expect when the attack was launched it took all of his self control not to be overwhelmed by the crazy things which were happening above and around him. He stoically tried to concentrate on what he'd been entrusted to do. He displayed the Governor Maximus insignia prominently on his tunic as he weaved through the scattering soldiers unchallenged until he reached the corral behind the camp where he witnessed a large number of men dashing around trying to harness the equally frightened animals for a quick getaway from the pyrotechnic display at ground level and overhead.

The dog had kept close to his master's side as they'd crept to within five feet of the tented accommodation wing where Adam had released the first spurt of flame. It had taken less than three seconds for the fire to take hold on the dry canvas and it elicited an immediate response from those inside which was screechy and panicky. The animated occupants could be seen grabbing weapons and possessions and most of them exited stage right and took to their heels and escaped to beyond the inferno. The flames consumed the canvas greedily and the bare structural framework was exposed in a flash.

Adam moved quickly on to the next unit and repeated the action and saw with the corner of his eye that Zeo was replicating his actions on the other wing of the horseshoe shaped enclave. They advanced stealthily along the curve until they met at the gap in the centre where the road passed through into the open countryside beyond.

Here Johnny had waited impatiently for his mates and regretted that he hadn't equipped himself with his own flamethrower and be able to speed things up but the plan had been that he should remain in the open space close to the entrance to the camp to monitor the response of the *custodis* and also see to it that the debilitated Euander passed through unhindered during the confusion and attempt to secure a horse and wagon. But Johnny's eagerness for action had made him stretch the rules of engagement a little when he'd positioned himself on the track between both wings of the tented dais where he darted back and forth waylaying any fleeing *custodis* who came nearer than a sword's length to him and very soon he lost track of the hits he'd scored in the unfolding tumult. Although everyone he engaged with appeared to be armed to the teeth they rushed blindly onto his sword as though he was invisible or even irresistible, similar he conjectured, to the incomprehensible sight of a herd of bolting wildebeests who couldn't perceive that they had the strength in numbers to win if only they'd stop, turn and utilize brute force and momentum on their attackers. But he didn't grumble too much because it gave credibility to his mantra of using *shock, awe* and *strike* tactics to defeat the enemy or on the other hand perhaps the strange all-black uniform and night-visions he wore didn't correspond with what their perceived opponent should look like, he mused, but whatever the reason was it worked a treat!

At the outer edge of the burning campus when the orange hue from above changed to a bright red tinge the human stampede intensified and the exit road from the chaotic compound became a free-for-all marathon track.

Soon the atmosphere of calamity pervading the camp had caught up with most of the men in the paddock where they gave up trying to harness the bucking animals and took flight from the field on foot and joined the others on the cobbled road leading to Ciro City.

Euander ignored the pandemonium surrounding him and continued purposely through the paddocks to the stables where he hoped to find his horse where he'd reluctantly left him three days ago to go search for Zeo in *Extremus*. But when he entered the faintly lighted enclosure he gasped with shock and indignation at what he saw.

The thickset *Centurio* in charge of the military outpost was about to mount Candeo, the pure white colt which was Euander's pride and joy. He bellowed at the captain to get away from his horse but the intending thief quickly pulled himself onto the saddle and unsheathed his sword and spurred the reluctant animal towards the open gate. He swung his curved blade wildly at Euander's head as he passed, yelling at him to do something which was alien to him and physically impossible for the young man to do. Euander followed outside and inserted two fingers into his mouth and gave a sharp distinctive whistle whereupon Candeo pulled up and reared on his hind legs and dumped the *Centurio* to the floor with a violent shake of his body. Before the stunned horse bandit could rise to his feet Euander decapitated him with one clean sweep of his sword just below the neck ridge on his helmet.

As the red flare began to wane on its way back to *terra firma* Johnny selected another white burner and sent it aloft but by now the encampment appeared to be pretty much deserted. Just then through the billowing pungent smoke from the smouldering wooden rostrum Zeo joined him carrying a blood smeared sword and shield with his flamethrower hanging from his waist belt. Without delay Johnny rotated on his heel and went in the opposite direction with Zeo in his train in search of Adam but they'd barely gone twenty yards when he and Zeo were confronted with a surreal almost mystical sight.

Within the wispy fog of drifting smoke and fumes several yards away from them the most spectral white steed stood gently snorting and rolling his head from side to side. But the grinning face of Euander in the saddle with Adam and Friday standing alongside them was equally gratifying and pleasing to the eye.

Brief victory salutes, handshakes and hugs were exchanged before they set about arranging the funeral pyre for those men who'd failed to escape and later when Zeo and Euander had finished the *exsequiae* rites they went to the corral where the animals had pacified now that the fires had subsided to just the occasional spark. Here they selected three lively ponies which had the appearance of being best of breed and rounded up four powerful cart horses and tethered them away from the drifting smoke and then returned to the paddock where they released the remaining pack to run free onto the grassland north of the camp. They explored the area and earmarked two sturdy four-wheeled wagons.

Meanwhile Adam and Johnny had hauled the rest of their gear from *Primoris* and had handpicked a quantity of the native weaponry from the camp's arsenal before they set it alight. They'd showered in the bathhouse which, like the armoury, had virtually escaped the conflagration being sited on the outside perimeter.

Johnny dutifully assumed the role of cook leaving the others to load the wagons with the equipment and supplies and at this point Euander took control of the logistics arrangement and decided on the location for the essential gear and the animal feedstuff on the cart. He linked both wagons in an articulated fashion with all four draught horses hauling the combined unit and by doing it this way the combo only needed one driver he reasoned. He appeared somewhat abashed when he admitted that until he was fully recovered he'd prefer the role of driver instead of riding on Candeo and that this way the others had the flexibility and freedom to reconnoitre the surrounding countryside unhindered on their own mounts. It wasn't lost on both Adam and Zeo that he was establishing his position to a more permanent role within their group but they didn't mind and in fact when the guy had been out of earshot earlier the three friends had decided then that they wanted him to remain with them for the duration. The decision was a no brainer for them, considering how he'd risked his life to get the warning from the Consul Primus to Zeo and then, though still in a parlous state from his injuries he'd managed to secure transport for them and had even dispatched the camp *Centurio* single handily in the process and it showed intelligence, commitment and stamina they concurred. The only downside to all of this was that he couldn't enter the Temple of the Gods and would have to remain outside but even that would be a good thing they quickly recognised.

Very soon the enticing aroma of percolating coffee which was wafting in their direction was overwhelmed by the mouth-watering whiff of a bacon fry-up courtesy of the camp's ample food store and Johnny's foraging and culinary expertise. It enticed them to where he'd prepared a triumphal breakfast feast, al fresco, though it was well away from the smouldering fort and funeral pyre.

And it was here...right on this very spot...that Euander savoured his inaugural taste of the most fundamental of brews essential to the quality of life and human fulfilment on this planet! Coffee!

And at this point Zeo informed Euander that he

was now *Optio* to Adam, Johnny and him.
The saliva-inducing breakfast revamped their energy reserves and though it was barely past the middle of the night they each had a celebratory glass of red wine.

Just before daylight they turned their backs on the smouldering scene of total destruction. When Euander climbed aboard the leading wagon and waited for the signal to go he reflected on what could be a life-changing and possibly an epoch-making venture he'd become involved in almost by accident. The sole purpose of the now defunct security post had been to capture Zeo and his friends when they entered *Oriens* but it had ended in abject failure and defeat for those who'd contrived the plan.
He still found it hard to believe that he'd played a small role in the opening scene by lending assistance to the son of the Consul Primus and the two *Praecipuus* of Sitantal and when he'd been told that he was *Optio* to all three heroes he'd gone week at the knees.
The scourge of 'Pravus' Sorus were alive and well and they were about to continue on their mission to the Temple of the Gods with a little help from him. And he was going with them as their *Optio*! Just imagine!
If only his parents could see him now!

As the linked-up combo wagon convoy with three outriders, a Labrador dog and a loosely tethered white colt moved south west from the charred compound in a remote corner of *Oriens,* almost one hundred miles away from this event an ominous procession of sealed black carriages exited the potholed road leading from the toxic swamplands in *Inferus Medius.* It headed due south and it too was on a mission.

The nefarious assignment was the product of the latest brainstorm of the usurper 'Pravus' Sorus and its intended destination was also the Temple of the Gods.

The passenger on the driver's bench on the leading black-curtained carriage was the vile herpetologist, Reptus Reptum.

CHAPTER THIRTEEN

The function of *Desperato Exspectatio Paenitentiarius* was plainly visible at first sight but once inside the place it exemplified the significance of its nomenclature precisely.

Rarely did anyone imprisoned in Hopeless Expectations Penitentiary come out contrite, reformed or for that matter even alive and no inmate had ever escaped from the place since the time when it was built. It was a gaunt austere superstructure which dominated the northern skyline of Vili City. It was situated on a steep incline and was isolated from the urban sprawl with only one narrow road linking it to the provincial capital. The ugly edifice could easily have been likened to a carbuncle on the outer city landscape.

There wasn't a single window or slit in its entire outer walls and the only view the inmates ever had was of its inner courtyard which could never be described as scenic or inspiring.

To the agreeable and law-abiding citizens of Vili City it symbolised *Purgamentum;* an earthly Purgatory; a cleansing place, but to the disagreeable and lawless it represented *Infernum in Terra*, Hell on Earth!

Below the hillside the fast moving flotilla, wagons and mounted troop had veered off from the main waterway and pathway into the slip channel which ran directly parallel with the road leading from the city to the prison complex and then past its grim forbidding and forboding entrance.

The Consul was perturbed to hear that there appeared to be no perimeter night-patrols on duty as they'd expected and he worried that the information he'd been given earlier was incorrect. Nonetheless he decided that they must continue; there was no going back, he'd come here to release the political prisoners and that was what he must do. He ordered his *explorator* to reconnoitre the prison site and to quickly report back to him.

They continued on the canal until they reached the extreme corner of the building and turned west.

Here the soldiers disembarked and readied their weapons and waited for the scout to return and some ten minutes later he informed the Consul Primus that all the night crew were in the communal room in the guardhouse which straddled both sides of the main entrance to the grim structure. They appeared to have abandoned their patrols and posts for the night and were waiting inside for the morning prison crew changeover.

The *century* of infantrymen split equally

with fifty of the Consul's men moving silently behind him up the incline to the guardhouse while the other foot soldiers followed the mounted troops who skirted round the rear of the building to the south side of the prison and positioned themselves near the connecting city road and here they waited in the shadows for the replacement guards to arrive. The Consul advised them to be prepared for stiff resistance and explained that the men coming on duty would have rested and were bound to be more resilient whereas he and his men would be facing those who'd been awake all night and probably less alert or prepared. He assured them that as soon as the guardroom was under control he'd join up with them.

    He and his infantry crouched in the long grass behind the unkempt guardhouse near the prison's main door and listened to the gabbling debate taking place inside. It confirmed what the *factotum* had reported the previous day, that Deputy Governor Pollux had left the province and was still with 'Pravus' Sorus and this he surmised was probably the reason that the prisons outer guard were taking it easy while he was away.

The men looked relaxed as they sprawled around the large table in the centre of the tatty room but right now they were moaning about being short staffed and having to work extra shifts because all the new recruits were being sent south to bolster the forces protecting *Urbis Capitolium*. They bewailed the fact that these raw rookies would be able to live the high-life in the Capitol and escape the constant grind of this place while they had to remain here and then, worse still, go home daily to snivelling kids, nagging wives or the same old boring, boring girlfriends, *ad nauseam!* It just wasn't fair!

The sound of glasses being topped up to drown their sorrows and help alleviate this perceived unfairness and injustice was duly noted by the silent eavesdroppers outside.

And as the Consul waited for the prearranged time he reflected on their journey across country during the night.

They'd made good progress after they'd despatched the four sentries at the canal junction without disturbing the sleeping village. He'd been certain that the reason the men were based there was that somewhere within the village there was a larger force of *custodis* billeted, otherwise there wouldn't be any point of having lookouts located at the canal intersection he'd concluded and if he was right in his guess then the billeted *custodis* and villagers would be in for a shock when they wakened.

He'd taken the advice of his younger son and his friends from *Terra Ferusum* of the advantages of spooking the enemy and whittling away at their morale and he'd arranged the dead sentries in such a way that would demoralise their comrades even more when they'd make the discovery at daybreak. Four hours earlier he and six of his cavalrymen had crept behind the nearest patrolling guard and had silently killed him and removed his body from the path and quickly replaced the sentry with one of their own men and they did the same with the next man in line until they'd removed all four without the alarm being raised; copying the scenario where Adam and Johnny had neutralised the sentries patrolling the camp in Nox before they'd rescued Camilla and Zeo from Gaius and the axe-man.

They'd then decapitated all four bodies and had propped them up in sitting positions facing directly into the village centre and had swapped the severed heads of each body so that the fattest man clutched the head of the thinnest on his lap and *vice versa* and again the other way round with the oldest man holding the head of the youngest soldier on his lap. They'd also arranged them with their eyes and mouths fixed wide open!

Recalling the grisly scene caused the Consul to shiver involuntarily all over again.

It was something that he'd never envisaged doing and even now it was spine-chilling just thinking about it. His reason for creating such a ghastly scene had been simply to frighten off any *custodis* who might be billeted in the village and could present a problem for them on their return journey to Esta City. The more he thought about it the more uncomfortable he became. He wondered if he'd ever sleep contentedly again.

He and his men had then rejoined the rest of the

cavalry unit and the flotilla where they'd waited further back on the canal and together they resumed the journey westwards. The curious crews in the *naviculae* had stood up when passing through the village and had craned their necks to have a look at the ghoulish sight they'd heard about from the returning cavalrymen but he had averted his gaze as he'd trotted past the deathly quiet settlement.

Standing on the top step leading into the forum in the central square in Vili City, less than two miles from Hopeless Expectations Penitentiary, the *Tempus Dico* announced the start of the active day while nearby the *Lanterna Extinctor* was snuffing out the city centre lights.

Just as the relief guard came within sight of the prison a silvery-blue dawn began to light up the countryside and when the Consul heard the clatter of his charging cavalrymen at the south side of the building he raised his hand and he and his men stormed into the guardhouse.

Tables, chairs, *amphorae*, bottles and glasses were sent flying in every direction and copious amounts of red wine were lost forever through the cracks in the wooden floor.

The soldiers displaying the *viridis, album* and *russus* insignia of the Consul Primus had the upper hand over those with the *album* and *niger* colours of the usurper 'Pravus' Sorus from the beginning. The prison guards were ill prepared to respond to the invasion of their space having casually laid their weapons here, there and everywhere when they'd settled back and relaxed to exchange gossip, gripes and grievances. But earlier in the intimate debate quite a few risqué jokes had been shared between them which, unknowingly, the Consul Primus and his men had missed out on because of their later arrival at the scene.

It took less than five minutes to bring the prison guards to heel. Twelve of the twenty-one men surrendered before long which prevented a total wipe-out taking place in the blood-spattered squad room. The Consul had managed to achieve a kill before he'd been surrounded by four of his own men who'd acted as a shielding *praetorian* guard and prevented the enemy getting too close to their leader during the violent though brief action.

As the bloodshed ended in the guardhouse and the surviving prison guards were being secured, several hundred yards away to the south of the building the vicious hostilities continued unabated on the second front and when the Consul left the base and witnessed this he dispatched most of his foot soldiers to the scene only keeping a handful back to supervise the captured prisoners in the guardroom. He moved closer to the combat zone and saw that the reinforcements were already making a profound difference and in less than two minutes the resisting guards threw down their weapons and surrendered to his captain.

Two casualties were sustained by his forces at the approach road battle, one trooper and one infantryman but the enemy had suffered fourteen casualties.

It took almost an hour to unlock all the cramped and squalid cells containing the political prisoners in Hopeless Expectations Penitentiary. The Consul found that the men, women and children behind bars were dirty, malnourished, and dehydrated and several of the younger men had visible signs of recent physical abuse, some of whom the Consul had known before the coup. He was shocked beyond belief when he saw how inhumanely these hapless people had been treated here, much worse than he and his fellow prisoners had been in Tabo City. He heard one harrowing story after another and grew angrier as he listened to details of injured and ill prisoners having been executed by the warden for no reason other than that they couldn't look after themselves or fight back. By the time all the political prisoners had been accounted for and debriefed and taken to the open courtyard he was incandescent with rage especially when he thought of the number of men who'd died rather than submit to the brutal warden. The Consul sent his captain to check if the man was among the captives and when he was brought before him he had the screeching man executed on his own gallows in the quadrangle.

The victorious troopers were split into two groups with one delegated to round up the abandoned horses and wagons and also to collect the weapons from the roadside and the prisons guardroom while the others secured the perimeter of the prison and organised the *exsequiae* rite for the dead. The infantrymen were given responsibility for the interior of the prison and charged with organising the new regime and to conduct an inventory of the armoury and the food stores to see how long supplies would last in the event of a counter response from the city's barracks.

A number of the captured *custodis* and prison guards were sent to the laundry to provide clean clothing to the freed prisoners while others were made to refill the overhead shower tanks again and again. The remainder were sent to the kitchens to assist in providing a substantial meal to everyone.

In the early afternoon when everybody had freshened up and dined the Consul sought out those who had previous military experience before their incarceration and those who were now prepared to join forces with him against Sorus but they'd have to be prepared to hurt and kill their fellow-countrymen without mercy to bring this madness to a conclusion.

He told the assembled men that he'd now decided to attack the city's central barracks and fully expected to meet resistance there but he believed that the lack of a counter strike by the city defenders so far had exposed a weakness in their command which he felt duty bound to exploit to the full. He knew that by now the urban population would be well aware of what had happened here when the night officers hadn't returned home after their tour of duty and furthermore the people who lived nearby were bound to have seen and heard the clash this morning and would have alerted the garrison that the prison had been breached and the prisoners released.

Even though the Consul recognised that he was taking a serious gamble and perhaps pushing his luck to the maximum by embarking on this action with his limited force he reckoned that it might be the only opportunity he'd have to encourage a *vox populi* debate between ordinary people before Pollux returned from the Capitol. The Consul was well aware of the power and influence the man wielded in this community and he couldn't ignore the fact that he'd turned a ragtag army into a fairly respectable fighting force within two years of taking charge of the military in *Occidens*.

He understood the need to treat Puto Pollux with caution and respect.

CHAPTER FOURTEEN

Just as dawn was breaking the tightly grouped articulated wagon-train accompanied by the three outriders and dog veered to the left from the main road to Ciro City a short distance from where they'd exited the thrashed surveillance camp outside the opening to *Primoris.* Zeo feared that they might encounter the *custodis* who'd dispersed following the midnight rout and advised his companions that it would be best to avoid any further contact with them. He reckoned that most of the gutless and contemptible deserters would be reluctant to return to their barracks in the regional capital for fear of punishment for their craven behaviour and ignominious retreat from the camp and they'd probably resort to banditry and pillage to survive from here on in he reckoned. He added that the last thing they needed on the journey southwest was to be harried and delayed unnecessarily though there was no certainties that even taking a circuitous route they wouldn't encounter them anyway; they could be anywhere in the locality at this stage he surmised.

As they cantered along the narrow stone surfaced road the three horsemen spent time getting acquainted with their new mounts and learning what if any idiosyncrasies the animals might have and also find out how responsive they were to their commands. But each of the three secretly eyed up Candeo with just a little bit of green-eyed wistfulness for what was a most handsome, graceful animal with intelligent blue-grey eyes which were forever alert as it trotted majestically alongside its rightfully proud owner.

As soon as Johnny and Adam felt confident in handling the ponies they trotted ahead of Zeo and the wagons along the nearly deserted road feasting their eyes on the landscape on all sides and just like the time they'd first seen Oppida in northern *Oriens* from the high vantage point they felt a similar thrill now, but this one was even better, they could reach out and touch the allurement at leisure in broad daylight without worrying that someone might see them. Their status as *Praecipuum* meant that no one should question or hinder them and even though they'd initially scorned the award they were now prepared to take full advantage of it to see everything that Sitantal had on offer considering that less than a month ago they'd been denied that chance when they had to leave the country at very short notice.

They bypassed several sleepy hamlets during the early hours and though they would've jumped at the chance to visit all of them they agreed with Zeo that they had to keep moving forward, but before nine o'clock they stopped on the outskirts of a pretty little village called Sala and led the horses to a nearby fountain where its circular lower basin rippled and overflowed with sparkling clear water. But their attention was immediately drawn to an uncomfortable and disturbing sight about twelve yards from the water feature.

An ancient grey-haired lady dressed all in black whose face was lined with more wrinkles than an elephant's ear, or so Johnny irreverently thought, stood wiping tears from her furrowed cheeks beside what appeared to be a recently demolished building.
Zeo approached her cautiously and enquired gently what troubled her and asked if he could be of assistance. She stopped dabbing the handkerchief and slowly raised her gaze. Her weary eyes explored the strangely dressed youth and though she'd never seen anyone quite so sinister looking in her life she showed no fear when she told him she wept because the village temple had been destroyed and the *augur* had been forcibly taken away *and* that *no* one had lifted a finger to stop it. She wailed that she just didn't understand what was happening to her country anymore.
As Zeo absorbed the plaintive lament he became angrier when he glanced at the pile of rubble and saw the remnants of a little brass bell scattered among the debris and he realised that Euander

hadn't been exaggerating after all when he'd said that he'd heard that the temples around the country were being desecrated. Now, and right here in front of him, was evidence of the sacrilegious act.

He was still glaring at the scattered masonry and charred timbers when Johnny warned him that several men were approaching and that they didn't look very welcoming.

The five-strong officious looking group, four of whom were in *custodis* uniform, came to a halt when they were about twenty feet away from the fountain. The oldest man amongst them, who displayed a prominent Governor Maximus insignia on his chest, drew himself up importantly and raised his hand towards his mouth and very aggressively cleared his throat. It appeared as if he was about to challenge the strangers but Zeo preempted him by raising the palm of his hand and motioned authoritatively for silence. He pointed to the mound of rubble and demanded to know who was responsible for the destruction of the temple. His actions and the tone of his voice confused the group and the four *custodis* looked at their leader for guidance but his only response was to move his right hand stealthily towards the curved sword hanging at his side.

With three giant bounds Zeo was right in front of him and slapped him so hard across the face the man crashed to the floor before his fingertips had even reached the hilt of his sabre. Adam and Johnny quickly stepped forward and withdrew their Taser guns in readiness for a reaction from the others but the four men seemed to be rooted to the ground in shock. When the recumbent official stirred and attempted to rise to his feet Zeo grabbed his collar and yanked him upright. As the dazed man swayed and tried to focus his gaze on his assailant Zeo ripped the Maximus insignia from his vest and crushed it beneath his boot and kicked the remnants from underfoot with contempt. Though the official's colleagues had been stunned to inertia by the initial assault on their superior this fresh affront enraged them sufficiently to make them act but that first shock they'd experienced a moment ago would be nothing compared to the next jolt they were about to receive.

They stepped back from the scene almost in tandem and fumbled rather clumsily to unsheathe their blades.

Adam ordered Friday to sit and he and Johnny darted further forward and they fired all four Taser guns in unison.

The old lady shielded her toothless mouth with her hand in surprise as she watched the men collapse in a heap together and writhe and twitch all over the place and she wasn't the only spectator who's mouth was agape at this stage.

As the tension had risen near the fountain it seemed that everybody in the village had become aware of it and had taken up vantage points to see what the hubbub was all about. If the body language was to be relied on, not one of the villagers appeared to be remotely sympathetic to the plight of the official or his men and the children were laughing and giggling at the sight of the four gasping, jerking contortionists on the ground and the adults made no attempt to rebuke them or to become involved, Zeo observed silently.

Euander had turned away from the horses at the drinking bowl and now stood alert with his sword at the ready but he too was just as stunned and mesmerised as all the others were by what was happening just yards away but he was loving every minute of it. He thought gleefully that the adventure gets better all the time.

Though the villagers were obviously nervous when Zeo approached them dragging the reluctant official by his sleeve they remained static and stoic. When he raised his free hand in greeting and asked if this was the man responsible for the destruction of the temple the old lady screeched from behind him that he wasn't but that he did nothing to prevent it either even though he was the village *praesum*.

While Zeo held onto the village chief and questioned the assembled crowd Johnny and Adam removed the Taser probes from the four men and proceeded to disarm them while they were still not fully recovered from the shock treatment though they were now trying to rise to their feet. When one of the dazed *custodis* attempted to stop Adam taking his blade he smashed him on the jaw with an uppercut which sent him back to the floor, but this time he made no convulsed movements; he was just out cold!

And Friday sniffed at the prostrate man's waxen face but made no attempt to lick it.

The villagers told Zeo that the temple *augur* had been taken captive by the band of *Mors Maniplulus* after they'd demolished the temple and that no one had seen him since. When he turned and asked the angry *praesum* what or who was this *Death Squad* he responded in a brazen arrogant manner that they were a special troop of fearless cavalrymen led by Commander Suga Cazo and they were popularly known as *"Removal Men"* established by Consul Primus Sorus.

When Zeo heard the official describe the outlaws almost with pride and refer to the dictator as *"Consul Primus"* he whacked him again across the face. The *praesum* rocked and swayed but he managed to remain upright as blood trickled from his now misshapen nose.

Zeo declared loudly that there was only one Consul Primus in Sitantal and that it was his father, Zeor, Consul Primus *Hereditarius!*

The watching crowd were obviously surprised at this but they remained restrained and offered no other response until the old lady in black pushed through the group forcefully and squawked shrilly *"Tu es Zeo?"*

He continued to face the villagers when he answered firmly "Yes, *Matrona*, I am Zeo, son of Zeor!" *"Auguribus dixit vultis venire!"* she said, as she approached him and bowed her head.

He was mystified when the old lady revealed that the *augur* had predicted that he would come to this place as he'd been dragged away by his kidnappers. Zeo bowed in response to the old lady but again he directed his words to the cluster of villagers.

He declared that Governor Maximus had aided 'Pravus' Sorus in bringing the country to the edge of anarchy where lawless gangs were now free to desecrate temples and abduct holy men and prophets at will. Surely the good people of Sitantal wouldn't want this to happen? What future would they and their children have under these traitorous villains and megalomaniacs? He pointed to the temple rubble and said that this was the result when evil went unchallenged. He announced that his father now controlled northern *Medius* and would advance to the south and to the east and west in the coming months and he would annihilate anyone who'd harmed their culture and their beloved country.

He informed them that this *praesum* was no longer in charge of the village but that he and the four guardians who'd allowed the destruction of the temple were now without lawful jurisdiction and must be held accountable for their collusion and failure in their duty and were therefore liable for the temples' restoration. He asked if there was anyone present who was willing to take on the responsibility for the wellbeing of the village under the authority of his father Zeor, Consul Primus.

Instantly one of the men in the crowd stepped forward and firmly announced his willingness and said that his name was Varus. He declared his readiness if the people agreed. He turned and bowed when all the villagers cheered in response.

Zeo saluted Varus and unbuckled the sword belt from the less than obliging disgraced official and he presented both belt and sword to the newly appointed *praesum* together with the weapons of the four redundant *custodis*. Zeo advised Varus to surround himself only with people he could trust and those who'd commit to protecting their village's wellbeing from now on.

He signalled to his three companions to come forward where he introduced them to the new *praesum* and the other villagers. Adam and Johnny tucked the pocket flaps behind the gold and enamelled insignia when Zeo mentioned proudly to the gathering that they were *Praecipuum* of Sitantal. All the adults and the older children in the crowd bowed their heads in acknowledgment as did Zeo and Euander and even the ex officials each gave a brief head bob.

    The ancient, wrinkled lady appeared to have discovered a new energy source as she fussed around the long table sited beyond the fountain. Every now and then she berated the young girls who were supposed to be helping her and the other village women in preparing the al fresco meal when the girls seemed more interested in checking out the four young newcomers who were seated nearby with the new village chief and a small group of men he'd selected to assist him.

A short distance away at the site of the temple ruins the deposed *praesum* and the four former *custodis* were sorting through the rubble and salvaging material which could be reused in its restoration but they didn't appear to be particularly happy or enthusiastic with their new career move. Though Euander watched and observed the ongoing debate he wasn't required to partake in it so he could allow his attention to stray without any fear of rebuke. Occasionally he was fortunate enough to make lingering eye contact with some of the pretty girls which made the sedentary activity less tedious for him.

But very soon Adam and Johnny became restless and bored watching the flirtatious primping antics of the very silly and very young girls and listening in on a conversation which was way beyond them, language wise, and they decided to stretch their legs and explore. They sauntered around the small village square when Adam eventually managed to coax Friday away from the generous ladies preparing the meal.

The pair paused at each house and feasted their eyes on the individual architectural styles that differentiated each building and observed that not one building resembled another and that they were all completely unique. They spent some time outside the village emporium which displayed an array of produce and products for sale which extended well beyond the front of the shop and onto the square and every possible requisite for the sustainment of life and limb appeared to be available there. The owner was nowhere to be seen so they browsed at leisure and recognised numerous things which they might have found in any supermarket back home though the labels had names which oddly seemed at variance with what they commonly called them, but when they tried to pronounce the written word it sounded more scholarly and less appealing to them. The only food item they found that had a nominal connection with their language was the display of lemons which had a label which stated *citrus limon*. The strange little symbols and digits on the labels they assumed was the cost of the item in the local currency which was something they'd need to discuss with Zeo later.

When they sauntered inside the open fronted store they were met with a diffusion of contrasting aromas, some they were very familiar with but there were others that were excitingly new to their olfactory senses and as they wandered around the emporium Adam believed that if he closed his eyes he could imagine he was strolling through a fragrant English country garden in high summer; it was calming but at the same time it was quite stimulating.

Johnny's nasal stimuli had a field day and the experience brought back latent memories of home and of his mother baking and cooking in their kitchen in the weeks leading up to Christmas or other special occasions like family birthdays though there was a possibility that it might be the numerous occasions he'd spent outdoors with his father when he'd smelt every plant and bloom and then had peppered him with questions on every aspect of botany that had popped into his inquisitive little brain. He'd thought the scents from way back then had been truly out of this world but here he had the pleasure of having them all together again in one big massive hit. The deluge of diverse perfumes surrounding him was so redolent of his childhood that he found it both tranquilising and invigorating in equal measure.

It was a generous though not a flamboyant meal provided by the villagers to the four visitors but Zeo made good use of the opportunity to again emphasise the need for the people to assert their patriotism and not allow malignant, radical individuals change their culture, freedoms and their way of life.

And Euander was feeling bright eyed and bushy tailed too and had all three ponies saddled in preparation for their departure. He climbed aboard the wagon combo with much more ease than before and felt totally rejuvenated following the session with the village *clinicus* who'd been coaxed by Zeo to attend to his recent injuries following his encounter with the Rootless creeping thorn-vine in *Primoris*. She'd assured him that in a few days he'd be good as new but insisted that he avoid any unnecessary scratching or exertion in the meantime. When they were leaving the small village Zeo saluted the assembled crowd and called out authoritatively *'Ero tergo!'* When he explained to Adam and Johnny that he'd promised the villagers "I'll be back!" the pair had exchanged knowing glances and burst into hyper laughter which puzzled and irked him and made him spur his mount forward and leave them behind, still in side-splitting fits.

They continued travelling southwest along the narrow road during the late afternoon and evening but avoided going to any of the other villages they saw in the distance when Zeo said if they visited all of them they'd never reach the Temple of the Gods and he was sure they'd find ample rivers and streams for the horses along the way. They encountered a few farmers and traders on the road but on these occasions the black dressed trio together with the dog took off into the surrounding countryside to avoid stirring up local curiosity more than was totally necessary. They hoped that from a distance they'd appear to be a hunting party which was exactly the idea they wanted to convey.

Before nightfall they pitched camp in a spinney adjacent to the roadside and at eight o'clock on Tuesday morning they pushed west again.

CHAPTER FIFTEEN

The neat and well maintained outstation which housed the *Beneficiarius*, the mounted military veterans whose function was to monitor and defend the environs and the approaches to the Temple of the Gods, was bustling with the constant arrival and departure of lightly armed men either going out on patrol or returning to the base from their tour of duty. The man in charge and responsible for maintaining law and order at the spiritual site was the widower General Exer Savus who for years had been the senior *Praefectus* guarding the Forum in *Urbis Capitolium* until his retirement twelve months ago. He'd been a personal friend of the Consul Primus who'd appointed him to this mainly ceremonial post with the honorific title *Dux,* just before the Consul had been ousted by 'Pravus' Sorus.

Only retired combatants who were either bachelors or widowers were eligible to serve in the remote posting for that very reason; its isolated position and its unsuitability to a normal, everyday family life. Their daily duties consisted mainly of rounding up errant children who'd given their parent or guardian the slip and had strayed into the no-go zone or even the odd artist who thought he or she might get a more intimate and particular view of the scene if they repositioned their easels a teensy-weensy bit closer to the object of their endeavours. Only rarely did the custodians have to contend forcefully with someone who was intent on reaching the venerated edifice and it was usually a starry-eyed zealot who'd had an *ignis fatuus* experience before arriving here. At times there had been some who'd become delusional and fanciful after gazing at the multi-coloured spectacular for too long and quite a few who'd sampled more wine than was good for them and imagined that the deity had invited them to call at the Temple of the Gods for a personal tête-a-tête.

But these hiccups aside, on the whole it was a job that every man in the unit relished.

The *Beneficiarius* were greatly envied by those retiring veterans who'd failed the induction test to the unit and would now have to go home to their respective partners and their families, so much so, it had been rumoured in the past that several retirees had even considered how to accomplish widower status from their mostly middle-aged but otherwise healthy spouses just to gain admission to the elite force.

      The skyscape in the vicinity of the Temple of the Gods was fading fast. The multi coloured hues would soon change to the evening turquoise blue when the convoy of black four-wheel transporters neared its north-eastern boundary limits where it ground to a halt.

Reptus Reptum waited until the wagon was stationary before he lowered himself to the ground while the driver alighted on the other side of the vehicle and inhaled deeply and satisfyingly for the first time since they'd set off on the last stage of the journey south in the early afternoon. The pernicious and overwhelming stench coming from his fellow traveller had prevented him from breathing properly for the duration of the journey and to make matters more unbearable a light breeze had fanned the noxious fumes in his direction for all of the torturous drive.

The thought had crossed his mind more than once already that anybody who smelt like this man would surely have been dead for some time. He was convinced that his lungs and olfactory sensory neurons would never be normal again.

With guidance from the herpetologist the coachmen manoeuvred the wagons into the densely wooded hollow about a half mile away from the perimeter of the exclusion zone where it was out of sight and well off the beaten tracks. The four wagon drivers quickly unharnessed the restless and still nervous animals from the parked wagons.

When they'd entered the snake breeder's compound in *Inferus Medius* two days ago the horses had become instantly agitated and unsettled in the malodorous enclave but then the animals had come close to mutiny and had attempted to bolt several times when the cargo was being loaded into the wagons they were hauling. All of the horse handlers had remained tight-lipped at the time but they were equally disturbed and spooked by what they'd witnessed there and especially when they'd seen what was being loaded onto the wagons. They were reluctant to reveal their true feelings to each other because individually they each imagined what their fate would be if their anxieties and revulsion became known or if they appeared to have questioned the orders of 'Pravus' Sorus.

All four drivers were certain that their future could be summed up laconically and perhaps even idiomatically if they were reckless or foolish enough to voice their opinions or concerns in public.

They'd probably end up doing one of the following unwelcome things; Push up daisies! Buy the farm! Kick the bucket! Rest in pieces!

And none of them had a penchant to do any of these things at that time!

They hurriedly led the unharnessed animals away from the sunken hollow and onto the dirt track a short distance from the wagons and without any discourse or signal passing between them they each mounted a carthorse and straddled the animal bare-back and immediately galloped off gracelessly into the blue twilight with scant re-

gard for their health and safety, dignity or even for horse-riding posture protocols!
Men and horses remained focused as one.
And there was absolutely no looking back.
Nay! Nay!
No way!

    Reptus Reptum flung the doors open on the first three broad-base wagons without so much as a glance inside to see if his human freight had survived the arduous journey but when he reached the fourth carriage he entered and carefully examined the vivariums to see how his slithery charges had fared. Unafraid, he opened each case and caressed the writhing creatures with the back of his hand and whispered soothingly and even lovingly to them for some time.
Eventually he moved to the other side of the wagon and checked on the water supply to the large enclosed crate containing numerous clamouring white mice. He scattered several handfuls of seed and grain on the floor of the box and watched them briefly as they scrambled and foraged wildly for the feedstuff.
He turned his back on the creatures and rolled one of the many firkin-size wooden barrels from the front of the wagon to the rear door and wedged it in place where he filled bowl after bowl with a grey coloured gooey mix with an intriguing aloe vera aroma which was somewhere between piquant and spicy. Even he would agree that the mixture looked revoltingly unappetising and he would also

concede that it smelled much better than it looked or tasted also.

It was a concoction he'd developed over the years, a combination of herbs, nuts, fruit and honey with a generous helping of sodium bicarbonate which altogether had an efficient antacid effect on the human stomach but with sufficient nutrient value to keep the recipients alive and at the same time protect his little darlings within their female couriers.

He distributed the bowls to each of the wretched looking women in the first wagon and waited until all eighteen diners, who looked more like disintegrating automata whose power source was on the blink, had consumed fully the rations in the dishes before he repeated the task in the second wagon and finally the third. Though it was a bit of a chore having to do this he knew he had to remain patient and alert.

Experience had taught him that his female nurturers couldn't be trusted when it came to taking their daily provisions and to utilising their natural mothering instincts and responsibilities even though they must surely be aware that what they were doing was for the benefit of all helpless Animalia and therefore it had to be for the greater good.

In fact, to his horror, in the past some of the more rebellious females had even tried to starve themselves to death and had caused their vulnerable internal protégés unnecessary distress and suffering which had really enraged him and had utterly disillusioned him no end. He'd found it totally incomprehensible that the supposedly gentler sex could be so cruel and heartless to the poor little darlings residing inside them.

What on earth had happened to their intrinsic maternal attributes of compassion and tenderness he'd questioned despondently?
It was a sad reflection on present-day female society he'd concluded.

CHAPTER SIXTEEN

The approaching daylight in conjunction with the sky-high flames coming from Hopeless Expectations Penitentiary helped to push aside the darkness which had shrouded Vili City. The Consul Primus led the cavalry, infantrymen and a long procession of timber and ballast laden wagons which trudged through the narrow silent streets towards the central square where the *custodis* compound was located. He, together with his captains and *Praefecti,* had spent hours last evening checking out supplies and reviewing the plans to destroy the prison but also to deplete the heavily manned city fortress which he'd calculated would disrupt the central powerbase of 'Pravus' Sorus and ostensibly the nerve centre of the rebellious province of *Occidens*. Since yesterday they'd wondered why the garrison hadn't responded to the attack on the prison and guessed that without Puto Pollux to tell them what to do they were ineffective as an offensive force. He'd thought again of Zeo and his friends' maxim of the need to inflict psychological blows against the morale of the usurper and his stooges at every opportunity. He wouldn't be surprised if by now Pollux had been informed of his arrival in the province and might even be on his way to confront him.

Though the Consul's initial goal had been to free the political prisoners and return immediately with them to Esta City the opportunity to inflict further damage to his nemesis couldn't be missed especially when he'd heard that Pollux was still out of town but would be returning soon to assemble more *custodis* to strengthen the defences in the Capitol. If he could disrupt this plan in any way then it might make a positive difference further on. He was well aware that he was taking a massive risk in this hostile territory but he felt that it was a case of *Non ausum, non lucrum!* Nothing ventured, nothing gained! The disaffected province was an integral part of Sitantal and needed to be freed from the malign control of 'Pravus' Sorus and brought back into the fold whatever the cost and he fervently believed that not all of the people agreed with what 'Pravus' Sorus was doing.

Earlier he'd supervised the repatriation of the freed political prisoners to Esta City who were physically unable to take an active part in his attacking force; the elderly and those who were ill together with all the women and children who'd been held captive in Hopeless Expectations Penitentiary had been escorted onto the fleet of *naviculae* berthed in the canal adjacent to the prison.

The Consul had reprieved several of the felons incarcerated in the prison for minor crimes and had inducted them into his force together with the prison guards they'd taken captive the previous day but eight hardened criminals convicted of unspeakable crimes were now shackled inside a prison wagon and were being transported to Esta City gaol by road. While he'd been engaged in the detail of their plans he'd dispatched a score of his soldiers to secure the city's central marina and to commandeer all *naviculae* and other craft moored there for their own use when they'd finally depart from here.

As they drew closer to the city centre he was aware of the youths darting along the side streets and alleyways and guessed they were on the way to alert the inner city population and the military ahead of their approach. There was very little he could do to prevent this happening without having to expend valuable resources and anyway, if they succeeded in stopping these children from getting through what could they do with them when they were only doing what they'd been ordered to do by grown-ups who didn't wish to take the risk themselves he'd warrant. He'd be very surprised if these youngsters had voluntarily left their beds so early on a morning and furthermore the Consul Primus was certain that the local population already knew that the prison had been taken and that the political prisoners had been released so the only thing they'd be unsure about was what might happen next.

As the trundling cavalcade neared the city centre the Consul paused when he saw the smoke blackened remains of a large domed building but it was only when he looked closer that he recognised traces of broken statuary and now he was certain that the ruined building had been a temple prior to the inferno. The images of the deities appeared to have been deliberately toppled and disfigured. He dismounted and cornered one of the boys who'd been ducking and diving in and out of the alleyways and enquired of him what had happened to the temple.

He was astounded when the cheeky lad retorted cockily that the temple had been destroyed by the *"Removal Men"* and that the Gods had been abolished by the new Consul Primus and that They didn't matter anymore. When he heard this blasphemy the Consul was sorely tempted to clip him across the ear but the lad had bolted into an alleyway before he got the chance to punish him for the insolence or even to ask him who these so called *"Removal Men"* were.

The *Tempus Dico* and the *Lanterna Extinctor* had fulfilled their duties and had departed the city centre when the Consul's force arrived in the principal square. The only people visible were the garrison guards in the towers at each corner of the solid looking outer walls which monopolised the north end of the wide cobblestoned quadrangle. The imposing studded steel doors into the barracks were well and truly shut as the usurper's colours fluttered in the gentle morning breeze above the corner towers. An identical flag adorned the grand legislature building and forum occupying the opposite side of the piazza and when he saw this the Consul Primus dispatched an *Optio* led *decem* of young cadets to remove the black and white banner above the forum and replace it with his own distinctive green and red standard with its central white rhombus.

His *explorator* joined him and confirmed that all three postern gates into the military fortification had been closed to them too but that access or egress could now be controlled by his soldiers if he wished. The Consul had already considered this scenario and had decided to allow any of the men inside to escape if they wanted to because there was no way that his men could manage to control large numbers of prisoners. It would be totally impossible and impractical for him to remain here to try and impose his authority on the city permanently with his already overstretched provisional army when it was obvious that the main campaign would be fought elsewhere, and more than likely that would be in *Urbis Capitolium*. Neither did he wish to punish anyone other than those who deserved it and even then only when it was essential for the security and the survival of his country. He strongly believed that if and when the usurper and his collaborators were utterly defeated the province would rejoin the federation willingly and all stirrings of insurrection would cease forever.

Just then he remembered the conversation he'd had with the youth at the burned out temple and ordered the *explorator* to get him all the information he could about who these *"Removal Men"* were, how many, what their function was and who controlled them?

Fifteen minutes later his scout reported back and shocked the Consul deeply with what he'd told him.

Just out of range of the barrack's defenders a number of the Consul's soldiers fanned out opposite the entrance to the fort and formed a wall of shields to protect the men now busily offloading the wagons behind them. From the corner towers and from along the fortresses' parapet a volley of *iaculum*, *globus filum* and *acus quattuor* missiles rained down from above but fell just short of the target. But when it became apparent that the barrage was totally ineffective the *custodis* ceased attacking and watched angrily as the construction behind the barrier continued unabated.

The raised voices of his engineers as they gave instructions together with the sound of hammers and handsaws echoed around the vast square. Meanwhile several of the leader's aides banged on the shop doors on the commercial sides of the quadrangle and demanded that the traders open up and conduct business as usual; that the legitimate leader of Sitantal, Consul Primus Zeor was in the city and that they were expected to show due respect and loyalty to him *or else!* Though they didn't elaborate on what might happen if they didn't.

It was almost midday when the din from the hammers and saws ceased and almost everyone within the square turned to inspect the massive wooden ramps leading to the raised oblong platform on top where several large improvised block and tackle gears were fixed in place within the framework. The structure occupied a great part of the north sector of the square and was directly in front of the entrance to the barracks where it towered at least thirty feet above the ground to its highest functional point which was about ten foot higher than the fortress's outer walls. An upright pole displayed the Consul's colours where it now fluttered in sync with an identical pennant on top of the forum building at the opposite side of the quadrangle.

From the high platform both ramps projected outwards in opposite directions and the shorter of the two ended about twenty feet away from the compound's main doors whereas the much longer and less steeply inclined slope extended almost to the centre of the square.

The Consul's infantrymen took up positions behind the protective wood-planking wall which encircled the base of the structure whilst the engineers cranked a modified iron-tipped ram-wagon up the lesser gradient to the top platform. Here the wagon was stuffed solid with ballast and both front and rear axle hubs were smothered with large dollops of fresh grease and when the ram-wagon was ready for use the Consul ascended to the platform with several armed men using their long shields to protect him. He stood and gazed over and into the barrack's inner courtyard below where row after row of battle-ready *custodis* were gearing up for an attack. The Consul Primus was met with obscene finger gestures and clenched fists followed by a loud chorus of derisory and bawdy remarks which were accompanied by a fresh barrage of missiles in his direction but they lacked sufficient velocity to reach the target.

He waited patiently until they realised that he was out of their range and gradually the clamour in the courtyard subsided. He then addressed the men directly and appealed to the fortress's military commander and captains to come out and parley with him and prevent any loss of life on either side. He assured them that soldiers who defected from the traitor 'Pravus' Sorus would be welcomed into his army without fear of repercussions but those who continued to oppose him would be held accountable for their treachery when the usurper was swept aside and he stressed that this was going to happen in the not too distant future.

The few shoppers and the just curious neck-stretchers who'd ventured into the central square were stopped in their tracks and the nervous merchants were standing in their shop doorways where they waited anxiously to see what response the Consul would get from those behind the walls. Even the unruly and disobedient children who'd ignored the orders of the Consul's men to disperse and return to their homes and parents for their own safety had stopped darting around and being a nuisance and now gazed in anticipation at the stronghold's parapet and corner towers looking for a signal or response of some sort.

From the high vantage point the Consul and his men could see a heated debate taking place between sections of the contingent of men gathered in the inner courtyard. Suddenly the altercations became physical and even the *custodis* behind the parapets and in the towers turned round to see what was happening below. The Consul couldn't be certain which faction was in favour or which was against his proposals but when he witnessed two men fall to the floor bleeding profusely from head wounds he knew then that his attempt at mediation had failed and the time for offensive action had come.

He moved to one side and signalled to the *Praefecti* waiting beside the steel capped ram-wagon and an order rang out. When the chocks were wrenched away the engineer and his men heaved the wagon's front wheels onto the edge of the ramp and pushed the tail end firmly and the heavily laden cart immediately lurched away and gathered speed as it rumbled noisily down the slope. The timber structure squeaked and groaned under the strain and when the wheels touched ground level the ram-wagon shot forward and scored a direct hit on the double steel doors with a dull clanging boom. The momentous force of the wedge-shaped ram caused the gates to buckle and split apart. The impact dislodged chunks of the supporting masonry frame where all of the hinges had been ripped clean from their brackets in the side walls. The only thing holding them upright was the dirt laden cart which had been placed directly behind by the fort's defenders in what the Consul had thought was a feeble and inadequate attempt to strengthen their defences when he took into consideration that they'd had the best part of four hours to do something more substantial though they probably assumed that the doors would withstand the shock.

Ten heavily armed men joined the Consul Primus on the high platform where they waited as a pair of drays was harnessed to the mobile ram below and hauled the damaged vehicle away from the opening. From the dais the Consul's men sent a volley of *iaculum* and *acus quattuor* at the corner towers and parapets to impede the defenders sniping at his men below and at this point a second pair of horses was harnessed to the buckled gates where they yanked them clear of the opening and in tandem with this action at various points along the outer perimeter wall his infantrymen stormed up ladders and over the parapet where they engaged in hand-to-hand combat to the left and right on the walkway in a concerted effort to reach the snipers in both end towers.

While all this was happening on the outer walls of the fort the infighting continued in the inner courtyard as the opposing factions clashed violently. Above the implacable din the military commander was heard to order his men to cease the mutiny and rally together to defend the fortress but his commands for the most part went unheeded. Seeing all of this from above the fray the Consul had his standard lowered from the pole and wrapped round a stone and thrown over the parapet into the courtyard below where it was quickly seized on by a *custodis* in the smaller faction on the left who then strung it round his sword and hoisted it aloft. He called out that his group would accept the Consuls terms but instead of attempting to reach the gates to escape they turned and faced their compatriots in the middle yard. The usurper loyalists angrily charged into the smaller group with extended swords and daggers and the Consul watched as his captain ordered his men to link up with their new comrades and counterattack the opposing side. At the corner towers his men had successfully forced the doors where they now set the internal wooden stairways alight which sent billowing smoke up the stairwell through to the top. It didn't take long before weapons were abandoned or flung over the sides and the spluttering and coughing *custodis* scrambled below and surrendered. Back in the fortress courtyard the pitched battle raged on and bit by bit the Consul's forces relentlessly pushed their opponents back and gained further ground. The scene and noise was chaotic as the casualty count mounted on both sides but just then the garrison commander called on his men to withdraw to the postern gates. On hearing the call to retreat the Consul ordered an immediate halt to the advance and ordered his men to pull back and allow the enemy to evacuate the fort without any hindrance. His captains and men were momentarily shocked and confused and turned to face him quizzically but he moved both his hands up and down in a calming fashion and called to them *'se relinquant!'* His order to allow them to retreat was still causing confusion among the adrenalin charged men and he signalled that he was coming down to join them.

Most of the Consul's soldiers and a few of his captains and *Praefecti* were still at a loss as to his reasons for what he'd just done when he joined them in the courtyard where he told them that the fort's commander had made the right tactical call and he reasoned that he'd have done the same if he'd been in a similar position bearing in mind that the *custodis* were plainly losing the battle. He guessed that the officer had considered the fact that since his only defences had been breached and having lost almost a third of their colleagues through defections the remaining *custodis* were dismayed, demoralised and probably psychologically unfit for further serious combat. The Consul then went on to say that they'd come to *Occidens* to free the political prisoners in Hopeless Expectations Penitentiary and had succeeded in doing that. The present operation at the city's barracks had been an opportunistic afterthought where he'd hoped to weaken the enemies resolve even further. But it was vital that they remember that the *custodis* they were fighting were possibly local people with friends and family living nearby and another thing they must always keep in mind at times like this was that these people were fellow countrymen; their own kith and kin with families and friends just like them and just because they'd been misled by a power hungry upstart didn't mean that they should be cruelly treated for this aberration but that everything should be done to make them see the errors of their ways and to try to bring them back willingly into the federation. They'd been indoctrinated with lies and had been led to believe that all their problems and privations were caused by him and the other provinces in Sitantal when in fact the mess was of their own making and in particular the egregious abuse of power by the Sorus family down the centuries. He stressed that a lot could be learned from how a victorious army behaves and treats those they have vanquished and this was one of those occasions. The good people of this city and province would eventually recognise this and realise that they've been duped and betrayed by Governor Sorus for his own glorification.

The Consul Primus detected no resistance or disagreement with what he'd told his men and he ordered them to allow their opponents thirty minutes for an orderly withdrawal from the compound but to remain on alert.

He moved away and climbed to the high platform again and waited patiently until the *custodis* had removed the usurper's banners and insignia from the towers and the fortress had been evacuated through the postern gates before he turned to face his engineers and the team supporting the assault operation directly below the platform. He was surprised and somewhat taken aback when he saw the large gathering of civilians grouped in clusters around the perimeter of the piazza.

The merchants and shopkeepers stood nervously in the doorways and even the unruly and ill-mannered children were now taking time off from their disruptive shenanigans to listen to what the Consul had to say. When he'd seen the large number of curious citizens waiting expectantly out there he quickly rethought and rephrased his message to them.

He greeted the people of Vili City and told them that he was delighted to be with them as their legitimate and rightful leader. He told them that he was sorry for having had to come to their provincial capital surreptitiously and bearing arms but because their Governor 'Pravus' Sorus had led them astray there just hadn't been an alternative. He denounced Sorus and advised them that the man thought only of his own personal aggrandisement and absolutely nothing of them. He pleaded with them to rethink and reconsider how much they or their city and province had benefited since Sorus had assumed the role of leader of the whole country. He asserted that they'd achieved nothing but death of their loved ones and the destruction of their heritage and culture. Here he cited as an example the recently burned temple near this square by Sorus's so called *"Removal Men"* and he poured scorn on the ridiculous notion that the Gods didn't matter anymore when they all knew that the creation and the very existence of Sitantal was because of Them. He reminded the listeners that their leader had been governor of *Occidens* for more than ten years and that before him his father had been in charge for thirty-five years and nothing good had come from him or, for that matter, his grandfather prior to that and so on going back for longer than anyone alive could remember. *Occidens* had been in decline for more than a century because of the brutality of the Sorus family and their collaborators and the local problems had nothing to do with the more prosperous areas in greater Sitantal. He pointed out that Deputy Governor Puto Pollux was Sorus's marionette and that things were no better with him in charge either but with the right leadership the province could have the same advantages as elsewhere. *Occidens* had been the Sorus' personal plaything and now the madman wanted to do the same with the whole country but he promised them faithfully that while he lived that would never happen. He announced that before he and his men would leave the city the now vacated garrison would be rendered useless as a military base just like the prison at the edge of town which was still burning. These sites would never be used for those purposes again and here he emphasised that the citizens had no need for a military presence in the very heart of their city no more than they'd needed a torture camp like Hopeless Expectations Penitentiary on their doorstep. He promised that new homes, businesses and places of learning and worship would replace these vulgar and evil monstrosities. New roads, canals and infrastructure would be commissioned urgently and he vowed that when he returned to *Urbis Capitolium* after the coup was reversed he'd decree that his younger son Zeo be the new Governor of *Occidens* solely because he was the right man to solve the challenges that faced whoever took charge here because of the brutality, corruption and the wanton neglect of the region. But Zeo would need the help of every man, woman and child to restore confidence and pride in their province.

He added that he believed that *Occidenians* would come to love and respect Zeo every bit as much as he did.

The Consul acknowledged the sustained applause from his men but as he was about to descend from the wooden platform he paused and listened to the faltering sounds of approval coming nervously from some on the edges of the quadrangle. He raised his arms aloft and bowed in respect at their bravery, very conscious of the danger they'd placed themselves in by making this very public gesture.

By late afternoon the corner towers of the garrison were no more than piles of rubble and all the inner buildings had the furniture, doors and windows removed to be used on the funeral pyre.

The Consul had his *scriptor* prepare a large notice which was fixed high on the outer wall of the fort where the scribe had written that the area was designated for new development which would commence when Zeo, younger son of Zeor was officially appointed and promulgated Governor of *Occidens*.

Decretum Zeor, Consul Primus Hereditarius.
Here the Consul had pressed his seal knowing that his decree would cause quite a stir when word of it reached 'Pravus' Sorus.

Psychological Warfare doesn't have to be bloody all the time he silently concluded.

The final act which the Consul had overseen was the dismantling of the wooden structure in the square before he and his men marched to the marina not far from the central square to return to Esta City.

Immediately behind them was a scene verging on industrious activity as the children who'd beset their operations from early morning were now busily hauling home the cut timber from the dismantled framework which the engineers had neatly stacked and abandoned close to the fort's wall with a scribbled *"gratis"* note attached.

The Consul thought silently that perhaps his words had a more inspirational impact than he'd allowed for and that maybe the people of *Occidens* could change the wildly held stereotypical trait they were branded with *"that tomorrow is a much better day to do something which actually needs doing straight away!"*

*

Puto Pollux had taken a diversionary route through southern *Occidens* to attend a wedding banquet on his way home to Vili City from *Urbis Capitolium*. He'd intended to avail of the sumptuous fare and then continue north but the rotund and avuncular host, who Pollux reckoned was a splendid fellow and a personal friend, had insisted that he and his ten man escort rest overnight and have *prandium* with him before they'd leave the next day. Though his brain told him to decline the tempting offer his belly voided the motion with little difficulty but instead of resting as he'd been advised to do he continued feasting late into the night.

It was almost noon on the following day when a messenger from the provincial capital disturbed the bloated and gaseous Commander with news that Hopeless Expectations Penitentiary had been breached by Zeor two days ago and that all of the political prisoners had been freed.

The news brought an end to the extended sojourn and without having as much as a mere morsel for *prandium* he and his men departed in haste for Vili City.

They arrived in the central square an hour before dusk.

His intention was to call at the garrison and get an update on Hopeless Expectations Penitentiary and to find out what his forces had done in response to the attack on the prison but when he arrived in the city's central square he had the biggest shock he'd had for a long time when he saw the destruction and the abandonment of the military base.

He threw a fit and demanded answers on how this could happen to a barracks which had a full complement of *custodis* manning it. He despatched one of his men to check with the local people to hear what they knew of the events leading up to this fiasco when he realised that there wasn't a *custodo* to be seen anywhere. Then he spotted the deposed Consul's colours fluttering from the top of the legislature building in the evening breeze and he became even more rattled causing his ruddy complexion to advance further up the rubicund measuring scale. He instructed the nearest man to go and remove the banner immediately from the forum but then his eyes caught sight of the sign fixed to the wall of the fort and he spurred his mount closer to read it. He craned his neck and convulsed and spluttered as he read it which made his previous outbursts look like minor tantrums as the terms of the written declaration sunk in. He angrily stood upright in his stirrups and used his unsheathed sword to try lever the offending billboard from the wall but because of his excess weight and his jerking movements his horse shifted its stance and caused Pollux to wobble and shift away from his centre of gravity. With one final upward prod with his sword he lurched sideways and tumbled clumsily to the floor. His lardy constitution cushioned the fall and prevented any noticeable injuries except to his dignity but his rasping, gasping demands for air could have created a destructive vacuum in the square had it lasted much longer, or so his *Optio* cheekily speculated, but silently. His men hurriedly dismounted to help him to his feet but they were irritably pushed away.

When he got to his feet he gazed round the square questionably and soon realised that there was something odd with the scene confronting him, something was amiss. All the shops and businesses were shut and there were no last minute shoppers rushing around as he'd remembered seeing them do in the past nor was there any sign of the young rascals who were a constant plague in the town centre. Today the place was totally deserted, like a ghost town. He wondered what the hell was going on here and what else had happened in his absence. The *Lanterna levior* was lighting the night lights when Pollux remounted his horse and crossed the square to the forum when he'd confirmed that the whole interior of the barracks had been razed to the ground and was now in ruins including the section that had been his own personal quarters.

For the first time in years the Deputy Governor of *Occidens* declined dinner claiming dyspepsia but the malady didn't stop him muttering and stomping ill-temperedly around the Governors official chamber in the legislature building. His *scriptor* sat nervously at the edge of the large desk surrounded by voluminous scraps of discarded notes at his feet and wondered if Puto Pollux would ever get his **'urgent'** message to Sorus finished and dispatched.

As the scribe scratched and laboured in response to the Deputy Governor's continuing attempt to embellish the hard facts of what would be a damming report to 'Pravus' Sorus on the debacle which had occurred in the dictators home town, his sworn enemy, the ousted Consul Primus Zeor was alighting sprightly from a *naviculae* in Esta City's central marina.

Zeor wondered mischievously if Puto Pollux had discovered his calling card by now.

CHAPTER SEVENTEEN

He was almost three hours into the journey southwest and Sala village was about twenty miles behind him when Euander noticed the approaching coach and outriders in the distance on the narrow road. He searched the surrounding countryside for any sign of his three comrades using the newfangled view magnifiers which Zeo had presented to him earlier but there was no trace of them anywhere. He refocused the binoculars on the fast advancing group and wondered if he might have a problem to contend with when he identified a long double-axle four horse coach being escorted by seven armed outriders wearing Governor Maximus insignia on their tunics. He edged as close as was physically possible to the left margin of the road and parked the wagons. He eased his sword from the scabbard and rested the hilt close to where he sat on the drivers' bench and re-located Candeo's tether nearer to him with a loose slip knot and guided the colt alongside the rear pair of dray horses nearest his box seat.

He waited and observed.

Thirty minutes earlier Adam and Johnny had been jog-trotting their mounts over the surrounding terrain and discovering new delights to savour on the picture-postcard landscape which surrounded them where they eagerly absorbed the diversity that was on offer to them, not just the abundant flora but the fauna too which had also captivated and thrilled them.
Never before had the pair seen so many different species of colourful birds in actuality. On their previous visit to Sitantal a large part of that time had been occupied travelling through *Extremus* and the only birds they'd encountered there were Spit-fire buzzards and those birds were anything but exotic or pretty. And when travelling through northern *Oriens* the only birds they'd got an up-close clear sighting of was a pair of cute preening bluebirds whilst most of the others had been too far away to fully appreciate. And in the permanent darkness of Nox there'd been no wildlife of any kind with the exception of the white wolves but they could hardly be described as wildlife when they'd been under the control of Erebus and not native to the region. But here now in southern *Oriens* they were spoilt for choice and Johnny had likened them to birds of paradise that he'd seen on a television documentary shot in New Guinea. The extra bonus for them was that these wild fowl showed little sign that they felt threatened by human proximity and the two ogling newcomers were chuffed that

they were able to get up close to the fabulous creatures before they took flight.

Both Zeo and Euander had watched the visitor's reactions with some amusement but also with great pride and satisfaction that they were so taken with their discoveries in Sitantal though Zeo asserted to his fellow countryman that *Terra Ferusum* was equally fascinating and full of quite amazing things too.

Euander had been the first to spot the plume of thick smoke rising from behind one of the many rolling hills in the far distance on their right and he'd immediately alerted Zeo who feared that Suga Cazo's *"Removal Men"* had attacked another temple and he called on Adam and Johnny to ready their weapons and join him to investigate the source of the fire. He'd told Euander to continue moving forward saying that they'd catch up with him in due course.

Euander reckoned that his anxieties had been well founded when the captain of the armed guard escorting the carriage unsheathed his sword and commenced calling out aggressively to make way when the coach and horsemen were still more than seventy yards away. He knew that his nearside wheels were tight up against the stone edging separating the road from the fast flowing shallow stream on the left and that there was nowhere else for him to move to without causing damage to the wheel rims and possibly his horses too. He believed that there was ample space for the coach to pass by if it was done with due care.

The captain spurred his mount forward ahead of the coach and the other outriders and came to a grit-grinding halt alongside the wagon. He was red faced and spitting out foul language as he gesticulated threateningly with his sabre and it appeared to Euander that he was just itching to use it on him.

But then quite suddenly the captain fell silent when his gaze fixed covetously on Candeo and his green eyes roamed up and down and covered every aspect of the colt. When he turned to Euander and asked to whom the horse belonged he responded that it was his and added emphatically that it wasn't for sale. Before the captain got a chance to respond to the rebuff the coach window was flung open with a sharp crack and an irate thirty-something woman leaned out and demanded to know the reason for the delay. But just like the captain had done, though maybe fractionally sooner, she diverted her attention to the white horse and immediately ordered the youth perched beside the older driver on her coach to open the door.

"I want this horse" she announced grandly to no one in particular as she approached.

"The horse is not for sale, my lady" Euander replied tersely.

"What? What did you say? Do you know who I am?"

"No my lady, but my horse is still not for sale"

"I am the Lady Dido, the daughter of the Governor of this province and very soon to be the wife of Sorus, the

new Consul Primus, so you'd need to bear that in mind when I tell you that I will have this colt, rusticus!"

Euander blushed and gritted his teeth in anger when he heard her call him a peasant and he knew straight away that he had to act right now because the position he was in made him a sitting duck.

Surreptitiously he undid the loose knot on the tether securing Candeo's reins and he quickly grabbed his sword with his free hand and leaped from the seat onto his horse before either the woman or the captain realised what was happening.

The lady Dido squealed with alarm but this quickly changed to rage as both horse and rider charged past her almost knocking her off her feet.

The six mounted *custodis* sprung into action when they saw what had just happened and before the captain got his wits together to instruct them what to do, they were doing it anyway and were now in hot pursuit of the runaway.

Contrary to everyone's expectations the fleeing bareback rider didn't flee very far at all. He swung round several hundred yards behind the coach and came charging back towards the chaotic scene on the narrow road.

The apprentice driver hastily climbed aboard the coach alongside his father and both sat and wondered with renewed interest on how this uneven contest would pan out. Even though the odds were stacked against the lone protagonist neither father or son would have taken a wager against him;

something about the lad convinced them that he wasn't going to be a pushover after all.

When the lady Dido saw that the captain was preparing to launch an *iaculum* at the fast approaching rider she screamed at him to stop in case he injured *her* horse.

Just as Euander was almost on top of the six charging *custodis* he veered acutely to the right and firmly gripping his outstretched sword he pierced the nearest man in the chest and sent him hurtling beneath the hooves of his companion's mounts scattering them all over the place and breaking apart their cohesion. He kept up the momentum of the charge along the road and raced past the confused captain and Dido for the second time and gave her the fright of her life when she thought that he was about to attack her too when he wildly swung his sword to the right and left. She screamed out in fear and hitched up her billowing robes and scrambled back into the safety of the coach, slamming the door behind her.

It was the first time in her life that someone hadn't performed this menial door-opening and closing task for her, which in itself was a novel experience and a credit to her!

And having witnessed this seminal event in the enlightenment of their mistress both coachman and his apprentice glanced at each other with raised eyebrows but quickly turned their attention back to the ongoing clash where first blood had gone to the underdog.

The captain signalled the remaining five mounted guards to join him near the front wagon where he'd just discovered the strange cargo under the canvas cover.
Euander sat astride Candeo further along the road. He waited and observed.
Then a young *custodo* dismounted and climbed aboard the wagon and proceeded to roughly offload the holdalls and when he tossed them to the ground Euander exclaimed loudly *"Don't touch anything; If you leave now you'll come to no harm!"*
This challenge brought an outburst of raucous laughter and derision from the *custodis* and even the coachmen couldn't resist a brief grin at what they reckoned was an impracticable threat.
Before his enemies had finished laughing Euander charged towards the stationary mounted group beside his wagons. They quickly turned to face him head-on and braced themselves with raised swords but when he was mere yards away from them he veered sharply to the nearside and into the shallow stream and felled the totally unprepared man who was standing upright amongst the remaining cargo on board the wagon. The soldier plunged forward from the cart onto the ground near his mounted colleagues with most of his viscera protruding from the long gash in his abdomen. The captain was so stunned and unprepared for this manoeuvre and deadly consequence he didn't react or do anything and neither did his men who only gawped at their gutted colleague

now dying at the hooves of their horses.
Of the three spectators watching the action from the coach only two were tempted to applaud the young man, but they didn't!
He continued along the road for a further hundred yards and turned sharply then stopped.
He waited and observed.
The lady Dido felt so sick at the ghastly sight she'd just witnessed that she collapsed back on the carriage seat where she swore coarsely and loudly that she'd find out the youth's name and have him, together with his entire family and his relatives and friends tortured and hung out to dry. The upstart's selfishness was so unreasonable and unkind, she raged. She was so perplexed and annoyed that it caused her voice to crackle in anger and frustration when she blurted out;
"Why is this *rusticus* being so mean to me? After all, the only thing I want is his horse!"
The father and son coach team heard this plaintive protest through the thin carriage walls and looked cynically at each other and then turned to see what might happen next on the open air stage.
The captain finally figured out what he would do in response and ordered his men to separate widely where they'd then encircle the young *interfector* from all sides and when the noose was tight and complete then they'd attack but only on his order. They must prevent any injury to the white horse because the lady Dido wanted the colt more than anything else and she'd reward them hand-

somely he promised.

The three friends and dog had reached the top of the hill where they paused and casually scanned the landscape below with their binoculars in search of Euander and the wagons. They'd spent the last hour helping a farmer bring an almost out of control accidental barn fire to an end.

In seconds Adam swore and yelled out loudly to the others as he galloped flat out down the hill with Friday running parallel with him. Johnny and Zeo spotted what had alarmed him in the distance and were now mere yards behind him.

Within minutes they'd cleared the slopes and had reached the flat fields and grassland below. They charged headlong towards the meadow where they'd seen Euander being outflanked on all sides by five sword bearing riders who were closing the gap separating them from their central target with every manoeuvre they took. Almost in unison the three friends dropped their visors, unsheathed their swords and hollered menacingly from the very depths of their lungs. Friday joined in the chorus and added an even more savage pitch to the clamour which echoed over the plains.

Though Euander saw and heard his friends approaching from afar it didn't tempt him to relax his guard and he continued to pivot and observe the features of his adversaries as he attempted to seek out the weakest link amongst them. Candeo gyrated faultlessly within the tightening circle and responded magnificently to every tug and nudge, whisper and whistle his owner had taught him right from the time when he'd commenced weaning him away from his dam. Now the colt's instant responses and agility had prevented the enemy overwhelming them thus far.

It was the approaching and ever increasing ruckus which finally broke the nerve of the *custodo* who had the least visual position to monitor the pending arrival of the three vociferous horsemen and dog behind him and he hastily pulled away and severed the ever- tightening noose. Euander had observed the imminent break in the chain a nanosecond before the deserter's colleagues were aware that a member of their group was about to balk and run. He spurred Candeo through the chink in the link just as the captain had been about to order the attack. Euander continued on the tail of the defector until he drew level with him near a green grassy knoll and struck him from the side with an upward swinging blow with his sword. Before the *custodo's* body had reached the ground he'd already steered Candeo on an acute left turn and had sped off to join up with his comrades.

The three friends had fallen silent when they'd seen Euander spring from the trap when they were less than four minutes away from reaching the scene and they pulled up and watched him chase down the deserter and end his rush to get away.

Adam's conscience had troubled him on the race back to help Euander and he reckoned that a plume of smoke shouldn't have deflected their responsibilities to work as a complete team and not to leave anyone exposed and unprotected such as they'd done with their new friend and colleague. As they waited for their new teammate to join up he told Zeo to tell him that from here on in the dog would remain with the wagon at all times as an extra safeguard and that they'd remain in close contact with each other whatever the situation in the future. He opined that because the countryside looked so peaceful and tranquil they'd have to continually remind themselves that evil stalked the land despite the beautiful setting and he guessed that both Johnny and Zeo were thinking just like he was about what had happened in their absence. The three horsemen remained where they were until Euander joined them where they congratulated him on his escape and the follow-up chase which they'd witnessed. He briefed Zeo on what had happened as they cantered through the meadow until they reached the clogged up road and the scene of the earlier action. On their approach they'd noticed that the captain had two men ride out and retrieve their dead comrade and the rider-less horse and then return with them to the roadside near the carriage. They'd already retrieved the other corpses and the unattached mounts and they now waited pensively beside the coach. Zeo had voiced his approval when he saw that they hadn't abandoned their dead or deserted the coach and he promised his friends that he'd go easy on them because of this.

When they reached the scene they found that the three *custodis* had already surrendered and had discarded their weapons onto the ground. But further along, close to the coach they witnessed an ongoing fracas involving the captain and Zeo's former aunt Dido, Maximus's daughter.

The lady had been incandescent with anger and inconsolable with grief when she'd seen what had happened out in the fields and had watched her escort returning empty-handed in defeat without her trophy. At that stage she couldn't decide whether to scream or to snivel in frustration, so she did a bit of both.

Without seeking the assistance of the apprentice or the driver to help her with the door she'd sprung from the coach in time to confront the returning captain. She'd been in her angry mode just then and had spun round and snatched the horsewhip from the font at the apprentice driver's feet and had attacked the captain with a vengeance which caused the driver and his son to wince every time a blow landed on the unfortunate man.

She eased off the onslaught only when a sharp voice behind her commanded;

"Madame, you will stop right now, and that is an order!"

The vigorous exertion to which she was unaccustomed had caused her to perspire profusely and by now the profusion of sweat globules together with her copious tears had caused her make-up to migrate to unintended locations on her face and had wreaked havoc on her appearance to such an extent she'd acquired the personification of an evil demonic being in her countenance.

She lowered the whip slowly but she spun round at speed to face the three black clad, helmet wearing men and a panting dog who had lined up in a row behind her. The facial contortions she now exhibited made her look even more devilish than a moment ago.

Adam and Johnny had to bite their lips and avert their eyes away from the comical sight until they'd regained a modicum of self control. Though she was visibly taken aback at the unusual sight confronting her, especially the two *PS* insignias now on display, she quickly regained her belligerent predilection and reverted back to type, after giving brusque nods to Adam and Johnny.

"How dare you tell me what to do? Are you as stupid as that rusticus you're assisting in denying me what I claim to be mine? Has he not told you who I am?"

At this point she glared at Euander who'd remained in the background astride Candeo.

Zeo spoke *"I know who you are Madame and you're very fortunate that I don't have you trashed with that whip you use so freely! Trust me lady, had there been a female in my company you'd be flogged to within an inch of your miserable life"*

The four *custodis* and the coachmen were astonished to hear this exchange involving a stranger and the woman who was feared above all other women in Sitantal. But all of those present who knew the lady Dido well could testify that she'd use every trick in the book until she'd had her way. They waited with bated breath for this to happen and it transpired that they didn't need to restrain their normal breathing pattern for very long.

The instant torrent of tears and the barrage of woeful wails could have softened the core of a cragged old stone. The disconsolate performance displayed by the lady reached crescendo levels when a black lace *sudarium* was produced with a theatrical flourish followed by a tour de force encore of fresh tears and wails.

From an audience which totalled ten the lady Dido failed to find one who empathised with her or who felt her pain.

"*That's enough Madame! Stop right now! Save the histrionics for your treacherous father Maximus and your future husband, the despot 'Pravus' Sorus. Your antics may work on them; they certainly won't work with me!*" Zeo coldly replied.

On hearing the insults to her father and her betrothed and the put-down of her well-honed artistic talents the lady Dido screamed and ranted as she charged at her tormentor with the whip flailing aloft but Adam and Johnny raced forward and grabbed both her arms and lifted her off the ground where they allowed her to dangle in the air. She screeched even louder and kicked out at them ineffectually with her delicately embroidered size eleven boots.

When Zeo removed his helmet at this point his

former aunt went totally berserk the instant she recognised him, to such an extent that her two handlers had to wrestle her to the ground to contain her. Had Adam and Johnny understood what foul names she'd been calling them they'd have been shocked, but only for a moment or so, though they laughed heartily when Zeo told them later that what she'd said was less than polite and ladylike.

At this point Johnny called on Zeo to have Euander bring him the holdall marked '*E*' which contained a bundle of plastic ties.

Had the coachmen and the *custodis* not been dependant on the lady's father for their lives and their livelihood they would have given robust applause and a standing ovation for the performance they'd just witnessed. But nevertheless they were still going to remember it with satisfaction for the rest of their lives.

When Johnny had the still agitated woman restrained he escorted her inside the coach and was amazed to see heap after heap and crate on top of crate of valuable looking stuff which was packed almost to the roof at the back of the coach. Here he called on Zeo to come and check it out and when he'd examined the hoard he remarked that he was about to debrief the men who'd travelled with the Governor's daughter and would find out more about it then.

While he and Euander gathered the coachmen and *custodis* separately and kept them well out of range of the lady in the coach Adam and Johnny returned to their wagons and fed and watered the horses including the animals that'd lost their riders battling with Euander earlier. They'd just finished reloading the dumped cargo when Zeo joined them and explained that all the valuables and coin stacked in the coach had been extorted from virtually every trader and wealthy individual and even some temples from here to the border with *Australis* whether the donors had been willing or not and more of these extortionary expeditions had been planned for the near future. He'd seen the inventory and it was breathtaking what Dido had extracted using her position and the fear of retribution from the two men in her life. All the goods and money collected were *Tributum dotis nuptialis,* a wedding dowry tax, and a "gift" from the donors to Dido and 'Pravus' Sorus. He told his friends that he'd confiscated the lot including the coach and he intended returning all the valuables and *cudos*, which he explained was the legal currency of Sitantal, to the rightful owners with the help of the driver and his son. The coach would accompany them to the most recent village which Dido had visited and then they'd make their way independently to each donor and restore their property to them, minus their own remuneration and any valid expenses incurred. He believed that the father and son coach team were decent honest guys and they had no desire to continue working for the Governor and the fact that the driver's wife, his co-driver's mother, had died almost a year ago had made this choice to relocate much easier for them.

Three of the surviving escort troop including the captain opted to quit the Governor's forces also and would now ride to Esta City to join his father's army. The fourth soldier had only agreed to escort the lady Dido to Ciro City because his young wife was there and expecting their first baby sometime soon and he needed to be with her.

Zeo believed the whipping and demeaning of the captain had caused great dissent and the defections within the escort and another factor the men couldn't tolerate was simply that because of Dido's own selfishness and her intention to appropriate Euander's horse they'd been prevented from using all available weapons in self defence even when he'd begun killing their colleagues. It had soon become obvious that the youth wouldn't allow his horse to be taken from him under any circumstances and was determined to kill again if he had to and yet all the lady could think about was her selfish desires and nothing else mattered to her.

    Before three o'clock in the afternoon the coach and wagons had been manoeuvred into line and now faced southwest and though the lady Dido had demanded the return of her personal travelling case Zeo had refused point blank to yield and retorted that most of its contents were probably stolen and anyway there was no way she could ride a horse safely and carry a delicate case at the same time and neither could her escort. This further reminder of her reduced travelling comforts brought on a new offensive of spit and spleen and Zeo advised her that if she needed assistance from any of the villagers on the way home to her *proditor* father in Ciro City she'd need to practice some good manners and a lot of humility along the way.

Without her vanity case the lady didn't have access to a mirror or cosmetics and she now looked like a disaster zone survivor and quite scary too, but she wasn't aware of this and no one had thought fit to mention it to her either. Initially she'd resisted mounting the horse until Zeo advised her that she could walk home if she wanted to that it didn't matter to him either way and the choice was hers to make. The stark advice helped her to change her mind but she struggled and swore vociferously and eventually managed to be seated on the saddle. Zeo had relented when he'd given her the most docile mount of the three available but only after Adam had exerted a lot of pressure on him to do it.

The remaining party watched with relief as she departed east on horseback followed by the lone *custodo* who they could see was keeping what he presumed to be a safe distance of two lengths between them.

Shortly after her departure the captain and his men rode northwards across the open fields and meadows. They each carried a recommendation to the Consul Primus and the captain had been entrusted with a sealed message to be delivered to his father from Zeo.

At this juncture when there were just the four guys and the coachmen remaining at the scene they all opted for a break when the coach driver opened a well stocked hamper which the lady Dido had secreted within the carriage for her personal delectation. While they ate the tasty treats and savouries the coachman gave a meritorious and vivid account of how Euander had singularly wreaked havoc on their unprepared escort. The subject of the salutation blushed profusely and when Zeo explained the gist of what had been said to Adam and Johnny it was obvious to everyone looking on that the bashful guy wished he was anywhere but there.

But it didn't stop him thinking; if only his parents could see him now.

The coachman and his apprentice rode the riches laden coach a short distance behind the three black clad riders along the narrow road heading west. Both father and son whistled a favourite family tune in tandem and they realised that this was the first time in years that they'd felt carefree and happy and they also knew that they'd never be at a loss for a risible conversation piece ever again. They believed that what they'd witnessed today was the stuff of anecdotes and folklore for decades to come.

Euander's articulated wagons took up the

rear of the departing convoy where he sat close to the end of the bench seat and patted and stroked Candeo affectionately every now and then as the colt walked alongside. His sidekick Friday sat upright on his left and stared straight ahead. Tethered to the back of the combo wagon were two of the three horses whose riders he'd killed earlier and whose bodies were now on board wrapped tightly in canvas coverings. This unpleasant addition to the cargo manifest was needed until they reached the nearest village where they'd part company with the coachmen who'd agreed to arrange the *exsequiae* rite for the dead.

Deliberately discarding these morbid details Euander relaxed and reminisced about the amazing but crazy things that had happened earlier.

Today had been like no other day for him; ever.

Never in his wildest dreams or even nightmares for that matter did he have to fight for his life or for his horse and to do just that and win against all odds was sweet, even more than sweet, it was delicious. All through his childhood and early teens he'd listened to both his father and mother tell him of the adventures they'd experienced in their younger years and he'd been thrilled and overawed and couldn't get enough of it. But having heard their tales of derring-do it had given him the will and confidence to face up to anything where it mattered and to never be cowed or fearful especially when you believed that right was on your side. He acknowledged more than ever just how much he owed his parents and he totally believed that their maxim *"exspecto et observo"* to wait and observe, had been the determining factor in his victory today.

He realised at that instant that he'd have to write a daily account of his adventures lest he'd forget even the smallest detail. He knew that his parents would wish to hear of the action as it had happened with everything in and nothing left out when he returned home.

The two cousins and Johnny chatted and laughed as they trotted forward and all of them wondered how their actions today would be received by Governor Maximus and 'Pravus' Sorus when they'd get the report.

But on a more serious note Zeo cautioned that they couldn't allow events like yesterday and today to delay them in future on their mission to reach the Temple of the Gods.

*

When the lady Dido reined in her horse near the sparkling fountain at Sala village almost three hours later she was met by a group of small children who immediately screamed when they saw her and ran crying hysterically into the small square. Mothers dashed from their homes to check what was happening to their little ones and were instantly alarmed by what they saw and they immediately gathered stones from their front gardens and pelted what they believed was a child-snatching witch on a horse. Very soon Varus, the village's *praesum*, arrived to check on the commotion and roughly ordered the diabolical looking horsewoman to clear off using language which she was very familiar with and totally understood though it wasn't in the polite vernacular.

The children then mimicked their mothers when they found plenty of rubble to lob near the site of the reconstruction work at the nearby temple and they thought it great sport.

The lady's lone escort had waited further back from the fountain having fully expected a reaction like this but he didn't care anymore. He'd made his mind up along the way that he and his pregnant wife would leave this province as soon as he reached Ciro City. As far as he was concerned he'd seen and heard more than enough to do a lifetime.

Zeo and his friends would only learn of this event when they'd meet the *custodo* again during military action down the line.

CHAPTER EIGHTEEN

The Governor of *Oriens*, Ballio Maximus lay listlessly on the deep-pile velvet *torus* in his private den in the late afternoon where he attempted to steer his thoughts away from what had happened overnight within his province. He tried to think of something he could do to change the dynamics of the catastrophe which had occurred, anything which would deliver a fortuitous alternative experience or even a miniscule favourable storyline with a happy ending would have been more than welcome right now.

When he'd heard the news that the renegade, his contrived grandson Zeo and his two collaborators from *Terra Ferusum* had escaped from *Primoris* after they'd thrashed and dispersed the men he'd sent there to prevent their entry into Sitantal proper he could barely believe his ears. Fortunately for Maximus the *Centurio* in charge of the post had been one of the many fatalities in the fiasco otherwise he personally would've had the *tegunt* strung from the nearest tree on his front lawn though his stomach wasn't up for that sort of thing right now. He'd declared this to the nervous messenger when he'd recounted to the Governor what had happened during the night at the security base in the east.

When he closed his eyes he suffered a fit of the jitters as he envisioned what awaited him when his daughter Dido returned from her trip to collect *Tributum Nuptia* to add to her dowry from the towns, villages and wealthy merchants in the south of the province. Though he dreaded the lashing he'd get from her sharp tongue his main concern was how Sorus would react to the news of the morning's debacle in *Oriens* for which he believed without doubt that he'd be held personally responsible. He'd long ago suspected that Sorus only tolerated him because he was soon to marry his daughter. But he was also aware that the dictator needed his influence with him being the only legitimate Governor still in office in the federation to further his quest to be declared the next *de jure* Consul Primus rather than his present *de facto* situation, a protocol that could only happen when they'd finally succeeded in removing Zeor and his family from the scene for good.

Maximus believed that he'd have to watch his back from here-on-in and this vigilance would need to be maintained long-term into the future, regardless of the proposed family alliance in marriage.

It crossed his mind again as it had done in the past that his daughter would need to remain wary too when she married the dictator even though there were times he reckoned she was more than capable of looking out for herself and perhaps Sorus should be the one who'd need to watch his back as far as Dido was concerned.

He'd tried vainly to dissuade her from the marriage and he'd reminded her more than once of the rumours that still persisted throughout the country of the sudden and peculiar circumstances relating to the mysterious disappearance of Sorus' first wife, Semele, about six years ago. Very few people had believed the man when he'd cried despairingly that the love of his life had been swallowed alive into an uncharted sink-hole in western *Occidens*. At the *inquisitio* into her reported demise Puto Pollux had affirmed under oath that he'd witnessed her being swallowed alive as she'd skipped joyfully over the grassy moorlands with her dear little pooch picking wild flowers a short time after the pleasant and carefree picnic she'd enjoyed with her husband on the open range, and all this had happened despite her devoted husband's heroic attempts to save her. Pollux had informed the *iudex* enthusiastically that the tiny dog had scrambled from the pit and had survived but that the poor little animal missed his mistress terribly, as did her distraught and grief stricken husband.

The *magistratus* did little to mask his sceptical mien when he'd ruled that the lady had died as a result of a rather anomalous incident in a hole that had materialised out of the blue and curiously, a hole that no one had been able to locate since that inauspicious day.

The germane question *but who am I to judge anyone?* flickered like a flash through Maximus' brain and was gone. He rang the little pewter bell on the side table and had the aide bring him supper and a large *amphora* of red wine to the inner sanctum where he intended to take advantage of the calm before the pending storm while he still had the benefit of priceless peace and time on his side.

But his attempt to divert his thoughts onto something more congenial and benign or alternatively drown his worries in the fruits of the vine proved to be ill conceived when his irksome retrospections didn't succumb to the smooth caressing nectar but instead brought him back in time to an event he'd long ago consigned to the dustbin of history. Though he didn't want to recall any of it his thought process appeared to have a different angle and itinerary and it held stubbornly firm.

It just wouldn't be diverted or obscured.

On that late winter's day over fifty years ago when he was a young ambitious officer he'd been summoned to this very mansion, the home of his predecessor and father-in-law, Governor Ursus of *Oriens.* His emotions had been all over the place when he'd galloped at speed on horseback to the meeting and on several occasions he'd come close to colliding with strolling pedestrians and with children who'd been playing *trigon* in the paved streets of the provincial capital. Though he'd been puzzled why Ursus wanted to see him so urgently he'd worried that the Governor had learned of his countless grubby infidelities since he'd been married to Belvia, the provincial ruler's only child and heiress. As he raced to the mansion he earnestly vowed to the Gods that he'd change his ways from this day forward if they'd only give him one more chance though it conveniently slipped his memory that he'd already made a similar commitment when his daughter Junia was born eighteen months previously.

     Almost three years prior to that fortunate day when he was just a dashing young *Optio* and obsequiously manipulating his rise to the top he'd first met Belvia in the arena at the city's equestrian school. He'd struck up a conversation with the naive and not so pretty young girl and had engaged in great machinations to ensure that it wouldn't be their last encounter. Whereas Belvia had believed that this first meeting was one of those random serendipitous events, a lucky fluke, it wasn't and she'd been badly mistaken but worse still she was being dreadfully deceived.

He was a cad and he knew it but he didn't care.

Within weeks of that first meeting he realised that he didn't have to manoeuvre his duties constantly to be at the riding school when Belvia was expected there after he'd learned that she was also checking the roster to coordinate her visits to coincide with his sessions.

The news was like triumphal music to his ears

though he had already seen the passion and fervour in her eyes.

The next conquest in his sights was her father the Governor who he'd guessed could be a more difficult task when he already knew him to be deeply devout and virtuous and a very strict disciplinarian.

During the time he'd been reeling Belvia into his net he'd resisted all the spicy temptations that had been constantly available to his insatiable lust for gratification which went hand-in-hand with the pursuit of his ambitions. He'd unashamedly used every talent and attribute he possessed to gain another foothold on the ladder going up to where he wanted to be. It mattered not a jot to him what he had to do to get there so he did it and had never regretted a single thing and he would do it all over again if circumstances required it and his physiology allowed it.

For his *modus operandi* and *artibus* he was totally indebted to the wisdom of his mother who'd continually reminded him of the need to utilise his good looks, his lean chiselled body and all of his other inborn attributes and talents but only where it benefitted him. She'd prevailed on him to learn to scrutinise the eyes of the people he met because everything they desired or conspired was lurking within for him to see. She'd emphasised that the eyes were the windows to the soul. He must also look his best at all times no matter where he was or what he was doing and that he needed to bathe regularly using tinted rose water. Also it was imperative that he dress with fresh underwear daily.

Because of this credo and her avid attention to detail in his early childhood he'd stood out like a beacon in the night. And when he attended *schola* his peers, boys and girls, had all wished to be his best friend and wanted to touch him at every opportunity and even his *magisters,* male and female, young and old were beholden to his every little whim and likewise he to theirs; reciprocity was so easy for him. His excellent yearly grades, though academically well deserved, reflected his total generosity to those who'd awarded them to him because he knew they also had desires for something pleasing and exotic too, just like him.

Continuing into his teens his popularity encountered no boundaries nor did his immorality and in early adulthood when he enlisted in the military academy he burgeoned well beyond his wildest expectations. His conquests multiplied in a place where he'd thought his talents would be superfluous and unwanted and his rewards had been both pleasurable and tangible in equal measure. His resourcefulness gained him fast-track promotions through the ranks and he also enjoyed becoming an extremely wealthy young man in the process.

But now that his ultimate goal was within his grasp he'd become almost boring and reclusive and he ignored all the pleas and entreaties to have some fun and diversion, so much so that his immediate colleagues thought that he was ill. His new-found abstinence from worldly pleasure and his publicly flaunted humble piety was observed with much scepticism by the few who knew him better than most and they wondered what his motives could be. Those who hated him, and there were a few, believed it was a ruse and that someone would pay dearly for it, one way or another, just like they'd done in the past. When they eventually discovered the reason for his perceived conversion and deliverance from depravity and decadence it was much too dangerous to try to do something to prevent Belvia marrying him because they knew that if they acted now it would assuredly bring about their own social destruction and demise or maybe worse.

They were well aware of his cupboard full of fetid skeletons which at anytime could rattle out their names, their foibles and their transgressions.

Oh Yes! He knew it all because he'd been there!

When he'd reached the mansion his previous thoughts and worries vanished from his mind when he saw the absolute mayhem close to the stables adjoining the paddock to one side of the large complex. He leapt blindly from his mount and without securing the horse he ran headlong towards the overturned and wrecked carriage knowing that something very bad had happened there.

The death of his little Junia almost broke his heart and resolve but the life threatening injuries to his wife were of less importance to him.

It took weeks for him to re-establish even a semblance of his previous life but he did stick to the solemn commitment he'd made to the Gods and had avoided all social contact outside his home. And not only had he to contend with the death of his daughter but the injuries sustained by Belvia would prevent her ever having children again and he guessed that over time this could cause problems with his inheritance if his father-in-law should renege on the covenant he'd made with him when he'd married his daughter.

Junia had been his guarantee to become joint Governor of *Oriens* together with Belvia when Ursus died. But now that their child had died and him having no chance of fathering other children with Belvia the Governor might turn to a male relative to continue the bloodline. The thought that this might happen drove him into a deep seated anger with his constantly snivelling wife and it took all of his willpower to refrain from shaking her from her grief when he believed that it was he who could lose the most in these circumstances. Even though he began to scorn her he still needed her if he was to stand any chance of keeping Ursus on side, though if he was being totally honest he'd admit that it was for these reasons only why he'd avoided any extra-marital affairs since the accident rather than his hypocritical promise to the Gods. The pressure began to get to him when he decided that he had to get away from there for a short time to clear his head and to figure out what he could do to prevent Ursus denying him his well deserved entitlement. He discouraged Belvia from telling her father or anyone else what the *medicus* had told them because he reckoned the doddering old ass hadn't a clue what he was talking about and was totally wrong in his prognosis.

Maximus actually didn't believe anything of the sort and was just buying time until he'd collected his wits together again and figured out how he could salvage and consolidate his inheritance for good.

Now that he was a senior commander in the military he had the freedom and authority to virtually do what he wanted providing the Governor agreed. He mentioned to Ursus that a patrol was due to leave to do the regular audit in the second and third sectors of *Extremus* and that he'd like to command it so that he could refresh his focus from the recent trauma in the family. But he also felt that his wife needed a change of scene to recover and he'd arranged for her to spend some time at a spa in *Australis* and visit the Temple of the Gods. His father-in-law heartily agreed and commented that it was a very meritorious and loving thing that he was doing and that they both had his blessing.

Maximus had searched the Governor's eyes as he'd said this and was reassured when he didn't see any signs of duplicity there.

Before the week was out he'd watched with impatience when early one morning Belvia departed for

Australis and an hour hadn't passed when he and four hand-picked young soldiers whom he knew intimately together with a stable boy had set off east on horseback along the cobblestoned road and rode into *Primoris*.

Commander Maximus and his men continued their journey through *Secundus* on foot when the stable boy departed with the horses to Ciro City. The boy had been charged to return to this point in eight days when the survey in the latter two sections of *Extremus* should be completed.

Neither Maximus nor any of the others had ever been further than the end of the cobblestone road before this day and for the first few hours they were so enamoured with their new surroundings that time flew. By late evening when they'd neared the east sector of *Secundus* their enthusiasm had waned somewhat and the sight of numerous white rabbits frolicking about or Spitfire buzzards cruising overhead no longer grabbed their attention other than to note the event. And in time the continuous brightness began to irritate their eyes.

The survey in *Secundus* and *Tertius* was performed annually though if there was a perceived increase or decrease in the wildlife there or if it was discovered that there was a variance to the lighting, water or alluvium it could be repeated more often to ascertain the cause, effect and possible remedy. Thought *Extremus* was anomalous and of no visible benefit to greater Sitantal it was officially believed that the regions were an essential part of their whole ecological system and any changes there could affect the entire country over time. *Primoris* was treated as a separate entity because of the more inhospitable terrain and thick vegetation and was evaluated more infrequently with a different conspectus which usually entailed a protracted period and much more manpower.

    As the auditors tired and neared the end of the first day Maximus felt that he'd made the right decision by coming here and joked with his men that perhaps they should do this more often. Within the group he was at ease with his four younger peers having got to know them all socially since they'd entered the service and he didn't have to pull rank because he guessed that they were more than happy to be in his company and would do anything he asked of them without hesitation. Before they dined they stripped and bathed in one of the deeper streams near their campsite and then spent their first night in the bivouac downing prolific amounts of wine before they eventually slumped one by one in a tangled heap to the floor with the devilish commander somewhere in the middle of the human jumble.

    At the end of the third day's trek they pitched camp near the entrance to *Tertius* but collectively settled for a wine and activity free night when they perceived the dreary environs which now confronted them. The five spent the next day trying their best to manoeuvre through the bleak interior of the last sector and still remain alert and note what they saw around them, but without having previously experienced a task such as this they wondered at its effectiveness when the wildlife they didn't want to encounter were the actual things they were expected to see. But when on the final leg of the journey they were shaken and shocked by the unexpected approach of a *Tresdentus mus-anguis* but luckily for all of them the cadet nearest the attacking animal had his sword drawn at the time and managed to strike the slavering creature by swinging wildly and injuring it sufficiently to bring it down. As it trashed about on the wet floor Maximus pierced its brain and finished it off. They didn't hang about and quickly sidestepped the carcass and left the scene in subdued silence and shortly reached the large chamber where *Extremus* ended. They all breathed a sigh of relief though they sat down with a degree of trepidation knowing that very soon they would have to go through the whole miserable experience of traipsing back through *Tertius* again.

Though Commander Maximus and the others knew that it was forbidden by law for anyone to open the exit into *Terra Ferusum* he couldn't resist the temptation to do just that. He felt comfortable and believed that his colleagues would never breathe a word to anyone about the capital offence.

He moved the counterbalance and waited pensively as the massive rock slid silently inwards and the chamber lit up immediately as if there'd been a hundred lanterns ignited in unison. But as they were about to have a quick look outside to see what was out there they heard the sound of excited chatter in a strange language coming from nearby. Maximus silently signalled to the others to remain still and inside the vault as he edged cautiously through the opening. He listened tentatively and realised the voices were coming from a broad granite outcrop above him. His curiosity was stronger than his fear of discovery and he climbed bit by bit through the deluge of water whooshing through the rugged fissure between the sheer rock face and the large prominence where the voices appeared to be centred. At the top he crawled behind a clump of stunted gnarled scrub and when he gently eased a section aside and peered out he saw a group of strangely dressed people with their backs to him gazing outwards, pointing and gesticulating to something elsewhere under a brilliant blue sky. But behind them and nearer to him were two small children, a boy and girl, sitting on a blanket giggling and poking excitedly at the grass. He almost gave his presence away when he saw the little girl but he managed to stifle the groan just in time. Her hair was blonde and curled and as she sat with her back to him he imagined that he was looking at his little Junia.

Without any consideration or forethought he sprung from behind the shrubbery and snatched her faster than the blink of an eye. His arm and leg muscles must have acted without any impulse or input from his brain because he was sliding down the water chute before it registered with him what he'd just done. Or so it seemed to him at the time.

As he raced into the chamber with the little wriggling bundle in his arms he heard frantic cries coming from overhead. He signalled his men to close the rock door immediately.

The little girl began to cry and his four colleagues stood open mouthed with shock as they looked on in horror and incredulity at their commander and involuntarily recoiled from him as if they were facing someone who'd gone mad. But it was the look of censure that hit him where it hurts and he knew there and then that he couldn't trust these young men anymore. Even in the dimly lighted chamber he'd seen these reactions and the dissenting emotion in their eyes and this grim revelation would seal their fate.

 The commander offloaded his backpack and made a makeshift harness for the sobbing frightened little girl and he had one of his men secure her to his back where she eventually slept, probably induced by the constant movement as they zigzagged their way through the boulder strewn dank interior. Maximus noticed the muted behaviour of his fellow travellers and guessed that it wasn't all down to their surroundings but he didn't give them reason to feel that he'd perceived their critical inner voices and he continued to project a happy-go-lucky attitude.

Later in the evening he selected a reasonably dry space where they settled for the night and at this point the little girl broke the silence of the vast grotto with ear-piercing cries which unnerved everyone even further except the commander who'd heard similar protest from his own child in the past and was able to accept it more patiently. Again exhaustion finally sent her to sleep which allowed Maximus to do his best to steer his men onto a more relaxed theme when he discussed the abnormal features surrounding them in *Tertius*. When they dined he'd insisted they have more wine than they'd wanted and he pretended to match them drink for drink but surreptitiously he tipped his share behind the rock he was sitting on without being discovered. Later when his four erstwhile friends succumbed to sleep he sneaked from the camp and returned to the spot where the snake-rat had been killed on the outbound journey.

The carcass had been virtually stripped of all its flesh as he'd fully expected that it would be but the poison tipped tail which projected from its back had remained untouched and it and the venom sac were still intact. With meticulous care he squeezed the poison from the gland into the little vial, sealed it and quickly returned to base where everyone including the child was still sleeping soundly.

They reached *Secundus* late the following evening where Maximus took the little girl and bathed her gently in the nearest stream and wrapped her in his own unworn clean clothing and then encouraged the frightened child to nibble a small cake and sip a little water. He washed her clothes and hung them to dry on a white cactus-like plant nearby. He guessed the pitiful child was severely traumatised and he hoped that with some care and attention she would recover and forget all about the ordeal she'd suffered. But he had no regrets about the action he'd taken and was confident that it was a gift from the Gods and that good would come from it in time. He settled the child down for the night and turned his attention to his four comrades who'd finished erecting the tent. Before the evening meal he casually eyed them as they bathed and mentally noted where they'd incurred abrasions and scratches on the exposed areas on their hands, faces or legs while they'd been trekking. He also reckoned that since they'd entered the more pleasant ambiance of the middle sector they'd shaken off the morose mood which had gripped them from the previous morning.

The generous praise and flattery he lavished on them during the meal for the excellent work they'd done over the past days was believed and was well received and very soon the four became smug and almost conceited about their achievements and their leader praised them even more. He mentioned more than once that he had exceptional and life changing plans for each of them in the future. He happily decanted the last large *amphora* of the strongest and best wine and the festivities very soon became a rollicking spirited jamboree where some of them even tried to tease from him his plans for them and if it would bring them really high-grade promotions and privilege.

He watched them drift into sleep one after the other and saw that each had a peaceful contented smile and he believed that their dreams were happy ones. He retrieved the little bottle and a small cloth from his bag and carefully soaked it with venom and ever so gently applied it to the still raw scratches and abrasions on his compatriots. Several times he had to pull away quickly and feign sleep when the sleeping rookie stirred and shifted position. He would then wait for a little while and repeat the application. By midnight he'd applied the toxin at least six times to each man and by now he was seeing and hearing subtle changes in all of them.

He left the comatosed men for a short time and checked on the sleeping girl and placed an extra blanket over her and ran his finger gently through her silken blonde hair.

The peaceful expression on her angelic face brought a smile to his lips and several tears of total happiness flowed freely down his cheeks.

He returned to the other tranquil scene and applied more dabs of venom to each perspiring man again. He listened attentively to the laboured breathing and observed odd muscle spasms on different parts of their bodies. He then sat down nearby and gazed with deep affection at his dying friends and colleagues and he cried copious tears of sadness for their plight. He was heartbroken with grief but very soon this changed to annoyance with them for being disloyal and forcing him to do this despicable deed though he'd loved them all.

He stood up and paced back and forth and berated the unresponsive bodies and he snivelled and sobbed that they shouldn't have been so fickle and perfidious but should have been overjoyed along with him that he'd become a father once again.

It took him the best part of two hours to move the four corpses into the slimy depths of *Tertius* where he hoped the carnivore inhabitants would soon erase all evidence of his contemptible but unavoidable act.

He bathed in the stream and returned the small bottle to his pack and then attended to the needs of the little girl and dressed her in her now dry clothes. His previous stress soon dissipated and he hummed and crooned and tickled the frightened child without success and she just cried even louder. As he packed his bag he was about to throw the single pink baby shoe away but shrugged his shoulders and placed it with the rest of the stuff in the pack. He ate a hearty meal and did his best to encourage his new daughter to eat but she shrunk away from him as if he was evil and she continued to cry.

He wrapped her neatly in the blanket and placed her gently in his makeshift shoulder sling and set off through *Secundus* before seven in the morning of the seventh day of the audit in *Extremus*. It took him a little while to adjust to the relative silence which now surrounded him compared to the jollity and camaraderie of the outbound journey.

He made great progress and restricted his rest periods to the very minimum and caught sight of the opening into *Primoris* before six o'clock in the morning of the eighth day. Though he was completely exhausted the precious bundle he carried numbed any discomfort that he felt at that moment and he resolutely continued forward.

He'd just passed through the opening into *Primoris* when he spotted the stable boy with the string of horses trotting towards him down the cobblestone road.

When he presented their new daughter to his wife she was so overwhelmed that she was lost for words and didn't ask who she was or even where he'd found her. She held the infant so tightly that Maximus tried to prise them apart but the little girl clung to her new mother and didn't want to be separated. In her excitement Belvia kept calling the child Junia until Maximus stepped in and insisted that she have a different name. Eventually they agreed that it should honour the month when she'd come into their lives.

Her new name would be Aprilis and she was the apple of his eye.

Fortunately for Maximus shortly after the new arrival to his family, the seventy-one year old

Governor Ursus of *Oriens* had a mental episode during his sleep one night and had wakened in the morning believing that he was a young boy again. He'd rushed from his bedchamber and had straddled the highly polished spiral banister a short distance from his room where he'd skimmed down almost three floors whooping all the way. But as he gathered speed he didn't quite make it to the ground floor when he'd crashed off at the last bend on the stair and had fractured his cranium in three places, the *medicus* had confirmed.
There were some in *Oriens* who didn't believe a word of this.

Maximus and Belvia became joint Governors instantly on his death and while she spent the following days, months and years doting over her daughter he'd taken to his new role and to the mansion that went with the exalted position just like a fish to water and in no time at all he'd returned to his old degenerate ways. Though Belvia was well aware of her husband's infidelities and capers she chose to ignore it and she spent most of her time with her darling Aprilis.
This arrangement had worked a treat for more than two decades until one day Maximus realised that he'd fallen in love with his then mistress. In fact he was totally besotted with her and when she declared that unless he married her she was leaving him for good he began the process of ridding himself of his wife of twenty plus years by searching out the little *ampulla* of snake venom taken

from the *Tres-dentus mus-anguis* in *Tertius* on that fateful day such a long time ago.

It had taken almost two years for him to achieve his goal and during that time relations between him and his supposed daughter Aprilis had become increasingly fractious due to her gnawing suspicions that somehow he was responsible for her mother's decline into ill health and eventual death and within one week of Belvia's passing Maximus had married his mistress. Shortly afterwards Aprilis had removed herself from the Governor's mansion and had relocated to *Urbis Capitolium* where she'd subsequently met the heir to the then Consul Primus and they were married two years later. Meanwhile Maximus' second wife had one miscarriage after another until she successfully delivered their daughter Dido.

Maximus was ecstatic and had celebrated her birth profusely and very soon the little girl was the new apple of his eye and the previous apple became an outsider in her old home.

    He groaned wearily and his shoulders sagged despondently. How ironic for him that the abducted child's younger son Zeo was now threatening to bring all his schemes and dreams to an nightmarish end.

An age old axiom '*Ventum seminabunt et turbinem metent*': *Sow the wind and reap the whirlwind,* continued to reverberate inside his brain and wouldn't go away. Eventually the recurring thought was swamped by his alcohol intake and his recollections blurred and drifted away from events of the past. His hands trembled when he decanted another large goblet of red wine. He dined, dozed and drank in his den for almost seventy-two hours where he'd reminisced and regurgitated the dark deeds of his past.

Maximus wakened to the screeching sound of his daughter Dido's voice as it reverberated down the hallway leading to his den. It crossed his fuggy mind that she must have heard of the debacle at the security point at *Primoris* which had allowed the fugitive Zeo to re-enter the country again and he braced himself for a thorough tongue lashing knowing that she always blamed him when things went wrong.

When the door crashed open he was astounded by the appearance of his normally fragrant and immaculately attired daughter. He gawked in disbelief before averting his gaze with embarrassment at seeing her in such a state.

Dido looked like a discarded bag of rags and she reeked to the high heavens too. Her face and hair was a mess and she was the epitome of filth and dirt right down to and including the remnants of her delicately embroidered size eleven boots.

She launched herself across the room and before the unprepared Governor had time to move from the *torus* or fend her off she was on top of him and pummelled him on his chest ineffectually with her closed fists.

Eventually he managed to grab her wrists and

push her away from him as she screamed frenetically that he should have killed the *spurius* Zeo when he had the opportunity almost six months ago.

It was only when he managed to get her to settle down beside him and explain in detail what had happened on her journey home that Maximus was able to understand his daughter's pent-up rage and when he'd garnered all the facts his anger surpassed Dido's by a long mile. He stormed from the den and grabbed a flunky and told him to have the city's *Praefecti* come to the mansion right away.

Rather than wait for the opportunity to randomly meet the pup who had disrespected his daughter he'd mobilise his forces and the whole province to hunt him and his two guilty accomplices down wherever they were.

He'd make them regret what they'd done to his darling Dido.

CHAPTER NINETEEN

When 'Pravus' Sorus had received the news of the assault on Hopeless Expectations Penitentiary and the release by Zeor's forces of the political prisoners being held there he'd flown into an uncontrolled rage and had lost all self discipline completely. He'd beaten the messenger black and blue; so much so, the man was still receiving treatment at the local *valetudinarium*.

He regretted it later but only because he'd been reminded that the runner was one of the best at his job and that he'd also been the link to his agent in Esta City. His gross and intemperate rashness was magnified even more when the replacement courier had taken four days to bring the follow-up message from his deputy Puto Pollux about the retreat, the abandonment and the razing of the military garrison in Vili City. He'd been given this galling information as he'd reached the top step leading to his palatial office and it threw him into a further frenzy but this time, rather than assault the messenger he attacked one of a pair of large ornamental urns beside the grand entrance when he heaved it from its pedestal and sent it flying down the many marble steps where it smashed into a zillion pieces on the plaza below. When he read the section where Pollux had dictated verbatim the notice which Zeor had publicly posted in the city decreeing that his son Zeo would be the next Governor of *Occidens* and vowing that the fortress which Sorus' grandfather had built would be razed to the ground to make way for such developments as educational and cultural study centres he veered close to apoplexy and raced across the path to the other matching urn on the left side of the doorway and sent it and its base crashing to the bottom.

On seeing this further outburst the runner took to his heels down the debris strewn steps now feeling what had happened to his predecessor could be about to happen to him. His next thought added wings to his flight when he recalled a rumour he'd heard several months ago of another messenger who'd been killed in this same building when he'd delivered bad news to the dictator. He was scared for his life and he now didn't give a rat's behind about the job anymore. He'd go north where he reckoned he might stand a better chance of survival. The way he figured it out right now was simply that this lunatic was bound to have more bad news coming his way in the future and he was determined not to be the one to deliver it to him; No way, *Hôrae!*

Sorus recognised the mistake he'd made in allowing Pollux to remain with him in the Capitol when they'd been alerted that Zeor was planning to free the political prisoners in Vili City but supposedly at a much later date. It was now obvious to him that they'd been fed misleading information deliberately and therefore the enemy must be aware of the agent in their ranks.

The audacious attack on the prison and then on the barracks had haunted him since he'd been informed of it and for the first time ever he had a niggling doubt about Puto Pollux, his *fidus Achates.*

He crossed the room to the large map on the wall and traced the latest movements of Suga Cazo from his most recent report. When he realised that Cazo was less than forty miles away he summoned a runner and sent his hit-man an urgent recall to the Capitol. He dispatched a second courier to Reptus Reptum and plunged into a further tantrum when he was informed that another messenger had debunked a short time ago and there was no one else available until the following day.

He sat down impatiently behind his ornate desk and drummed his fingertips irritably on the polished surface as he pondered how to reclaim the initiative and bring the fledgling countercoup to an end. It was close to midnight when he climbed the ornate staircase on his way to his bedchamber clutching his papers. He now knew what he had to do over the following days to get his plans back on track.

Having just unilaterally prorogued the senate Sorus had declared a state of emergency throughout Sitantal. The self appointed Consul Primus had ended the fractious gathering with the senators in the forum and sent his personal *factotum* to have the city *Praefectae* come to his office immediately. He made a conscious effort to conceal his pent-up irritation with the senators from the flunky having finally realised that nervous personal staff talked to each other and to their contemporaries in other places in a less cautious fashion than was good for him. Plus there was the added problem of finding reliable and trustworthy overland and local messengers as he'd found out when not one but two of the replacement runners had messed up recently with verbal instructions, one where Commander Cazo had killed the wrong senator and the other to his Deputy Governor Pollux in *Occidens* which though it didn't have such fatal consequences, nonetheless had caused problems. He was now in a situation where he had to dispatch all his orders in writing with the added danger of them being intercepted by his enemies though not forgetting the extra workload this now placed on him having to dictate constantly to a *scriptor*.

The Capitol's senior *Praefectus'* demeanour was inscrutable when he stood in front of the dictator, that is, until he was ordered to conscript every male who was sixteen years old and older in the city and in the provinces into his army.

Those who refused to join up would be thrown into prison along with their parents and younger siblings until they'd complied. Sorus directed that anyone with an eye in their head, a hand to hold a weapon and a leg to stand on was now required to enlist with the exception of those in academia, those engaged in essential works and services or active in his administration being exempt from the draft.

The officer's lower jaw had dropped so much so that a passing swarm of bees could easily have established a hive in his wide open mouth, or so the *factotum* smugly imagined as he listened in on the conversation but nonetheless he was very relieved to hear that he'd be one of the fortunate ones who'd be exempt from the draconian directive. He vowed silently that he'd be more conscientious in his duty to his master from this day forward.

    The message rack on the usurper's desk had several scrolls awaiting consideration but before he touched them he called on the pageboy to fetch wine.

He waited until the nervous youth had decanted a generous measure into a large goblet and signalled him to leave the room before he selected the missive bearing the seal of Governor Maximus. It was dated four days ago and related to events which had happened at the security base guarding the opening to *Extremus* on the day prior to its dispatch.

The cut glass vessel smashed in umpteen particles

against the opposite wall and the page peeked nervously round the door but he quickly withdrew back into the anteroom where he trembled and quaked in his black patent leather boots with shiny buckles. He ruefully wished he'd listened to his parents when they'd pleaded with him to continue his studies at the academy.

'Pravus' Sorus had ditched his short-lived self imposed sanction on his temper tantrums for good and now sent the *amphora* in the same direction as the goblet had gone before. He re-read the message then tore it into shreds before unrolling the scented frilly page from his fiancée Dido who'd written him from someplace in south *Oriens* he'd never heard of where she was on her way home to Ciro City.

He noticed that it had been dispatched to him on the same date as her father's infuriating letter had been penned.

It oozed with declarations of devotion to her lover and she enthused about her large coach laden with *cudos* and valuable gift's which the generous citizens of south *Oriens* had freely donated in celebration of their forthcoming wedding. She promised him that by the time she'd finished her tour of the provinces he and she would be the wealthiest couple in Sitantal besides being *super omnia*; the first family of the nation! Just like nobility! Imagine it! It was such fun and so nice to know that everyone loved her so much. She'd signed off with his and her initials romantically and regally intertwined which were enclosed within a glowing heart symbol wreathed with cute little forget-me-nots. He wondered, but only for an instant, what he'd look like wearing a chaplet on his head.

Her tender innocence, selflessness and fidelity almost brought a tear to his eye. The love letter from his *inamorata* and the good news of the valuable gifts lightened his dark mood for a moment or two until he eyed the shredded report from her father strewn on the floor detailing the rout of the security camp near *Primoris* by the little *merda* Zeo and his two cronies from *Terra Ferusum*.

He opened the report from his spy located near the Temple of the Gods with a distinct lack of fervour. This soon changed to a positive note when he read how just three days ago Reptus Reptum and his female snake bearers had completely annihilated the *Beneficiarius* in the exclusion zone without a modicum of mercy being shown to them. It proudly added that no one had escaped the total wipe-out.

The last message sent by him to the snake breeder had ordered the old man to forgo the previous instructions to take Zeo and his companions alive so that they could be executed in full public view as a warning to others whereas his new orders were to kill them on sight and send their bodies to the Capitol. Sorus had decided that if he needed to torture someone at any time there were plenty of candidates in the senate whose early demise would equally satisfy his lust.

The note continued that the presence of the herpetologist and his *Vipera Dominam* were now discouraging regular pilgrims from the area and they'd be ready for the pending arrival of the three particular pilgrims on the dictators most wanted list.

Sorus rubbed his hands in glee at the pleasing thought and called the young page to fetch another *amphora* of wine. He gave the pasty faced youth a handful of silver coins when he returned and told him that he could have the rest of the day off to go down town and have a good time. Though the boy was startled by the uncharacteristic generous gesture shown by his master he didn't have to be told twice and literally danced out the doorway in his black patent leather boots with shiny buckles. Thirty minutes after the youth had left the building Commander Suga Cazo was shown into the dictator's chamber which coincided with the delivery of the latest message from the agent in Esta City which he noted had taken three days to reach the Capitol.

Sorus scanned the message avidly and pointed Cazo to the vacant chair opposite the desk as he re-read the contents of the paper.

    Suga Cazo played his subservient role with genuine deference as he sat in front of the man who'd saved his neck on the gallows some time ago. Though he was well aware that the dictator had reprieved him for his own nefarious reasons nonetheless there were plenty of others in prison he could have chosen who were known to be just as psychotic as him. But the more he'd gotten to understand the dictator the more he realised that they were two of a kind, birds of a feather even. Never in his life did he, or anyone else for that matter, think that one day he would be appointed a Commander and have one hundred and fifty fellow felons at his control or that they'd be able to loot and pillage to their hearts content especially where temples, *augurs* and their acolytes were concerned. Already he'd accumulated enough spoils to see him comfortably into his senior years and perhaps beyond, it was a win win situation for him in every sense and it satisfied his lust for blood and lucre all at the same time. But the icing on the cake was that he could conduct the banditry under the auspices and protection of the *domitor* of Sitantal.

CHAPTER TWENTY

They separated from the coachmen, the corpses, the riderless horses and the treasure filled coach at the first village they reached and continued southwest for the next three hours and then they rested overnight in a sheltered glade alongside a rambling, babbling stream.

They continued onwards early next morning and the three horsemen deliberately bypassed the villages at the roadside and larger towns in the distance whereas Euander was able to pass through with his combo wagon without raising much curiosity. They ignored the stares from the few people they did encounter on the way and all the three mounted men avoided those they could by trotting off into the nearby orchards and meadows.

On the third day after leaving *Primoris* they reached the *Australis* boundary mark at noon when Zeo indicated a simple Latin script road sign. At this particular point neither Adam nor Johnny could see any perceptible change in the landscape; it was just as idyllic and peaceful as the province they were now leaving behind them except that in the distance to the far right they could see where the undulating terrain rose sharply to the skyline. At the next junction they angled off in a northwest direction towards the jagged expanse. Zeo assured them that on the other side of the towering ridges they'd be able to get their first glimpse of the Temple of the Gods.

Late in the evening they reached Merusa, a small village with a number of dwellings, an inn, bakery, wheelwright, a busy little coaching halt and an equally busy marina which was linked to the first canal they'd seen for several days. Further from the hamlet was the four-road intersection where they'd go north. Though the two outsiders were itching to take a closer look at the pretty chocolate-box scene they did agree with Zeo that it was best to avoid it right now and keep away from people they didn't know. Several hundred yards from the village they located a small siding near a narrow rivulet and parked up for the evening where the long pilgrim's road dissecting the ridges in the north began. Being the only one in their group who was dressed in the indigenous fashion Euander strolled into the hamlet to buy crusty fresh bread and succulent fruit and as they ate they had a clear view of the surrounding area and were able to observe the steady flow of traffic coming and going over the double-track road which would bring them to their destination.

During the night watch they'd observed an intermittent trickle of traffic through the lantern lit hamlet where the marina, the coaching halt and village store remained open and were active all night long.

During breakfast they agreed to make an early start and when the horses were fed and watered the group moved onto the twin-track road marked with the directional sign AD TEMPLUM DEI just after seven o'clock. They'd barely travelled a hundred yards when they met the first of many pilgrims, some on horseback and others in small and large coaches and all were heading south. The worried and focused looks on some of the occupants attracted Zeo's attention and he rode across and spoke with one of the anxious looking drivers and asked if there were problems ahead.

Though the man looked even more nervous when the all-black attired Zeo approached him he agreed that there was something amiss near the perimeter of the exclusion zone, where strange sightings had been reported with unpleasant sounds and odours everywhere for several nights in a row but odder still there were no *Beneficiarius* patrolling the area as they'd expected. Their base had been completely deserted when they'd called to check and he and his family, along with many others, had departed early last evening because they'd sensed a malignant presence at the place. He told Zeo that he and his companions should turn round now and go no further, that there was definitely something evil afoot.

When Zeo explained to the others what he'd been told and relayed the stark warning from the fleeing pilgrim it spurred them onwards at an increased pace.

Throughout the day they witnessed coaches which they'd seen travelling north on the previous day now return south and by early afternoon the exodus of pilgrims had petered out and eventually they had the wide open road to themselves.

The mountainous gorge which the road ran through had widened out and the vegetation and trees now thrived on both sides inside the rocky chasm but the firmament above the stark precipices wasn't the usual azure blue they'd become used to since they'd re-entered Sitantal but was now a vaporous mix of coasting pastel vapours of every hue imaginable high above them. When they'd exited the rocky elevations on their right Johnny and Adam were confronted with the source of the most amazing array of vivid colours they'd ever seen above a landscape anywhere. Though they were still several miles away from the nexus of the spectacular phenomena Adam had no difficulty in understanding why the people of Sitantal would believe that this place was hallowed and though Euander and Zeo had visited the Temple of the Gods in their younger years they too joined the first-timers in using their binoculars to view it once again.

Nobody had spoken since they'd first perceived the spectacle and the only sounds around were

Johnny's faint whistles and Friday panting. Adam was blown away; it was much more than he'd ever imagined it would be and he'd be the first to admit that his innate artistry and imagination would be stretched to the max to do it justice if he ever attempted to depict the scene on canvas. Its sensational impact could never be overstated and the usual adjectives such as inspirational and sensational and others, like awesome and stupendous fell well short of the mark when describing something like this he mused as he filed the vision into his memory bank.

The Temple of the Gods ascended from within a series of jagged varicoloured rocks reaching up to its base. And even from this distance the massive and voluminous shards protruding from this lofty mount glowed and appeared to palpitate like they were freshly molten and pliable hot glass. These giant luminous projections gave the skyline its colourful and electrifying splendour but soaring up to the heavens from the centre of the multicoloured mount was the laser-like wonder which they'd been commanded to attend by the Gods of Sitantal.

Johnny had ceased expressing his astonishment with whistles, sighs and grunts and had now fixed his gaze on the soaring edifice which sliced upwards through the scintillating skyline in front of him. He believed that the answer to everything could be found in that place and his gut instincts told him that it was the real thing;

This is it!

Before him was the tangible proof that Sitantal was blessed and regardless of what anyone might say or do in the future to try to convince him otherwise; that there was no definitive evidence of an omnipotent Being out there, he knew they'd be wrong because he was looking at the manifestation of it right now and he'd remember and respect this for all time. And even though he was still quite a distance from the Temple he felt its influence right here and he believed it would become even clearer to him when he reached the awe-inspiring edifice. He concluded that anyone who was irreligious or nontheistic or even a Buddhist would have a difficult time in this place when they'd see what he was looking at and even the most diehard agnostic would be hard pressed to explain this phenomenon.

      Having spent almost ten minutes gazing into the far distance and just as Zeo was about to interrupt their viewing Adam and Johnny signalled to him that they were now ready to continue on the journey.

The three horsemen and the combo wagon moved forward on the totally deserted road and as if to emphasise their aloneness and the malign influence which had infused the sector which the departing pilgrims had run from, all birdsong appeared to have ceased and an eerie quietude had descended on the surrounding area. Euander was the first to mention this anomaly to Zeo who relayed the observation to his friends and the group came to a halt again and listened more attentively. The only noise they detected was the odd gentle snort from the horses but even they appeared to have muted the volume they normally ventilated. The guys continued forward on high alert as they scanned the landscape diligently.

With the road now empty except for themselves the three mounted a protective zone around the wagon and manoeuvred back and forth on each side allowing Euander to drive in the centre of the carriageway. They had yet to see any *Beneficiarius* who were expected to mount regular patrols to monitor the flow of pilgrims entering and leaving the venerated area which extended well beyond the Temple mount. It confirmed to Zeo what the retreating driver had earlier warned him that something definitely was amiss. As dusk loomed they came to a halt. Adam and Johnny were distracted again when they saw the Temple of the Gods and its rugged surrounds change from the multicolour hues to a uniform ultramarine blue and the transformation was bordering on phenomenal also.

They agreed to set up camp and form an enclosure in the middle of the deserted road, well away from the lush trees and tall flowery grasses beyond the verges. They corralled the horses between the two separated wagons where Euander had spread armfuls of freshly cut long grass from the abundant source nearby. He lighted the lanterns he'd expropriated from the security compound they'd overrun and after the meal they mounted a double manned five hour watch as they'd done on the previous night with Adam and Johnny taking first duty together with the dog who also remained on alert.

The *de rigueur* coffee was ready for Zeo and Euander when they rose to relieve the others at two in the morning but their lips had barely touched their steaming mugs when the dog gave a sharp warning growl and peered into the grassland to the right of the camp with his ears cocked upright. All four guys immediately sprung into action and separated and took up defensive positions around each side of their camp. Adam was closest to Friday when he broke into a continuous blitz of enraged barking and he pinpointed the area where the animal's gaze was fixed. He readied the flamethrower and aimed high.

The ball of fire shot twenty feet into the semi-darkness and lit up the cluster of trees with its orange glow and before the flash lighting petered out he saw what looked like a tramp scurry from behind the tree cluster ahead and out of sight into the thicker foliage behind.

It wasn't a sight that he'd expected to see and he quickly turned to Johnny who had just joined him. 'Did my eyes deceive me or was that just a raggedy old tramp lurking in the bushes?'

'I doubt it was a tramp somehow. No self-respecting bum would be out and about in the middle of the night, would he?'

Johnny's glib answer and question didn't elicit a direct response but Zeo thought that there might be some merit to the tramp explanation or that the night visitor might be a religious hermit hoping for salvation by living out in the sticks near the Temple and be as one with Mother Nature, just like a troglodyte.

Reptus Reptum battled his way back through the brush and undergrowth to his camp feeling irritable that he'd been discovered by the very people he'd been sent to intimidate and prevent from reaching the Temple of the Gods but at the same time he was pleased to have located the road they were using to approach the Temple. But other thoughts began to needle him and one was the fact that there were now four people to contend with and not three as he'd been told and there was also the added problem of a vicious dog to deal with, not to mention that the enemy appeared to have some sort of fire belching weapon. He vowed that Sorus would pay him extra to what had been originally agreed in their contract. The opportunity to extract more silver and gold from the dictator cheered him up quite a bit for the second time in three minutes as he stumbled through the thick brush.

Unknown to the four campers or to Reptus Reptum a spindly skeletal figure who was clad in olive green attire from top to toe and who'd been static during the entire incident now slunk further back into the bush behind the camp where he still observed the scene with intense interest.

Not only was his clothing made from green fabric his face, hands and hair were dyed to the same colour as were his socks and boots. The little faux green and brownish leaves attached to his tight fitting clothing fluttered in the faint night breeze and helped him blend in perfectly with the natural environs. Even from a short distance he looked like a scraggily old stump which had weathered a few storms in the past and this was something he was immensely proud of and could attest to.

Horses, cattle, pigs, boars and wolves had used him as a scratching post and he had the friction-burn scars and flea bites to prove it. Territory marking dogs had raised their hind

legs against him many, many times and he could remember with justifiable conceit and pride the morning a little bird attempted to build a nest in the moss cap on top of his head.

He rightfully claimed to be a master of disguise in the art of close surveillance.

After breakfast the four decamped and the journey north continued under the shifting kaleidoscopic ceiling. Before noon they reached the outstation at the perimeter of the exclusion zone without being challenged by a *Beneficiarius* or even seeing anyone else on the way here. While Adam and Johnny remained outside the station on horseback Zeo and Euander dismounted and cautiously entered the silent compound. Zeo called out enquiringly as they approached the main building in the enclosure and tentatively opened the door. Both guys recoiled with their hands covering their mouths and noses and hastily backed off. Neither Adam nor Johnny needed to be told what their friends had discovered inside and quickly joined them in the small grassy square in the centre of the quasi-military enclave.

The partially decomposed body of General Exer Savus was lying inside the door to the office. He was dressed in *Beneficiarius* uniform and was clutching a broken writing instrument. A thick ledger and a polished brass bugle lay abandoned near the desk.

Zeo had recognised the honorary *Dux* insignia still attached to the General's lapel and he explained to the others that he believed robbery hadn't been the motive behind his death and he was certain it wasn't natural or accidental either considering the marks on his face and neck and it tied in with what they'd been told by the fleeing pilgrim on the previous day. They checked out the other buildings within the compound and found seven more bodies in similar condition as the General's in different locations and ten agitated horses in the paddock and two in the stables all of them without feed stuff or water. Zeo directed Euander to attend to them straight away. Meanwhile Adam, Johnny and Zeo steered the wagons and their own mounts into the compound and unharnessed and corralled the animals when Zeo explained that they'd need to try and discover what had happened here and that there was also the added responsibility of the cremation and *exsequiae* rite to be fulfilled before they could leave.

When all the newly acquired animals and their own had been catered for the four friends ate a quick lunch followed by coffee and then prepared mentally for the unpleasant task of assembling the cadavers for the funeral pyre.

With the aid of a stretcher from the small medical bay in the station, one by one they loaded the bodies on a large four-wheel wagon found on site. Fuelled by a collection of furniture and bales of straw from the other buildings they set them alight in the remotest corner of the paddock as Zeo and Euander chanted the rite to the Goddess *Libitina*.

Immediately after they'd all showered Zeo browsed through the thick daybook which he'd found in the dead General's office when he suddenly thumped the table with his fist and exclaimed that the *Beneficiarius* had been killed by snake bites which explained the multiple twin puncture marks they'd seen on the necks and faces on the dead bodies. Four days prior General Savus had recorded in his ledger that three of his men patrolling the exclusion zone had been surrounded and attacked by a large group of women who had snakes protruding from their mouths. Two officers had been bitten and poisoned instantly but the third had reported back to base before he too had succumbed to the venom. He'd written that the guard had declared that the women assassins were virtually naked and he'd described them as being more *mechanicus* than human like and that they were being controlled by a filthy looking old man. The General had instantly summoned all his men to report back to the station but by the morning of the next day none had returned including the man he'd sent out to alert them. He was convinced at the time of writing the last entry that every member of his *Beneficiarius* on duty outside the station had perished somewhere in or around the exclusion zone and he hoped and prayed that he and his remaining guards could defend themselves and the station against this illogical and almost unbelievable threat.

Zeo and the others were at a loss as to how a group of what appeared to be fit and healthy ex-military could be overwhelmed and killed without any signs of a struggle. None of the victims had any defensive wounds and not one of them had unsheathed a sword in self defence. The complete slaughter baffled the guys especially when they considered that these men had been made aware of the approaching danger. It appeared to them that the men had simply succumbed without a fight.

At this point Zeo perused and flicked through the neat and well kept ledger almost forensically and he muttered and wondered why the subsequent two pages to the last entry had been roughly torn from the book. He searched the desk top and scanned the floor but failed to find the missing pages anywhere.

Both Adam and Johnny had sat and listened to Zeo's narrative of the General's last observations with a certain amount of scepticism and disbelief though Johnny was slightly preoccupied as he examined the highly burnished brass bugle and though he was sorely tempted to find out if he could extract a note from it he resisted and eventually placed it on the desk and concentrated on what was being discussed.

The idea of a band of naked women with snakes in their mouths and killing people was a tad hard to swallow for Adam and Johnny and sounded rather like a Grecian myth and the story verged on the delusional the more they thought about it. But they had to admit that they'd seen the puncture wounds on the bodies and they appeared to be similar to their expectations of what a snake bite would look like.

Zeo called an end to the debate as he placed the dead General's journal and bugle in a holdall in their cart and said that because it was nearing dusk he believed they should remain at the outstation for the night but that he thought it best to camp out in the open on the green rather than be confined indoors.

During the evening meal a still sceptical Adam grilled Zeo about the myths and lore of Sitantal and specifically asked if there were tales and fables about Gorgons or if women with snakes featured in any of their folklore. Both Zeo and Euander were adamant in their denials about such things and said they'd heard loads of legends but none which featured snake women...ever. They then discussed what options they had should the threat turn out to be true and what they could do if they found themselves in a similar position as the *Beneficiarius* had obviously encountered.

During the coffee break Adam insisted that regardless of their immediate enemy being women they had to recognise and accept that they had to treat them as being equally dangerous as any male protagonist they'd ever meet and that there was no room for queasiness or vacillation because of their gender. He stressed that he'd lived long enough to realise that women and even children could be just as dangerous and as evil as men. They'd already killed the *Beneficiarius* out in the field and probably those here according to this diary and he was convinced they'd done this to clear the way to get at them and stop them reaching the Temple of the Gods. He added that he guessed that 'Pravus' Sorus had something to do with it and he emphasised that their main focus should be to take out the controller in charge at the first opportunity they'd get. Here Johnny interjected rather dramatically; 'Yeah! Cut off the head of the snake!'

If Zeo was familiar with this expression he didn't acknowledge it and Adam also allowed it to fly. Unruffled by the lack of appreciation for his wit

Johnny remarked that the tramp they'd seen during the previous night was probably the man the General had said was controlling these creatures and more than likely he'd been searching for them at the time and now that he knew where they were they'd need to prepare for an attack starting right now.

They arranged their own wagons plus two others from the station's stableyard in the central grass square and formed an enclosure for their horses. They also laid out extra ammunition and weapons for easy access on each of the carts.

And because of the plethora of potential hiding places around them they changed the previous night-watch routine and through chicanery and sleight of hand Johnny managed to get the shortest straw which secured him the first three-hour rest period because he firmly believed that any attack would occur well after midnight and he wanted to be in the thick of it from the start; after all, he thought, it wasn't an everyday event where one had a chance to encounter a bunch of snake-spouting naked females who were determined to nibble at you. It promised to be a profoundly evocative occasion and he just had to witness every second of it.

CHAPTER TWENTY-ONE

The Consul Primus exited the forum ahead of his military advisers and strategists where he'd just ended outlining his revised plans to accommodate the growing influx of supporters to their cause. He and his *Optio* mounted their horses and traversed the city for the next hour, a routine exercise which they did daily after the morning conference.

Just over two weeks ago he'd returned to Esta City in triumph after the successful expedition to free the political prisoners in *Occidens* and not forgetting the *carpe diem*, the "seize the day" moment of the unscheduled victory they'd achieved against the military barracks there. Since that time scores and scores of supporters, both new and from the past had descended on the now overcrowded city and quite a few were from *Occidens*, the cradle of the insurrection which had brought 'Pravus' Sorus to power . Vast numbers of tents and temporary wooden buildings had sprung up on the meadows, grassland and plains beyond the city limits and teams of engineers were constantly building new roads and bridges and diverting streams, rivers and canals to cope with the demands of this human and animal influx. A continual two-way flow of *naviculae* and other craft navigated the canals connecting the city with the nearby towns and regions which transported men and materials either in or out of the sprawling conurbation. Large areas had been cleared and designated as military training grounds with an ever increasing provision for stables, paddocks and chariot tracks. The whole area was more active than an anthill and today, just like the preceding days, the Consul and his aide visited the city's boundaries to inspect the further changes and each time his heart filled with pride as he witnessed the stirring scene beyond the city's boundaries. His colours fluttered proudly from virtually every tent and building and the sight of all the young men and women in combat gear preparing to confront the usurper on his behalf made him feel humbled and totally unworthy. He'd silently invoked the Gods to treat everyone favourably who died fighting in his name in the forthcoming battle of good versus evil.

When the pair returned to the city centre Zeor junior, Livia and Camilla rode up alongside the Consul Primus and being in a public place, they saluted formally then dismounted and joined them. The Consul's son detached a large pouch hanging from the pommel on his saddle and presented his father with a personalised skeleton-stock crossbow together with a small bundle of quarrels. He allotted bows and ammunition to his sister and his fiancée and retained the last unit for himself. When they'd examined and admired the weapons and missiles Zeor junior convinced a local grain merchant to donate a bulky wheat sheaf which he then propped up against the nearest tree and each of them took turns on the make-do target. Initially the broad palm tree's base took the brunt of the action but after an hour or so the archery novices became more proficient at penetrating the bundle rather than the bark. Livia and Zeor junior out-scored their father convincingly.

    Later in the afternoon the Consul and his elder son rode out and visited each of the suburban training grounds and spoke with the captains in charge and got updates from the officers on the manpower and their effectiveness. They watched various cavalry, infantry and charioteer units being coached in sundry disciplines and the Consul surmised that if this level was maintained they stood an excellent chance of defeating his arch enemy regardless of what the usurper would throw at them in the future. The pair made the female training camp their last call where Livia and Camilla were posted. The first surprise they had was to find that there were now almost one hundred and fifty young women signed up for action and the second jolt to their preconceptions was to witness the sheer intensity and commitment to excel displayed by the trainee feminine warriors.

They spent the next hour enthralled by the prowess shown by the captain and her recruits and before they remounted to leave the field the Consul Primus informed Captain Electra that she was being promoted to the rank of General.

When father and son dismounted near the forum they were met by the Consul's *Optio* on the steps and were told that three defecting *custodis* from Governor Maximus' forces were waiting inside with correspondence to him from his son Zeo. After reading his son's recommendations the Consul welcomed the defecting captain and his two colleagues into his own battalion and bade his *Optio* to see to their immediate needs. He and Zeor junior quickly hurried home without opening the sealed personal message until the family were having *cena* where the Consul read the contents aloud for the benefit of everybody there.

Zeo's success in persuading Adam and Johnny to return to Sitantal was met with a prolonged round of applause from all those in the room but also from the little plump housekeeper who had her ear pressed against the perfectly devised and successfully proven eavesdropping slit at the family room door. Zeo's praise for the youth sent by Commander Otho to warn them that Sorus knew of their possible arrival through *Primoris* was effusive and his son requested that a message be sent to Euander's parents assuring them of his invaluable contribution to their mission and of his present whereabouts and his wellbeing. He informed his father that the youth would remain with them and would accompany them to the Temple of the Gods. The brief report on the defeat of the camp near the exit at *Extremus* contrived by Governor Maximus brought fresh acclamation from inside and outside the room but the account of the encounter with the lady Dido and of the confiscation of her haul of treasure resulted in so much floor thumping and clinking of glasses that Porcia was swept along by the euphoria now resonating throughout the house that she abandoned her spot at the door temporarily while she downed a celebratory beaker of red wine. She quickly returned to her vantage point in case there was more exciting news to be gleaned about her adventurous boys.

The Consul Primus then sent for the captain who'd deserted Maximus' forces and had him give a fuller account of what had happened when the lady Dido had met Zeo and his comrades in southern *Oriens* and when he learned the full extent of the confrontation the leader knew for sure that his younger son and friends would become the number one target when Sorus and Maximus were informed of what had happened to Dido and her treasure even though he guessed they were already high on the usurper's capture list anyway. But the encounter with Dido was bound to rattle their gall stones even more. At that moment the Consul Primus determined to assemble a troop of dedicated fighters and send them to *Australis* to covertly monitor and protect the four young men because he was certain the enemy would now retaliate with a vengeance and employ even more extreme measures and he'd warrant that a substantial reward would be offered for their capture dead or alive.

When the captain left the house both Zeor and his elder son were joined by Commander Otho and sat late into the night formulating and tweaking the emerging project which they codenamed *Virago*.

Just before daylight the Consul Primus summoned General Electra.

CHAPTER TWENTY-TWO

Livia and Camilla rode directly behind General Vita Electra as the five *turmae* of female cavalry cleared Esta City limits at first light. Two days earlier the Consul Primus had informed the General that her combined unit of one hundred and fifty raw combatants were being deployed to *Australis* to covertly protect his younger son Zeo and his two *Praecipuus* companions while they were at the Temple of the Gods. He believed that it would be at this time when they'd probably be unarmed with only the youth Euander and possibly not more than a *decurion* of elderly *Beneficiarius* on the outside to protect them that they'd be at their most vulnerable. The last message from Zeo had placed his party two or three days from the temple site and though he couldn't be sure how long they'd be inside he hoped that her unit would be there in time for their exit from the revered place.

At the conclusion of the meeting he'd presented her with the gold braided standard proclaiming her unit's induction and purpose; an *Or* rampant

Canis lupos protecting her litter on a background *proper* which now fluttered proudly together with the colours of the Consul Primus above the heads of the two *signifers* riding parallel to the General.

She was equally honoured that her pacesetters, the first female only army unit ever in Sitantal had been entrusted with this mission. It had been code named *Virago* and she and her troop were supremely motivated to justify being styled as valorous female soldiers.

Contrary to what the city's chattering classes and gossipmongers believed and expounded on, the Consul's secret orders to her were to go east for at least twenty miles and then veer west to support the notion that they were going to *Oriens* to garner backing in the province for the coming countercoup. The bogus assignment plans had been mentioned *sotto voce* throughout the city for the last few days in case their true destination should reach the Capitol and 'Pravus' Sorus before they'd made progress on their journey south.

Their covert route would bring them away from populated areas on the journey southwest and force them to reconnoitre thoroughly every inch of the way to remain undetected for longer because the Consul was certain that Sorus would be aware by now that the three young men had been commanded to visit the Temple of the Gods and he'd be preparing to stop them at all costs. Here he laughed as he recounted some of the wild rumours and schemes that were in circulation on how Sorus would do this but most were too farfetched and fanciful to be believed he reckoned. The General had been warned to avoid traditional roads, canals, navigable rivers, cities, towns and villages and she'd have to traverse lesser tracks, moorland and plains and where necessary travel during darkness to avoid detection or to offset any time lost on the way. To minimise needless contact with the rural population a wagon-train trundled along in the wake of the fifth *turma* of mounted troop and was piled high with provisions and equipment for the cavalrywomen.

The great procession stretched for almost one thousand yards and the entire cadre taking part were female including the *explorators* who were already scouting well ahead of the snake-like cavalcade.

Their destination was Abdo, a small settlement about a mile or so to the west from the Temple of the Gods exclusion zone. The hamlet consisted of some six houses, a store and an Inn which according to legend, from the day it had opened had never entertained an overnight guest. The place was so insignificant it didn't even warrant an entry on any map or guidebook and even the Consul Primus had only become aware of its existence when Porcia, his little plump housekeeper had informed him that she'd been born there and knew all about the place. He believed the location of the settlement in the middle of nowhere made it the ideal location for *Virago* to establish a clandestine base from which to patrol and protect the environs close to the Temple.

The tightly disciplined column made steady progress through the morning without encountering any obstacles or other human life on the journey south. By mid afternoon they'd skirted the borders of *Occidens* and continued south with only a fractured wagon wheel and an ancient shepherd who was tending his flock and who couldn't be avoided, disrupting the progress of the convoy.
The weather beaten herdsman was at pains to assure the General that he was a lifelong Zeor loyalist and patriot and anyway he'd be alone with his flock on the moors and going nowhere but to his isolated hut for the next two months. He also insisted on showing her a more favourable and obscure route which compensated handsomely for the earlier wagon breakdown delay.

An hour before dusk the cavalry and the entourage made camp in a sunken basin on the moors where a clear rippling stream surged through it. A small contingent of zealous *machinators* erected the tents and mess and prepared the evening meal while the main body of young female warriors stripped and bathed exuberantly in the cool crystal clear waters where they had great fun as they frolicked about.
The overnight *excubarum* kept guard on the surrounding hills.

General Electra's compact unit broke camp at dawn and continued uneventfully during the morning through lower western *Medius* sticking to the route the shepherd had recommended on the previous day. Only occasionally did they diverge from the newly chosen path and only when a scout returned to warn of a potential danger ahead; the first occasion being a hunter's camp nearby and another when an amorous couple were having some rather noisy fun-time in the heather satisfying a carnal desire. But the one occasion they didn't deviate from their route was when an *explorator* reported a group of ten *custodis* at an outlying hill farm dragging the farmer's young son away in shackles. The scout had pretended to be disoriented having become separated from her hunting party when she'd approached the group for directions. Here she'd discovered that the boy was being conscripted into the usurper's army and that if he hadn't agreed to this the whole family would've been seized and held captive until he'd complied.

The General hurriedly handpicked a squad of twenty cavalrywomen who'd excelled in fencing but also in close combat at the academy. The detachment which included Camilla and Livia followed the scout until they spotted the *custodis* and the conscripted youth further ahead and continued at the gallop. Without issuing a challenge or warning they attacked the guards from behind with drawn blades and in less than seven minutes following an intense and bloody sword fight they'd freed the conscript and had slain all the men without sustaining any casualties or serious injuries to themselves in the process. Though it had been an imbalanced two against one contest the cavalrywomen felt they'd have succeeded on a one to one basis anyway.

Camilla's third kill in six months was added to her account whilst the rookie Livia could now mark up her first.

General Electra had her scout immediately escort the shocked boy back to his family having cautioned her to leave him when they were within sight of his home and avoid having to explain who they were or why they were in southern *Medius*. She believed that because he was so traumatised and bewildered by the whole experience he'd be unable to give a cogent explanation about what had really happened on the moor and even if he could no one would believe him anyway she reckoned.

By late evening the convoy had reached the western regions of *Inferus Medius* where the rocky terrain rose unremittingly and slowed their advance with the heavily laden wagon train now reduced to a straggle.

At this point the General ordered a halt for the day. When the scouts reported later that the track ahead was blocked in several places by landslides and now totally impassable they were despatched hurriedly to find an alternative route. Eventually they located an uncharted cow track further west and on much flatter land. The General pondered and weighed up her options as she studied the maps and charts on her campaign table.

Though the new route would take them dangerously close to the chief roads and canals serving Helias City, the *Australis* provincial capital, the General decided that it was worth the risk considering the fact that it would knock one or possibly two days off the previous estimated journey time. She felt supremely confident that her unit could face anything that was thrown at them should they encounter the enemy even if they were outnumbered. Another factor in the decision was that she believed that even if Sorus was informed of their arrival in *Australis* he wouldn't have the time to dispatch a force large enough to prevent her troop reaching her destination now. Though the Consul Primus appeared to dismiss the bizarre and fantastical rumours sweeping Esta City about what Sorus was planning to do to stop Zeo and the two *Praecipuus* from reaching or leaving the Temple of the Gods she wasn't totally convinced that all the gossip was untrue or exaggerated. The despot was capable and liable to do anything and would stop at nothing to remove Zeo from the scene she believed. She was acutely aware that should anything happen to the Consul's younger son or his two friends from *Terra Ferusum* the whole counter insurrection would be dealt a catastrophic and perhaps even a mortal blow.

Though General Electra was almost twice as old as Zeo and had never met him personally she admired and respected him with fervour and believed that he more than anyone else could restore harmony and tranquillity to the nation.

She'd grown up as an only child under the influence of her military father and had listened to his warnings and complaints on how the country had become systematically weakened and how its proud heritage was being devalued by unscrupulous cliques and nothing was being done to confront this subversion. So it had come as no surprise to her to learn of the coup by Sorus and at the time she'd feared for the survival of Sitantal. That was until she'd learned that someone out there was causing havoc and fear in northern *Oriens* and also within the new regime in the Capitol. When it was eventually discovered that it was the younger son of the imprisoned Consul Primus who was behind the mayhem and terror it had made her sit up and take notice and when word reached her of his daring feats she knew for sure that he was the one and the only one who could save them from the abyss. It was incredible that he and two friends had annihilated a whole unit in the fortress at the entrance to the dark province and in a truly gruesome fashion too and then they'd put an end to Erebus and had banished his Pirates of the Dark from Nox. This had been followed by the rout of a relief convoy on the northern canal and finally they'd defeated the prison guard in Tabo City where he'd freed his family and all the political prisoners there. That stunning news had clinched it for her and she immediately set about forming her novel and exclusively female corps using all the knowledge she'd gained from her father in the past. Though she met with derision and resistance initially she'd argued successfully that a woman could be a true patriot and love and fight for her country just as much and as effectively as any man could do. She'd insisted that she felt compelled to do everything in her power to protect the culture and the constitution as enshrined in the Statutes of Sitantal.

She'd won the opening battle of wits with the old guard but she knew she'd be under continuous scrutiny and that she and her fellow fighters had to be equally successful in the battles of war to convince and convert those doubters.

She'd never tired of wheedling out information and anecdotes about Zeo and his two friends from *Terra Ferusum* in her spare time. She'd had a field day especially with Porcia and others who'd been prisoners in Nox who were now residing in Esta City and everyone without exception had confirmed that they were the bravest and noblest young men they'd ever met.

Simply; Zeo and his two friends were heroes of Sitantal and in her view they were the best!

She'd vowed to willingly sacrifice her life for them and for Sitantal if need be.

CHAPTER TWENTY-THREE

Johnny was wakened abruptly where he'd slept soundly on the deck of the cargo wagon by the horses agitated neighing and their shuffling, stomping hooves combined with Friday's incessant barking. But the animal noises were almost overwhelmed by another and a much more disconcerting and eerie sound. An oscillating pervading hum seemed to come from all around him which rumbled seductively inside his head. It took him a second or two to shake off the drowsiness and to collect his wits and when he peered above the side of the wagon to see what was causing the commotion and the uncommon droning noise his eyes almost popped from their sockets.

Just inside the entrance to the outstation's rectangular enclosure a myriad, possibly as many as fifty, of virtually naked women swayed slowly from side to side, pendulum-like. It was like a macabre cabaret enacted specifically for decadents in Hell and not a display where a chap would be tempted to exclaim *'Phwoar! Bring it on!'* Johnny thought. The almost complete nakedness of some was minimised by a few remnants of what appeared to be animal skins, straw and tatty rags arranged haphazardly on their gaunt physiques. Some two yards from the cargo wagon his three companions stood gawking, rooted to the ground and he guessed that the cause of their inaction wasn't just the erotic pageant in front of them but more than likely it was the incessant droning sound and the mesmerising rolling movement of the large troupe. His mates were spellbound!

He understood immediately that he had to neutralise the catatonic effect before it overwhelmed him too. He hummed loudly to himself in an effort to confuse the pervading sounds around him as he grabbed a water bottle and a cotton-wool pack from the first-aid kit and stuffed his ears sufficiently to block out the drone but still be capable of hearing more immediate sounds and now realised how the *Beneficiarius* had been so completely and utterly overwhelmed by this bizarre display. He cajoled Friday to join him on the wagon and bade him to wait there and not move.

Without further delay Johnny sprung from the cart and roared loudly at his three immobilised friends but got no response from them at all.

Euander was nearer to him when he slapped him hard across his cheek followed by a more than sufficient splash of water to his face. Without waiting to see if the stinging smack and cool deluge had worked he raced across and repeated the action on Zeo and then on Adam calling on them to waken up.

The shock treatment had the desired effect and Johnny roared a warning to the still groggy and soggy trio to blank out the droning chant as he thrust a wad of cotton-wool to each of them and indicated his plugged ears. As they followed his instructions he urged them to ignore the swaying movement of the group and he signalled to them to prepare their weapons and to go on the defence instantly.

Even though they'd been made aware of what to expect from the report in the dead General's journal the reality of their unorthodox adversary had shocked all of them to the core and sent shivers down their spines, it was truly an unsettling and surreal sight to see.

The slowly advancing and glaringly feminine ensemble held their arms outstretched in an outside calliper-like fashion and each of the four intended targets knew that it wouldn't be a happy-ever-after ending if any of them became entrapped in such an embrace.

The female horde were less than forty feet away from the centre of the quadrangle when without warning they halted and the seductive sonorous noises they'd made also ceased.

It was at that moment they saw the dishevelled figure lurking in the background close to the gateway into the compound and from the large throbbing canvas bag slung from his shoulder numerous viper heads protruded inquisitively. The grubby old man put his fingers to his sunken lips and issued a series of rasping glottal noises.

Abruptly and with obvious synchronised timing each of the women's mouths widened and a viper's head slid out several inches with its beady little eyes fixed forward. Their moist forked tongues probed the night air analytically and expectantly.

For the briefest instant Adam mused that no one would freely conjure up a scenario such as this and expect it to be credible and he reckoned that the résumé would be utterly lampooned and dismissed out of hand by a sensible person as the ravings of an out-and-out lunatic.

But nevertheless the graphic evidence was real and was massed in front of them and was bearing down menacingly on their position right now.

Suddenly about a score of the snake spouting women broke away as one from the main formation and lunged wild-eyed toward them.

The moment the guys had dreaded had arrived but on this occasion there was no agreeable adrenalin surge in anticipation of the sortie they were about to launch to defend their post. All four swung into action unenthusiastically but nevertheless well aware they would be engaging the enemy in a fight to the death.

Zeo opened fire and was the first to register a kill when his quarrel brought a snake-woman down. To add to the discomfort of watching her die as she collapsed to the floor the resident green viper inside her wriggled quickly from her mouth and scurried out of sight.

As this scene unfolded another attacker hit the floor courtesy of Johnny's crossbow and a third became the first casualty of an *iaculum* launched by Euander.

Adam was last to shoot and kill.

All four reloaded their weapons and discharged barrage after barrage and though each of the missiles fired scored a direct hit the ever dwindling number of the forward section continued to advance over and around their slain companions almost zombie-like. In a very short time all of the leading faction lay dead on the floor and the only discernible movement near the corpses was the scuttling evacuating reptiles and the numerous red rivulets of blood seeping into the tightly packed gravel.

The dirty old man dashed crazily back and forth behind the rear cluster of nude assassins squeaking and gesticulating wildly. The four guys wondered momentarily what he was up

to until Zeo managed to pick up more clearly what he was saying beyond what mostly sounded like gobbledygook and snake-speak.

The wretched controller had just ordered the next formation to collect the loose vipers and to spread out and attack from all sides. No sooner had Zeo told his friends of the old man's plans for the new onslaught of naked assailants the snake-women had fanned out and each of them now brandished a vicious writhing viper aloft.

On learning of this tactic and fearing that they might be swamped by a downpour of venomous reptiles Adam jumped onto the cargo wagon and grabbed the flame-thrower and quickly swept the area between them with a continuous jet of fire while the others sent a volley of bolts and *iaculum* through the flames into the group. The searing heat and the salvo had an immediate effect and the advancing party halted just yards away from the grassy central island. The hand-held vipers contorted so much in the heat that the handlers were unable to hold onto the slippery creatures and very soon they wriggled free and dropped to the floor where they made a second retreat to the rear to rejoin their master.

By now the gravelled space in front of the camp was a scene of deplorable carnage where almost two thirds of the snake-women who'd entered the compound now lay dead but the old man showed no sign of retreating and seemed hell-bent on pushing on regardless in his attempt to defeat them. Realising that the crazy old coot was prepared to sacrifice all of the women to achieve this Adam swapped the flame-thrower for his crossbow and aimed at the skulking wretch in the shelter of his remaining female clique but he missed his target by a mere fraction when the man lurched away from the trajectory of the missile at the very last instant and was now lost from sight.

Frustrated and totally sickened by the abominable

battle he was engaged in Adam called out to Zeo to have Euander mount his horse and circle behind to try and reach the old man and kill him and end this repulsive contest. A fleeting thought spun through his brain that Zeo's Gods expected far too much from him and Johnny.

As Zeo was about to speak with the youth one of the older snake-women within the centre of the remaining group broke ranks and clumsily pushed her way through to the front and into the killing zone.

On seeing the sudden movement and believing it to be an immediate threat Johnny took a step sideways and realigned his bow and shot the woman point blank in the chest. With blood oozing from her wound a two foot long viper emerged from her mouth and the green reptile slithered down her naked body and then zigzagged across the gravel and out of sight. As the dying woman sank slowly to her knees she fixed her blood-shot eyes on her killer and both marksman and target locked gazes for the briefest instant. She then bowed her head to him and demurely smiled. Her last voluntary gesture in life was to deliberately thrust a wad of scrunched up papers in his direction as she collapsed face forward onto the ground right in front of him.

Johnny's throat had become as dry as the Mojave Desert and his gut churned faster than a butter-making tub as he stood motionless and gazed at the dead snake-woman almost within touching distance of him. He was aghast and totally unnerved by what had just happened and he couldn't erase the image of that demure smile from his brain, it had had a beguiling and provocative essence, just like the Mona Lisa, he thought. Not only was his stomach churning so were his thoughts: *What am I doing? What have I done?*

Zeo had seen the fleeting interaction between Johnny and the dying snake woman and had rushed in front of his friend and hurriedly retrieved the papers. He noticed that they were similar to the missing pages from the dead General's ledger.

When he rejoined the others he quickly scanned the scribbled notes and gasped audibly several times as he read. He solemnly announced to them that all the snake-women had to die, that they each were *Vipera Dominam*, Mistresses of a Viper and that this abomination had been forced on them by a man named Reptus Reptum. They'd been deceived, defiled and dehumanised by him at the request of others and on these pages were the names of each *Vipera Domina* and the identity of the people who'd betrayed her. The vipers living inside them would continue to force them to attack and kill anyone the snake controller decided should die and there was nothing anyone could do to save them. Their bodies and spirits could never recover from what had been done to them and the only freedom for them now would be in death and *only* in death.

Zeo paused and read the final line with a breaking, disbelieving voice;

Gratias dirimendae tormenta nostra. Deum vobiscum! Ego sum Semele, uxor Sorus.

An ashen faced Zeo turned and faced his two friends but he concentrated his gaze on Johnny "Thank you for ending my torment. May the Gods go with you! I am Semele, wife of Sorus".

The bombshell statement, especially the fact that the snake-women killed by Johnny was the wife of 'Pravus' Sorus, hit all the guys like a sledgehammer though Zeo was shocked for a second time when he saw other names on the list that he recognised. They became aware that the bloody battleground was eerily still and realised the snake-women hadn't tried to advance further since Zeo had recovered the notes nor while he'd narrated its message. They now stared intently at him though their resident reptiles were protruding even further from their mouths with their toxic fangs exposed. The green creatures jerked from side to side as if they were enraged by the delay and wanted their transporters to move forward but their hosts ignored the agitation and remained defiantly still.

From the far corner of the compound near the entrance Reptus Reptum reappeared from the shadows and angrily urged his fighters forward in a rasping voice that had more of a hiss to it than a natural vocal sound would have and it soon became obvious to the four guys that he was now speaking more to the reptiles than to the women.

Euander quickly mounted Candeo and guided the colt between the parked wagons and circled round the bodies of the dead *Vipera Dominam* and those still standing but when he reached the area there was no sign of Reptus Reptum; the old man had vanished into the shadows. Though he extended his search beyond where he'd last seen him near the entrance into the outstation he was unable to locate him and he reluctantly headed back to the compound.

  The remaining snake-women were advancing forward again but now they moved without their arms being outstretched making it obvious their fight was over and that they were prepared to die.

Zeo, Adam and Johnny looked desperately at each other before unsheathing their swords just as Euander returned to the bloody arena where he guided Candeo around the edge and dismounted and secured the colt before he rejoined the others in the bloody purge.

  He swung his sword intently trying his best to envision a masculine enemy instead of women and girls, some of whom were not much older than he. But this ploy was an impossible and futile stretch to both his imagination and his senses when most of the enemy had their delicate femininity exposed for him and for everyone else to see. In all of his young life he'd never felt so saddened as he did right now.

  Adam watched as one woman after another

near him slumped to the floor at the end of his sabre. The shivers running down his spine became violent tremors and his weapon wobbled in his hand where it felt heavier by the second to such an extent that he believed that he'd soon have to drop it to the floor. His innate scruples kept urging him to cut and run from the ghastly slaughter but deep within he knew he had to continue to the very end; that there was no way out for him and he was in it for the long haul and once again he thought of Sisyphus on the hill, which made no sense at all to his mixed up brain.

Johnny faced each of the wretched women he was going to kill with abject despair and anger and though each thrust of the blade into the throat of the woman snuffed out her miserable life it also severed the viper which had made her its slave. But this brought little comfort or balm to his frayed nerves which still beset him following the fateful and unsettling encounter with the wife of 'Pravus' Sorus. Even now as he looked into the forlorn eyes of these wretched women he could see Semele's modest mien.

Zeo had moved down the left flank of the slowly moving line and tried to reach the soul of the woman he would kill. He softly revealed his name to each one and stressed how he loathed what he was about to do but he solemnly promised that those who'd perpetrated this evil deed on them would be exposed and would one day pay with their lives. He'd uttered '*Ego sum* Zeo; *Paenitet,*

Promitto qui hoc est tibi moriendum. Vale!' five times before he lowered his blood coated blade for the last time in the battle.

The four guys stood silently to one side and viewed the aftereffects of the wanton butchery which they'd been part of and all of them were distressed beyond revulsion by the sight they observed. Never, not even in a million years could any of them have ever envisaged something as horrific and incomprehensible as this. Only someone with a sick mind and who was under the aegis of 'Pravus' Sorus could conjure up something as vile and repulsive as this to use as a weapon of war. The stratagem deployed here to prevent them reaching the Temple of the Gods had been simply barbaric and obscene and they believed that there was only one way they could ever remotely expunge themselves from the part they'd played in the god-awful deed.

They had to find Reptus Reptum right away.

Adam, Johnny and Zeo slipped away from the outstation while the countryside was still bathed in the turquoise glow from the temple mound which dominated the whole region. Euander and Friday remained at the base to protect the horses, equipment and supplies but the earnest youth vowed that he'd also prepare the stables and the other flammable buildings for the mass cremation of the *Vipera Dominam* pending their return.

The three hurried along the northern stretch of the pilgrim route checking the tall grasses at both sides for any evidence that the snake controller might have veered into the brush after he'd fled the battleground. A short time into the search they found a trampled track about a half mile from the outstation leading off from the road and downwards into thick brushwood and a tree clustered hollow. They crept stealthily forward for fifteen minutes until they reached a broad clearing at the end of the dirt path where four large covered transport wagons were parked up to one side. A faint glimmer of light leaked from the wagon nearest the track and a nauseous stink exuded from the unkempt site.

Zeo quietly gave the others the thumbs up, certain that they'd found the fugitive's lair and they waited in the undergrowth until the heavens brightened before they approached the broad steps leading up to the double doors on the end wagon and from where they'd earlier seen the chink of light.

    They'd been followed from the outstation by the spindly green man who was now less than ten yards away from them and the four parked wagons. Here he waited patiently with his ears peeled, a penetrating encompassing gaze and a controlled shallow breathing regime which sent sufficient oxygenated blood to all parts of his body that needed it. His years of practice and artistry came into play and he was quite calm and collected as he monitored the occasion.

But he had itchy green fingers!

With helmet lights on full beam, visors fully lowered and sabres and daggers in gloved hands Adam and Johnny watched as Zeo wrenched open the double doors. They recoiled immediately from the escaping stench and the sight that assailed them.

Reclining on a leather *torus* was Reptus Reptum where he was covered by a living blanket of green snakes right up to his neck with only his hands and head visible from within the animated covering. He continuously stroked and caressed the snakes covering his upper torso with his gnarled and dirty hands and appeared totally unperturbed by the arrival of the enemy into his den.

Johnny uttered a sharp whistle followed by an astonished *'Cor blimey!'* while the others just stood on the threshold gawping at the freakish scenario. Zeo quickly recovered from the initial shock and curtly ordered Reptus Reptum to step outside the wagon to receive the punishment he deserved for what he'd done to so many innocent women.

The old man seemed unfazed by the threat and without a flicker of fear he displayed a toothless gummy smirk and whispered a series of hissing sounds and the vast majority of vipers raised their heads with their fangs bared and faced the three standing at the door.

Each of them realised immediately that their blades would be ineffective and that there was no way they could reach Reptus Reptum safely while he was protected by such a large nest of venomous snakes which they reckoned was close to one hundred in total.

Adam unholstered his Tasers and warned the others to be ready to make a quick exit if his plan went awry. When he fired both stun guns into the centre of the reptiles the three watched as all hell broke loose inside the large transport wagon and because none of the guys were familiar with snake sounds other than the archetypal hiss the ear piercing shriek that ripped through and beyond the wagon caught them totally off guard and forced them back a pace onto the outside platform at the top step.

And even the spindly green look-alike post sited thirty feet away wobbled more than a fixed pole would be expected to do in such a delicate early morning breeze.

But what the trio saw unfolding inside the wagon held them rooted firmly to the floor boards at the doorway.

    The layer of vipers covering the old man had mushroomed up almost two foot from the *torus* and were spitting and spurting venom as they bounced and some of the poisonous spray reached the visors of the three rapt spectators. The reptiles spilled back in a writhing shambles on top of their stunned controller who appeared to be still dazed by the electric charge. The mass of creatures slithered and squirmed crazily over and under each other as if looking for sanctuary and almost immediately one of them found the gaping mouth of the old man and took refuge inside. His old bony frame contorted and his eyes rolled in their sockets as he gasped for air. He tried to grip the slippery creature with both hands but by then a second viper had squeezed between his ever widening lips. When the third snake pressed into his mouth his arms slumped down and he ceased resisting. Within seconds more and more vipers tried to gain entry until the man's mandible was brutally stretched about five inches away from his maxillae and the epidermis and dermis split and haemorrhaged blood all over the pressing creatures. At this stage it appeared as if the old man's head had been replaced by a giant octopus with throbbing red tentacles but still other vipers appeared resolute on gaining shelter inside the dead herpetologist's body.

The three friends withdrew from the wagon and closed the doors firmly where they paused for a few seconds to get their thoughts back on track. Though they were extremely satisfied but still in awe at what had occurred inside the wagon Johnny was the only one to voice his feelings aloud.

'Hal-le-lu-iah! You got what was coming to yah!' He paused and gazed at the others 'My word! That was an unexpected but pleasing conclusion, don't you agree? How sweet is it that the wretch got his just desserts from his own creation?'

All three touched ground with leaps from the narrow platform but when Zeo told Johnny that he couldn't provide him with a Latin word for serendipity he stopped in his tracks and gaped at him in amazement and disbelief and he looked genuinely disappointed too.

They collected anything flammable they could find and stacked it around the wagon and set fire to the heap and waited long enough to see the flames take hold before departing the hollow knowing that they had a more solemn conflagration to enact when they got back to the outstation. Both Adam and Johnny had noticed that Zeo hadn't treated the burning wagon as a funeral pyre nor did he petition the Goddess *Libitina* to intercede on behalf of Reptus Reptum and they fully understood the reason why.

The spindly green man could barely wait for the three to vanish out of sight on the tree lined hillside before he scrambled up the steps of the burning wagon where he flung the doors wide open and peered into the smoke-filled interior. He concentrated his gaze on where he'd discoveredced the hidden repository less than a week ago when its owner and his *Vipera Dominam* were hunting down and killing the *Beneficiarius*. Since that time he'd schemed how to appropriate the cache in such a way that no one could ever point a finger at him. And now deep within his lanky bones he felt that his ship had finally come in.

He could see sufficiently through the smoky haze to confirm that the herpetologist was dead and that the reptiles had succumbed to the fumes but the thing he wanted more than anything else in the world was still in its place and appeared secure and intact. Taking a deep breath he covered his mouth and nose with one hand and dashed through the fog and behind the *torus* bearing the remains of the bloody snake lover and his deceased darlings. He gripped the heavy ornate chest and dragged it to the door and gasped greedily at the fresh air and then heaved his prize down the steps. He scrambled through the sparks the chest had stirred up on its way to the ground and he speedily hauled the heavy box into the bushes.

His life-long career as a master of disguise in the art of close surveillance was now over for him thanks to the avaricious and parsimonious Reptus Reptum; deceased!

CHAPTER TWENTY-FOUR

The orange and yellow flames rising from the burning *Beneficiarius* base couldn't outshine the showy multicoloured skyline above the sombre procession which headed west following the mass cremation of the *Vipera Dominam*.

The three guys had reluctantly returned to the grotesque execution-suicide scene at the outstation which had been forced on them during the night but they knew the distasteful task had to be done for the sake of the unfortunate victims of this irrational and heinous crime and just thinking about it gnawed cruelly at their senses as they'd trudged back to the bloody battleground from the sunken hollow. They firmly believed that the depraved actions of Reptus Reptum had the imprimatur of 'Pravus' Sorus all over it and that he'd arranged and manipulated the incident to thwart their attempt to respond to the commands of Zeo's Gods. The defeat of the snake women and of the sicko controller would enable their progress to the Temple in the short term but each of the guys felt that it had been a pyrrhic victory for them and the inhumanity of the deed had caused them to soul-search more than they'd ever done in the past.

The cremation and the *exsequiae* rite was a ritual Adam and Johnny were now getting used to though they could never play an active part in the panegyric-type ceremony but on this occasion they'd lowered their heads and had reflected silently during the solemn incantations. It had been a conscience thing for them and they'd felt that it was the least they could do for those they'd slain so that the wretched victims could regain their dignity and freedom in death.

In the early afternoon as the three horsemen escorted Euander on the combo wagon with Friday up front beside him they came to the point near the exclusion zone where the pilgrim road ended. They were outside the entrance to an extensive rectangular enclosure, three sides of which were colonnaded with twenty-foot high columns on pedestals and topped with capitals. Standing majestically in the middle of the enclosed area was a domed marble baldachin shielding a golden image on the inner plinth.

The four guys dismounted at the entrance and entered the imposing but rather spooky site.

The abandoned area reminded Adam of a deserted genteel holiday resort in mid-winter back home where the hurdy-gurdy had fallen silent and the candyfloss and ice cream vendors had decamped until next season.

Dotted around the precinct was an array of little huts, bench tables and several active fountains where the cascading watery mists constantly refracted a host of dispersing tints from the cragged and dominant mount to the south of the arena. This side of the rectangle was column free and allowed an uninterrupted view to the Temple of the Gods where it soared heavenwards in the far distance. Behind the north perimeter of the public viewing space was a large paddock with numerous water troughs and animal pens and what appeared to be a shuttered, deserted emporium with a large rectangular building with shower and toilet cubicles and there was a scattering of other nondescript buildings nearby.

Adam and Johnny crossed the smooth cobblestones to the viewing area on the open south side and gazed through the iridescent colours drifting cloud-like around the Temple of the Gods. Though they adjusted their binoculars to the max they were unable to see how far the triangular smooth form soared into the blue troposphere above or see if it actually ended there at all.

From their vantage point it appeared to reach infinity and beyond.

They shifted their focus to the supporting miniature mountain below the tower and scanned the different coloured cragged shapes which added to the beauty of the whole display. Both of them agreed that the steep serrated mound looked similar to the afterglow from a volcanic eruption millennia ago but instead of expelling what became the usual blackened lava on the surrounds this outburst had disgorged a massive patchwork of luminous molten crystal which still sparkled and gleamed to this day.

Whilst Euander tended to the horses in the paddock beyond the arena Zeo joined Adam and Johnny where he waited patiently as the pair marvelled and absorbed the wondrous sights beyond. When they eventually lowered their glasses and prepared to move away he escorted them inside the domed marble monument.

Sited on the solid raised plinth in the middle of the floor was a giant replica in gold of the sculpture which Zeo had used when swearing them to lifelong secrecy almost five months ago and which he'd later presented to Johnny's parents on the eve of their previous departure to Sitantal.

The various pastel hues drifted under the arches and into the inner chamber where they danced merrily on the raised contours of the image and virtually energised the robust piece which appeared to give it a life of its own.

    Following a short coffee break they moved each of the horses except for Candeo into the paddock behind the emporium and then left Euander and Friday to guard the supplies and equipment. The three guys left the arena and crossed over into the brush and bracken below the colourful jagged semi-mountain in search of the route to the

Temple which they'd been unable to locate using their glasses. They happened across several trails crisscrossing the ground between the giant boulders which Zeo presumed had been used by the *Beneficiarius* when they'd patrolled the area in the past. Eventually when they explored a wide crevice which appeared to have been traversed more than the other tracks they discovered that it ended quite abruptly at the bottom of the most convoluted flight of bluish coloured steps that weaved upwards through the coloured luminous reefs and crags which towered above the narrow stairwell.

Here Adam knowledgably told the others that the colour of the stone steps was known as *Carolina Blue*.

The stressful events of the previous night and the lack of sleep forced them to abandon further exploration of the steps until morning but they did continue to look for a safe place where Euander and the animals could be based whilst they were away. They discovered a reasonably large space where a quick flowing water gully passed through the secluded cleft which was surrounded by massive green, orange and blue boulders.

Back at the camp they spent a few hours discussing and sorting out what they'd need for the next phase of the journey and also what Euander would require while he and the two animals were confined to the crevice while they were at the Temple.

Just after dusk they laid the sleeping bags on the smooth surface next to the baldachin and where

the sculpture was still glinting but now it was a monochrome blue like everything else in the vicinity of the temple mount and it appeared to be as motionless as a statue should be.
It too looked as if it had settled in for the night Johnny quipped as he nestled down bleary-eyed in his quilted bag.

The temporary camp buzzed with activity from seven in the morning as the guys showered, shaved and had breakfast before packing everything away.
Candeo was laden like a packhorse by Euander and now carried all of the essentials which his owner would need while holed up within the rocky mound. The guys shared the rest of the gear between them and very shortly the small procession moved into the thick brush at ground level.

The three spent a short time in Euander's secluded refuge offloading the baggage where Adam and Johnny agreed to go unarmed into the Temple of the Gods when Zeo explained that it was the proper thing to do; that even in a less important local temple it would be considered a breach of protocol to bring weapons into a place of veneration. Each of them had a small bottle of coffee and a few chocolate bars for this stage of the odyssey and after a final brew they bade farewell to their friend and his companions.

The adrenal bounce was short lived and the initial stages of vigour and aplomb became less noticeable and the three slowed to a more sustainable pace. They deliberately idled here and there on the way up and gazed through some of the larger gaps in the rocks and through the various tinted hues swirling across the northern panoramic scene below and beyond the mini mountain. They knew they were looking at something that very few people had witnessed in the past and more than likely never would. They gradually climbed above the lower strata of vibrant coloured boulders and though they tried to spot the place where Euander was based they were unable to figure it out in the medley of coloured mounds and shards below.

Johnny had been counting the steps but very soon he'd lost track and gave the exercise up as a waste of time and oxygen but he protested that it was because the air was getting much thinner with each step upwards when Adam teased and derided him for throwing in the towel so soon.

By mid morning they estimated they'd climbed at least two thirds of the stairs though they didn't have a clear view to the top of the mount but the expanding views of the wider countryside were absolutely awesome and encouraged them onwards and upwards with them guessing that there was even better to come.

As they climbed higher the cragged shards became more numerous and more tightly pressed together and the opportunities to see beyond the confines of the stairs were for the most part totally restricted but when they'd exited a narrow passage-like shaft they gasped aloud when they saw what awaited them beyond the fissure.

The flight of *Carolina Blue* steps had become a stair bridge over a yawning gorge which was at least forty foot wide and eye-wateringly deep. The serrated architecture looked more like a buttress rather than something they should climb. Though the stair bridge spanned a wide chasm there appeared to be nothing supporting it other than the pressure each step exercised on the other and though neither of the three would ever be classified as being fat or even slightly overweight they all mentally wished they'd eased off on the carbs more often in the past. But it was the lack of any kind of barrier or balustrade on either side of the configuration that really knocked them for six and when they craned their necks forward and looked over the edge they groaned aloud in sync.

'I knew it was too good to be true and there had to be a bummer somewhere on the way'

Johnny grumbled, more to himself that to the others.

Rather than prolong the suspense or the debate Zeo dropped to his knees and edged slowly up the serrated incline and even though he'd inwardly vowed that he'd keep his eyes peeled on the next level and look nowhere else but there he couldn't resist the urge to have several sneaky peeks over the edge at the other physical peaks down below. But he wasn't alone in his morbid curiosity; his two friends had similar hankerings to see what was in store for them if the thing collapsed or if they slipped up, or, being rather pedantic, if they slipped down, Johnny thought.

Adam was the last to scale the stair bridge and when they were all together again on the upper side of the chasm they took one last look into the crevasse to see what they'd just conquered. They continued climbing hoping that the bridge had been the first and the last of its kind on their ascent to the top.

For the next hour they only had occasional views of the wider outer regions beyond the mini mountain such was the lack of clear spaces between the soaring shards nor could they see the temple above as the steps weaved deeply in and out between the sharp gagged crystal rocks but just when they were becoming dispirited they emerged onto a radiant white alabaster plateau but it wasn't this which got their immediate attention, it was the flawless white windowless skyscraper towering upright in front of them.

They'd finally arrived at the Temple of the Gods and they weren't disappointed.

The temple was colossal and so perfectly crafted that both Adam and Johnny whistled in tandem as they gazed along the outer wall and then upwards as far as they could see. The differing rays of colour coming from the miniature mountain on which they stood atop cast ethereal pastel forms on the smooth glossy wall where the colour changed from second to second as the trio ogled it and it appeared to them that the shafts of differing colours partly filtered through and were absorbed by the colossus.

Adam checked and noted that they'd spent more than five hours on the blue steps. He turned to scan the structure with his binoculars but the extraordinary piece appeared to have no end and went on and on and up and up forever. He couldn't comprehend how this could be when he considered that they were in a place which was in the depths of the earth and therefore had to be finite. Perhaps it was an optical illusion he allowed but logically the Temple must have a nadir and a zenith and couldn't continue into perpetuity.

He'd been up close to many superstructures in the outside world but he'd never ever seen anything quite like this, anywhere. He had yet to go inside and he wondered what other surprises and conundrums awaited him there. And to make things more baffling for him was the fact that Zeo had told him that this towering mass had been here for as long as Sitantal had existed and yet it appeared totally fresh and contemporary and wouldn't look dated or out of place on a new development back home.

Though Johnny searched thoroughly for quite a distance along the outer wall and its base he could find nothing to suggest that the structure was man-made. He couldn't find any seams, joints, tool marks or blemishes anywhere and he had only to think about the amazing glowing crystal-like mini-mountain the Temple was structured on to realise that the whole caboodle defied logic as far as he was concerned. He wondered briefly to what extent humankind and especially the present-day smart aleck's and the so called *"scientists"* and *"experts"* back home had got things wrong about Creation. At that moment he realised the Big Bang Theory had been just a load of made up balderdash and codswallop and was on the same level as the dross the charlatans spewed out that *Homo sapiens* had originated in continental Africa where ancient ape bones and organic debris were manipulated and fabricated to be other than what they really were. Square pegs in round holes came to his mind at this point. Recalling these esoteric pronouncements he deemed them to be possibly misguided, erroneous or duplicitous but whatever it was it didn't really matter here. In fact he now believed that there hadn't even been a *Little* Bang never mind a big one and that the Genesis of life and of everything else had come about over an aeon of time and had been designed and shaped in a carefully planned deliberate sequence with no bangs, clangs or prangs of any kind and with absolutely no shafts of lightning spritzing from ethereal fingertips either. He concluded that this place was supremely different from anywhere else on earth and was well beyond the realms of mankind's understanding and competence. To his mind the human being hadn't yet been born who could explain this place and this included the leftie academics who believed that there was no

one on the planet smarter than them and also the so called *illuminati* from the past and those presently out there who had a similar belief in their own infallibility. These people believed that they knew the answers to everything and because they were so clever they couldn't bear to think that they might be wrong and that there might be an omnipotent creator out there after all. The fact that this *supremo* hadn't made itself obvious to the intelligentsia such as them was ridiculous and unthinkable so therefore it just couldn't be true.
Johnny didn't have a shadow of a doubt that this colossal architectural form wasn't of this world and that it was utterly extraterrestrial.

Zeo gazed with reverence and awe on what he knew was something which had been divinely created and an object that was forever part of his birthright. But now that he was actually on the threshold of the revered place it made him question once again his fitness to be there and he couldn't help but sigh deeply in anticipation of what might await him inside. No matter how much he'd tried to play down his concerns that the Gods might be disappointed, perhaps even angry with him, it still loomed large in his mind. But he accepted tranquilly and dispassionately that if this was the end of the road for him, then so be it.
The decision would be the Will of the Gods.
His paramount concern was for his two loyal friends, Adam and Johnny and if they came through this experience safely then his fate was of

little importance, *in grandi rationem ordinis rerum:* in the grand scheme of things, he concluded.

Without prompting and even though the three were still absorbed in their own reflections they strolled the short distance to the north facade of the triangular monolith to where the only entrance to the structure was reportedly located but it took the best part of thirty minutes for them to reach the entrance in the centre of the north elevation and when they saw the size of the opening it knocked them for much more than a six and in fact almost over the edge of the unprotected precipice when they stepped back to appraise the extent of the massive portal into the Temple of the Gods. They viewed the broad lettering on the lintel above.

SEMPER TECVM

Zeo translated the relief petroglyph for his two companions as meaning **"ALWAYS WITH YOU"**
The portal was surrounded by a gargantuan representation in gold of the symbol that Adam and Johnny now identified with Zeo's gods and they felt that it was by far the most awesome and impressive doorway any of them had ever seen.
And the huge crystal-glass doors were ajar.
The trio made wide-eye contact with each other and without further debate they walked stoically through the vast opening, side by side.
But what they'd gleaned from the outside didn't really prepare them at all for what they found

within the interior of the vast structure.

CHAPTER TWENTY-FIVE

When they emerged from the foyer and into the main building the first impression Adam and Johnny had was as if they'd stepped right into the centre of an animated rainbow. The combination of swirling rays of colour which penetrated the great edifice from the outside and from the crystal floor beneath their feet was mind boggling. The colour waves which permeated through from the outer walls were wispy pastel-like, whilst those radiating up from the glass floor were more vibrant and sharp. All the disparate hues mingled together and swirled around the interior where they coalesced and brilliantly highlighted the amazing array of life-size crystal fabrications which virtually filled the whole area which dazed all the guys, but especially Zeo. It was just like they'd arrived at the biggest, most colossal conceptual and reality fair of all time where a prototype of every conceivable object that had ever been made was here on show, but these exhibits were manufactured in glass or crystal and they looked just perfect and to scale. The swirling beams of textured colours enveloped and caressed them and virtually brought them to life.

Automobile, van, truck and tram with bus, train, motorcycle and bicycles were on show as was farm and industrial machinery, with diggers, dozers, cranes and such like. But away in the far background were replica ocean liners, yachts, and even a submarine together with familiar towering structures like America's Statue of Liberty, One World Trade Centre and Trump Tower; Australia's Sydney Opera House; London's Tower Bridge and "Big Ben"; Tyne and Wear's Angel of the North; Rome's Coliseum and St Peter's Basilica; Canada's National Tower; Moscow's Kremlin; New Zealand's Beehive building; France's Eiffel Tower and Japan's Yokohama Landmark Tower and these were just some of the distinguished architecture the newly arrived visitors could identify with and were recognisable as being man-made structures which were part of the Modern Era and they were absolutely certain that there were other familiar global landmarks to see further beyond in this impressive show.

The ginormous display didn't stop at floor level either they quickly discovered.

In the soaring heights above the three newcomers there were a number of various types of aeroplanes, helicopters and drones but even higher still they could see satellites and even a space module and rocket. It was as if this gargantuan tower had no defining boundaries restricting its height, depth or width and though Adam and Johnny were shocked to the core to find such an infinite contemporary display even though it was wrought in glass here in Sitantal it was Zeo who found it the most difficult to comprehend knowing that none of the things featured here had been created in his world.

For him it was too weird to absorb in one session and it was just simply too complex to understand. Though he knew that the Gods had the power to do anything, not in a thousand years would he have envisaged something like this, and so close to home. It gradually dawned on him that this was a personal message more to Adam and Johnny than to him. It was showing them that the Gods weren't solely confined to Sitantal but had relevance in *Terra Ferusum* also, but he decided that he must allow them to figure this out for themselves.

Deep within the building and in the midst of the enthralling display but directly in front of their observation point they could see the most exquisite broad staircase sweeping upwards as far as the eye could see and though none of them could be certain how many levels the stairway served they felt that because of its size that they must be numerous.

They moved away from the foyer and passed through the forever changing colours and none of them could resist the temptation to touch and caress the crystal concepts as they passed by. They marvelled at the precision and scale of actuality and authenticity they encountered and as they peered through the vehicle windscreens they saw that everything that one would expect to find in a real life model was there, seats, consoles and steering wheels, right down to thin glass seat belts and even the solid crystal tyres were engraved with tread-like patterns and air inlet valves. It was breathtaking and mind boggling.

Adam was totally mesmerised by the sheer beauty and artistry of the sculptures and he continued to wonder how any human could have created these works of art. It made him feel that his own talents were of little consequence and totally inadequate in comparison. And the more he saw of the assemblage the more humble he became.

As they slowly weaved through the collection of objects they had glimpses of the exterior skyline beyond the tower and yet when they'd been outside they'd been unable to see anything within and it baffled them briefly and left them at a loss as to how this could be. But being able to see beyond the edifice gave the effect that they were in the open air again and that this whole panoply was being staged in a gigantic al fresco theatre high in the heavens.

They reached the clearance in front of the wide stairwell and noticed for the first time two separate giant vertical white gossamer-like screens dangling at right angles to each other from aloft though what supported them was unclear to the guys from where they stood and it seemed they were levitating freely in mid air. They paused and viewed the screens when the circling colours wafted across the vast area in the direction of the fluttering gossamer-like drapes where they formed intricate and multicoloured images with every one different from the previous and all of them were sublimely delightful to their visual senses and were almost hypnotic. And just like it had started so it ended when the coloured rays drifted away and continued circling through the atmosphere at random leaving the fluttering screens totally blank.

Zeo couldn't explain what any of the images or symbols had represented and suggested that perhaps they were meant to help them relax and dispel any fears they might have.

When the visual show had ended the guys became aware of the open space below the screens where they saw, and again it was for the first time, a selection of crystal glass furniture studiously arranged below the screens. The area was enclosed on three sides by an intricately crafted opaque glass reredos which created a recess away from the displayed objects and artefacts.

The furniture suite consisted of an oblong crystal block table with three smaller contoured seats arranged alongside and with a crisp white fabric robe neatly folded on each seat. An empty glass repository had been placed close by which they guessed was for their clothes. Three sparkling goblets and a carafe filled with a clear translucent liquid rested in the centre of the solid plinth and all of them knew the beverage was for them.

It didn't go unnoticed to Adam that the robes immaculate white fabric was the first item they'd encountered that wasn't made from glass since they'd entered the Temple of the Gods with the possible exception of the two suspended wispy screens though he couldn't be sure what material these were made from.

They moved between the reredos and the altar-like slab and changed from their black garb into the white robes and though Adam or Johnny had never worn anything like this before they slipped into them effortlessly. Rather strangely though none of the guys were of the same stature or girth the robe fitted each of them like a glove even though they'd randomly selected them but maybe it was just a coincidence Adam reflected as they dropped their clothing into the repository. They stood whilst Zeo filled each goblet with the brilliantly clear liquid and clinked the cut glass together in salute. The musical tone echoed round the vast space and though they guessed that the libation was anything but *aqua pura* they sat down and sipped at the honeyed tasting fluid without hesitation.

It tasted just like what they imagined nectar should do; soothing yet stimulating!

And in less than three minutes the glasses were empty.

They rose in unison and turned to leave the recess

and discovered that all around them everything had been transformed, nothing was the same as before.

*

    They believed they'd been translocated somewhere but hadn't a clue where to or how it had been done but when they gazed into the distance all they could see was the blackest of blackness they'd ever seen in their lives. The deep-deep black canopy overhead was punctured with bright star like dots and all of them had the feeling that they'd ascended to the top of the Temple of the Gods or maybe even to the top of the world. The air felt thinner here and all around them was a vacant emptiness and arid nothingness but uneven rugged rock at their feet which expanded outwards in every direction and out of sight.
They moved forward over the barren and rough landscape aware that there was more activity above them than at ground level, which they assumed and hoped to be *terra firma* and here Adam bent and touched the granite to check that it was real and then checked his watch and saw that the time hadn't changed from when they'd arrived at the top of the mount. Though he shook it and tapped the dial the minute hands refused to move and eventually he gave up and vowed to have a few words with the jeweller when he returned home. Every now and then the heavens above them lit up

briefly by what they thought were shooting stars or comets whizzing by. Johnny exclaimed that he was sure that they were at the edge of space and above them and out there was the solar system. He admitted that he couldn't identify any constellations he was familiar with though he could see that there were some which appeared to be very close compared to the ones he'd seen in the past from their garden with his father. But neither Zeo nor Adam responded to his hunch because their brains were already overtaxed trying to assimilate the entire visual geological stratum surrounding them on the bare bedrock.

Later on and quite a distance away from their starting point they reached a descending slope and when they arrived at the next stage below they saw that it was no different to the one they'd just left and the heavens above were still visible and what had happened to the landscape they'd just traversed none of them had a clue. This anomaly continued as they descended to other levels and confused and bewildered all three even more. Each ramp and new level were virtual copies of all the previous stages and this was the case until they'd descended no less than ten flights down. Here Adam declared that Johnny had been right about being on the edge of space and he believed that what they'd seen so far was an absolute image of how planet Earth had been at the beginning of time, when the

globe was just a barren rock careering through

space with nothing biological in its makeup and if his thinking was right each level they'd been on represented a portion of Megaanni, meaning the millions of years since the Universe had been formed. They should reach more interesting and recognisable phases very soon he promised them with tongue in cheek.

On the downward journey he tried fervently to recall the Periods, Eras and Epochs he'd learned of and what he'd read about them in the past and when on the next level they saw anemones and corals he announced that they'd reached the Ediacaran Period and the beginning of primitive life on Earth. On the next floor down they found signs of fish and molluscs which he thought was in the Cambrian Period. The following level introduced them to insects, sharks, scorpions, reptiles, beetles, plants and conifers. Several floors down from there brought them to the Triassic Period where they witnessed ichthyosaur, dinosaur, turtle and crocodile. Adam's two companions were now impatient to hear more and when Johnny learned that they should reach the Jurassic Period presently he virtually bounded down to the next tier calling out that he'd seen the film twice.

Here they perceived allosaurus, carnosaur and the first flying birds.

On the Cretaceous level they observed the creation of the oceans of the world, the arrival of bees and the formation of Australia which all together was an exhilarating sight to see.

They reached the Palaeogene Period where the emergence of camels, primates, rhinos, whales and elephants was evident and to make it even cosier they saw cats and dogs and the very first lush grassland.

Further down on another plane they witnessed giraffe, kangaroo, horses and the mammoth in the Neozoic Period and just as they were about to depart for the next floor they were stopped in their tracks when they spotted a Homo Erectus in the near distance. Upright Man also came to an abrupt standstill and raised his hand above his eyes and returned the stare before he lumbered out of sight behind a cluster of conifers, though whether he'd spotted them they didn't know for sure. They also had sightings of other Homo erectus on distant continents further from Africa, convincing Johnny that hominids had not been exclusive to any particular continent but had developed in various parts of the world simultaneously.

When the nearest Homo erectus had vanished out of sight Johnny was sorely disappointed that he'd been too gobsmacked to give the only biped of the species that he'd ever seen up close a cheery hand-wave in greeting. It might have revealed to him if the individual was extinct or extant at this particular time he mused and it would've been a nice gesture he believed. But he did utter a hearty laugh when it dawned on him that what he'd just witnessed would be a fly in the ointment to the old duffers and duffettes in white coats and their unsubstantiated guff and fiddle-faddle about the Origins of Man originating only on the African continent.

Adam's chagrin was that they'd failed to see a Neanderthal on this level.

As the guys descended further into the Cenozoic Era and its Tertiary and Quaternary Periods and into the Pleistocene Epoch they viewed the last Ice Age together with Homo sapiens, and not only in Africa but also in Europe, Australasia and the Americas too. Though Johnny had been tempted to jump up and down and wave to the ancestors in the far distant past he realised that he'd be distracting them unnecessarily when he saw that his trans global forebears were exceedingly preoccupied trying to catch their next meal.

And when the guys arrived at the Holocene Epoch they'd reached the penultimate level where they could see below them the awesome crystal glass reproductions and the representation of their world in the Present Era.

All of them were still enthralled by what they'd experienced. By now Adam and Johnny had concluded that Zeo's Gods had brought them on this journey to show them that They were not restricted to this part of the world only but were very much part of theirs. Here Adam recalled Zeo telling him during a debate in The Grumpy Old Beggar in Trident Vale that his Gods had known of him and Johnny and he now believed this to be so.

They descended the awesome stairs to the ground

floor and made their way to the recess below the hanging veils and immediately saw the flitting wafts and beams of colour veer towards the screens once more.

CHAPTER TWENTY-SIX

It was barely past midnight when operation *Virago's* General Electra led her troop of cavalrywomen ahead of the supporting supply wagons along the narrow causeway. They were only a few miles away from the north-south principal canal and some fifty miles from the *Australis* provincial capital. She'd had her scouts traverse the twenty-one mile track through the miry flatland during daylight hours identifying possible problem areas until they'd been able to mentally envisage the path like the backs of their hands. The place was an inhospitable expanse of open marshland where during daylight hours the raised causeway could be seen for miles around but using it as a shortcut could knock at least a day off the scheduled journey time to the Temple of the Gods. Some two hours earlier she'd dispatched two separate *decurion* units of cavalry to monitor from a distance those villages close to the track when her company would pass by. They had strict orders to prevent or neuter any witnesses to the troop's movement overnight. Each wagon wheel and all of the horses' hooves had been muffled with hessian and straw before they set off and a relay of mounted horsewomen carrying lighted tapers in miniature shades lined one side of the track and assisted the wagon drivers to steer accurately along the narrow road. The faint light was concealed from the wider countryside and villages by the horse's bulk as they moved in sync with the almost silent procession. Very much to the General's satisfaction a wispy veil of low marsh mist had descended and now shrouded the whole area and the only noises breaking the nocturnal peace were the odd animal squeak or splash of water in the dark marshland. Their challenge was to ensure that the convoy cleared the expanse before the first labourers arrived to harvest the abundant supply of produce available in the lush ecosystem where it was there for the taking by those who were prepared to make the effort by wading almost knee deep in the squelching mud. One of her *explorators*, a woman who knew the area well told her of the game, vegetables and minerals galore which could be harvested by early risers. The General was anxious to avoid the villagers and the entrepreneurs who came from the area and much further afield where they laboured diligently and profitably on the wetlands and who might talk elsewhere of the military movements so far south.

Mid way through the overnight trek across the causeway and just as the convoy was skirting one of the smaller settlements close to the passageway an inebriated young man was weaving his way home when he spotted the gossamery silent procession approaching the raised parallel track through the fog. His woozy brain tried to absorb the topsy-turvy thoughts and images it was receiving from his confused sensory nervous system and in the muddle he recalled something his late dear grandmother had cautioned him about a long time ago: Beware of ghouls in the middle of a misty night especially the *Temere Palus Mortis Conquisitors*; the Random Marsh Death Seekers; who were really fiendish phantoms who targeted anybody who drank too much.

In panic he cried out 'Yikes! Just go away! Find someone else and leave me alone!' He stumbled off the main track and into the nearby alleyways in an attempt to throw the procession of vaporous demons off his trail. He vowed loudly and plaintively to the Gods that if he could give these monsters the slip tonight he'd never leave his wife and children to be with his mates down in the tavern again, ever!

The *explorator* who witnessed this enlightened reversal of the drunkard's lifestyle allowed him to continue his journey home without having to intervene and help him forget what he'd seen during the night near his village.

A half hour before daybreak the slow moving caravan reached the end of the causeway several hundred yards from the main highway leading to Helias City. The popular and normally busy roadway hadn't yet come to life and the nearest settlement was at least a mile from this point. The procession quickly crossed the road and traversed over the plains until it reached the rarely used trail through the middle of the ancient forest of *Silvanorum* on the border of eastern *Inferus Medius* and *Australis.* And in this verdant idyll General Electra ordered a six hour break when they were several miles along the shaded trail. But during that time she had her scouts reconnoitre the entire route through to the other side and at three o'clock in the afternoon the cavalry and supply wagons were on the move again. They made camp for the night at the eastern edge of the forest which was less than ten miles from their destination at the little known village close to the exclusion zone. In her desire to reach the village and be as close as possible to where her charges were at the Temple of the Gods the General was initially tempted to continue through the night but the *Optio* advised her that the horses were showing signs of exhaustion as were the troop. She also pointed out that it might be better to arrive at Abdo during daylight hours rather than in the middle of the night like an enemy might do. General Electra concurred with the advice and ordered a halt until daybreak but for no longer she stressed.

Though it was very early morning Abdo's entire population which numbered about thirty adults and twelve children were lined up nervously behind the *praesum* as the *Virago* force rolled into the tiny village square. It was obvious from the sombre reception that the apprehensive people had been warned in advance that an army was coming their way and they felt safer standing up on their feet rather than being caught sleeping in their beds. The cavalry and wagons filled the square separating the few dwelling houses on the east end from a tiny emporia and inn on the west side. General Electra instantly observed the debris strewn site of the village temple on the south side and realised that the usurper's *"Removal Men"* had visited the hamlet in the recent past.

The village chief was the first of the assembled party to identify Consul Primus Zeor's standard but he was at a loss as to the identity of the military division when he couldn't recall ever having seen the *Virago* uniform or their colours on parade before. Though he relaxed a little when he saw that the entire force was female he silently prayed to the gods that they weren't another anarchist gang like those who'd terrorised their village and had destroyed their little temple just four weeks ago because the way things were going in his country right now nothing would surprise him anymore.

General Electra informed the small crowd who they were but she declined to reveal the true reason why they were here only to say that they would be protecting the Temple of the Gods from the ungodly. When the villagers heard this she was greeted with relief and a harmonious chorus of applause and as if to emphasise the easing of worry and tension the people began to straggle back to their homes. But when the troop's leader enquired of the *praesum* if there were any nearby meadows with fresh water available to hire his eyes lit up as did others in his group and when she enquired if there was rental accommodation available for her and her *Optio* within the village the chief had to resist the temptation to perform a *saltatus* around the village green.

It transpired that the *praesum* was also the *taberna* keeper and now the first female General he'd ever known was about to break his duck. At long last he would have an entry in his dusty visitor's book and he briefly fantasized about what this very important army person's endorsement could do for him. Who knows but it might make his inn the *in* place to be. The *praesum* virtually drooled when he informed General Electra that he was delighted that she and her division would be using Abdo as their base.

With the aid of the village chief the General helped to secure the area surrounding Abdo and she dispatched her scouts to reconnoitre the exclusion zone at the Temple of the Gods and in particular to check for signs of Zeo and his companions. During *prandeo* with the inn-keeper the General elicited the details of when the village's temple had been destroyed but she soon put this event to the back of her mind when he told her of what had happened in the weeks since then when the fear of the

"Removal Men" returning had waned.

The villagers had suspected for some time that something peculiar was happening in the Temple's exclusion zone when a local huntsman reported that a sinister looking and foul smelling, four wagon convoy had pitched camp away from the regular pilgrim sites some weeks ago. Then there had been sightings of a dirty old man with numerous snakes hanging from his shoulder bag and one villager swore he'd seen several naked women and each of them had a viper protruding from her mouth. Because of that report the locals spurned the place and mothers refused to let their children out of their sight even though most of them didn't believe it. Some of the villagers thought that the wildlife appeared to have deserted their regular habitats during that time too.

But what were initially rumours and gossip amongst the villagers became more serious on the discovery of the remains of several dead *Beneficiarius* and their riderless horses who'd been on guard duty near the Temple of the Gods. The visual marks on their bodies suggested that they'd been bitten by snakes prior to their deaths and this had exemplified and even justified a lot of what had been just hearsay and rumour up until then. The circumstances of how they'd been killed had caused alarm and sleepless nights for everybody in Abdo and for the past three weeks virtually nobody had left the village and very few had ventured from their homes on their own. But just over a week ago when nothing further had occurred that they were aware of, and the wildlife seemed to have returned to normal, the village chief had sent two volunteers to reconnoitre further afield and to gather what information they could and on their return they'd told him that the exclusion zone was totally devoid of pilgrims but they'd met a very scrawny fellow dressed all in green on horseback and with another heavily laden mount in tow behind him. He was heading west from the zone and appeared to be in a great hurry to get away. The oddly shaped man had told them that an old man named Reptus Reptum from lower *Medius* with about fifty women who had vipers living inside them and were known as *Vipera Dominae* had been sent by the dictator to stop a son of the ousted Consul Primus from going to the Temple of the Gods. But the scheme had gone belly up for them when all of them had been killed by this guy called Zeo and his three companions when they'd been attacked by the snake women who'd tried to poison them when they'd arrived at the *Beneficiarius* outstation. This had happened only days after the women and the old man had murdered all the Temple guards in the area which had left the holy site unprotected for the first time in history. When his men had asked the green dressed stranger how he'd witnessed all of this and yet he had escaped unscathed he'd become evasive and pleaded a pressing appointment in Helias City and had quickly ridden off.

General Electra rode from the village with two *turma* of cavalry and the scouts who'd located the burnt remains of the *Beneficiarius* outstation in the early afternoon and when she dismounted she realised immediately that the entire complex had been used as a cremation pyre and when a scout relayed the fact that a further cremation site for the slain *Beneficiarius* had been located in the paddock nearby the General was impressed that Zeo had displayed strength, decency and honour for friend and foe alike, even when under pressure.
She could imagine that he and his companions were anxious to obey the command to attend the Temple of the Gods and then rejoin his father's campaign to help in the fight against 'Pravus' Sorus. Though they'd been attacked and delayed when they'd arrived here they'd still found time to do the honourable thing where others might have just turned away from the task. This indefatigable gesture of respect shown for the dead emphasised to her once more that Zeo was the one who had integrity and could save her country from descending into barbarism.
As she rode away from the poignant scene she suddenly reined her horse in and came to an abrupt stand-still much to the surprise of her unprepared colleagues who immediately went into combat mode fearing that she'd spotted danger ahead. But it had just clicked within the General's brain that though she was aware that four young men had been at this site recently only three of them were

due to visit the Temple of the Gods, so the questions were; where were the three friends who'd been summoned to the Temple and where was the fourth man now? She gazed towards the crystal mount and edifice in the distance and pondered silently. She remembered from her only visit here as a child that there wasn't access from this side so she assumed that Zeo and his companions had set off to the Temple some distance north of here and she reckoned that she should concentrate the search for him there. She guessed that the youth was in hiding somewhere nearby whilst he waited for his colleagues to return, that is if they hadn't already departed so it was imperative that she establish that they were still here.

At this point the General dispatched her most capable scout to reconnoitre the northern area and check for any signs of activity in that sector and to report to her later in Abdo.

An hour after dawn General Electra together with a full complement of mounted troop and accompanied by her chief scout rode out from Abdo village and arrived at the viewing arena below the Temple mount fifteen minutes later where the troop separated and spread out. They concentrated their search efforts initially from horseback but after an hour of fruitless endeavour they dismounted and proceeded on foot through the nooks and crannies between the colourful stratums. Just before eleven o'clock they discovered the blue steps and within a few minutes they'd found what appeared to have been a hideaway close by which they believed had been vacated only a short time ago but it was only when they checked out the old barn and found that though the wagons were still in place all the supplies had now disappeared since the previous afternoon and here they paused to re-evaluate the position.

The General pondered over this development briefly and concluded that the youth waiting for Zeo and the others had probably known that his hiding place had been discovered and had re-located elsewhere. She recalled her troop to the viewing area and addressed them from the saddle and told them they need search no more. She was now positive that the three pilgrims were still at the Temple of the Gods and that the fourth member of their team was still in hiding somewhere nearby waiting their return. This was all they needed to know and now they could concentrate on defending the site and the surrounding area and from here on in they would spend less time in Abdo and establish a two mile secure perimeter, being certain that any threat to Zeo and his companions would come from the northern approaches. She instructed her scouts to expand their search area over a ten mile radius day and night because she was certain that 'Pravus' Sorus would know by now that the *Virago* corps were here in *Australis* to protect his most bothersome opponents and that Reptus Reptum and his snake women had failed to stop them reaching the Temple of the Gods.

CHAPTER TWENTY-SEVEN

Two days after his comrades had ascended the blue steps Euander rode Candeo several miles south of his hideout which was something he'd done since the others had gone to the Temple. Not only did he and the colt need exercising daily but so too did Friday who appeared to enjoy the freedom outside the pen. He had to allay the boredom of being cooped up and it wasn't only for him because he was certain that the animals were affected by the monotony of the claustrophobic enclosure just as much as he and all of them needed to keep fit anyway. The wounds he'd sustained from his brush with the Rootless creeping thorn-vine in *Primoris* had healed and he could now enjoy the pleasure of putting Candeo through his paces without the fear of opening the old wounds.

On the previous day when on one of his outings from the shelter he'd discovered an underground cavern on the east side of the crystal mound, or rather the dog had found it, and though it wasn't as close to the steps leading up to the Temple as the other place it offered more cover and would be harder to find should anyone try to seek him out. Since the three guys had gone he'd had plenty of time to think about things and one of the main worries for him was that those who were trying to do harm to Zeo and the two *Praecipuus* would know that whilst they were in the Temple that he'd probably wait for them within close range of the steps to look after the animals and equipment and during this hiatus he and the others would be at their most vulnerable to attack when they left the Temple. He guessed that Zeo would have commented; *Est nulla cerebrum!* It's a no brainer!

The trio were approaching their base within the colourful rocks when Euander spotted movement in the far distance. He focused his binoculars and could clearly see that a lone horsewoman had ridden from the east and had dismounted at the entrance to the viewing area below him and the fact that he was certain that it was a female rider added to his surprise and consternation, it just wasn't what he'd expected to see in this place right now. She tethered her mount and proceeded to thoroughly search within the colonnaded arena and then moved on to the surrounding paddocks and buildings. She spent a long time in the distant barn where they'd concealed most of the unessential equipment and supplies which wouldn't fit into the shelter behind the rocks and Euander guessed that she'd discovered the stash. Before she remounted she made notes and he assumed they were of what she'd observed. When she counted the number of horses grazing in the paddock it became obvious to him that she was recording the information for another party. As he watched her ride west about a half hour later he knew that he'd got no time to lose and without further delay he returned again and again with Candeo to his shelter near the *Carolina Blue* stairway and transferred all the equipment to the newly discovered refuge underground and without pausing he repeated the evacuation of the animal feedstuff and all the other equipment they'd concealed in the old barn until he'd relocated everything but the combo wagon into the cave.

He remained ever watchful to see if the female rider returned but he saw nobody during the late afternoon and evening. As he kept lookout on the western approaches he placed as many obstacles as he could find in the area surrounding the new bolt-hole just to make it more difficult if anyone approached their hiding place.

Before dusk he searched the rocky terrain near the cave until he found an area where he had a discrete but commanding view of the north, east and west access route to the steps.

Euander's body clock had alerted him that in fifteen minutes it would be dawn and while he awaited daylight he fed and watered his two charges and then sat and munched cookies and sipped from a large mug of steaming coffee, something he'd become more than fond of and he wondered briefly what was in the beverage to make it so invigorating and pleasing. Here he wrote his latest observations in the notebook donated him by Zeo.

He and Friday climbed to the vantage point where he lay flat out with the dog alongside and trained his binoculars on the viewing ground almost a quarter mile to the north where he waited and observed.

The surprise he'd had on the previous day when he'd realised that the person surveying the immediate area to the north was a female was nothing compared to the impact to his system when within an hour of taking up position on his vantage point the arena-like field in the distance was abuzz with an entire regiment of female cavalry milling around the viewing area and they were displaying the colours of Consul Primus Zeor. His initial exhilaration on seeing the colours was short lived and though he was relieved to see that the soldiers appeared to be allied troops he became suspicious and sceptical and decided to stay detached from them until he could establish their intentions and the reason why they were here at the Temple of the Gods.

Before he'd enlisted into the army of the Consul Primus and during the short period between being dispatched to *Primoris* to warn Zeo by Commander Otho, he'd never heard of an all female unit in the army, ever! And the last thing he wanted to do would be to lead his companions into a trap. Just because they marched under the Consul's colours didn't mean that they were legitimate as far as he was concerned and just because they were women didn't mean they couldn't be treacherous and dangerous too and here he recalled the encounter with the *Vipera Dominae* to justify his scepticism and mistrust.

As he viewed the scene below he was pretty certain the woman conversing and indicating different places to the officer in command of the force was the same individual he'd seen surveying the area on the previous day. He watched as the horsewomen separated and set about exploring the immediate terrain surrounding the base of the mount and later on he

perceived that they'd found his former hiding place and he exhaled a long sigh of relief.

He observed the detachment of riders fan out around the exclusion zone and he knew they were searching for him but with the help of his binoculars he was able to keep a constant watch on their movements and continue to take evasive action to avoid the search parties. He patted Friday continually and whispered at him softly to remain calm and quiet when the seekers were in the immediate area and he wondered momentarily how the animal understood what he was saying when Adam spoke a different language but perhaps dogs recognised the tone rather than the spoken word he figured.

He observed the search parties return sometime later and join their leader but was unable to deduce what was being said but he emitted another long sigh of relief when he saw them ride north and out of view. He returned to the hideout and brewed his second coffee to celebrate that he'd managed to avoid being discovered by the persistent all female hunting pack.

CHAPTER TWENTY-EIGHT

Yet once again the young pageboy was shaking in his black patent leather boots with shiny buckles as he clattered across the richly patterned marble floor in the grand office of 'Pravus' Sorus. The reason for his nervous disposition was that each messenger, agent, *Centurio, Praefectus* and commander which the dictator had received during the morning had angered and stressed him further and the tension in the room had gone from bad to worse. The youth wondered which visitor would eventually be the catalyst who'd precipitate the punishment he invariably took when the supreme leader was having a bad day at the office.

Just then the dictator's personal *factotum* popped his head around the door and announced that a very skinny man on a crutch sought entry. He'd refused to give his name except to say that he was the master of disguise in the art of close surveillance. He'd insisted that the Consul knew him and that he had urgent information he'd want to hear. The youth holding the quivering silver jug thought; *Oh meus Deus!* Could this be it?

His trembling escalated and he almost spilled the fresh water the leader had demanded of him a few minutes ago. Somehow he could feel in his young bones that whoever the man might be that he was bearing more bad news. And when he saw the spindly man hobble into the room on his makeshift crutch his fears were heightened tenfold by the doleful look on the man's weather-beaten and haggard face. There was no way that this guy could be bringing anything but bad news with a countenance like his the worried pageboy surmised as he scuttled away from the ornate desk and when he reached the relative safety of his bolthole in the anteroom he left the door slightly open to listen in on the exchange so that he'd be better prepared for any fallout that might happen between his master and the master of disguise in the art of close surveillance.

When 'Pravus' Sorus heard the news that Reptus Reptum and all of the *Vipera Dominam* had been killed by Zeo and his three companions near the Temple of the Gods he thumped his desk in shocked disbelief and anger and sprung backwards from his chair though coincidentally a scintilla of relief had flickered through his brain as he'd reacted thus; the fact that his wife Semele had now gone from his life for good was a welcome and timely event which had removed permanently any potential difficulties to his forthcoming nuptials. But back on a singular track again he cursed

all four of the *bastardae sordeda* who were responsible for this and vowed that he'd torture them without mercy when he got his hands on them and before he'd finished with them they'd prefer to be in the hottest zones of Hell. He continued stomping furiously around the room filling the air with one expletive after the other until he'd almost exhausted his impressive collection before he returned and stood behind his chair and glared unsympathetically and sardonically at the apparently disabled agent with his knobbly home-made crutch. Recognising the derisory and sceptic look on the dictators face the skinny man cried pityingly that the snake breeder hadn't been alone in his grave misfortune and that he'd personally suffered a debilitating injury to his back on that assignment and would be unable to take on any more commissions. The dictator glared across at him with contempt and gripped the back panel on his chair so tightly that his knuckles drained of blood but he regained control of his fury and signalled dismissively that the meeting was over. With a flick of his wrist he disdainfully directed the skinny man to get out of his sight.
Sorus sat down behind his desk again and finger-drummed the top with his right hand and reflectively caressed his lips with the other but just as the hobbling spy reached the outer door the dictator stopped him in his tracks by demanding to know what had become of the dead herpetologist's valuables and money.

Though he was now retired from his profession, the master of disguise in the art of close surveillance managed to mask his shock and fear and instantly depict an image of incorruptible innocence and anguish. He assured the dictator that he knew nothing of the poor man's meagre possessions but he would hazard a guess that perhaps they'd been destroyed in the conflagration which had left nothing but a massive heap of ashes on the forest floor but there was also the possibility that Zeo and his accomplices had discovered them before they'd torched the camp.

He was ever so sorry but he just didn't have a clue. The master of disguise in the art of close surveillance had lied twice in succession without batting an eyelid.

When 'Pravus' Sorus dismissed his former spy for the second time he mentally noted to have Suga Cazo check the man out in the future to see if his circumstances and his bad back had miraculously recovered. He'd found it intriguing that the seemingly crippled man hadn't once pleaded for assistance or a stipend to help him through his sudden and unexpected disability especially when he could remember being bombarded tearfully for help by everybody else who'd found themselves in a similar situation in the past.

His dark deliberations were interrupted again by the busy *factotum* who announced the arrival of a courier with messages from Governor Maximus and the Lady Dido.

The young page breathed a sigh of relief and moved away from the door when he learned where the courier had come from because his master had always mellowed and lightened up quite considerably when he received a *nota-blanda* from his sweetheart.

The boy sat on his little padded stool in a far corner of the room and daydreamed how his job would become so much more pleasant when his master and the Lady Dido were married. In his heart he was certain that the lady must be a very sweet and gentle person to have such a calming effect on the leader.

He fantasized that she had to be the most beautiful and refined lady in Sitantal.

The demented bellow was quickly followed by the sound of the silver water jug crashing against the anteroom door and the clang was succeeded by a metallic clatter as it landed on the marble floor.

A trickle of water snaked underneath and into the room and with that the pallid faced page swooned and slumped off his little upholstered stool onto the floor.

The news from the Governor and his daughter was so devastating it tipped the letter's recipient further over the edge and into a more virulent echelon of insanity but when he saw that both messages had been penned and dispatched to him five days ago he exploded again and he contemplated having the messenger hanged instantly for his utter tardiness and gross dereliction of duty. He only put the plans to the back of his mind when the *factotum* interrupted him to say that the *scriptor* had arrived in the building.

As the dictator attempted to sort the papers strewn on the desk he called loudly to the page to fetch more water but when he got neither response nor libation he stormed from his seat and across the room where he had to sidestep the puddles and kick the dented silver jug out of his way before he charged into the anteroom. When he saw the youth sprawled on the floor he became even more enraged and bent over and grabbed his tunic collar and pulled the semiconscious youngster upright and slapped him hard on the face. He dragged him by the scruff of his neck like a rag doll across the marble floor and burst through the door where he slammed into the startled scribe and sent his writing accoutrements flying from his hands. Sorus ordered the anxious *factotum* to immediately escort the boy to the captain of the guard and have him conscripted into the army right away and barked that it might make a man out of the snivelling runt.

The aide was anything but happy to leave his station and trudge through the extensive building to the guardroom at the front entrance but the pair had barely gone five yards when the diminutive pageboy wrenched his arm free and bolted down the wide corridor like an imp out of hell where he made resounding rat-a-tat-tat noises on the marble floors with his black patent leather boots with shiny buckles.

Though the angry assistant chased after the absconding youth he was unable to catch him and eventually he lost sight of him in the maze of passageways. He gave up and returned to his station where he was relieved to see that his master was engaged with the *scriptor* and would hopefully soon forget about the brat with so much happening elsewhere.

The leader's brain was spinning with the vast amount of reports and information which had arrived during the morning and a lot of it had been hard to stomach and some of it had even been difficult to believe.

He reread the censorious letter from his *inamorata* though it was the most painful thing to do especially the part where she'd blamed him and her father for allowing the felon Zeo to create havoc around the country and to put in peril the putsch which had brought him to power. She wanted him to post the biggest reward ever for Zeo's capture, dead or alive, and believed that every *custodis* under his control should be mobilised at once for that purpose and to launch an attack immediately on his father in Esta City to bring him to heel now that he didn't have Zeo and his cohorts to advise or protect him. She'd said that this should have been done when the prisoners had been set loose from the tower in Nox and before they had time to mobilise and establish a counterrevolution. More should be done right away to destroy the *nothus* and the interlopers from *Terra Ferusum* now that they knew where they were and where they were going. For too long, it seemed to her, these outlaws and bandits had been able to traipse around the country at will. She also believed that the two outsiders who'd been elevated to *Praecipuum* status by Zeor which had forced her to bow her head in homage to them whilst they'd robbed and assaulted her was an utter and absolute travesty. But an even bigger outrage was the fact that no one could ever rescind the *Praecipuum* honour from the pair once it had been bestowed.

The mere reference to the young pup Zeo and his co-conspirators who'd thieved from and humiliated his future consort was more than Sorus could bear to read. Angrily he repeatedly clenched his fingers and cracked his knuckles, an exercise which made the scribe twitch every time he heard the leader's joints pop as he fiddled nervously with his writing instruments.

Governor Maximus' latest report had a litany of new excuses for his failure to capture the villain Zeo when he'd passed through *Oriens* on his way to the Temple of the Gods and with the resulting traumatic experience for his daughter as she'd travelled home. He wrote that he'd immediately put his troops at the ready and if Sorus ordered him to follow and hunt down the highway robbers while they were in *Australis* he and his men would set off right away. Following the ordeal they'd inflicted on his darling daughter he felt it was essential that something be done to restore law and order and respect for the elite class especially when he'd already heard that bawdy songs were being composed and sung in taverns throughout *Oriens* about Dido's encounter with Zeo and there were rumours now circulating that schoolchildren were penning cheeky rhymes and ditties too. These insults had to be stopped before they became commonplace.

But before Sorus had dictated a word to the scribe the dutiful *factotum* was at the door again with an urgent message from the dictator's secret agent in Esta City.

This report detailed the recent clandestine despatch days ago of General Electra and her all-female unit to the Temple of the Gods to protect the three special pilgrims there. Zeor feared for their safety believing that they would be very vulnerable on their way to and from the Temple regardless of the presence of the *Beneficiarius* and the agent could confirm that the former ruler's only daughter Livia was an active combatant in this unit. This news caused the dictator to snigger scornfully and he reckoned his enemy must be finding it hard to get recruits when he had to resort to enlisting women to fight his battles. He resolved to have the female warriors' attributes, endowments and credentials checked out in due course. It also pleased him to know that Zeor was unaware that the *Beneficiarius* had been erased from the region and now there was only a collection of women to protect the three of them.

A postscript to the agent's note included the latest rumour within the city circulating that the ousted Consul Zeor together with his elder son were in the final stages of launching a campaign in northern *Oriens* and he could verify there was increased troop movement in the holding camps outside the city and he was certain that the information was true.

When Sorus appraised the spy's report from Zeor's base in Esta City his first instruction was penned to Suga Cazo and his *"Removal Men"* which commanded them to abandon the raids on the temples and also the other clandestine assignments he'd previously given them and all of them, as a matter of urgency, must leave for the Temple of the Gods in *Australis* immediately.

And with the news that Zeor was on the move in the north and was about to launch an incursion into *Oriens* his next message was to Governor Maximus telling him to forgo his plan to pursue Zeo to the Temple of the Gods, that he had his own ideas on what to do about the little *merda*. He insisted that the Governor remain in *Oriens* and defend his province and his capital against the new threat at all costs and to hinder, harass and repel Zeor's forces as soon they set foot in his province to prevent them gaining further territory or support but also if he could pin him down within the province and delay him from returning to Esta City it would be even better still. An addendum to the note explained that his strategy would become clear in time to Governor Maximus.

His third dictation was to Puto Pollux outlining what he wanted his Deputy Governor of *Occidens* to do for him on his way back to the Capitol. His adrenal glands began to pump faster and faster the more he cogitated over his embryonic scheme and by the time he'd finished dictating the instructions he'd developed a hyperactive energy flush which rippled through every part of his body including his loins. He'd spent more time on this directive than he'd spent on the other instructions combined before turning to the notary to transcribe his final letter which was to his lover Dido.

    The *scriptor* squirmed and he almost threw up as he listened to the leader outline his sentiments to his *amoris*. He blushed so much so his face turned a vivid shade of red and not only that but his toes began curling up tightly in his sandals as he penned the final message of the day. It was the first time ever that Sorus had had him write on his behalf to his lover and very early into the lustful letter the scribe realised that both the dictator and his bride to be were licentious perverts and reprobates. He was shocked and embarrassed to the core to hear what debauchery the dictator was planning for their next tryst but he was also profoundly relieved to know that his wife and daughters were far away from the central hub of politics and governance and seldom ventured into this part of the city.

And following this ghastly discovery he'd insist from now on that they never would.

When the scribe departed his office Sorus bade the still diligent *factotum* to seal and despatch the mail promptly with the runners and then call on the *dispensatrix* and have her find a new page-boy to attend his office daily. He instructed the aide to warn the doddering old housekeeper that she'd be in serious trouble if she saddled him with another useless wimp.

Sorus leaned back in his chair and considered afresh the morning's events. Though he tried to compartmentalise his deliberations and concentrate on each specific problem individually the haunting spectre of Zeo and his companions infiltrated his thought process time after time making the task virtually impossible. Eventually he gave up and sprung from the chair and hurried from the room.

CHAPTER TWENTY-NINE

During *cena* five days following the departure of *Virago* from Esta City the Consul Primus was with his wife and son Zeor junior where he'd just informed Aprilis that both he and junior would be leaving the city before daybreak at the head of his army. They'd march north and then east to Oppida and if and when they'd secured the town from the usurper's grip they'd continue from there into central *Oriens*. He explained to his wife that the goal was to replace the Governor's stooges in every town and village in the province with men and women loyal to him. Before the week was out, and if all went according to plan, he hoped to be within sight of the provincial capital which would mean he'd come into direct conflict with her erstwhile father Ballio Maximus and his daughter Dido. He promised to do his utmost to take both of them alive to stand trial for high treason but if they resisted or if they became a danger to anyone he would execute them without hesitation because, but for them, 'Pravus' Sorus wouldn't have had sufficient backing to engineer the coup against him and plunge the country into turmoil and he was inclined to think that it was Dido who'd encouraged Sorus to stage the coup, that she was jealous of her half sister being married to a Consul Primus. And from rumours circulating he was convinced that Dido actually wanted to be even more than the wife of a Consul Primus, possibly even noble and she now insisted that she be called the *Lady* Dido.

From Ciro City they'd march on the Capitol to face 'Pravus' Sorus but in the meantime he thought it best that she remain here in Esta City which would be under the protection of Commander Otho. Aprilis nodded her assent and said that she'd use the time to study the *Promptorium parvulorum.* She planned to have a proper conversation with her nephew and his friend when everything was back to normal and before they'd depart for *Terra Ferusum.* There was so much she wanted to know about her biological family and Lo Garrantraa and she believed she'd never have an opportunity to do it again. The Consul Primus raised his glass and proposed a toast to the success of their campaign in *Oriens* and they both committed to sending a weekly report to each other with the latest developments in their part of the world.

At her favourite listening post behind the door Porcia dabbed the tears from her eyes at the thought of not having the Consul and his son to care for. Just thinking about it made her sad and lonely already even though her work load would be reduced considerably now that there'd only be one member of the family to look after while the Consul Primus and his children were engaged in different exploits in far flung places.

The night watch in Esta City had become accustomed to early morning troop movements in what had become a garrison city but this was the largest operation they'd ever witnessed and it was a most impressive sight to behold from their high vantage points. The flat plains to the south pulsated with activity as heavily armed infantry lined up to board the vast numbers of *naviculae* moored on the Trans-*Medius* canal while the cavalry took to the saddle and manoeuvred their steeds into formation in the main training grounds. A forty-strong paired fleet of charioteers armed with multiple short *pili* lined up behind them and to the rear was a long train of supply wagons with a squad of engineers waiting at the edges of the plains to take up position in the huge movement of men evacuating the city. The introduction of two-manned chariots, which were normally confined to sporting events into an active battle role, was a new concept promoted by the Consul. He believed their prowess in the chariots could be used as an independent force but could also remove wounded comrades speedily and efficiently from the combat zone.

The throbbing mass of humanity and animals were joined on the plains by the Consul Primus and his son shortly before dawn where differing bugle and trumpet sounds echoed over the lands as the *Bucinators* and *Tubicens* relayed fresh instructions from the Captains and Commanders to their men while *Signifers* and *Tablifers* brightened up the approaching silvery daylight with a magnificent range of colourful banners and insignia.

When the City's *Tempus Dico* announced daybreak the Consul Primus together with his son and personal standard bearer rode to the small hill at the edge of the flats and faced his army where he proudly saluted his men and signalled with his baton to go north after the city's *Pater Antistes* had invoked the Gods to bring success on their mission and protect them all on the campaign.

The marching drumbeat replaced the roar of approval that had swept over the plains.

Aprilis and her little plump housekeeper Porcia stood outside the city limits surrounded by crowds of women and children where they dabbed at their eyes and fluttered their lace *sudariums* at the departing men.

The Consul led the cavalry to the outskirts of Oppida and waited there until the engineers had opened the abandoned canal gates. The flotilla of fully manned *naviculae* raced along the short stretch to the central marina where the armed infantry disembarked in front of the town's forum and here they were met with a barrage of *iaculum, acus quattuor and globus filum* from the barricades arranged around the civic building facing onto the square and marina. The town's Mayor, the *Summus,* reputed to be a slavish Maximus supporter, issued orders nonstop to the defending *custodis* and initially his men were successful in holding the infantry off until the Consul led the cavalry through the square where they charged forward and mounted the steps with drawn swords and dispersed the resistance from behind the barricades and forced the survivors including the mayor and his *Praefecti* to retreat indoors.

Though the General, *Optio, Praefecti,* commanders and even his son expected the Consul Primus to order an immediate attack on the ancient building he resisted and called to the mayor and the defenders to surrender and save themselves and the town.

He promised them that if they complied they'd be safe, losing only any official status they presently occupied until they recanted Maximus and Sorus.

He met the mayor and *Praefecti* below the steps where they surrendered Oppida and yielded up their badges and insignia of office. They told him that about twenty *custodis* had fled but those remaining wished to change sides and join his army. As they negotiated terms the Sorus and Maximus colours were lowered and burned on the marina concourse and the red, white rhombus and green banner of the Consul Primus was raised above Oppida's civic buildings.

    The Consul left the town in the afternoon

feeling satisfied with the early morning conquest having suffered only one casualty but inflicting two on the opposing forces though the enemy had sustained two critically injured plus several less so but having achieved a surrender he'd prevented a more painful result. His aim was still to conduct the counter coup with caution where this was possible. He had to remember at all times that these were his people and as Consul Primus *Hereditarius* his main responsibility was to render a remedy giving the fairest outcome to any problem where one was feasible, whether it was a minor dispute or even in civil war and it was a policy he wanted his son Zeor to embrace one day when he'd succeed him.

He'd promoted one of his officers to the rank of Commander with a force of thirty men to administer Oppida on his behalf and the former *Praefecti* would now be his second in command. The mayor had been re-sworn and then reappointed by him but was now subservient to military orders. And even though the townsfolk hadn't danced in the streets in celebration he was certain that in time they'd realise that the outcome could have been more destructive and painful for them and their town.

The main road and canal network connecting Oppida with the provincial capital meandered through central *Oriens* where they ran almost parallel with each other. The Consul's cavalry and infantry entered several villages en route but met with no blatant resistance until they approached Venura some one hundred and twenty miles north of the provincial capital and the birthplace of Ballio Maximus.

The scout had informed the Consul that a large force of *custodis* and diehard cohorts of Sorus and Maximus now guarded the town and had dug in and appeared to have prepared for a long siege.

He met with Governor Arrol, the captains, commanders and scouts and agreed that if they wanted to achieve complete control of the province they'd have to address the challenge and remove this threat on the western edge of *Oriens*. He called a halt for the day and made camp about a quarter mile from the obstinate town and arranged a cordon in place to prevent anyone now entering or leaving unless they were showing the white mark of submission. When darkness descended a detachment of infantry rode out and encircled Venura where they kept a constant vigil on all access routes while numerous *Lumen Peditatus mobilis* shone quivering beams of light towards the towns' boundaries.

Venura was essentially a light industrial town, neither large nor small, and was without permanent fortifications but whoever was in control there had obviously prepared for an assault and once again the Consul wondered who the agent might be who was passing information to the enemy. It was obvious to him that there'd been advance warning given because there was no way the defences could have been fabricated quickly, there'd been a considerable amount of time and labour involved he could see.

Hugh wooden framed towers had been erected around the town's perimeter and tightly interspersed between the structures were sectors with high wooden palisades and latticed criss-crossed spikes and spears projecting outwards in anticipation of a cavalry charge and as the scout had reported last evening, all roads and canal channels leading in and out of the town were similarly protected.

The Consul understood why Ballio Maximus would want to do everything possible, short of manning the defences himself, to prevent his birthplace falling to his enemies, it was a psychological thing and Zeor believed that even though Venura was very important to Maximus his enemy's main objective would be to protect his capital at all costs because he'd know that if he lost Ciro City then he was finished and would have to run to Sorus.

The Consul's infantry marched from the overnight camp to the outskirts of Venura with Zeor junior in the vanguard flanked by a *signifer* and *tubicen.* The cavalry was split into right and left wings with the right detachment under the command of the Consul Primus and the left company under the control of General Arrol, the elderly Governor of *Australis,* who'd gained a fine reputation in the military and had been made General before he'd succeeded his father as Governor

of *Australis*. And now though seventy years old, he was still agile and fighting fit and raring to go.
Remembering Zeo's psychological mantra the Consul had kept the circular cordon in place surrounding the town, preventing egress or entry and now he proposed to use the space between the town and the cordon as a form of track for his charioteers and cavalry.
The infantry's *tubicen* sounded a sharp note on the command of Zeor junior twenty yards from the town's defences where the legion split into multiple ten-manned *contubernia*. Smoothly and almost robotically they used their long shields to form numerous *testudos* and then edged forward until they were about twenty feet from the wooden stockades and towers. Almost immediately each *testudo* was battered incessantly with missile after missile of one form or another; spears, *iaculum*, *acus quattuor* and even *globus filum*. But unseen and unknown to the enemy, an archer lurked within each *testudo* with a pair of the many reproduced skeleton stock crossbows of the type Zeo had given his brother before he'd gone to *Terra Ferusum*. Each archer had an aide to assist loading each bow speedily and seamlessly. Zeor junior had spent every moment of his time with thirty of the most promising recruits practising their skills with the new weapons. The infantrymen behind the shields waited several seconds before returning fire and directed their missiles only at the *custodis* beyond the palisades at ground

level.

As the onslaught commenced Zeor junior sheltered within the *testudo* close to the west end of the town and together with his aide he prepared and aimed the crossbow.

Meanwhile the Consul's mounted troop waited patiently until the infantry on the western approach to Venura had formed the continuous chain of *testudos* and faced the town.

He then raised his baton and the cavalry responded to the *bucinator's* trumpet fanfare and with helmets on and spears uncapped and ready, both cavalry detachments charged in opposite directions with the Consul branching off to the right whilst General Arrol's contingent veered to the left of the town. They charged past the manned towers and palisades on the north and south sides of Venura without pausing or using their weapons and when they reached the eastern side they galloped past each other and continued to circle until they ended up at opposites poles to where they'd started from, near the western elevation behind the front line of *testudos.* They repeated the sally again and again, confusing the defenders even further each time they charged past.

So far Zeor junior had managed to score nine direct hits in both towers sited beside the main arterial road leading into the town which allowed his infantry to breach the palisades and the stockades to reach the unprotected rear of the outer defences where they gradually advanced further along the front line clearing one section after the other.

Zeor junior's armour protected *testudo* moved to the right and halted at the next manned tower where they repeated the exercise until all the west facing towers and palisades had been cleared of *custodis*. At that point both wings of the cavalry reformed and charged through into the town while the infantry detached and dismantled the *testudo* formations and swept forward to engage the enemy still holed up behind the north, south and east barricades. At great speed teams of cavalry dismounted and looped a rope to a tower support which was tied to their saddle pommels and rode forward tugging the tall edifice noisily to earth with the occupants on board whose screams on the way down added to the mayhem and pandemonium all around.

The Consul Primus allowed the unbridled violence to continue as stores and workshops were engulfed in flames and only the dwellings were spared. The destruction only reached a definitive conclusion when the surviving enemy combatants had finally capitulated and had thrown down their arms. Though this was in direct contrast to his previous sentiments at Aleppo he believed that this town had gone to great pains to thwart his campaign and to inflict maximum damage to him and his men right up to the end. They'd thought that they were untouchable and they just wouldn't give in. They'd acquired the reputation of being out and out diehard supporters of Sorus and Maximus and now there could be no doubt about it; they'd all died hard!

Before dusk the rebellious town was conquered and subdued.

The captured *custodis* were detailed to arrange the cremation pyre for their fallen comrades but the Consul's men insisted on a separate pyre and *exsequiae* rite for their dead and though he protested that everybody was equal in death he eventually conceded to their request.

Two large funeral pyres on the outskirts of Venura lit up the surrounding countryside as the Consul Primus and his son met in their camp compound where the Consul addressed his victorious army. He congratulated them fulsomely and assured them they'd be well rewarded in time but tonight they'd have to remain clear-headed and vigilant. And like the previous night the town would be under curfew with absolutely no one allowed to enter or leave. At daylight a thorough house to house search for weapons and fugitives would be mounted. He and his senior commanders, advisers and strategists would meet then and plan the next move forward.

CHAPTER THIRTY

Seated alone and below his own personal screen Zeo had gazed back into prehistory, to the very conception and birth of Sitantal. The time line was set immediately after his ancestral fatherland had been submerged below the waves following what had been the most destructive event to beset the most beautiful island on planet earth since the creation of the cosmos. His homeland had become engulfed by the huge deluge but just when the population were in abject despair and had resigned themselves to an imminent, deep watery grave a colossal translucent dome had appeared above them from out of the blue, some even thought it was a giant bubble that would burst anytime soon but as the island land-mass continued to sink into the depths of the ocean the only thing between them and certain death was the glass ceiling. When the calamitous event had finally concluded and the land had stabilised at the bottom of the deep blue sea the only link between this new world below and the old world above was the inhospitable sector called *Extremus.* And even though the people didn't know or appreciate it at that time this extremely unpleasant and hostile link to surface planet earth was the essential umbilical cord which would keep their new under-water continent alive. They were also ignorant to the fact that if ever the extreme region ceased to function or exist so too would Sitantal.

The populace had barely come to terms with their divine deliverance or with their new circumstances below mountain and sea when without warning the whole country had shook and trembled in sudden convulsion. It had sent young and old fleeing in every direction seeking cover and some hid in the most peculiar and useless places. But nonetheless the people were united in their fear and had cried out to the Gods to save them once again.

And just as if They had heard the heartfelt pleas anew a truly magnificent display of every colour on the spectrum slowly filtered out and enveloped the entire land for a short time and then the tremors gently receded and were gone. This colourful fanfare missed no part of Sitantal, north, south, east or west. The chromatic splurge radiated and penetrated everywhere and anywhere, even reaching into *Extremus* but just as the ground vibrations had ceased eventually, the billowing, colour-imbued mist gradually faded and was gone. Word quickly spread out from *Australis* that something magical, even miraculous, had happened there on the day their country had trembled and that it could be *casus fortuitus.* The fantastic news encouraged droves of curious people to head south

from every corner of the land to see what some had described as an act of the Gods and others had pronounced it as being dark magic. When the people saw the enormous edifice on the multi-coloured magma mount they were overwhelmed and shocked by its magnitude and splendour but when they saw the auspicious inscription "SEMPER TECUM" above the permanently shut doors their confidence in the future was restored and most were now reassured that they were not on their own, that Sitantal was indeed a special place and that they were, without doubt, a chosen people.
Here was the proof that their new homeland had been created by the Gods for them alone and therefore their country must surely be blessed.

Zeo's journey through the ancient past continued and took him into a frightening period after the extraordinary birth of the new nation to a time when there was great uncertainty and turmoil within the confined population with those who believed that their deliverance was a permanent thing and the doubters who thought it was just a temporary respite and the Gods would desert them eventually. If that happened they'd be subsumed by the oceans above and they would all die. Whilst these negative emotions persisted it prevented the country from thriving and it cast a nasty shadow of ill will and malevolence throughout the land. And during the formative and evolving years a plethora of warlords brought constant grief and strife to vast sections of the interior but eventually when they grew tired of killing each other a form of feudalism replaced this carnage and mayhem. Though the new system brought a semblance of stability and less bloodletting there was an underlying feeling of fear, separation and inequality within the general populace. Eventually and at a time of extreme discontent over two thousand years ago, a group of trusted representatives, elders and the righteous from all five provinces had met in conclave at *Campus Concordia.* Here they'd drafted a bill of rights and laws enshrining every facet of life in the country. The historic document was officially titled *Praeceptis Sitantal Liberatum,* the Statutes of the Liberties of Sitantal and the people who'd devised and compiled it were known as *Sodalibus Condita,* the Founding Members.

Included in the covenant was the pledge that the provincial Governors would be held to account if they transgressed or exceeded their powers and it also proscribed individuals or groups who tried to usurp lawful authority for their own selfish gain against the wishes of the population at large. To safeguard against such abuses it was enshrined in law that the Governor of *Medius* would be *primus inter pares;* first among equals in an *aequabilis;* an egalitarian society and he or she would be hereditary supreme leader of Sitantal and would be the sole Councillor and arbiter in all major civil and constitutional disputes.

The holder of this office would be styled *Consul Pri-*

mus Hereditarius.
Every adult, whether they were a patrician or a plebeian and who could sign their name, was entitled to vote on the agreement and very soon the Statutes of Sitantal had been enacted as the constitution and the law of the land.
The chief administrative city would be *Urbis Capitolium* and seat of the Consul Primus.
And this is how it had remained until 'Pravus' Sorus had overthrown Zeo's father.

But in all the intervening time between the new beginning, the turmoil and the plebiscite no one had been prepared to fully investigate or put their lives at risk by visiting or exploring *Extremus,* citing that they and their ancestors had survived an epochal and cataclysmic experience when their island had been swallowed by the sea and even though they guessed that the dangers lurking in the extreme region were nothing in comparison to what had occurred in that distant time, as far as they were concerned enough was enough.
Plain and simple! Let someone else explore the place in the future if they wanted to but not them and definitely not now! Never disturb what you don't need to; just let it be!
And this adage had become the mindset of the population of Sitantal for many, many centuries and it was still the prevailing attitude when the first Consul Primus had led an expedition into the unknown territories where he'd identified, surveyed and named the three different regions he'd

discovered there.

He'd forbidden anyone from ever tampering with the physicality of the inhospitable place or its environs, being certain that it played an essential role in the wellbeing of Sitantal. When he and his party had reached the last chamber in *Tertius* he'd had his engineers stabilise, balance and counter balance the boulder door securely into place, a system of protection that was still adequate and useable up to the present day.

He declared it would be a capital offence for any Sitantalan to open the outer door except in a case of life or death without authority from him or his successors. He attested that the isolation of the people, culture, flora and fauna of Sitantal was the personal conception of the Gods and were separate, unique and distinct to the land below mountain and sea and should never be exposed to the corruption and barbarism which he firmly believed to be rampant in the primitive jungle beyond that point and that the Gods had despaired on redeeming the place before *Aestimatio Die;* Appraisal Day, that the Evil One was already too imbedded there. He professed that it had been like this since Genesis; from the beginning of time!

From that day and for those reasons the outside world had been known as *Terra Ferusum*.

Since the era of the first Consul Primus and a forebear of Zeo, forty-seven great-great plus-plus grandparents of his had held the position until it passed onto his paternal grandfather before passing from him to his father Zeor twenty odd years ago. Some of these men and women had been more capable and successful than their kindred who'd predeceased them but on the whole most had made a difference for the better in Sitantal, with a few gaining in death an honorific *Great* suffix after their name whereas some had been sufficiently successful to achieve a *Good* appendix. Fortunately none of the deceased Consuls had gained a truly negative appellation though three had come precariously close to causing a blot on the lineage including a ruling but wayward great-great-plus grand-mother several hundred years ago who'd had a wandering eye and a propensity to be more touchy-feely with other women than what was considered *aptus* at the time.

Though a lot of the early history was new to Zeo and some of the later events had been exaggerated or at times sanitised in the family records, quite a few puzzles and doubts he'd had about parts of the family chronicles had been revealed but he didn't believe that the Gods had commanded that he come to the Temple of the Gods with Adam and Johnny to browse Sitantal's old history alone, there had to be another reason for it he was sure. As if They had detected his growing restlessness with these revelations about historical subjects the animated fluctuating screen moved to contemporary events when he saw his father and his brother in central *Oriens* as they marched across country towards Ciro City. Then his sister Livia appeared to be with an all women unit and oddly from what he could make out, she appeared to be in *Australis*. His anxiety changed to disquiet when the images on the screen billowed and contorted and the scene was a city in flames and it looked like Esta City to him. He was further shocked to see the Honorary Governor of *Septentrio* and father to the renegade Gaius appear from the shadows and point out a villa on a tree-lined avenue but just then the images vanished for an instant. When the image returned his heart sank further when he saw the body of Commander Otho sprawled lifelessly near the portal of his family's interim home which was also ablaze. Instantly he knew that Castor, the Governor of *Septentrio* had turned traitor. Like father, like son!

He gasped aloud and shifted his position closer to the continually changing images but he drew back in horror instantly when the image of a frightened lady in shackles appeared.

It was his mother and she was in a careering, bouncing coach somewhere very far away!

CHAPTER THIRTY-ONE

When Johnny and Adam had settled and gazed at the strange configurations on their personal mercurial medium they wondered what was happening and what they were meant to do now. Johnny had been about to whisper irreverently to his friend that he'd seen more action in a grotty fleapit cinema but just then it became clear to him that they were observers of some sort of ethereal visual chronicle of Homo sapiens emerging signs of intelligence and enlightenment when ancient world history was first noted. They both realised in concert that whatever was going on here had to have a serious meaning to it and they were intrigued to find out what it might be. It soon became apparent that they were in fact viewing events almost from the outset of recorded time on Earth starting well after the Ice Age and leading up to the Bronze and then the Iron Age; those defining Era's not visited on their recent adventure above this place, which had portrayed the evolution of the planet.

They witnessed a fledging cuneiform script in

the East and the transition of Mesopotamia and Babylon, Egypt, India and the Dynasties in China. They saw Solomon in Jerusalem and the division of Israel and Judea and the inception of the Old Testament. Sometime later Confucius shared his wisdom in China. The two guys were transfixed by classical antiquity and what was happening in Greece with Homer's *Iliad* and *Odyssey* and in Olympia they were present at the first Olympic Games.

They saw Romulus on the Palatine Hill and the dawn of the expanding Roman Republic and they sat forward in their seats when they witnessed chariots in tourney competition.

On the other side of the world they watched North America, Mexico, Brazil and pockets elsewhere in the south, come alive.

The two friends shifted in their seats as they viewed one bloody slaughter after another on every continent on Earth and they observed the rise and fall of kings and kingdoms and

the demise of emperors and empires. They saw great swathes of the emerging world resort to savagery and barbarity, some of which lasted right up to the present day.

When Gaius Julius Caesar came on the scene and on their screen everything changed, in south-western Europe, in Gaul, on the Hispania Peninsula, Britannia and right up to the waters of the Rhine. His influence extended into the Middle East and North Africa and further afield. They saw him and his legion cross the Rubicon but the pair of viewers braced themselves for what they already knew from the annals of history and of his friend's vengeful betrayal on *idibus Martiis,* the Ides of March.

They gazed on ruefully as the great Dictator-for-life died alone on the bloodstained steps of the senate while the treacherous Marcus Brutus and his henchmen skulked away into the back streets of Rome.

They saw a young man struggle with a rough wooden cross up a sun-baked hill as mobs jeered and laughed while others cried out plaintively and sympathetically along the way.

Adam and Johnny witnessed the onset of the Roman Empire and building commence on the Great Wall in China.

They observed the countries of Europe advance more than any other place on Earth; militarily, technologically and in every other field including the sciences and the arts and though the Europeans had copied a thing or two from the Orientals they soon surpassed them just as the power of the Roman Empire began to wane.

Without any preamble the colourful scenes on their screen changed to depict a shimmering desert and then panned onto the image of a stooped, bearded man emerging from a cluster of Halophyte-type reeds as he plodded purposely over the sand.

Both friends exchanged querying glances and they

each grimaced and shrugged their shoulders, quite bewildered as to where this latest historical episode was taking them when the robe-draped man came to a standstill directly opposite the largest orange coloured King Cobra they'd ever seen.

The reptile stiffened and shimmied and rose until it was almost erect and near level with the desert traveller's sun-toasted face. It was a surreal sight to witness and the pair of viewers sat open-mouthed and in awe. But rather than recoiling from the reptile as they expected him to do, the man moved closer and spoke directly to the creature and when they saw that the cobra appeared to interact they were dumbfounded. As they watched the more than peculiar encounter between man and snake and witnessed the dialogue between the aberrant communicants they wondered what part of the first millennium *Anno Domini* this weird segment alluded to. Their puzzlement continued until the man bowed his head to the snake and departed the spot. As they stared at the still erect cobra both guys gasped with shock as the snake altered its shape for the briefest moment into a grotesque beast-human like form but it was the look of pure evil and contempt it directed towards the departing robed man which had appalled and stunned them more than anything they'd seen so far. But before they had time to recover from their shared stupefaction the beast-like-human-like figure turned and faced them head on and stared malevolently at each of them separately as if it

knew it was being observed, causing them to gasp loudly and flinch in horror and disgust. But in less than an instant, equivalent to the blink of an eye, the abomination transmuted back to its reptile form and slowly descended to the sand where it slithered out of sight and off their screen.
Adam turned to Johnny to check that his eyes hadn't deceived him or that he'd imagined what he'd just seen and without having to ask his friend he knew immediately that Johnny had seen it too. The last disturbing image the two had of the robed man in the desert was of him shuffling towards the setting sun where he cast an evil dark snake-like shadow, moving concertina-like on the sands, directly in his wake. The sight of this unsettling anomaly delivered a further shock to their senses.

The two friends sat and stared blankly at the screen deep in churning thoughts and emotions as live vivid scenes appeared from the second millennium *Anno Domini*; images of the Crusaders, Genghis Khan, Magna Carta and of the Black Death as it swept through Europe from its source in Asia barely registered with them though the sight of the first coffee beans being harvested caught their attention but only momentarily. They looked on as new dynasties were formed and reformed on every continent and the pair shook off their reverie but only briefly when they were shown Dante Alighieri writing *Commedia* with the ghostly image of Virgil acting as *cicerone*. They recognised the Aztec's at war in Mesoamerica and saw elegant Constantinople fall to vulgarian Turks. The screenplay also depicted the Incans in action in their part of the world.

Tobacco and potatoes became must-haves in Europe and elsewhere and influenced the great adventurers like Marco Polo and Christopher Columbus. Master artists were seen in action all over Europe with Leonardo Da Vinci followed later by Michelangelo at the Sistine Chapel. The sight of these renowned painters and sculptors at work had Adam's full attention but as soon as the subject changed he reverted deep into his previous rut. Joan of Arc only just caught their eye though Galileo Galilei stirred both viewers interest anew when he appeared on screen with his eyeglass pointing to the heavens.

Fleeting action, faces and places filled the screen continually, some which they instantly recognised whereas others were lost to them forever.

Eventually they began to recover from that earlier dire and disturbing scene from the first millennium *Anno Domini* which had since preoccupied and troubled them more than they were prepared to admit. They became more relaxed and at ease and were now able to concentrate more closely on major events and figures disinterred from the archival history of mankind long since gone. They perceived the United States gain Independence and saw Francis Scott Key pen *"The Star-Spangled Banner"* at Fort Mc Henry. They got another fillip when they saw the first steam engine on the screen. The two were enthralled as they listened to the magical music of the young Wolfgang Amadeus Mozart and had a further resounding buzz when they tuned in to the first scratchy telephone transmission. They grinned as they saw the very first steam locomotive chug on the Liverpool to Manchester line and were further exhilarated to see the Wright brothers soar into the skies at the outset of the Twentieth century.

Then Henry Ford filled the roads with his Model T. But to witness the wanton hurt and pain of World War One brought their spirits down, big-time, and then to see the Bolshevik Revolution was further depressing for them.

The invention of Television had people excited and optimistic until World War Two came along with only a few nations on Earth escaping the bloody carnage.

The Post War World spawned treaties, conventions and organisations that promised much but delivered little, leaving most countries on the planet to wallow in the corrupt cesspits they'd emerged from with similar unprincipled and fraudulent leaders as before. The exemplar on the screen depicted the assassination in Nineteen Sixty Three of the Thirty-fifth American President by the Thirty-sixth.

For the next forty plus years the ensuing technological and social changes on earth did little to promote peace or goodwill but in fact added to the rotten quagmire and gave an uncivilised horde new ways to terrorise and expedite an evil ideology.

Then a full screen view of a rotating Earth appeared and the guys wondered at the switch and it was only when Adam detected Johnny leaning forward and stare intently at the screen did he also see the little black minute snake-like shadows waggle over a vast number of countries but the main concentration was in the parched and the gerontogeous regions of the world although the wriggling black micro blots could be seen infiltrating civilised, sophisticated areas of the planet. Then on a date between the first quarter and the middle of the Twenty-first century *"Mundus Bellum III"* flashed across the panel and the little black snake-like specks scuttled eastwards in their multitudes where suddenly a huge, blindingly bright orange flash filled the screen. But when the images returned, in the Middle East and Asia, major states and especially the desert lands were now boiling and bubbling like a seething tide of molten glass. The cataclysmic immolation was an absolute holocaust where, in a nano-second, more than one fifth of the Earth's population had been totally obliterated and the dark snake-like dots had vanished completely from the globe.

The apocalyptic revelation was still deeply imbedded in their thoughts when the world vision changed again and now on the screen they surveyed sylvan landscapes they'd recently become reacquainted with as they realised that they were looking at present day Sitantal.

They saw the Consul Primus and his elder son on horseback in a pretty town somewhere and the next picture on the screen almost caused Johnny to groan aloud when he recognised Livia in combat uniform astride a fine bay horse but before he had time to do a double take on the beautiful girl he and Adam were confronted with the dead body of their one-time adversary Commander Otho outside a burning building. They then saw Aprilis weeping as she clutched the battered volume *Promptorium parvulorum* in what appeared to be a fast moving carriage where an iron shackle and chain had been attached to her ankle but before the guys could refocus on the surreal images they'd disappeared from the screen and it took them several minutes to figure that the action they'd just seen was possibly contemporaneous and actually occurring in real life, or at least very recently. Johnny and Adam sprung from their seats just as Zeo dashed from his viewing area to join them. He was about to cry out to his friends to come see what was on his screen but they were already hurrying across the crystal floor to join him. When he saw the look of concern on their faces somehow he guessed they'd just seen the same scenes as him but before they had a chance to exchange a word their eyes were drawn back to the overhead valance where the floating coloured beams swirled and merged again and formed the words "ERIMUS VOBIS!" on both diaphanous backdrops. Zeo didn't have time to translate the Latin when the words "WE WILL BE WITH YOU!" appeared in English directly below and caused all three onlookers to gape in total astonishment. It was truly an incontrovertible moment of truth for both Adam and Johnny to see this message and to realise that it was addressed personally to them.

Zeo was the first to recover from the surprise and whispered that they must leave right away and added that he believed their visit to the Temple of the Gods had now ended.

They moved behind the reredos and quickly changed back into their S.W.A.T. clothing in silence and with a final glance at the super-magnificent interior the three visitors walked through the now wide open doors and into the turquoise eventide.

They'd experienced spells of excitement, enlightenment, euphoria and awe but there'd been several segments which had shocked and alarmed them acutely and had forced them to ruminate more than they'd wanted, but now as they exited the Temple of the Gods all that Adam and Johnny could think about was the disturbing image of the chained Aprilis and they believed that Zeo's mother was in great danger from the despot 'Pravus' Sorus. And they were sure that there was no time to lose.

CHAPTER THIRTY-TWO

Puto Pollux paced back and forth mumbling to himself as he repeatedly scanned the message from his leader and idol. He'd never ever queried an order from his leader in the past, but this was peculiar and what his hero had instructed was confusing him, big time. As far as he was concerned it lacked specifics and was devoid of clarity too, and he really liked clarity.

The Deputy Governor of *Occidens* had spent the last couple of weeks criss-crossing the province going to numerous towns and villages recruiting, conscripting, coercing and bribing rookies into his force and after he'd procured them he'd inducted them into intensive combat training from early morning till late at night by using all the bullying and pressure that he could conjure up. Not only were the men exhausted but so too was he and already he reckoned he'd shed at least *libra triginta* through hurried and missed meals and along with this supreme sacrifice there was the inordinate amount of agonising time he'd spent on horseback daily. There had been consequences and they had impacted on his belly. And to highlight the shrinkage of his bulging gut he'd noticed when he was dressing that morning that he'd been able to see both sets of toes at the same time when he stood upright, a feat which had been impossible for years. He'd been tickled pink to see his lower digits again from this perspective and had hailed them with a chirpy *"Salve!"*

But the new directive from Sorus though bereft of clarity and background detail was unequivocal in one regard; in forty-eight hours from now he and all his available men, which was just short of a *dimidius* legion, must march north from Vili City up through *Occidens* for one day and overnight they must swing due east into northern *Medius* with a closed coach and four. During the daylight hours they were to wait at upper *Medius Minor* until a second messenger would give him the final details of the plan Sorus had contrived which had to be acted upon without delay on that precise night. He and his troops must be in place and ready to move instantly when the second order came through and the men must be rested, sober and ready for action.

The Deputy Governor was perplexed with the message from Sorus and wondered what was behind all the cloak-and-dagger stuff his leader was planning but nonetheless he'd be prepared.

*

The plump little housekeeper had been wakened by the trumpet call close to the Consul Primus's villa and though she was still groggy she realised it was the military's *classicum* alert for clear and present danger.

She quickly stepped from the divan and slipped on her robe and took one of the night lights spaced out along the long corridor and hurried as fast as she could to the apartment of the Consul's wife.

As she neared the chambers she heard the sound of breaking glass, clashing steel and raised aggressive voices within the lower house and she rushed into her mistress's bedroom without any polite preliminaries. She closed the door firmly behind her and slid an ornamental bureau up against it and only then did she pause as she sucked in a lungful of oxygen.

The Consul's wife was rendered speechless with fright and sat upright and peered towards the night light but before she had time to enquire what had happened Porcia told her to rise and dress at once because she believed that the house was under attack.

As Aprilis rose from her *lectus* and donned her robe heavy footfall approached the room and the sturdy ornate door burst open and smashed against the bureau behind it and sent it tumbling to the floor with a splintering crash. She grasped the hide bound *Promptorium parvulorum* tome from the tiny table as a means of defence when four heavily armed *custodis* sprung forward and roughly gripped the two trembling women now clinging to each other in fear as Puto Pollux stood out on the gallery and viewed the abduction with a deadpan stare at the captives. Aprilis still gripped the book as she and Porcia were rushed from the room and along the corridor and then down to the front portal where here they passed the bodies of several dead and injured soldiers sprawled in the foyer and on the outside there was more carnage on the blood smeared front steps.

Porcia gasped and cried out when she saw that one of the bodies inside the portico was Commander Otho.

The women were shackled and bundled into a four-horse drawn closed carriage which waited in the middle of the avenue where it was protected by a *contubernium* escort of ten mounted *custodis*. Five saddled horses were alongside the coach and on hold for Deputy Governor Pollux and his four henchmen.

Less than one minute later the abductors turned the corner at the end of the avenue and sped south as flames swept through the Consul's villa.

The entire operation had been executed in less than fifteen minutes and without a word being exchanged by anybody during the enterprise.

The flames and billowing sparks from countless other burning buildings lighted the ancient skyline of Esta City and Puto Pollux felt that he'd succeeded in delivering a valuable prize into the hands of his leader and a deeply wounding blow against those who schemed to overthrow his hero and it had been achieved with one strike.

When the courier had handed the sealed roll to him earlier at *Medius Minor* he'd torn it open impatiently. Having waited almost twenty-four hours to find out what Sorus wanted of him had been the most frustrating time he'd ever passed. When he'd read the leaders proposals he'd been speechless for the best part of five minutes as the daring plan registered fully with him. It was nothing short of a brainwave he believed. But there was one thing in the message he was less than happy with and that was his destination when they'd completed the mission successfully, in fact he'd rather spend a month in the *Tertius* region of *Extremus* if he had a choice but Sorus was his master, and when all was said and done he was his chief facilitator. He gazed momentarily at the old key enclosed with the note before slipping it into his pocket. Five hours later when they were almost sixty miles from Esta City, Pollux called a halt to the overland dash at a roadside staging post where he commandeered four rooms in the *Caupona* in the name of Consul Sorus.

The two frightened prisoners were bundled from the carriage and locked inside a ground floor room and though it wasn't yet dawn the Deputy Governor compelled the owner to provide a freshly prepared meal for him and his *Optio* and captain with food befitting a triumphal celebration. As he waited for the feast he dispatched a messenger to Consul Sorus with the news that the mission had been successful and that the catch was in the net.

In the late afternoon on the next day the horsemen and carriage laboured up the zigzag avenue to the hilltop and eventually came to a standstill beside the crumbling steps leading to the entrance of the decrepit building. From the extremely high-ground elevation Puto Pollux could see the sprawling metropolis less than a mile away to the south. *Urbis Capitolium* was beginning to sparkle as the city's *Lanterna Illuminas* lit up street after street and he wished he was down there right now rather than up here but his leader had specifically instructed that he and his force guard the valuable prisoner night and day.

As soon as Aprilis stepped from the carriage and looked at the ruin of the forbidding tower her heart sank some more. She heard the stifled groan of fear from her companion who was looking at the enormous stone built mass for the very first time in her life. But the Consul's wife had seen the Arx from a safe distance many times in the past and was aware that the citadel had been declared unsafe by Zeor's great-grandfather more than a hundred and forty years ago when dry-rot was discovered together with a colony of *Uni-corniger perforo-vespertilio* on the uppermost floors but she didn't share the grim news of the wood rot or the bats with her trembling companion. Since then its doors had remained sealed and a fifty foot radius barrier had been constructed on the surrounding site to keep picnickers and strollers from the dangerous ruin. She was bemused as to why they were here but then the thought hit her instantly; surely Pollux wasn't thinking of putting them in such a death trap?

But he was and he did, or rather he got his *Optio* and captain to do it.

The two prisoners were ushered down the rickety flight of steps into the dank dungeons of the Arx. All around them they heard the agonising grind of scraping masonry and tortured timber intermix with the shuffling sounds of agitated bats in the murky shadows.

Both women sat side by side on the thin *stragulum* on the floor beside the lantern where their shadows loomed large on the graffiti daubed walls of the cell. The plump little housekeeper had pleaded with their gaolers to fetch them another blanket but they'd curtly replied that there was only the one available and that was that.

Before the guards departed they'd warned them not to leave the room if they wanted to stay alive, that the rest of the place was on the verge of collapse and that they were in the safest part of the building though there were no actual guarantees that it wouldn't crash in on them. For good measure they told the trembling wide eyed pair that there was just the one stairway to the dungeon which they'd just used on the way down and it was the only way to reach the solitary entrance to the tower which would be locked and guarded day and night.

They'd concluded that each of them would be given one bowl of *pulticula* and a jug of water daily. The *lanterna* would be refilled when needed and they shouldn't ask for anything else but be very thankful that the Deputy Governor had allowed the removal of their leg irons.

When the captors had finished outlining the do's and don'ts they left the dungeon quickly and they didn't look back.

The iron-clad door which was once an obstacle to freedom from their cell was no longer fit for purpose as it hung uselessly from its rusted hinges. Aprilis stood and peered down the dark narrow corridor leading to what she guessed were more cells. Porcia joined her and together they toured and scanned the writings on the wall which appeared to have been written by someone centuries ago when they'd used an old fashioned lexicon which was no longer in use. The fading graffiti depicted the usual flippant remarks; *so* and *so was here* but there were others that were derogatory such as; *Marcus est asinus*; Marcus is an ass, and *Adipem Marcus est porco piaculo*; Fat Marcus is a piglet. Then, *Marcus mox moritur!* Marcus will die soon!

They discontinued reading the unflattering memoirs of the previous occupants when they noticed another remark about this fellow Marcus, a person who appeared to have had few friends inside the place, when they partially read; *Marcus porci sunt! Tua tam obesa mater est...* Marcus you are a pig! Your big fat mother is a...

They immediately averted their eyes and returned to the blanket and embraced. They wept silently until exhaustion overcame them when they sank onto the thin cover and slept side by side.

CHAPTER THIRTY-THREE

For almost two miles the scout had tailed the large group of heavily armed and unruly riders as they galloped south and it was only when they'd halted at a small hamlet some eight miles from Abdo that she closed in on the gang. When she heard them demand food and wine of the frightened residents or they'd take any valuables they possessed she knew for sure that they weren't regular army but a bunch of thieves and criminals on the make. Her intuition that they might be the lawless Death Squad aka *"Removal Men"* was quickly proven true when she heard the leader, a thickset and ignorant looking brute, brag who they were and then boast that they worked directly for the new Consul Primus, Sorus. And if anyone in the hamlet had any doubt in the veracity of their credentials they were very quickly jettisoned when they witnessed the ransacking and demolition of their little village temple as they waited to be served.

She sneaked closer to the loudest faction until she could hear their raucous exchanges where she learned that their mission was to kill or capture Zeo and the others at the Temple of the Gods. Having heard enough the scout quickly sidled back into the laneways and left the village and raced south to inform her General.

Virago took up position where the road dipped and dissected the woods beside a pleasant rippling rivulet three miles north of Abdo. There were no banners or insignia raised to flutter in the early afternoon breeze nor bugle sounds to interrupt the birdsong in the trees. General Electra had told her troop that she would signal silently when it was time to attack but after that they could make whatever noise they wanted to but preferably they should shriek and screech which might unnerve and distract the enemy.

In tandem the entire troop donned helmets and withdrew swords and waited for the Death Squad to approach. Barely twenty minutes had passed when the approaching discordant sound of hoofbeats and ribaldry shattered the tranquillity of the verdant woodlands as the would-be killers of Zeo and his friends rode down into the peaceful hollow which General Electra had specifically selected as the ideal location to launch an ambush. Though head for head, her opponents outnumbered her regiment by at least thirty cavalry she was supremely confident in her female warriors and she'd enjoined them that they mustn't show fear no matter how thuggish or brutish their opponent appeared to be.

On the General's signal her soldiers charged downhill from all sides, from the north and south ends of the road and from the tree lined slopes on each side of the track. In the initial surprise and shock stage of the fringe attack on Cazo's men they were hacked down from their mounts by the swarm of screaming female soldiers before they were fully aware what was happening. The tumultuous clamour merged with the cries from the baying, neighing horses together with the bewailing panic stricken men where it ripped through the air and tortured the eardrums of all who were there. Birds and wildlife scattered from the scene in their droves but the so-called *"Removal Men"* had nowhere to remove to or escape from the deadly trap. Cazo raged and drove his horse deeper into the middle of his struggling men urging them to, *Kill! Kill!* But the complete and utter pandemonium engulfing his squad made it near impossible. Dead and injured horses and mortally wounded men and women soon littered the confined space and prevented a sustained counterattack or even offer the besieged men a way out of the cramped internecine bloodbath.

When Suga Cazo spotted the rider on the edge of the conflict who he perceived to be in command of the attacking force he spurred his steed furiously towards the mounted General who was facing away from him. He sent his men sprawling as he charged through their ranks but the momentum of the animals' lunge forward was beyond his control and such was the sheer fury and force behind the rush that his terrified horse collided heavily onto the rump of the General's mount and sent her flying headlong from the saddle to the ground. The impact of the fall left her injured and stunned and as she lay sprawled out in pain at the edge of the road Commander Cazo leapt from his mount and switched his sword for his dagger and bent forward to render the coup de grâce. But mere seconds before this happened Livia had spotted the pending danger to her leader from six yards away where she'd instantly dismounted and had readied her crossbow as she prayed to the Gods that her aim would be true.

She cheered as the quarrel sunk deeply into Cazo's neck where he slumped lifeless on top of his quarry but she wasn't the only one to witness the dispatch of the Commander of the Death Squad; several of her colleagues and a number of the Cazo's team observed the act and the causal effect on *Virago's* opponents morale was utterly devastating and all those men who'd seen their leader die tried again to find a gap in the tightening *Virago* vice.

Before the ambush on 'Pravus' Sorus's Death Squad General Electra had issued orders that no prisoners would be taken or clemency shown to these criminals and that is precisely how the endgame concluded and the babbling, bubbling brook which meandered through the sunken hollow was now running red with blood.

The *bucinator* used her bugle to summon the *capsarior;* medical orderlies, and the stationary wagons where they'd waited further back in the thick woodlands during the course of the battle to approach the bloody scene as the uninjured *Virago* troops searched the carnage for fallen comrades. Though General Electra was in obvious agony with what she suspected was a fractured or dislocated *clavicula* she sobbed and cried copious tears as she recognised each and every woman who'd died for their beloved Sitantal, including the beautiful and brave Camilla.

While the bodies of her compatriots were being placed on board the wagons, General Electra had sent to Abdo for every able-bodied man to attend the battle ground to collect and cremate the corpses of the Death Squad out of view in the adjoining woods. The *Virago* cremation pyre would be arranged close to Abdo and well away from this foul, contaminated site she'd declared.

Abdo's tavern keeper's wife and their teenage daughter had transformed the little inn into a field hospital to treat and care for the injured cavalry. Though her husband, the village *praesum* was deeply saddened by the loss of so many young women he and everyone there were delighted that Suga Cazo and his criminal gang had been exterminated and would never terrorise Abdo or anywhere else ever again. He'd informed General Electra while she was having a shoulder sling fitted by the medical orderly that there'd be no charge by him or the other villagers whilst she and her colleagues recuperated from their injuries, that everything they needed would be *gratis*, courtesy of the little village. The generous offer was genuine, gracious and heartfelt for the sacrifice *Virago* had paid to rid the country of the godless terrorists but the inn keeper and the adult villagers also realised that their little place in the middle of nowhere might now become famous and perhaps destined for the big league as far as tourism was concerned when Sitantal was at peace again.

The General tried her best to console Livia on the death of her best friend who was also her eldest brother's fiancée but she'd found it to be a near impossible task and no matter what she said it brought no comfort to the wretched heartbroken girl. Even when she informed her that she'd been promoted to the rank of *Optio* in the *Virago* corps and would be recommended for the Emblem of Merit it had no consoling effect. The General had thought it best not to mention then that the previous *Optio* had died in the hollow, a detail which could be rectified at another time in the future.

CHAPTER THIRTY-FOUR

A little after dawn on the fourth day since his colleagues had gone to the Temple of the Gods Euander climbed to the vantage point to check if the cavalrywomen would return to search the area again. And after waiting in vain for more than an hour he was convinced they'd given up. Part of him was disappointed at the no-show inasmuch that when they'd been nearby he'd begun to enjoy the hide and seek exercise but there was also another reason for his downer and that was the solitude and the aloneness which was beginning to get to him and the presence of a stranger, just another human being close by had been something to look forward to in the circumstances. In his hideaway he'd spent hours whispering to Candeo and Friday and occasionally they'd stirred and at times had even twitched their ears or wagged tails as if they'd understood what he'd been saying but that was all he got from them. There had been no rejoinders nor had he expected any.

He returned to the cave and brewed his

second coffee of the morning but before long he became restless and unsettled again and he saddled Candeo and rode west with Friday bounding alongside. He stayed well away from the more frequently used lanes and tracks and kept to untended and what looked like remote and isolated areas but just as he turned a bushy blind corner he almost collided with a pretty young girl who'd been holding a flower basket with purple and yellow blooms which she'd dropped in fright. Her collection now lay scattered on the grass.

He reined in Candeo abruptly and leapt to the ground and apologised to the frightened girl and quickly bent and carefully retrieved the stems and placed them in her basket. As he did this he became puzzled as to why she was collecting Arnica and Foxgloves when he'd learned from his parents when he was a child that these plants could be dangerous and he'd been warned not to meddle with them.

Though she still looked shaken by the fright she shyly thanked him but slightly averted her gaze away from his as she spoke. He introduced himself, then Candeo and Friday who seemed delighted to be stroked by the young stranger in the lavender pink robes. Euander reckoned her to be about thirteen or fourteen years old and though he was still slightly unsettled by the unexpected encounter he was curious as to why she was in such a remote place without adult supervision and collecting such hazardous plants, so much so that he asked her directly.

She responded by pointing to several rustic roofs and chimney stacks just visible above the treetops about three hundred yards behind him. She revealed that the settlement was Abdo village and that it was her home and that her name was Isselle. Defensibly and rather pertly she announced that she lived at the village Inn with her parents and younger brother and came here regularly to gather herbs and plants for her mother and that she knew how to handle them safely. She was collecting these particular plants to make a 5special unguent for a very important lady General who'd been thrown from her horse in battle only yesterday and who was still in great pain.

Though Euander was a bit rattled to discover that he'd come so close to this village without being aware of it until now the latter part of the young girl's motive for being here rid him of those thoughts and moved his interests in a different direction and a half hour later and before he bade the now chatty Isselle *"Vale",* he'd elicited all the details about *Virago* and the battle with Suga Cazo and the *"Removal Men"* and also the reason why the cavalrywomen had been dispatched to the Temple of the Gods.

On the ride back to base he diverted and checked his previous hideout again to see if his colleagues had returned from the Temple but he left disappointed and wondered how much longer they'd be away and he vowed to scale the steps on the following morning to make sure that there was nothing amiss further up. Four days in the Temple seemed a very long time to him and he wondered once more why the Gods had insisted Zeo and his companions visit there but there had to have been a good reason to do so whatever it might be he speculated for the umpteenth time.

As Euander sipped the dark brew in the dimness of the cave he mulled over the news that the Consul Primus had despatched the all new female corps *Virago* as an added protection for his son and the *Praecipuus* and by association even for him and to learn that the cavalry corps, though they'd suffered heavy casualties in the battle on the previous afternoon, had nonetheless succeeded in destroying Suga Cazo and the Death Squad.

He now regretted that he'd not made contact with them when they'd been searching near the Temple. Had he been aware who they were then perhaps he might have been able to help them in some way in the ambush on the *"Removal Men"*.

He was so deep in his reveries that the sudden yelp and scramble by the dog caught him off guard as Friday scampered from the cave before he had time to stop him and when he reached the entrance the dog had vanished from sight. He raced back inside and grabbed his sword and helmet and set off to find him and was still at a loss as to what had stirred the animal. But being unsure which way the dog had gone he opted to go north and had only gone a few hundred yards when he saw Friday prancing madly in front of the three returning pilgrims as they headed in his direction.

The four had a quick group embrace though Euander detected a slight edginess as if something was troubling all three and as he led them into the cave he told Zeo why he'd relocated from the mount and rather breathlessly said that he had something important to tell them while he prepared coffee.

Zeo retorted that there were more urgent things to do right now and whatever he had to say could wait until later.

Euander frowned and was taken aback by the tetchy disregard of what he'd thought was something that they'd all want to know about and he was on the point of returning the Moka pot and the coffee to the holdall when Adam sensed the tension and asked Zeo what was bothering Euander.

Zeo turned impatiently to the youth and irritably enquired what was so important that they needed to know right now but his countryman glared back defiantly and related what Isselle had told him earlier and without hesitating Zeo crossed the floor and embraced him and apologised for the slight and explained that his mind was in turmoil since he'd learned that his mother had been taken captive and could barely think straight anymore.

Zeo told the others about the complete rout and defeat of the Death Squad by a regiment of cavalrywomen sent by his father to protect them while they were at the Temple but that quite a few of the all female troop had died in the battle.

Johnny interjected 'Didn't you say that Livia had joined your father's army and that you'd also seen her in uniform just like we did on the screen in the Temple? Could she be in this *Virago* unit?'

The last question hit Zeo like an uppercut and he recoiled in alarm and when Adam saw this he signalled to Euander to continue with the coffee, telling them that this news had to be assessed properly and that they needed to get all the facts before leaving the area and though it was vital that they didn't waste precious time they'd have to remain overnight.

Zeo had Euander relate all he knew about the battle between *Virago* and the *"Removal Men"* and the female General. He ended by telling him that Electra had been injured during the bloody clash with Cazo and was regarded as a heroine by the people of Abdo.

As the two compatriots talked Johnny and Adam prepared a quick meal from the dried rations and it was only when they smelt the spicy food did they truly realise how hungry they were. Johnny grinned and whispered to Adam 'This is a bit like slumming mate, eh? Just think about it, Adam, only a few days ago we were supping *ambrosia* with the Gods!'

'I'm still trying to get my head around the fact that we were so long in the Temple. We must have spent quite a few days in the Prehistory period alone with the rest of the time viewing the recorded history on the screens I reckon. I didn't get a chance to tell you this before but as soon as we'd gone back to the beginning of everything at the edge of space I checked my watch and time had stopped but the seconds counter had continued to rotate as per normal. It was only when we exited the Temple that my watch began displaying real time again. Oh! And another thing, the date indicator had advanced forward when we came outside. Is that weird or what, Johnny?'

Euander had been busy since before daylight and had the horses including the drays and combo wagon tethered as near as he could get to the cave where they loaded the equipment and supplies and in less than a half hour they passed through the colonnaded viewing area as they rode north-west to Abdo.

The female mounted watch posted on the outskirts of Abdo village brandished unsheathed upright swords and bade the approaching riders to halt. Zeo quickly told Euander to mount Candeo and ride forward without his weapons and identify himself and his party as friends and to seek permission to speak with General Electra and the village *praesum*.

He explained to Adam and Johnny that he didn't want to cause alarm in the village, that Abdo would be on a knife-edge following the recent events and the S.W.A.T uniforms might worry them even more, while not forgetting that there was bound to be quite a few battle hardened cavalrywomen billeted close to the village.

When General Electra arrived with the *praesum* she supported her left arm in a sling and it was obvious that she and the village chief had been caught unawares by the early morning visitors and both seemed anxious and wary when the three horsemen dismounted and approached.

Zeo saluted and greeted them in the name of his father Zeor, Consul Primus *Hereditarius* and told them that he was his younger son Zeo and his two companions were *Praecipuum* of Sitantal. He mentioned that they'd recently attended the Temple of the Gods and then introduced Euander on the white colt as their *Optio*.

Though General Electra endured a stabbing pain in her shoulder and at times felt dizzy and nauseous she was determined to muster every ounce of grit and resolve to meet her champion face to face without looking weak. She held onto her dignity and saluted him smartly in return and bowed deeply to both Adam and Johnny who each returned a courtesy bow. The *praesum,* who was excited and awed much more than he'd freely admit, briskly bowed separately to all three and turned to do the same with Euander but managed to curtail his enthusiasm at the last second.

Zeo acclaimed the General on her victory over the usurper's Death Squad but stressed that he regretted to hear of the heavy losses her troop had incurred. His heart pounded and his lips were dry when he asked if his sister Livia served in her unit and if so, could he meet with her?

His friends were well aware of how Zeo had walked the floor in the cave for most of the previous night where he'd fretted for his mother as he traversed one way and then agonised over his sister on the return route, nonstop.

General Electra allowed a few seconds to pass before she replied that Livia was here but that she was much traumatised on the death of her friend Camilla.

Zeo gasped loudly not only with joy that Livia was safe but in sorrow also to hear that Camilla had died which caused his emotions to run helter-skelter inside his brain.

He couldn't celebrate nor could he commiserate; in an instant his spirits had soared and then they'd crashed.

When Johnny and Adam heard the name Camilla and the grave word *mortem* so closely linked together they didn't have to be told that she was dead.

The two inhaled and exhaled noisily as both recalled the beautiful young lady in black whom they'd fantasized about a few months ago on the eventful journey from the Erebus settlement to Tabo City and they remembered being told she was the sister of Zeo's friend Marius. The fantasy only ended when they'd learned of her betrothal to Zeo's brother but Johnny recalled how gentle she'd been to him when he'd been badly slashed at Tabo City.

The guards stood aside and allowed them to pass

into Abdo where most of the residents had lined the tiny street when they'd heard the news that a son of the ousted Consul Primus together with two *Praecipuum* had arrived in their village. An audible murmur rippled over the confined space when the black-garbed trio dismounted in front of the *taberna* but this soon became a chorus of titters when Isselle dashed from the Inn waving frantically and called out '*Ave*, Euander! *Ave!*' The blushing recipient of the greeting was less excited by the encounter and after a very brief wave he concentrated his efforts on guiding the drays to the water trough on the village green.

Zeo and Livia were reunited in a separate room where they spent a tearful half hour until he called Adam and Johnny to join them.
It wasn't the type of reunion with the girl he'd fallen for that Johnny had envisioned in any of the daydreams he'd had in the past, in fact it was a disaster and he was certain that she'd barely looked at him or Adam either, for that matter, though her eyes were so puffed up and water logged it was hard for him to know for sure. It was only later on when they'd departed Abdo that he'd been able to fully comprehend the trauma she'd suffered in just a few days with the sudden death of her friend and then learning that her mother had been taken captive by the enemy. The news would surely be enough to send anyone into the pits of despair he'd conceded.

Though they were anxious to continue

north General Electra pressed them to have *ientaculum*, the local breakfast, with her and Livia. Together they might agree a common strategy that could be beneficial in defeating 'Pravus' Sorus, she proffered. Zeo accepted the invitation but insisted that Euander be there also, he was an integral part of their team.

Adam and Johnny ate the freshly baked bread amply spread with nutty tasting butter and then tucked into cherry laden pancakes. They washed it all down with a large tankard of sweet *mulsum* while Zeo and the General engaged in urgent discussion beside them occasionally breaking off to get their opinion on a particular point. Johnny tried to give the impression that they had his full attention but he couldn't stop his eyes drifting to the crestfallen figure of Livia on the other side of the table as she nibbled absentmindedly at her food. His frequent casual glances in her direction soon became stares and glares when he noticed that Euander, who was seated next to her, was now offering her little dissected portions of the cherry pancakes which she accepted and ate quite readily. But what made it particularly irksome for him was that every time she'd taken the offering she'd looked directly at the youth and had whispered "*Gratias*" with a gentle smile.

Zeo had agreed with the General to provide two of her best people, a courier to take a message from him to his father in *Oriens* and a scout to covertly accompany them wherever they went for as long as needed but who would remain *sine nomine et obscuro*, anonymous and obscure, to them to protect her cover. She would also act as a runner between *Virago* and their group if required. And if the search for his mother brought them to the Capitol she had contacts there and could be invaluable in getting information on his mother's location. They'd only come in contact with her on a need-to basis with Euander the conduit between them. General Electra had convinced Zeo to leave the combo wagon in Abdo until they actually required them, food and supplies for the animals could be obtained en route which would allow them to move at speed with Euander on horseback and off-road where necessary. It was also agreed that Friday should remain at the inn.

The General expected that most of her unit would be battle-ready within a week and would join them if they needed them otherwise *Virago* would join the Consul's campaign in *Oriens.*

Euander could barely wait to ride his white colt alongside his comrades though he secretly wished he was dressed just like them, not realising that it was for that precise reason he'd been picked as the go-between them and the covert scout.

The four horsemen took leave of the General, the *praesum* and Livia just after nine o'clock and rode north to the border between *Australis* and *Medius*. The shadowing scout was nowhere to be seen but they were confident that she was already at work.

CHAPTER THIRTY-FIVE

'Pravus' Sorus leapt from his chair and thumped the air. Yes! At long last he had positive news to bring his supporters rather than the litany of dire problems he'd tried to disguise and brush aside to obscure the true position for the past three or four months. He now had Aprilis in a place where anyone attempting to free her would probably kill themselves in the process and her as well.

Without having being told in the note from Pollux how he'd executed the incarceration of the prisoner in the dungeons he'd bet his last *cudo* that his Deputy Governor hadn't put a foot inside the building but had made others take the risk in the hazardous ruin, but he didn't care and chuckled loudly.

Not only had he got her but if everything went according to plan he hoped to hear soon that Suga Cazo had rid him of the little *merda* Zeo and his two cronies at the Temple of the Gods and also the bunch of silly women who'd been sent there to protect the brat.

He sniggered even more as he swaggered around the room and thought of the effect the news would have on the ousted Zeor and his supporters and guessed that they'd be gutted and totally demoralised and he wouldn't be a bit surprised if they came begging to his door for mercy but they'd be sorely disappointed if they did, he vowed. They'd find out then that compassion wasn't his strongest attribute, that is, if they hadn't already figured that out.

He left the hilltop building with a spring to his step and walked briskly to the forum where he remained quite cheerfully for several hours and fobbed off any searching questions and sneered openly at any murmurs of doubt or discontent from the benches. Though he'd prorogued the senate of its powers and now ruled by executive orders, his supporters continued to use the chamber as a meeting place to update events and socialise. Just after midday he returned to the mansion in an even better mood than before where he looked forward to having a substantial *prandium* with a vintage red wine.

The normally gruff and unsmiling leader was extra pleasant to the people he met en route; even those who he believed opposed and detested him at heart.

He waylaid an aide in the lobby and ordered his favourite dish be brought to him and even said '*Gratias!*' to the youth as he sped off to the kitchens. Sorus hummed as he climbed the broad stairs sprightly and then gave his sentinel *facto-*

tum a cordial smile at the door to his grand office where a sealed scroll had been placed on his ornate desk which he nonchalantly unrolled as he sat down.

The agonised roar sounded like a lanced bull and filled the large chamber and oscillated further and reached quite a few other rooms normally out of earshot. The new pageboy peeked from the anteroom as did the *factotum* at the main door.
Sorus blared again but this time it seemed to be even louder as he smoothed out and reread the creased parchment.
He wanted to hurt someone right there and then.
It was the worst news he'd received so far and was totally incomprehensible and it just didn't make sense to him at all. He glared at the report again to be sure his eyes hadn't played tricks with his brain but his retinas and optical nerves had functioned properly and the message was real, very real;
Suga Cazo and all one hundred and seventy hard men in his Death Squad had been totally annihilated by a bunch of wannabe female recruits barely out of training; novices in fact.
It was embarrassing just to think about the debacle and he could see no way how he'd be able to whitewash over this abysmal defeat to those in the forum, even knowing that most of them were staunch supporters of his. And when they'd learn that the *irrumator* Zeo had escaped unscathed from the *Vipera Dominam* and had managed to enter the Temple of the Gods and then exit the

site unhindered they were bound to be sceptical of his promise that things would only get better and were under control. But when they'd hear that Cazo and his *'Removal Men'* hadn't even managed to reach the Temple before they'd been wiped out by a lesser number of an all women cavalry unit and that Zeo and his companions were now heading this way he wouldn't be at all surprised if some of them would think that the *bufo* must have the Gods on his side and therefore the coup was doomed to failure leaving all of them in fear for their lives. He could envisage quite a few of them citing a personal crisis which needed them to vacate the Capitol for their homes in the country but he'd have none of it. No way!

As his temper and his blood pressure fractionally stabilised he began to mull over the only piece of information that might restore some balance in the ongoing erosion of his hold on power and that was that the source of most of his problems was now coming this way. As he dwelled further on this and wondered what the mangy rat was up to when he'd assumed that he'd join up with his father in *Oriens* if he managed to escape the traps he'd laid. Surely he couldn't know at this stage that his mother was now a prisoner near here. There just wasn't a way where a spy could have passed the news of his mother's capture before even he knew in the Capitol. He again checked the dispatch and saw that it had been written and sent on the previous evening which could mean that the brat might know that his mother had been taken captive before Pollux had informed him, but how could that be possible he asked himself again and again.

He scribbled a note and ordered the nervous *factotum* to despatch it immediately to Puto Pollux at the Arx.

CHAPTER THIRTY-SIX

The four cantered across country rarely using the intersecting roads or lanes except when they needed to reach the other side of a deep river or canal. Only a few startled farmers and workers in the many vineyards and fruit orchards they traversed witnessed them race past. By mid day they'd crossed the border into *Medius* and continued north-west for a further hour where they had their first real break since leaving Abdo. Though Adam and Johnny would have preferred to spend some time in the towns and villages they'd avoided they were continually rewarded nonetheless with the eye catching vistas of the undulating blooming countryside around them and their olfactory senses were constantly enriched with new and exotic fragrances as they'd passed from one scenic idyll into another.

Complimenting his role as the trio's *Optio* and without been asked, Euander had taken on the role of cook and now brewed the coffee expertly each time they rested to water their mounts. And before dusk as the others searched for a secluded place for the night he'd scoured the surrounding meadows armed with his *Dirigo* and *iaculum* and very shortly returned with a large plump rabbit which he skilfully skinned, dressed and spit roasted as the others waited impatiently for the savoury unexpected feast in the woods.

He wore night visions as he paced back and forth on first watch around the canvas lean-to makeshift tent where his companions slept. He was deep in thought when the pebble glanced off his arm and startled him but instantly he went into defensive mode and brandished his sword as his gaze swept the area but he saw nothing. Then the stillness of the night was disturbed by the faintest whisper *"Psst! Euander"*. The hushed call came from a thick clump of brush about twenty feet from the camp and instantly he knew that the tone was feminine and quickly moved to the source.

The whisperer remained unseen when the night sights failed to penetrate the dense shrub where she told him that Sorus had mounted a continuous day and night watch on almost every road, tract, river and canal leading north to the Capitol. There were groups of mounted guards patrolling constantly overland on the lookout for them with everyone anxious to collect the very substantial reward posted for information leading to their location and capture. She stressed that it was imperative that they trust no one from here on in.

She was unable to tell him where Aprilis was being held captive but she hoped that when she'd reach the Capitol in the morning that might change. She told him that he'd find a white lace *sudarium* attached to the bush which he should attach to the pommel of his sword if they needed her assistance at any time in the future.

As soon as she'd relayed this message she disappeared into the night, leaving only the delicate trace of the floral perfume on the handkerchief to indicate that she'd ever been there.

The encounter with the shadowy scout had excited him. Even with the night visions he'd been unable to get the slightest glimpse of the person behind the voice behind the bush and he'd been so absorbed in what she'd told him he'd barely responded and now that she was gone he could think of lots of things he could have said.

    For most of the second day's journey across open country they split up and maintained a wide distance apart giving them a broader panoramic view to the right and left which also made an enemy ambush more difficult to mount they reckoned. They kept to the remotest, higher countryside as they moved north to *Urbis Capitolium* and paused on every hilltop to view and scan the landscape below. Though the repeated halts were time consuming they still managed to cover half the distance to the Capitol where they found a secluded spot to spend the second night in the open countryside.

Euander mounted first watch as he'd done previously but the inconspicuous scout failed to make contact with him or the others during the night.
After daybreak the four continued across country separately and on two occasions had to take evasive action to avoid contact with enemy units during the early morning, the first being when at least two *turmae* of mounted troop cantered south on one of the many narrow roads. The other was when they spotted a *custodis* camp on the outskirts of a small village where armed men were posted on both road bridges straddling a canal confluence. Several coaches and boats were being searched as they watched.
They altered course and gave the area a wide berth and steered further west. Late in the evening they took sanctuary deep in one of the larger rolling forests less than eight miles west of *Urbis Capitolium*.

The shadowing scout brought the news that Zeo's mother and her housekeeper were being held in the Arx, a ruinous tower north east of the Capitol, which was now heavily guarded day and night under the personal supervision of Puto Pollux. She gave him the address of a safe house in the suburbs of the city less than a mile from the citadel where the owner would accommodate them and their mounts but it was important to remember that there was constant troop movement in the area.
The scout departed as stealthily as she'd arrived and within fifteen minutes of being given the news where Aprilis was being held captive all four

had decamped from the forest.

Zeo had recognised the address as being the equestrian riding hall where he and his siblings had trained to ride at an early age. He led the way cautiously down to the flat lands below. They steered east across country until they came to a little used track and were able to increase the pace and circled round the western boundary of the metropolis.

Three hours into the night trek they reached the main north-south arterial road leading to the Capitol where it passed through dense coniferous woodland. They were about to bypass the brightly lit turnpike at the city's boundary line when Adam bade them halt and take cover when he saw a two horse coach bearing south with its mirrored lanterns quivering as it sped across the paved surface. They held back behind the inactive toll booth at the tree line and observed the handler alight and move to the coach window which opened noisily as he approached. An antsy hand shot out and thrust some coins to the driver before the window was slammed shut. Zeo whispered to Adam and Johnny that the coachman appeared to be more trustworthy than his passenger. They watched as the man ambled nonchalantly to the night-time honesty box attached to the long balanced cantilever barrier which spanned the broad roadway.

All four horsemen refocused their gaze when the coach window was loudly wrenched open again as a middle-aged man called irritably on the driver to *'Festinare!'*

Zeo frowned and exclaimed in shock *'Et non credidistis ei!* He gasped 'I don't believe it!' and spurred his mount across the low wall between the darkened building and the road and sprung from the saddle alongside the coach. The visibly alarmed passenger saw him coming and quickly withdrew his head and slammed the window shut again.

Zeo's three companions raced to join him on the thoroughfare where Euander reined in his colt and prevented the startled driver from returning to the coach.

Though neither Johnny nor Adam fully understood what was happening they knew that Zeo's odd behaviour had something to do with the passenger on board and they quickly dismounted beside their friend and watched as he drummed his sword blade against the thick glass and called out *'Aperire!'*

When the window opened a fraction Zeo spoke to the ashen-faced man cowering inside *'Ai, Gubernator* Castor, *velit exire!'*

The Honorary Governor of *Septentrio* reluctantly followed Zeo's command to exit the coach. He was shaking like a leaf and almost stumbled from the step but when Zeo removed his helmet the abject fear in Castor's demeanour changed to utter horror.

'Appares magna festinatione ad Urbis Capitolium, Gubernator!'

The chilling derision and contempt in Zeo's voice when he remarked that the Governor appeared to be in a great hurry to reach *Urbis Capitolium* solidified the terrified man's worst fears that somehow Aprilis' younger son knew of his involvement in her abduction. But how could that be when he knew for certain that the youth had been several hundred miles away in *Australis* at the time? The vexing question rebounded around his brain cells and he just couldn't think straight anymore but nonetheless, deep within his befuddled cerebrum he reckoned that the game was up for him; it was over, period! He felt he had nothing to lose when he sneered disdainfully and retorted that Zeo was no better than the very people he sought to oust and that he was just as unprincipled as anyone else when he too killed his opponents in cold blood and he was convinced that he'd murdered his brave son, Gaius. The story of him being killed by a dog was utter bilge and bunkum and was calumnious fiction and a blatant cover up, he raged.

Zeo stepped back and challenged *'Proditor! Defendo te!'*

Not only was the Governor taken aback by the challenge, so too were the four observers to the evolving confrontation.

Though Adam or Johnny hadn't understood the extent of the exchange between Zeo and the traitor they did understand the command to Castor to defend himself and neither could believe that Zeo was taking such a risk and giving this opportunity to the man who'd betrayed his mother when they'd have been perfectly happy had he dragged

the creep from the coach and gutted him on the spot.
They immediately closed in on Zeo as he removed his jacket and protested vehemently and told him that he only had to give the word and they'd sort the dirty scumbag out in seconds, no problem! But Zeo raised his free hand and said 'Not only did betray he my mother but his name also is on *Vipera Dominam* list and the promise I made to them must I keep. A better way is this for one whose forbear was a Founding Member of Sitantal and because he the last of that ancestral line is I will their memory not dishonour more than he and his traitorous son already has done. Trust me my friends, fight for his life will he but Castor today will surely die'.
Together Adam and Johnny silently embraced their great friend and stepped back but each of them covertly unclipped a Taser holster flap.

Meanwhile Euander struggled with his emotions and his obligation to remain close to the coachman even though he was sure that the driver had absolutely no intention of becoming involved in the drama a short distance away. He wanted to plead with Zeo and tell him that he'd take his place in this deadly duel so that the mission to free Sitantal wouldn't falter or fail. But he knew that he'd be rebuffed and decided that the best way he could help was to wait and observe and to pray to the Gods.

A huge surge of relief had shot through

Castor's system when the initial shock he'd experienced had eased off and he'd realised that he'd been given an unexpected chance to come out of this alive but it would also give him the added satisfaction in avenging the death of his son. As he reached into the coach for his sword he almost laughed aloud at how easy it had been to get the cocky little rat Zeo to take his bait.

Being a redundant Governor of a defunct province with no official role to play he'd spent all of his leisure time over the years hunting, shooting and fishing but also fencing and practicing the art of swordsmanship and he had no qualms in claiming to be one of the better duellists in the land. And to top it off he must outweigh his opponent by at least thirty pounds and perhaps even more and he knew from past experience that no matter how skilful one was in swordplay that the power behind the strike was an essential ingredient in wearing your adversary down before going in for the kill.

    Daylight was only moments away when Castor turned from the coach and faced Zeo with his unsheathed sword and a derisory smirk on his lips. Immediately and without a preliminary sound or gesture he lunged forward but Zeo nimbly did a *pass back* out of range. The traitor made a diagonal move and swung his blade with a swift downward sweep and Zeo swept upwards to deflect and the weapons made first contact with a sharp ringing and vibrating crash. As Zeo swiftly did a *pass forward* he adroitly flipped his sword to his left hand and attacked from the unexpected angle almost catching his rival off guard. Without pause to his momentum Zeo switched his weapon back and advanced further and then adroitly pivoted to the right of Castor where he launched a flourish of nifty jabs, stabs and slices. Very soon his opponent's smirk waned after a series of *pass back* and *pass forward* actions by Zeo and Castor's initial smug demeanour was now an angry scowl.

Adam and Johnny were rooted to the spot as they watched their friend dance rings around the burly man and as the duel continued the more captivated and engrossed they became, though the butterflies fluttering around in their stomach didn't completely migrate from their innards. The traitor became more frustrated and enraged and had begun to sweat inordinately, so much so, he constantly wiped his brow with his tunic sleeve. His frantic lunges, slices and footwork now verged on the clumsy and predictable and Zeo *parried* them away almost effortlessly and in contrast to his heavier opponent he skipped lightly from *fade* to *empty fade* positions and appeared to have added wings to his springs. At this stage Zeo's pivoting steps forced the Governor to rotate and face every point on the compass continually; giving the spectators the impression that Zeo was now playing around with his foe, almost like a cat with a mouse. Eight minutes into the deadly joust a reckless reverse thrust by Castor left him momentarily exposed and Zeo seized the narrow opening and deftly sprung forward in a *long point* movement and plunged his blade deeply into the traitor's chest.

Before the now recumbent and haemorrhaging Governor took his final breath Zeo dropped to one knee beside him *'Nam mater prodo meam ut Sorus, et ut omissae amator apud Reptus Reptum'*. When Zeo told the mortally wounded man that he died because he'd betrayed his mother to Sorus and the woman he'd enslaved with the herpetologist, his eyes glazed over briefly and then rolled back in their sockets as he expired.

Adam and Johnny rushed forward as Zeo stood up and they did a group embrace for the second time in ten minutes but this time they were smiling and Johnny remarked 'Wow! That was something else Zeo and you don't even have a mark or a scratch to show for it, do you? You're a dark horse, old bean. And that's for sure!'

Though Zeo was confused by what sounded like mixed metaphors to him nevertheless he figured that it was probably complimentary so that was okay. He grinned broadly as he turned and beckoned the edgy coach driver.

When he learned that the coachman had simply been hired to drive the Governor to the Capitol on the day after Esta City had been torched, he directed him to turn round and convey the corpse to the nearest town north of the turnpike but to only reveal Castor's identity if it was absolutely necessary. He permitted him to use whatever valuables or money the Governor had in his possession as remuneration for his time and labour and he passed him a sealed message to forward to the Consul Primus when he reached his home base.

When the four horsemen cleared the thick copse on the other side of the roadway the panoramic views opened up before them and here Zeo pointed to the larger of the rolling hills about two miles further to the north where the grim bulk of the stone citadel domineered the whole of the countryside. On the flatlands below the relic and to its right were the outer suburbs of the sprawling metropolis. They used their binoculars and were able to explore the large encampment spread out all over the hillside below the Arx.

Now that they'd lost the cover of darkness they were constantly forced to stop and take cover from a bevy of *custodis* or supply wagons either coming from or going to the security outpost at the citadel. Almost three hours after the fatal bout beside the turnpike the four horsemen arrived behind the old riding school.

The silvery-haired *Matrona* Minula slowly escorted Zeo to the large indoor equestrian arena several hundred yards from the rear of the extensive villa where she'd resided alone since the death of her husband some years ago and whom she obviously still mourned being totally robed in black and without the faintest trace of colour of any kind to be seen on her austere ensemble. She enquired about the health of his brother and sister but never once mentioned his father or mother or the political upheaval besetting the country or the reason why he needed to covertly use her property. When Zeo opened the broad double doors and entered the building she remained outside but told him that there was abundant hay and straw within should he require it and at the rear of the building there were fresh water filled troughs linked directly to a nearby stream. She pointed to a pair of black-painted carriages, one larger than the other deep within the building and told him to use them if needed. She insisted on returning alone to her home but asked him to deliver the key to her when he no longer needed the facility.

The polite but terse exchange between Zeo and his former riding instructor left him fazed but only for a few moments when he recognised that in these uncertain times only a zealot or the foolhardy would become openly involved politically at such an advanced stage in their life and he believed that the lady was neither of these.

CHAPTER THIRTY-SEVEN

On the morning after the capture of Venura when the Consul and his experts had put in place the team to administer and retain control of the subjugated but still belligerent town they were browsing and reviewing the charts and maps for the next stage in the campaign further south when they were interrupted by the messenger from Abdo.

When the Consul Primus rejoined the group he was ashen faced and beckoned his son to join him away from the assembled officers where he broke the news to him that Camilla had died in a clash with Suga Cazo and his Death Squad and that his mother had been abducted when she'd been betrayed by Castor, the Honorary Governor of *Septentrio*.

The still stunned Consul escorted his traumatised son to his tent and had his aide remain with him while he returned to the waiting team where he informed them what had happened since they'd departed Esta City. He told them of the death of his son's fiancée at the hands of the Death Squad in *Australis* and of the seizure of his wife, done with the complicity of Castor who, they'd remember, had withdrawn from the current campaign at the last minute citing torturous *podagra* in both feet. The appalling and devastating news had come directly from his son Zeo who was now en route to *Medius* to try to discover his mother's whereabouts.

The leader assured the company of advisers and strategists that he was totally confident that Zeo and the two *Praecipuum* were capable of securing his wife's safe release; if there was a way to do it then they would find it he asserted, then adding that his son believed that if the Consul's army became involved at this stage it might place his mother in even greater danger and that he and his friends had a much better chance by operating covertly. Zeo thought it best that the Consul remain in *Oriens* and continue with the campaign but if he needed help to rescue his mother he'd let him know.

The news of the death of Camilla and the betrayal and abduction of Aprilis had caused the jubilant atmosphere in the Consul's team to sink into a sombre mood and had delayed them further as they reassessed and realigned the plans previously drafted. Though he'd thought of sending his older son back to Esta City to apprehend the traitorous Castor and review the situation there he'd decided that in the circumstances it wouldn't be wise and instead dispatched the Governor of *Australis,* General Arrol with a detachment of men to take charge and organise the city's recovery, insisting that they owed it to the people there who'd remained loyal to him and who'd willingly given sanctuary to many of them when they'd needed it after their escape from Tabo prison.

The betrayal by Castor had dismayed and hurt the Consul more than he was prepared to admit to anyone, even to his son Zeor. He remembered being told how his great-grandfather, the then Consul Primus had stood loyally by Castor's great-grandfather the then Governor of *Septentrio* when it had suffered the catastrophic loss of light even though there had been some evidence that he too was involved in the explosive experiments being illegally conducted there. From early childhood everybody in Sitantal learned how their country had been miraculously created by the Gods and they were made aware that the only thing between them and oblivion was the crystalline canopy overhead and for that reason all experiments involving volatile substances was totally forbidden. And anyone who disregarded the warning faced instant retribution. Despite the rumours of complicity in the crime his forbear had promised the exiled and redundant Governor that in time if one of the governing families became extinct or if a governorship became vacant for any other reason, either he or his heirs would secure it. In fact only recently he'd privately pondered the possibility that if the present campaign was successful in removing Maximus from *Oriens*, Castor would be granted the province. He wondered briefly if his betrayal had something to do with the death of his traitorous son Gaius. Perhaps they both had more in common than he'd allowed. He recalled an old proverb; *non longe ab arbore pomum!* The apple doesn't fall far from the tree!

With a shrug he resolved not to dwell on it further but consign the vile episode to history.

The march through *Oriens* continued during the early afternoon and proceeded on the following day where the Consul's advancing army passed through several towns and villages without any resistance. In one of the larger towns the mayor admitted that up to that very morning a large contingent of Governor Maximus' *custodis* had been stationed there for several months but when the news that Aleppo had surrendered to Zeor and hadn't experienced the fate of Venura, the *custodis* had been ordered in no uncertain terms to vacate the town by him and the townsfolk and to go and fight their battles elsewhere.

The town's population wished to save their homes and livelihoods and wanted no part of the 'Pravus' Sorus power seizure. The mayor firmly believed that most people in *Oriens* were totally disillusioned by what had happened to the country since the usurper, with the connivance of their Governor and his daughter, had seized control but they'd been too afraid to say it openly when they knew of some who'd voiced disapproval and had then mysteriously disappeared, especially when the *"Removal Men"* had been in the province.

The Consul was surprised that news of what had occurred at Aleppo and Venura had reached this place especially after they'd imposed a curfew on Venura preventing anyone entering or leaving and as if to emphasise this failing, immediately after the messenger from Abdo had delivered the news of Aprilis' abduction, a runner had arrived from Esta City informing him of the dire events there which had made him wonder how Zeo had known about it so soon afterwards. How he knew of Governor Castor's involvement in the dastardly deed, or for that matter, how he'd known that the messenger from General Electra would find him in *Oriens* baffled him further and he couldn't figure out how his son was aware that he'd launched a campaign in the province even though he was hundreds of miles away at the Temple of the Gods at the time.

He was puzzled some more to learn that word of his army's advance into the province had reached well beyond central *Oriens* and virtually every town and village in their path had shown little defiance or resistance, in fact in most places it was quite the opposite and on the occasions he'd been informed that the local temple had been desecrated he'd secured a solemn commitment that it'd be restored to its previous glory before he'd return in the future.

Less than a week after his forces had swept into Oppida the Consul's colours had been hoisted on civic buildings in every town in the north, east and west *divisus* of the province as the expanding force marched relentlessly south towards Ciro City. His scouts told him of the continual retreat of Maximus loyalists where they constantly clogged the roads further south as they fled from all areas as they fell back to the capital.

On the eighth morning of the campaign in *Oriens* the Consul used the still novel binoculars to gaze from the highest hill at the enemy troop formations defending the handsome city further south in the lowlands. He was impressed with the approach taken by Ballio Maximus to protect Ciro City but he remained confident and resolute that he could resolve the issues before him.

The provincial capital city had been conceived and had evolved in more peaceful times and was without manmade fortifications of any kind. The proudly elegant and orderly urban areas were divided and subdivided by a plethora of streets, avenues, canals, rivers, pools and lakes which not only dissected but virtually surrounded the idyllic and scintillating city. The shimmering waterways were crisscrossed by the most extraordinary assortment of fine arched spans and bridges imaginable. Precision planted borderlines of deciduous and coniferous trees together with shrubs and verdure of every variety and hue thinkable dangled over and softened the sharp edges of the multiple incisions in the lush topography.

On any given afternoon the city's waterways and pools attracted large numbers of young and old alike from every corner of Sitantal. It was a favourite spot for the carefree retired but also for the love-struck romantics and those newlyweds having a good time together before passing from their nonchalance years to the new age of parenthood which would eventually restrict their freedom to *frigus* and relax.

The Consul would agree fulsomely with those who'd say that it was the most tranquil and serene city in the entire federation and if someone was looking for an exemplification of peace and harmony they only had to come here to discover it, he acknowledged.

In his heart he knew he couldn't allow his men to despoil or damage this beautiful jewel.

As he looked southwards on the now inactive capital where nothing moved on the canals, rivers, streets or on the rural roads radiating into the central hub it occurred to him that the tourists must have heard of his march on the city and had departed for home but he wondered if the city's civil populace had also abandoned the place for somewhere safer or maybe they'd just secured themselves indoors. But less than a quarter mile from the urban boundary line, sizable details of cavalry and infantry had been stationed behind formidable defensive barriers of palisades on the solid ground between the waterways, lakes and pools and immediately he could see that Governor Maximus' military prowess and talent had been utilized to the full.

As Zeor reflected on how the rebellion by Sorus and Maximus had made him theorize, rationalize and conceptualize militaristically, things he'd never envisaged doing when he'd inherited the office of Consul Primus more than twenty years ago, his train of thought was diverted by the arrival of a runner from Esta City with news that Zeo had killed the traitor Castor and that he now knew that his mother was being held captive in the Arx. He promised to keep him informed of any further developments.

As Zeor absorbed the positive report from his son he was joined on the hilltop by one of the many scouts he'd sent to search out vulnerable points in the city's defences which could be reached and possibly breached during the hours of darkness and when it was revealed that the man had found such a place on the western flank all three riders returned to the camp and convened the strategists and advisers in *consilium.*

From late morning and well into the afternoon the *Praefecti, Decurionis, Decanus* and captains moved multiple divisions of men down onto the plain where they deployed them into a semi-circular position facing the northernmost point of Ciro City. On signal the men marched to the centre of the wide open space and manoeuvred into a solid Quincunx assault formation and paraded menacingly back and forth for an hour and then regrouped to form numerous *testudo* and other protective configurations. They continually modified and tweaked their positions from one area to another on the now dust choked plain and in full view but out of weapons range of the enemy forces holed up behind the barricades, Zeor junior had his archers practice on several erect lifelike dummies. They spurred each other on by chanting loudly and menacingly *"Invenire in corde inimicorum!"* 'Aim for the heart of your enemy!'

In a further effort to rattle and confound the foe and to portray the image of a much larger force than actuality, the Consul had the engineers construct rows of tents and huts, though the vast majority were bogus and merely one sided set-ups, facing south. They arranged these quarters on higher ground towards the western corner of the plains at a sufficiently far flung distance to make the deception harder to detect. Here plumes of smoke snaked skywards from fictitious kitchens and mess tents and a fleet of horse-drawn wagons entered the canvas encampment from the west end and filed out at the east side only to return some thirty minutes later to repeat the procession. To add to the apparent industrious bustle in the camp a blacksmith and his apprentice took turns to clout an anvil with their hammers for hours on end.

A vast array of various regimental banners and insignia fluttered in the gentle breeze as the *Bucin-*

ators and *Tubicens* frequently added to the noisy and dynamic hullabaloo.

And meanwhile, in the forward zone of the vast ground between the opposing forces, the charioteers mounted wave after wave of forays almost to within touching distance of the
pointed staves on the palisades before veering off in a wide circle without attempting to launch *pili* against the enemy. And as each operating module rested another unit doing something completely different would replace them and at no time was the billowing dust in the amphitheatre able to settle and before long all of the participants in the outdoors military operations looked like they'd just emerged from a chalky sepulchre. The robust action went on and on unceasingly as each of the crews re-entered the field and repeated their warlike performance without letup. The Consul and his team had contrived the almost pageant-like tableau for the sole purpose of unnerving and debilitating the enemy and hopefully convince their leaders that an attack could occur at any time soon and when that happened it would come from the north.

This endless blitz on the enemy's sensory nervous systems continued well after dusk when banks of lanterns lit up the night sky and added shadowy depth to the illusory phalanx of troops as they moved across the flats. This incessant action on site extended past midnight and was still happening as the Consul Primus exited the encampment from the farthest point west ahead of four *maniples* of infantry together with Zeor junior in command of fifty archers as the rearguard of the slow moving column.

The Consul and the company of heavily armed men had spent the late afternoon and evening resting in a secluded ravine well away from the contrived tumult at the edge of the city. As they crept closer to the spot where the scout had identified as the most vulnerable part of the city's defences the Consul wondered if the constant clamour had had the desired effect on the defenders that he'd hoped for which was to wear them down and sap their morale before the first weapons were used in anger. That Maximus, with his military expertise, was in charge of the defence force made a quick and neat outcome much less certain but the Consul was emboldened when he saw no signs that his rival had prepared to do anything other than hunker down and wait it out.

They approached the deep dry ditch which the scout had explained to the Consul earlier had been put in place some fifty odd years ago when one of the larger rivers encircling the city had burst its banks and the torrent had flooded a *cryptoporticus*, an underground passageway which passed from the city centre to the western perimeter. Thirteen people had drowned in the tunnel.

Even with the new overflow channel in place to prevent a recurrence the city dwellers and visitors had refused to use the underpass again and the gates were shut at both ends and in time they became smothered and clogged up with *hederae* and other clinging creepers and ultimately were lost to the world and totally forgotten about. That was until the scout had recalled the tragedy from his early childhood when he remembered a cousin who'd been one of the victims of the deluge. He'd secretly checked the site at first light that morning and had eventually found the opening.

When the Consul heard of the events concerning the passageway he estimated that it was around that time Commander Maximus had lost his first born daughter and reckoned that he'd been too consumed with his own misfortune and what had happened elsewhere in the city was probably of little importance to him right then. The Consul hoped those advising Maximus on the urban defences were unaware of the disused tunnel beneath their feet.

The scout led the way down the weed and lichen smothered steps to the totally concealed portal where they waited as a small team armed with sharpened *forfex* snipped, clipped and prised away at the tangled growth until they'd uncovered and wrenched open the rusting gates.

The procession of men trundled through the dank tunnel until less than ten minutes later they reached the city end but here they allowed the vines to remain attached to the gates but sliced along the edges as they gently eased the ivy enmeshed structure to one side.

The Consul Primus and his men exited from the subway into a darkened empty park not far from the city centre.

Six hours earlier when darkness had enveloped the valley Governor Maximus had stood on the raised dais between the second and the third defensive line and peered north into the hazy lantern-lit flatlands beyond and wondered what the enemy was up to. As far as he was concerned the whole operation being orchestrated outside his capital was a waste of time and energy and it flew in the face of all the tactics he'd learned in the military academy and was tantamount to a crazy charade without rhyme or reason. From his point of view, a siege was a siege, period! It was just a waiting game and was simply executed by massing your forces outside the target site and biding your time for the people inside to run out of supplies or lose their nerve and as sure as night follows day it would be either one or the other of these events in the majority of cases. There was little need for these brazen theatricals and if they thought for a second that this craziness would rattle him or wear him down before they'd launch an attack they'd be sorely disappointed. But even as he'd promoted these positive notions he was well aware that his men were nervous and were already on edge. He'd assured them *ad nauseam* over the last twenty-four hours that the deep trenches, the multiple pointed palisades, the copious deep-water impediments and the soggy marsh-lands were more than enough to hold the enemy at bay and the city had enough supplies to last six months or more. And he was certain that he had more manpower than the opposition should they decide to strike. But there was one thing which could bring this stupid extravaganza to an end without confrontation was the news he'd had two days ago from Sorus informing him that he'd seized Aprilis and was holding her hostage until Zeor surrendered and sued for peace. Though this was good news in itself there was no way of knowing for sure when the enemy would capitulate so there was a strong possibility that the siege could continue for some time, Maximus allowed. One way or another he didn't care, the longer the blockade on his capital lasted the more time Sorus had to get the result that would give them all that they desired. As he mused and peered into the waxing and waning shadowy lantern beams in the distance his brain thumped with a sudden and frightful premonition and when he descended from the platform and mounted his horse he just couldn't shake off the notion that they'd missed something in the format they'd devised and that his capital might not be as secure as he'd believed it to be and the vexatious feeling remained with him as he dismounted outside the Governor's mansion twenty minutes later where he made a mental pledge to convene his devisers and surveyors, Generals and Commanders first thing in the morning to review every aspect of defence and peruse the charts and maps of the city inch by inch for the slightest weakness in the fortifications. His instinct told him there was a fault, big time!

He was joined at dinner by Dido and though he'd tried to keep the conversation upbeat and away from what was happening outside she'd constantly sniped and ridiculed his initial response to the invasion of *Oriens* by Zeor. She raised her voice to a much higher decibel when she turned her anger to more recent events when she berated him about how the city was under siege because of his abject failure to confront the counterrevolution sooner when it was miles away from the capital and only the Gods knew what might happen next she exclaimed. When he told her he'd been following orders from her know-it-all lover Sorus who'd ordered him to hold off now that he had Aprilis as hostage and he intended using her to bring Zeor and his supporters to heel. With a shrill scream she leapt from the couch gritting her teeth and snarled and said that captivity alone just wasn't good enough for Aprilis, that she wanted the *canicula* dead along with the rest of her family.

When Maximus fanned both hands in a COOL DOWN, gesture Dido stomped up and down on the mosaic floor in anger and the pink tassels on her fluffy size eleven slippers flicked back and forth *in tempore* before she dashed from the room in tears.

The Governor grabbed the carafe and goblet and fled to his den but he'd barely taken a sip when Dido stormed his refuge and demanded that he launch an attack now and kill the entire rabble outside the city which had forced every emporium to close and prevented her from preparing her trousseau for her impending wedding. She screamed and thumped her father numerous times and cried out that the plebeians were so mean and selfish to do such a rotten thing just now when they must be aware of her forthcoming glorious event.

CHAPTER THIRTY-EIGHT

Inside the relative dimness of the equestrian training arena they took turns to rest until two hours after twilight when Zeo, Adam and Johnny slipped from the building and headed northeast. Using night visions they traversed gardens, yards, meadows and lanes and some ninety minutes later they had the greatly illuminated tiered hillside in their sights. On each level, multiple cabins and tents had been erected and the whole place looked like a giant candle-lit three layered wedding cake that had been colonised by a swarm of ants, or so Johnny professed.

Only now was he and Adam able to see the true size and defined outline of the massive edifice and rather than being cylindrical and circular as they'd assumed it to be from the distance they found that it was hexagonal in design. Its six stone rendered sides tapered out from the vertical as it stretched into the heights with its only door on the western side elevation directly above the tiered incline on where it had been built. Its upper battlement level was domed and was as much as three feet wider than the diameter at ground level and the huge and oddly designed column reminded Adam of two upright multi sided containers, with the larger unit atop the lower smaller section and altogether he reckoned the tower to be more than one hundred and fifty feet high. When he focused his binoculars under the central and uppermost cantilevered protrusions he was able to see the underside of the overhanging embrasures used by the defenders in the past to repel attackers directly beneath them. Although the construction of the structure appeared to be a contradiction to the laws of physics and gravity it didn't appear to be as ruinous or as perilous as Zeo had led him to believe. He'd told him and Johnny earlier that the Arx had been built well over two thousand years ago by one of the dominant warlords and had never been breached in all that time. But all of this was before the whole of Sitantal had been finally united by his distant ancestor, the first Consul Primus. For subsequent centuries it had been used as a secure lockup for the insane and for dangerous criminals and nobody had ever escaped from its impregnable and notorious confines with its single access and egress equally strong. They observed the changing of the watch at ten o'clock and then moved well away from the roadway leading to the hillside's broad winding avenue occupied from end to end by the tents quartering hundreds of *custodis.* They moved further along a disused track on their right until they were at the south east elevation near where the citadel hill sloped abruptly and vanished deeply into a tree choked chasm behind the steep bluff. After surveying the scene they went deeper into the undergrowth and debated until they finally agreed on a strategy and then returned to the site and explored and uprooted, cut and levelled thick scrub until they'd cleared a narrow strip between the furze and the rugged edge near the thick conifer growth rising from the crevasse at the rear of the tower's east wall. They each took turns to labour on the clearance while one of them kept lookout further along near the southwest face of the Arx.

Midway through the night when they'd finished clearing a pathway they climbed to the base of the tower and crept along the outer southern walls until they had the citadel's front elevation in sight at the tower's base level and viewed the sprawling custodis encampment concentrated on the tiered hillside below the concourse and it became clear to them that Puto Pollux must believe that any attempt to reach the prisoners could only be attempted at the western side where the structure's only entrance was located.

Further along the broad forecourt the guards remained stationery on the top step at the double doors for most of the time but every fifteen minutes or so they separated and patrolled to each angle of the west wall and then both returned to their post. The guys reckoned that it was more to do with assisting their circulation and relieving boredom than actually guarding the site. This routine suited the embryonic plan they were hatching and provided this routine remained in place and didn't change for each watch they'd put their game plan to the test in less than twenty-four hours.

They returned to the arena and detailed to Euander the role he would play in the rescue operation as they sipped at the extra strong coffee he'd prepared.

The three rested throughout the morning and well into the late afternoon until the ever ready Euander prepared the evening meal and then they honed, enacted and tweaked the tactics until some three hours later they harnessed the strongest of the three dark ponies to the small coach when they'd all agreed that the handsome Candeo could attract unwanted interest which might make things more difficult for them should they meet anybody in authority on the journey to the Arx.

With Euander at the reins the coach exited the entrance to the villa and complex where he did an immediate turn into a rarely used route. His three companions were seated inside.

Johnny nudged Adam and whispered that he felt like the King of England and that he had an irresistible urge to wave regally out the window if they should see any of the great unwashed along the way.

Adam elbowed him in the side in response and told him to be quiet.

In less than five minutes they reached another unpaved road leading north and here all three passengers alighted to ease the load but also to keep an eye and ear out for other night time travellers. The three wayfarers blended into the shadowy brush and vegetation on each side of the track and kept well out of range of the beam from the single carriage lantern.

They'd travelled almost half a mile and were approaching a small junction on the narrow track when a *decem* of mounted *custodis* suddenly emerged from the left laneway and when they confronted the approaching coach the leader signalled his men to stop. By now the black dressed pedestrians had vanished deep into the brush where they waited with bated breath and crossbows at the ready and listened as the captain of the troop challenged Euander. The officer dismounted and approached with his sword unsheathed and enquired why he was in such a remote place during darkness.

Euander recited the story he'd rehearsed with Zeo earlier; that he was training the skittish animal to get used to night-time journeys; that his brother and his sister-in-law worked for *Eius Praestantis*, Consul Primus Sorus, as *facilius* and *auctor* respectively and they often worked late into the night and didn't have time to train and discipline the filly themselves.

The reference to the dictator as "His Excellency, Consul Primus Sorus" had the desired effect on the ambitious captain who was well aware that outside the leader's inner circle of staunch supporters very seldom did anyone refer to him thus and recently, as each day passed, it had become even less common as news had filtered through of one setback after the other. And it was very probable that this young man was connected directly to the elite otherwise he'd have been conscripted into the forces by now he silently conjectured as he remounted his horse and amicably and respectfully signalled Euander to continue without confirming who he was or even checking inside the coach.

When the mounted *custodis* had vanished into the dark Adam and Johnny emerged from cover and congratulated Zeo on his smart idea and they also gave the thumbs-up to Euander for pulling it off.

They proceeded north until they reached the thick woodland several hundred feet from the southeast sector of the citadel a little before midnight where Euander unhitched the pony from the coach and tethered him further back in a grassy area to graze.

All four crept noiselessly along the lower path at the bottom of the citadel mount and viewed the now inactive and somnolent camp scattered along the three tiers on the west side of the tower. Further up from the camp they watched the two sentries separate and move infrequently from the only doorway into the pile and patrol the width of the front elevation and then turn back to an *at ease* position on the steps as before.

The guys returned to the forest edge and scaled the path they'd cleared on the previous night and five minutes later they took cover in the shadows of the southeast wall of the ancient towering pile. Adam reviewed the tactics with the others and was happy with their readiness for action before they crawled stealthily from the east around to the southwest wall. They remained glued to the ground when they saw the forward moving shadow cast on the ground by the approaching sentry but they breathed a great sigh of relief when he pivoted to the west without looking in their direction and he was gone from view in seconds.

It was almost twenty minutes later before the guard returned and as soon as he reached the angle Adam and Johnny yanked him from the pathway where Euander quickly detached and affixed the man's helmet, shield and sword and casually ambled onto the path adjusting his clothing pretending that he'd just taken a call of nature. He stopped at the edge of the south slope and then stooped down and held the long shield at an angle which covered much of his body and casually called to the other sentry, but just loud enough that only the man would hear; *Amicus! Veni et videamus hoc!*

In the meantime, as Euander played out his role, Adam and Johnny had dispatched the captive and now waited for the other sentry to approach. Zeo hugged the wall with his crossbow loaded and was ready to step out and shoot him if he ignored the request or showed any signs of alarm or suspicion.

Euander repeated his passion laden appeal to "Come and look at this!" and added "This is amazing!" as he pointed to an imaginary spot on the ground near his feet when the curious *custodis* came up behind him. Johnny and Adam sprung into action again and repeated the snatch and grab exercise followed by instant execution and without pause they removed the large key to the citadel's door from his belt.

Euander and Adam hoisted a dead sentry under arm between them and proceeded towards the entrance to the tower which was an action they'd practiced and rehearsed numerous times at their base earlier but now they were able to use the *custodis* long shields to baffle and distort their silhouette as much as possible. At the double doors they held the corpse upright and secured it to the hinge's scrolled design with plastic ties and for extra effect they attached a lance to his lifeless hand.

Zeo lay at the edge of the concourse in front of the Arx and scanned the multi tiered encampment below him and searched for movement within the vast array of *cubiculum* knowing that within two hours the peaceful scene would change when the *domesticum* arrived to prepare the morning meal.

Whilst all this was taking place near the only doors into the tower two very frightened women huddled together in the dungeon below where every noise they heard impacted on their everyday life such was the effect of being in virtual isolation for days on end but Adam was unaware that the suppressed sounds made by him trying to unlock the door in the middle of the night had filtered below and was now causing abject terror with both women certain that something unspeakable was about to happen to them.

They passionately beseeched the Gods to save them.

With the second body now hoisted into place at the other side of the doorway Adam, Johnny and Zeo edged cautiously through the partially opened doors while Euander crawled across to the verge to monitor the tented quarters below the concourse.

The first thing Adam was aware of inside the tower was the overhead rustling of bats and the noxious reek of bat guano filtering down from above. With the aid of his torch he and the others crept down the uneven steps in single file and very shortly they saw a dim light escaping from a narrow opening on the right. They withdrew their swords silently as they neared the source of the glow not knowing what they might find awaiting them beyond.

Zeo warily peered round the corner and saw his mother and the plump little housekeeper where they were huddled together and both were staring wide eyed from the furthest recess in the cell. He hastily whipped off his night goggles and helmet and dashed into the room where the women burst into tears and sprung from the corner to meet him.

Zeo was being smothered in kisses and hugs when Adam and Johnny joined them and instantly both sobbing women reached out to them and all together they embraced to the sound of whimpers and squeals of delight. Porcia eased off a little and gazed fondly at Johnny and whispered *'Gratias, meus paulus puer'*

Adam signalled that they must leave immediately as Aprilis retrieved the copy of the *Promptorium parvulorum* and handed it to Zeo and without further delay the group moved along the corridor to the steps. Adam lit the way through the eerie building and briefly directed the pinpoint beam aloft and noticed how rotten and unsafe the tower actually was, contrary to what he'd thought about the structure from the outside. When they'd reached the top he whispered to Zeo that he had devised a little plan but that he and Euander must get the ladies away from here as quickly as possible. He added that he and Johnny would stay behind and would allow them ten minutes to reach the coach before he'd put his idea into action. Though Johnny was mystified about what was afoot he nodded his head agreeably and fussily ordered Zeo to hurry up.

The women averted their eyes and shivered when they passed the bodies strung up outside the door and quickly followed Zeo and Euander away from the gruesome scene. Adam and Johnny waited until they'd turned the southwest corner of the tower before returning inside where Adam quickly explained that he planned to set the building alight when he'd noticed that every floor and the rest of the interior was timber based and that the ground floor was as dry as snuff to make it easier. He also reckoned that the higher floors were swarming with bats and there had to be loads of guano which was rich in nitrogen, phosphates and potassium and would be ideal for a combustible reaction he felt. He added that he wouldn't be surprised if the whole thing exploded because he'd read of a place somewhere in Texas that did, therefore they'd need to beat a speedy retreat. Another point, he added, if this did happen, 'Pravus' Sorus would think that Aprilis had died and wouldn't search for her which would give them more time to get away from the Capitol.

'What a superb idea! You're ever so smart, no matter what others might say, my friend. Let's do it and see what happens' Johnny gushed as he patted Adam on the shoulder.

While Johnny remained at the partly open door Adam went down to the dungeon and got the still half-filled lantern from the ladies former cell and moved deeper into the bowels of the creaking building until he found a spot where the upper floor had collapsed in a thick mangled heap into the space below. He splashed the oily liquid over the pile of dusty dry timber and set it alight. And when the flames took hold he moved speedily down the passageway and up the steps to Johnny. At this juncture the flames were breaking through to the ground floor and the pair unhooked the corpses from the hinges and bundled them unceremoniously down the steps and closed the doors behind them. They raced to the first corner of the octagonal tower and along the south base to the downhill path and were very surprised to find Zeo and the others waiting on the track below. Adam ushered the ladies into the coach and indicated to Euander to move forward instantly and in less than seven minutes a thunderous boom sent shockwaves rippling through the trees on both sides of the trail and almost simultaneously a bright orange glow lit up the night sky behind them. The sudden blast and flash caused the pony to buck nervously until Euander subdued her with soft whispers and caresses.

Aprilis and Porcia sprung from the coach in fright and were in time to witness the crazy and fantastical display to the north. Several smaller booms and bursts quickly followed the first and in the distance they saw chunks of masonry spew skywards and then rain back to earth like confetti and even at this distant point from the *custodis* encampment they could hear cries of terror and pain filter through the trees.

Though he was just as fascinated as the others were with the pyrotechnic display Adam cleared his throat and warned of the possibility that survivors from the camp might flee in this direction and without further coaxing they turned their backs on the still blazing ruins of the Arx on the

hill. As they reached the coach everyone, with the exception of Adam, stopped in midstride and glanced wonderingly at Johnny when he fervently exclaimed;
'Veni, vide, vici!'

CHAPTER THIRTY-NINE

'Pravus' Sorus sprung from the divan in alarm and was now wide awake. He rushed over to the north facing window of his bedchamber to where he believed the rumbling blasts had come from and when he wrenched back the drapes his jaw sagged as he stared in disbelief at the faraway flame-spurting hilltop. If the thunderous boom in the north hadn't already roused them, the sharp warning blasts from the *Cornicen* horns now sounding all over the city was bound to have stirred the sleeping population a half hour before the *Tempus Dico* was due to perform the daily wake-up call anyway. Before Sorus had time to rearrange his muddled thoughts into a neat and manageable sequence, an unrelenting rattle of knuckles on his apartment's door forced him away from the window.

His personal *factotum* breathlessly gasped that he believed that something very strange had just happened at the Arx.

As the pending dawn diluted the nightscape eleven horsemen galloped at speed through the streets of *Urbis Capitolium*. The senior *Praefectus* impatiently informed each night watch patrol they encountered on route to make way for Consul Primus Sorus and his escort. They raced along the north-south arterial road and all of them ignored the fist waving and almost apoplectic toll collector who'd just arrived for duty as they spurred their mounts and skirted the cantilever barrier at the turnpike and continued north east towards the erratic dwindling flames on the citadel mount. As they neared the site they met odd groups of panic stricken men as they fled from the hill some of whom had *One-horned boring-bats* still clinging to them apparently unaware or even caring that they were now being sucked dry of their lifeblood as they stumbled to reach a safer and better place. Some of the injured were barely able to move but nonetheless they were glaringly determined to escape the apocalyptic scene and when they saw the horsemen looming through the smoke one cried; *"Oh Meus Deus! We've displeased the Deities and now they're being vengeful! Hellfire, Brimstone and Bats! It must be the end of the world! We're doomed! Doomed, I say!"*

Although 'Pravus' Sorus had no idea what he'd find when he reached the place where the menacing citadel was located he was totally unprepared for what he encountered.

The Arx had vanished and the tiered hillside was a scene of chaos and utter carnage.

Though the presence of guts and gore had never caused him to bat an eyelid in the past the sight before him took his breath away and forced him to recoil as two of his escort quickly dismounted and regurgitated noisily most of what they'd eaten for late supper on the previous evening.

Multiple canvas fuelled fires continued to flare up on what remained of the tent covered hillside and the entire citadel mount looked like it had been peppered with hundreds upon hundreds of cut stones and other objects, animate and inanimate, some of which were the most gruesome things imaginable. Though the landscape was a hotchpotch of debris, a confused shambles, there was one commonality and that was that everything on the high hillside was uniformly spattered and sticky with blood.

The sight before Sorus and the others was too repulsive to bear and they averted their eyes continually and they got some respite from the gut churning scene but they had no way to blank out the spine chilling cries from crippled *custodis* unable to move nor could they mask the noisome stench of burning human flesh, hair and blood that merged with the smoke that polluted the atmosphere.

Sorus called out to several men who stumbled aimlessly along the path if they knew the whereabouts of Commander Pollux but they'd either been rendered deaf or were still concussed and ignored his enquiry completely as they continued silently on their focused wide-eyed search for safety. The lack of reply or even acknowledgement of the question irked the dictator and it required a super human effort of self-restraint on his part not to inflict more pain on these wounded individuals. His growing anger and frustration at what had transpired here and its impact on his recently devised strategy was beginning to clash with his thought process as he tried to assess the ramifications of it all. There was no doubt in his mind that Aprilis and her companion had died in the dungeons in the tower but that wasn't the real reason he regretted what had occurred; simply, it was the loss of the valuable bargaining tool which he'd intended to use to bring the counter revolution to a speedy end and to finally get the chance to finish off the *tegunt* Zeo, once and for all.

     He had six men from his escort remain on site and begin a search for Puto Pollux while he and the others returned to the city to organise a company of men to rescue the injured and recover the dead for cremation. During the early morning his *factotum* was kept busy deflecting one anxious senator after another as they sought assurances that what had happened at the Arx didn't mean that Zeo and the two *Praecipuum* had arrived in the Capitol. He'd stressed that the citadel had been so well protected that it would have been impossible for anyone to get past the cordon and what had happened there was simply an accident and probably caused by the two prisoners messing around inside.

He quickly ushered them away and Sorus remained closeted in his office with his senior military commanders and *scriptor* and stubbornly refused to meet with the numerous nervous politicians who still milled around the corridors of the vast building well into the late afternoon.

*

At the time 'Pravus' Sorus and his escort had been dashing from the Capitol along the arterial road leading to the burning citadel that morning, several miles further east on the many, almost inaccessible and unfriendly lanes and tracts well away from the normal routes, the unlit coach driven by Euander weaved south with its two nervous but relieved passengers on board.

Zeo, Johnny and Adam scouted ahead on foot on the lookout for patrolling *custodis* or people who'd been disturbed from their sleep by the incident on the northern hills overlooking their homes.

When they reached their hideaway just before dawn they were surprised to find *Matrona* Minula waiting for them inside the arena where she insisted that the two women should accompany her to her villa to recuperate and until such time when they continued their flight to freedom.

Over celebratory extra strong coffee all four guys debated and strung together a plan and very shortly afterwards Euander left the building on one of the dark nondescript horses displaying the white lace *sudarium* given to him by the secretive scout assigned to them by General Electra. As the flimsy fabric fluttered prominently from the pommel of his sword he trotted at random through the avenues and laneways and passed numerous groups of residents where they chatted and gesticulated, some exaggeratedly, towards the smouldering hill in the distance and they were so engrossed that they barely looked in his direction. Hours later when he could feel that his mount was beginning to tire he returned to the refuge only to find the elusive spy who he'd been searching for was waiting for him in plain sight as he dismounted.

He recognised her instantly though he'd never actually seen her before. She was truly alluring and delightful as was the perfume she exuded which had revealed to him her true identity because it was the same fragrance that was still detectable on the lace *sudarium* attached to his sword. When Johnny opened the doors to Euander he had to muster all of his fortitude not to fall headlong in love with the pretty woman who was standing there.

Once again he mentally bemoaned the fact that he was unable to speak in Latin and until that changed he'd be deficient and would be forever in Limbo he realised. There was so much he wanted to say right now but all he could do was groan in frustration.

He and Adam were introduced to the svelte female scout who told Zeo her name was Ailia and together they sat and swapped ideas on how their group could exit the Capitol undetected and some thirty minutes later they'd agreed on a plan.

Shortly after Zeo and Ailia had gone to her home *Matrona* Minula came alone to the arena and spoke with Euander briefly. As the silver haired lady turned to leave and before Euander had time to move to do the chores she'd outlined, she demurred briefly and then turned and approached Adam and Johnny. She bowed deeply to each of them.

'Salve! Tibi gratias ago pro auxiliis familiae Zeo'

The guys guessed that the lady had complimented them for helping Zeo's family and both bowed respectfully to her in return. Somehow they knew that she'd been made aware of the language barrier and wasn't expecting a reply from them but as she pivoted to move away they responded almost in unison; *'Gratias, Matrona* Minula!'

The lady in black paused and glanced sidelong at them with a quizzical sparkle in her now smiling eyes. She nodded her head again in their direction and Euander stopped abruptly in his approach and eyeballed them thoughtfully before he exited the door behind her.

Both Johnny and Adam were quite chuffed with their combined effort of communications and struggled to suppress the urge to high-five each other.

When twilight had progressed into fully fledged darkness the two-horse, four-wheeler, elegant carriage departed through the equestrian centre's rear entrance with the four horsemen leading the way along the deserted avenue. A casual glance at the drivers' lofty box could make a casual observer think that the reins-man was a delicate young fellow wearing a loose ill-fitting tunic, gloves and hat which was the impression the travellers were trying to portray.

Ailia steered the horses at a steady unhurried pace as the three passengers on board gazed nervously into the varying blackness beyond the carriage windows.

Earlier when the pretty female scout and Zeo returned from the villa he said that the intention was to move his mother and Porcia from here and then to Abdo. Adam insisted that *Matrona* Minula must also leave with them, that he was sure that eventually word would filter back to the Capitol that Aprilis and Porcia had survived and had escaped from the Arx and what had happened there hadn't been an accident at all but a deliberate act.

If it became known then questions might be asked and there was a strong possibility that anyone could have seen them here at the arena or on their way to and from the citadel but had thought nothing of it at that point and if they were quizzed afresh they might recall having seen them near this place at the time of the incident at the Arx. Another thing which shouldn't be forgotten was

that Euander had been challenged using the coach by the *custodis* patrol only a short distance away on the night of the event. He added that there was no way they could be completely certain that the carriage might not be observed leaving the house this very evening. Finally, he stressed, the good lady had been placed in great danger by them and therefore had to be protected now and that was that, period!
Though the elderly widow had protested stridently, eventually Aprilis had succeeded in convincing her to travel with them.
During the afternoon Euander rounded up two sturdy black shires from the equestrian paddocks and readied the pair and the larger coach for the lengthy journey ahead and then focused on changing his beautiful Candeo into a nondescript pied old nag by splashing muddy water and daubing him all over with cold brown coffee. By the time he'd finished with his pride and joy he was saddened by the sight but certain that absolutely no one would bother him or be covetous or envious and would probably feel sorry for him and the horse.

  Though it added an extra thirty some miles to the journey south the convoy kept to the east of the Capitol when the scout-turned-driver confirmed that security around the city was concentrated on the southern approaches to the west with less scrutiny being paid to outgoing traffic. Three hours later when they'd cleared the city limits by several miles without incident Zeo directed Ailia to a roadside Inn and *Caupona* for the night while he and his three friends camped in the little spinney nearby where they took turns to keep watch.

With the Capitol now in their wake the procession continued south and in contrast to the previous day it now depicted a more leisurely, even relaxed pace, whereas before this the carriages' three occupants had looked distressed and sombre in their *palliolum luctus.* The mourning veils and the all black garb they were attired in was meant to portray a group of grieving mourners on the way to a dear relative's funeral in *Australis* should anyone in authority enquire the reason for their journey south. This only occurred on two occasions when they'd come to a halt at a military checkpoint. They'd been quickly waved through by the sentinel on duty when the three occupants of the carriage had launched a nonstop soul destroying boohoo of lament for the dear departed.

From a watchful distance Johnny observed this spectacle being acted out for the second time that day and the drama confirmed to him something that he'd heard about in the past and that was that a majority of the population, if given the choice, would prefer to engage in one of the following challenges; *"Run a mile; Suck a boil; or Eat a bag of scabs!"* rather than listen to or be in the company of somebody with selfish whinging and cringing gripes like so; 'Oh! Woe-is-me! Look at me! Now cry for me because I'm a victim too!'

Before dusk and less than forty miles from the *Medius Australis* border they spent the second night in another roadside Inn and *Caupona* and the four man escort remained al fresco and out of sight but still on guard a short distance away.
Early next morning as the three ladies finished *prandium* and were about to don their black lace mourning mantles and leave the dining hall a shrill voice rang out; *'Domina! Ego credebam te convivam ducis alibi!'* Aprilis, together with her two companions spun round to see who had remarked "Madame! I thought you were a guest of our leader elsewhere!" The wife of the Consul Primus found herself staring into the surly enquiring glare of Senator Brisus, a well known crony of 'Pravus' Sorus and also an unprincipled adversary of her husband. Before she had time to respond Ailia stepped forward and ushered all three startled ladies outside the room and into the waiting coach. She was aware that the senator stood at the entrance and observed them driving south.
When out of sight of the hotel Ailia beckoned Zeo alongside the carriage and told him what had happened at the hotel and she was sure that the senator had noted the owner's mark on the carriage and had possibly spotted him and the others waiting for the carriage further along the road. When he informed Adam of this he complimented him on having made a good call when he'd insisted that *Matrona* Minula vacate her home. They all agreed

that the senator obviously hadn't heard of the destruction of the citadel otherwise he might have created a fuss and tried to prevent Aprilis from leaving the building. They made for the border with renewed urgency guessing that it wouldn't be long until Brisus heard what had happened to the Arx. In the early afternoon the group neared Porcia's home village of Abdo and close to the hamlet's boundary one of the many patrolling *Virago* guards challenged them and then sped off to announce their arrival.

    A breathless Genera Electra and the *praesum* were waiting together with Livia to greet the party outside the village inn, as was a slurping, dancing and prancing Friday.
The village chief and innkeeper could barely contain himself when he learned that two of the ladies in the carriage, one of whom was the wife of the Consul Primus *Hereditarius* of Sitantal would be his guests for some time to come and only a little disappointed to hear that Porcia would lodge with her cousin who still lived just beyond the village green. Nevertheless he rubbed his hands with glee as he went to speak with his wife but also to tell his darling daughter Isselle that her new best friend Euander was here again but not on the handsome colt Candeo. He guessed she'd be upset and disappointed to see that he was now riding a shaggy old nag that didn't appear fit for purpose. Though he wasn't savvy in equine matters the animal looked as if it should be sent to the knackers' yard, *extem-*

pio!

Before they dined Electra dispatched Ailia with letters from Aprilis and Livia and a report from Zeo to the Consul Primus. The young woman had volunteered to be the courier and insisted that she'd never ever visited *Oriens* and always wanted to see Ciro City ever so much. Zeo had messaged that he and his friends would soon join him in the province and gave the rider a sketch outlining the route that he and his friends intended to take to reach *Oriens* so the she could join them on her return journey and let them know where the Consul Primus was based.

It was also agreed that General Electra's *Virago* would now remain at Abdo and establish a more permanent base there to protect Aprilis and the others in case a further attempt might be made by the usurper to seize her or maybe even Livia to hold hostage.

Adam figured that there'd be consequences when 'Pravus'Sorus discovered that the captives hadn't perished in the citadel after all and especially if he learned that his three accursed tormentors were responsible for the rescue and the total destruction of the tower. Something like this might drive his anger to a higher level. And adding salt to the wounds would be the psychological impact stemming from the audacious action though he'd assembled a massive security presence at the Arx under the control of Puto Pollux. Keeping all of this in mind they had to be ready for anything

Sorus might throw at them he declared. Zeo also agreed when Johnny suggested that the *Virago* corps should be used to guard the Temple of the Gods in place of the defunct *Beneficiarius* at least until such time that another system for protecting the site could be established on a permanent base.

    The rest of the afternoon was spent preparing the supply wagons for the return journey to *Oriens* to meet up with his father and when everything was organised they returned to the *taberna* and prepared to meet the ladies and Livia. It became a party-like event when the three chattering ladies and the four guys who'd helped them escape the Capitol three days previously, gathered to have *cena* in the cosy dining room on what would be their last day together. It became obvious to everybody there that the widow *Matrona* Minula was now relaxed and was actually enjoying the adventure which had been forced upon her when she'd agree to allow her home to be used as a launching pad to free the two prisoners and she sat and avidly listened to the tales that both Aprilis and Porcia related to Zeo and the others about the night of their capture and their confinement in the dungeons of the Arx.

At daybreak the four departing overnighters were surprised to find that almost the entire village population were waiting on the little street and some of the ladies and a frantic Isselle, waved *sudariums* as they bade goodbye to the group including a red faced Euander.

As ever, Friday stared straight ahead from the box seat.

They went east to retrace the eventful route they'd travelled a few weeks ago to attend the Temple of the Gods.

CHAPTER FORTY

Puto Pollux was reposed on his belly and was entirely naked. He was convinced that he'd expired and had completed the inevitable cycle from birthday suit to deathday suit and worse still he guessed that he'd been condemned to the meanest part of *Tartarus* and he was dead angry about that too. Why he'd ended up in the main torture chambers of Hell seemed rather incongruous and severe to him considering the fact that he'd personally known others who'd committed the most horrendous deeds much more often than him. And he was convinced that the torture being inflicted on him was at the upper end of the punishment scale and if the other lousy miscreants only had to endure what he was now suffering it didn't seem fair or equitable to him at all. He was positive that no one and he meant absolutely nobody had ever been dealt the heinous abuse that was being levied on him right now. The familiar pious parables; that *'death was the great equaliser'* and that *the punishment should fit the crime,* blah, blah, blah, was just a bunch of hyperbole and humbug as far as he was concerned. Just then he noticed a dissolute, in fact, a most evil looking man who seemed vaguely familiar to him was lurking about in his sector and it gave weight to his belief that the revered and august Gatekeeper to the Gods, who was commonly known as the *Soul Control,* had been much too harsh with him when they'd banished him to this part of the underworld in the company of rascals like so. Was it possible that those at the higher and spiritual echelons of the system could be unjust or maybe even bent, he wondered? He tried his best to shrink away as the horrid spectral figure approached because even in these darkened shadowy surrounds he could tell that this stranger was bad news and here he remembered another compelling old adage from his erstwhile worldly existence; *a man is judged by the company he keeps!* He groaned plaintively and muttered *sotto voce;* "*Oh, go away! Give me a break! Puleaseee! If Diabolus, the Devil thinks that we know each other I'm totally toast!*"

But Puto Pollux found that he couldn't move from where he lay, not even an inch! He believed that he'd been restrained on a spiked bench which pierced every part of his body and held on to him like a *mendicus* to a *cudo* which prevented his escape. The despicable spectre bent down to his level and glared into his eyes and when he spoke it sounded like they were both in an echo chamber and the question he posed *'How are you?'* irked Puto Pollux, no end. His puffed up bloody hands curled into fists in anger and had he been free and upright he'd have sucker punched the ugly looking irritant on the spot for sounding so blasé and insincere.

Here he was in the Other World being tortured and abused and this wise guy comes along with a facile and insensitive question at a time when it was obvious to anyone with an eye in their head that he had more than enough to contend with trying to figure out what the blazes was going on and how he'd ended up here in the first place. He was being abused horribly by the ghouls who laboured in this hellhole and to make matters worse for him, in his prone position he couldn't see what these fiends looked like but maybe that was for the best, he reluctantly figured.

The visitor exited the room where the *medicus* had earlier informed him prior to going in that the patient had been given a large beaker of poppy juice and that they were waiting for the onset of narcosis before they'd extract the multitude of wooden game pegs and splinters from his back and upper legs.

As Sorus continued along the corridor of the busy *Valetudinarium* he had great difficulty in erasing the image of an *albulus hystrix obesus*, a fat albino porcupine, from his brain.

    It was in the early period of the fiery blast in the dark that the Deputy Governor of *Occidens* had encountered portions of good fortune along with misfortune. Unfortunately for him all of these segments were in conflict with each other on the citadel hill when the tower and everything in it had been blown into smithereens.

His first and *numerus unus* piece of misfortune had happened as he'd struggled to don his helmet while he was rushing headlong from his tent to see what was causing the loud hellish noise and pandemonium on the hill behind him when he got walloped down the span of his back by a large antique wooden board game called *Duodecim Omnibus,* which roughly translated as "Twelve pops for Everybody"

Unfortunately for him the myriad of tapering tipped pegs which were essential to play the once popular game were still in situ when the table-like top impacted his body which was *numerus duo,* the second piece of misfortune to afflict him that morning. Though the Deputy Governor was excruciatingly pricked and punctured from his shoulders blades right down to his thighs he valiantly tried to stand upright and prise the game board away from where the pegs were imbedded in his body but if only he'd remembered that these nasty things invariably occur in three's he might have avoided the next misfortune that assailed him, but with everything that was happening around him he genuinely forgot the age-old warning and was severely punished for the lapse when he was clobbered on the crown of his helmet by one of the horde of rocks raining back to earth courtesy of its gravitational pull. The tremendous impact which was the third, *numerus tres,* stroke of misfortune sent him crashing into a hollow dip at the edge of the winding track and though he didn't know it at the time this was the very instant that his luckless run of misfortune had taken a turn for the better.

When he'd collapsed into the void in an inert heap the long *Duodecim Omnibus* board was dislodged and flipped one hundred and eighty degrees before it landed. The spiked side now faced upwards and the smooth wooden underside came to a rest on top of the prostrate Commander and protected his head and torso from the barrage of aggregates that were still teeming down on the campsite. When the bombardment had stopped and the dust had settled on the recumbent and unconscious Puto Pollux he'd been covered from top to toe by almost one hundred and forty-five pounds of loose rubble, timber and cut masonry.
The toll collector at the turnpike was kept busy throughout the morning as the bleak and sombre wagon trains trundled back and forth to the city in three specific forms; firstly, the wounded, then the mortally wounded and lastly, the much smaller group; the lucky ones. Meanwhile back on the hillside the senior *Praefectus* and his team of searchers increased the effort to find the Deputy Governor and no place was left unchecked for the missing man, including the smouldering remnants and the gaping crater on the hilltop. He formed a second team and extended the probe in a broad sweep that included the gorge on the eastern side and onto the private property, woods and common land adjacent to the site and as nightfall approached he'd

virtually given up hope of finding Puto Pollux alive and had proffered several different scenarios on what might have happened to him, none of which were pleasant or good. It was only when the last remaining pack horse, which was being led along the side of the litter strewn zigzagging path, decided to jettison the entire contents of its bladder right there and then that the mystery was finally solved. When the almighty whoosh and splish-splash of steaming liquid hit the particular spot at the edge of the track a noisy spluttering and gurgling reaction ensued and several chunks of masonry were dislodged from the pile which caused the frightened animal to buck and shy away in alarm from the shifting ground beneath him. The officer quickly cleared the pile of rubble until he'd uncovered the unconscious blood and urine soaked Pollux underneath the gaming tabletop. He quickly moved the comatose man to level ground and transported him in the fastest open top carriage to the nearest *Valetudinarium* in the north of the Capitol and here the *Praefectus* had set off immediately to inform the leader that his Deputy Governor had been found alive but injured and that incidentally he'd been located thanks to a copious flush of good fortune.

When 'Pravus' Sorus returned to his office from the *Valetudinarium* he summoned the page to bring him a goblet and a large *amphora* of wine and then dismissed the youth for the rest of the evening and as he savoured the smooth fruity juice he wondered if his right-hand man would ever be the same again. There was no way for him to know for sure if it was the influence of the poppy drug or if his deputy had completely lost the plot due to the battering he'd endured on the hillside but he couldn't banish from his thoughts the very strange squint in the naked man's eyes. He was pretty certain that his colleague would have attacked him at that time had he not been strapped to the surgical *leictica* to prevent him running amok around the facility and doing damage to himself or to others.

But immediately he put the concern to one side and made a list of people he had to see and things he needed to do first thing in the morning. He was convinced that now was a good time to pursue an offensive against the enemy rather than be pro active to events.

Though there were scores of people still in the building the place was now as quiet as a sanctuary for retrospection and this allowed Sorus to browse and review the events of the past twenty-four hours. Although he'd lost his valuable hostage in the explosion at the Arx he nevertheless felt a surge of satisfaction that in a convoluted way he'd managed to inflict great pain and anguish on the pup Zeo and better still, the death of his mother couldn't be blamed on him directly, it was just an accident and could have happened to anybody in the vicinity at the time.

He was convinced that others would think him cruel and vindictive but he couldn't give a *fimus* what they thought of him or how they felt about the women who'd died and he was more than happy that the persistent thorn in his side had suffered the most heartbreaking loss that any young son could experience and he hoped to give him a lot more to feel sorry about in the future. And the fact that the three mangy dogs hadn't succeeded in reaching the Arx in time to free the two women was *ohe sic dulcis!* Oh so sweet!

He was sure that the sycophantic supporters of the ousted leader's son and his two cronies from *Terra Ferusum* who thought that they were super human beings and capable of doing the most otherworldly things would now see that their heroes weren't as smart or as clever as they'd thought them to be. He refilled the crystal goblet and snarled spitefully, '*Quoque nocens! Illud modo possunt exsugere!*' Too Bad! They can just suck it up!

It was almost midnight when he ascended the stairs to his private apartment and he was in a more optimistic and light-hearted mood than he'd been when he'd broken the seal on the now empty jar.

Over the next two days 'Pravus' Sorus received written daily bulletins on his Deputy's progress from the hospital but his *factotum* noticed that they remained unopened on the leader's desk. During that time he could see that his leader was preoccupied with what might be happening in *Oriens* when he continually enquired if any runners had arrived.

Though he'd sent news of the capture and imprisonment of Aprilis at the time and had advised Maximus that it was only a matter of time before the enemy would want to negotiate a settlement to secure her release he'd yet to have a response from him. He'd ordered the Governor to keep him informed of Zeor's progress within the province on a daily basis but he hadn't had a report in over four days. The last *communicare* he'd had informed him that Zeor's forces were less than ten miles away from the provincial capital Ciro City. And to make matters more unsettling for him he'd had no letters from his sweet *inamorata* Dido for ages either.

During that period Puto Pollux had given the hospital staff a difficult time and on one occasion he had to be restrained in a padded *cubile* until the poppy juice had rendered him more agreeable again.

But on the third day following the inferno at the Arx the Deputy Governor wakened early after an opiate free sleep and shuffled to his feet and demanded his clothes and a horse. Though he ached in areas on his body which up to that time he'd never known to exist he finally managed to mount the animal and he looked a sorry mess as he set forth. Luckily for him some of the insignia denoting his rank was still attached to his tattered and torn military uniform as he made his way through the numerous checkpoints to the centre of the Capitol. When he dismounted at the steps leading to the *Domus Magnus,* the stately colonnaded mansion on *Collis Capitolium;* Capitol Hill, which was the official residence to each Consul Primus for the last five centuries, the on-duty farrier attendant was about to order the household guard to remove the bedraggled, smelly man and his animal from the grand piazza but then he recognised him just in time and relieved him of his mount. He could barely conceal his smirk as the tatty Deputy Governor slowly but determinedly climbed the steps to the main entrance.

At the grand portal the captain of the guard used all his courtly skills and diplomacy and finally convinced Pollux to wait in his office while he requisitioned suitable clothing to replace his torn and ammonia reeking uniform before he allowed the Deputy Governor to proceed further.

When the *factotum* ushered Puto Pollux into the room the leader rose slowly from behind his desk and greeted him rather warily and analytically before he indicated that he should take a seat. He called on the page to bring some *acetaria* and a fruity white wine for the wasted looking visitor and while they waited for the salad and beverage Sorus enquired *"How are you?"*

The simple question was the catalyst that brought a new awareness and clarity into the confused and turbulent memories swirling around inside the head of the Deputy Governor and he began to recall and calibrate more of the events of the past few days which had beset and befuddled him to such an extent that there were times when he'd thought that everyone around him was non *compos mentis* and that he was in a madhouse. He was just about to rise from the chair to embrace his hero for further aiding his deliverance from the fugue and fog of this freakiness when the young page arrived with a heaped platter of mouth watering and nostril dilating cuisine and wine which instantly caused him to defer his emotive impulses from his epicurean disciplined mind for the time being, but he'd give his true friend a big, big embrace later he silently vowed.

Sorus glanced witheringly as his colleague groaned, moaned, munched and swigged his way through the serious treat and meanly imagined jets of wine spurting from the legion of punctures that he knew the man had sustained from the *Duodecim Omnibus* game board only three days ago which he was certain wouldn't have yet healed.

He averted his eyes away from the gobbling gourmand and allowed his thought to dwell on the meeting he'd organised with his Commanders and *Praefecti* within the next hour but he'd barely had time to adjust to a military thinking mode when the *factotum* peered around the door and announced that Senator Brisus needed to see him urgently.

Though the Senator was fully expecting his leader to react angrily when he relayed to him of how he'd arrived in the Capitol just that morning to learn of the horrific incident at the Arx and to hear that the casualties included the wife of the former ruler, the very person he'd met on the previous day at the *Caupona* as she was heading south in the company of two other women and their driver. When he added that he'd observed their departing carriage being escorted by four young horsemen and that he was convinced that one of them was her son Zeo he was quite unprepared for the sequence of perfidy, infamy and butchery which followed the disclosure.

CHAPTER FORTY-ONE

Governor Maximus wakened from a troubled four hour sleep just before Ciro City's *Tempus Dico* was due to announce the start of a new day. The same gnawing suspicion that he'd had before the fitful slumber was still with him and as soon as the aide had responded to his bell he bade him to have the *assessor protelum*, his advisory team assemble at the northern observation post without delay and emphasised that they all had to be there with maps and charts to every section of the city. Though he heard Dido call to him from her bedchamber on the first floor he hurried from the mansion to the stables and in less than three minutes he was exiting the main gate. With the nagging concerns still with him when he'd risen he'd forgotten to check his upper body but he knew for sure that his ribcage would be black and blue from the pummelling he'd received from her last evening. His genteel daughter had no idea of her own strength, he allowed, and didn't realise that her little prods packed a lot of punch and once or twice recently he'd almost forgotten his chivalrous disposition and had been on the verge of smacking her back such had been the stinging soreness she'd inflicted on him and another more tiresome upshot of her shrewish behaviour since she'd returned from her pre-wedding tour in the south was the fact that he'd been unable to join his lady friends and colleagues in the *thermae* to rollick and splash about in the altogether in case they'd question his mottled and bruised upper body.

As Maximus rode down the deserted *Via Fons* the sparkling fountains which adorned the city's main commercial thoroughfare failed to lift his bleak mood. All around him he could hear the early birds tentatively begin the rehearsal for the dawn chorus but even that did nothing for him. He'd almost reached the end of the wide impressive avenue when he saw a baby's *mitra* lying near the kerbside and the bonnet reminded him of the sickening scene in which his little Junia had died so many years ago. At that instant he gasped and almost tumbled from his horse when the recollections from that time hit him like a lump hammer. The Governor sharply reined his mount to the left and galloped towards *Parcum Viridi* and his heartbeat frantically thumped in harmony with every beat of the horses' hooves on the paved avenue.
He circled round Green Park until he reached the creeper covered protrusion that had concealed the opening to the underground passageway for decades and saw the ivy entangled gate propped up to

one side exposing the gaping opening to the tunnel. He groaned aloud knowing there wasn't much else he could do and his heart couldn't sink any further when it was already in the pits.

It was patently obvious to him that a large force had come through the tunnel, the scuff marks on the grass was all the evidence he needed. He knew the enemy was now within his capital.

Ciro City was lost!

Totally dispirited he turned his mount away and left the park and guided the animal south along the avenue, back the route he'd taken a little earlier. Inside the mansion he searched out the housekeeper and told her the enemy was in the city and to wake his daughter immediately and help her pack, that she must leave right away for *Urbis Capitolium* and added that he'd already organised her coach and driver and that it would arrive shortly. Maximus advised the elderly lady that she should accompany Dido as her *patrona* to the Capitol and handed her a sizable purse and wished the shocked and tearful woman *"Vale"* as he turned on his heel without waiting for a response.

On the way to his den he detoured through the kitchen where he selected a large *amphora* of vintage red and a sparkling crystal goblet.

He avoided the velvet *torus* in the *sanctum* and slumped in the seat behind the ornate desk where he broke the seal on the *amphora* slowly and methodically filled the goblet to the brim. He sat and stared into space and waited for Dido to come charging through the door which she did less than two minutes later.

Her fists were clenched, her face was red and she was exceedingly exasperated and angry. She became even more irate when she saw that her father wasn't on the couch but was at his desk where she couldn't get close enough to thump him. Though she was on the verge of screaming an expletive she paused briefly and snarled an expanding onomatopoeic *"Grrr"* through gritted teeth whilst flailing and clenching her fists aggressively as she vented off.

Maximus slapped both palms on the desk top and told her to be quiet; that she had to see that it was *termino,* over. Period! Ciro City had fallen and she'd better leave right now before the enemy forces arrived or she'd end up in chains just like her stepsister Aprilis. He doubted that her brother-in-law Zeor would have much sympathy for her especially if he'd been made aware of what had recently happened to his wife.

She ground her teeth even harder and kicked the desk with her exclusive size eleven hand-stitched riding boots but Maximus ignored her and withdrew a compact gilded casket from a concealed alcove in the depths of the desk and told her that there was sufficient gold, gems and adornments to keep her in comfort for the rest of her life but to refrain from telling Sorus about the treasure.

It was only at this juncture that Dido realised that things had changed dramatically and immediately she knew that this was the last time that she'd see her father. She snatched the casket but stood deadly still for an instant and gazed directly into his eyes before she turned and fled from the room clutching the jewel box possessively to her chest.

From the same secret compartment in the desk Ballio Maximus collected the small glass *ampulla* which he hadn't touched since the death of his first wife Belvia more than thirty years ago. With the venom from the *Tres-dentus mus-anguis* and the full goblet of fine wine he moved to the plush velvet *torus* where he sat and then comfortably reclined.

An hour before Maximus had departed the mansion the Consul Primus ordered the heavy vine laden gate be moved to one side and he and his company of men exited from the underground passageway into Green Park and moved purposefully north. And as daylight broke through the gloom his infantry was less than a half mile from the rear of the capital's second inner defence line before the alarm was raised and at this point the Consul Primus ordered his standard be unfurled from the high building nearby.

As this was happening in the north side of the city, some three miles further south a twin-horse coach with two ladies on board sped past the night guard at the city's southern boundary without stopping. The coach headed west past the *Urbis Capitolium* road indicator. Both females were extremely nervous, with the older woman who'd been asked to escort and chaperone the lady Dido on the journey now fearing for her own safety because of the disturbing behaviour of her hysterical charge who'd plead to the Gods for protection from bandits on their drive to the Capitol in one breath and then in the next instant promise vividly explicit excisions and dissections of the most intimate body parts of her enemies both male and female, for having cruelly inconvenienced her wedding preparations but also for ruffling her exemplary and ladylike disposition which she believed she exuded to all and sundry, including mere plebeians. She announced that there were those who'd also vouch for her irreproachable and altruistic lifestyle and she was quite adamant that there was not one person in all Sitantal who could match her simple humility and anyone who'd say otherwise was a lying good-for-nothing *obtrectatio,* a detractor, and deserved public disgrace and inexorable punishment until the slander was recanted. The elderly minder now deeply regretted accepting the commission from the Governor and was busy planning how she'd avoid completing the journey with her scary ward.

The besieging army's Commander of operations on the northern plains saw the Consul Primus' colours billow aloft behind the enemy lines and immediately sprung into action. He signalled the *bucinator* and at the sound of the bugle all forty broad wheel-base double manned chariots swept wide from behind the assembled cavalry and infantry and raced forward and swung alongside the central wall of palisades where the operator behind the driver of the leading unit launched a three-pronged *lucitationis hamum.* The grappling hook was secured to the end of the sturdy rope attached to the chariot's solid chassis and snared the wooden structure and hauled it away, sending tufts of turf sky-wards in the process. The procedure was emulated by the next speeding unit behind.

During the thirty minutes exercise to brazenly purloin the spiky barriers in full sight of the enemy only minor injuries and hiccups were inflicted on the attacking forces. The raiding charioteers made no attempt to engage the enemy behind the barricades but concentrated their efforts on clearing a path through the defences and though some of the harnessing forays failed occasionally, eventually one whole expanse of palisades was cleared giving the Consul Primus' static infantry and cavalry access to the outer defensive line. A double *maniple* of infantry was met with strong resistance by the city defenders and the sound of steel on steel added to the enormous mix of human and mechanical sounds blasting across the valley as the Consul's men swarmed through the breach. When the field Commander saw a foothold had now been established he signalled the bugler again and when the series of staccato notes blared out all of the infantrymen on the flatlands in the northern combat zone struck their shields with their sword's pommel in sync with the *bucinator's* blare which added a new dimension to the battlefield's acoustics. In seconds the entire valley echoed to the rhythmic beat which resonated and reverberated much like the advancing march of an approaching legion. The echoing thunderous clamour was both awesome and fearsome to hear but more so to the *custodis* behind the barricades. Meanwhile further back and close to the populated outer urban area of the city the Consul together with his son and his company of archers attacked and chipped away at the rearguard defences and as they edged forward it became obvious that their confined opponents were beginning to crack and were getting close to desertion as the predicament they faced became more pressing and unnerving for them by the minute.

Above the cacophony of the battle a wavering trumpet note drifted through the discord and the Consul's own *cornicen* was able to tell him that it was the defenders calling for assistance from the forces in the eastern sector and immediately the Consul ordered Zeor junior and his archers to fall back to the eastern defensive points and prevent any *custodis* relief or realignment.

In tandem with the call for assistance from the northern sector the defending force there was well aware that their front line had been breached and that their foe was also behind them and getting nearer to them by the second and unless help came straight away they were finished. They were being

squeezed vicelike from both sides and from this critical position most of them could only see one escape route from the grip and that was to make a dash south where there were fewer opponents and less hardware to contend with as far as they could make out. As they weighed up their options the incessant *thump, thump, thump* tempo from the north loomed large and saturated the atmosphere around them and this was the catalyst which sparked the near collective mad rush for freedom.
The deserters abandoned most of their heavy arms and only wielded swords or *pugios* knowing for sure that a *dirigo* and its ammunition were of little use when they were in a flight rather than a fight for their lives. As the *custodis* in the vanguard became aware that their rearguard colleagues had abandoned their positions and left them perilously exposed on their south flank within seconds of this realisation the remaining lines began to break and fragment. The comrades in arms became cronies in retreat as they dispersed in every which way but north when they deserted the theatre of combat.

    As the Consul Primus and his men weaved from east to west and then back again neutralising the few rabid pockets of resistance they encountered they allowed the *custodis* who'd decided to flee from the conflict clear passage but only if they were unarmed, an action which had caused some irritation within the ranks until the leader explained that quite a few of these men had been coerced and conscripted into Maximus' or the usurpers columns by force or by other nefarious means and never had a desire for a military life. And he'd also wager that most of the men had no quarrel with him or with anyone else for that matter and would probably prefer to be with families or friends right now rather than being caught up in this internecine struggle between people they had little or no association with normally. It was no great surprise to him to see that they didn't have the stomach to die for something which they didn't really understand or believe in. He insisted that his men should focus on rounding up the leaders and less effort on the regular *custodis* unless they were deliberately engaged in actions that were posing a threat or if they wilfully tried to harm anybody or destroy property. If these *custodis* fled from here only to join forces with 'Pravus' Sorus then so be it but, he stressed, that he was sure that the desertions were a result of cowardice rather than a pre-arranged tactical move on their part and if his assumptions were correct then there was nothing for them to worry about because these men would still be afflicted with the lily-livered condition for the rest of their lives wherever they went.

As the morning progressed the Consul Primus surveyed the evolving scene and he was at a loss as to where Governor Maximus and his senior tier of command were as the city was being slowly squeezed into submission.

When both parts of the Consul's army regrouped in the northern sector now completely under their control he had the charioteers continue the task of removing the palisades and barriers scattered around the eastern and western perimeter and he commanded that they do it slowly and with care to avoid damaging the landing decks, esplanades, bridges and water features throughout the elegant and winsome city and to be careful not to frighten the local citizenry but if they were met with resistance to call in the cavalry and neutralise the threat.

Before noon virtually all resistance to the Consul Primus' forces in Ciro City ceased and a sizable portion of his infantry, cavalry and archers accompanied him and Zeor junior on the *Via Fons* towards the Governor's Mansion in the city centre. Elsewhere the core of the Consul's army escorted the *custodis* who'd surrendered during the battle to the barracks in the eastern sector of the capital. The procession included the Governor's advisory team, the *assessor protelum*, who'd been found hiding under one of the many ornate bridges in the northern suburbs bearing a collection of maps and diagrams of the city and each one of them contained a faint broken-line segment showing the location of the disused *cryptoporticus*.

During the Consul's journey through the capital's streets the residents cautiously exited their homes and some proffered drinks and food to the victorious army along the way.

There were no guards or security detail

outside the Governor's Mansion and the imposing building looked oddly gloomy and ineffectual even though it was embellished with potent statuary and symbols displaying its power and importance. An ancient liveried retainer warily emerged from the main entrance and apologised to the Consul Primus that Governor Ballio Maximus was indisposed indefinitely and that the palace was totally deserted but for him. He politely requested that the Consul accompany him inside where he would see for himself the nature of the Governor's indisposition.

As the Consul Primus followed the equerry through the eerily silent building he was informed that the lady Dido together with the housekeeper had fled the mansion for the Capitol very early that morning. When they reached the open door to Governor Ballio Maximus' personal sanctum near the rear of the building the Consul observed the lifeless body of his onetime father-in-law reposed on the deep-pile velvet *torus.* An empty crystal goblet and a tiny glass phial rested on the thick woven *stragulum* beside the couch and both vessels were empty. The Consul appraised the scene from the open doorway without entering the room and he dispatched the manservant to have his captain and four soldiers join him where he had the body of the deceased Governor removed, still on the *torus,* before sealing off the room. He commanded the captain to build the funeral pyre at the remotest part of the large grounds and said that he'd personally conduct the *exsequiae* rite at dusk.

The Consul had the elderly retainer invite the panic-stricken staff to return to duty where he assured them that the defeat and death of their Governor would not affect them in any way and invited them to attend the funeral ceremony to show their respect for their late leader.

While he and his son Zeor junior together with his most senior officers were in the process of taking up residence in the mansion the messenger from Abdo arrived with the letters from his wife and daughter and the report from Zeo. When the Consul learned that Ailia had assisted in the flight to safety from the Arx he insisted on hearing all she knew of the rescue first hand and pressed her to have refreshment with him before she departed. And when he heard that she planned to leave Ciro City in the morning to meet with Zeo and the others en route he penned a note lauding his son and the others for their success and he advised him that his army would rest for a week in the city before marching on the Capitol where he expected him and his three colleagues to be part of the force. Following the cremation rite for Maximus he and Zeor junior, although they still mourned the death of Camilla, toasted privately over *cena* all the positive things that had happened since that awful deed.

Later on both rode to the regional barracks together to celebrate the army's triumph which he'd determined they fully deserved for the restraint they'd shown when subjugating Ciro City.

CHAPTER FORTY-TWO

The combo wagon with Euander and Friday on the bench seat and Candeo alongside the drays, stopped behind the three horsemen when they reached the colonnaded viewing area below the Temple of the Gods to allow Adam and Johnny to have what they all believed would be their last chance to view the wonder again. They all dismounted and while the *Praecipuum* of Sitantal sat sipping their steaming coffee on the steps of the baldachin and remembered their amazing visit and feasted their eyes on the majestic pile and on the rays of colours surrounding it, Zeo and Euander speculated on when the civilians might return on pilgrimage to the revered place and hoped that it would happen soon. They moved on in fifteen minutes and within the hour they'd passed the burnt-out shell of the *Beneficiarius* out-station and all of them bowed their heads in remembrance of the *Vipera Dominam* and General Exer Savus and his men who'd died there three weeks prior.

The overhead hues had changed to ultramarine

blue when they made camp for the night on a grassy patch where they reverted to the quarterly night-watch rather than the double-man team they'd used on the initial inbound journey in the past.

Following breakfast at dawn the group continued northeast and through the cliff enclosed gorge without stopping until they reached the east end of the pilgrim's road, a place where'd they'd camped overnight on their way to the Temple of the Gods. They remembered admiring Merusa, the charming hamlet nearby with its few dwellings, inn and *caupona,* bakery, emporium, and a wheelwright with blacksmith, all set back from but parallel with the canal and marina.
Zeo remembered his friends' obvious chagrin when they'd given the place a miss the previous time they'd passed by and he rode alongside Euander and instructed him to drive into the hamlet and to call at the smithy and wheelwright and have the horses and wagons checked over while they dined. Adam and Johnny were about to guide their mounts past the short road into Merusa when Zeo beckoned them to follow him. Neither needed to be asked twice and the pair of friends smartly steered their horses to the right and were more than keen to experience what was on offer there. When the riders dismounted outside the inn Zeo asked Adam and Johnny to display their *Praecipuum* insignia prominently and to continue wearing their swords until they'd established

where the villagers' loyalty lay.

Euander steered the wagons into the wheelwrights' yard and instructed both men to check the shoes and all the wheels and to make whatever adjustments or repairs required, including his three colleagues' mounts, while they were at the inn. The avuncular crafts- man agreed to look after Friday whilst they were away.

They entered the *Caupona* together leaving behind several curious onlookers at the roadside marina.

Inside the large scrumptious smelling dining room mine host was gobsmacked and stood staring at the three men in black but he ignored Euander completely as if he was invisible to the naked eye.

Zeo stepped forward and introduced himself and then the others but it still took a few moments for the information to register with the innkeeper who remained gawking with his mouth hanging open until Zeo raised his voice and again requested a placement and food. As if he'd been stung by an angry bumblebee the landlord sprung forward and grasped Zeo's hand and shook it so much that Zeo had to prise it off in the end. He then bowed so deeply to Adam and Johnny that they both reckoned that he was on the verge of tilting over but he still ignored the fourth member of the team.

Zeo beckoned Euander to come close and re-introduced him; stressing that he was their *Optio* and stated that it appeared to him that the innkeeper hadn't heard him accurately and that must be the reason why he hadn't greeted his officer correctly. The abashed man blushed and acknowledged Euander with a respectful bow and then fussily guided them to a set of couches arranged around a broad low table opposite the bay window overlooking the marina and the undulating variegated landscape on the other side of the berth.

All four lounged on the upholstered chaise longue type divans and were barely settled in when a pretty young woman with lustrous blonde hair and bright blue eyes and a figure that any female would surely die for approached with four large silver tankards of sweet frothing *mulsum*. Johnny almost fell head over heels in love again, especially when she bowed her head and upper body ever so deeply to him and then to Adam who was also momentarily seduced by the revealing and agreeable act and both smiled appreciatively in thanks.

Though none of them had felt very hungry before stopping at the village the appetising aromas within the inn hit their olfaction receptors and now they felt ravenous, so much so, they all slugged at their tasty mead-like drinks to satisfy the needy pangs.

As they gazed absentmindedly through the window at the picturesque idyll beyond, their viewing was interrupted by a crowd of people, young and old, small and tall, staring curiously at them and most of the wide-eyed oglers nodded and waved excitedly when they saw that they'd got their attention.

Zeo rose and went outside and spoke briefly with the inquisitive observers and with that they dispersed grinning and nudging each other good humouredly and when he returned he told the others that he'd agreed that they'd all speak with them before they left the place provided they'd let them eat in peace.

The table was barely big enough for all the silver platters and bowls spread out in front of the four diners but what really impressed the two strangers most of all was the two large dishes in the centre. They were huge but so too were the roast boar and venison joints that were partially enclosed by golden brown pastry enclosing the lower part where they rested on the trays. A collection of glazed vegetables arranged in smaller dishes and what looked like a fricassee of various white meats in a large silver vessel were placed alongside numerous boats and bowls of diverse sauces and herbs. The largest and most ornate *amphora* of juicy red wine Adam and Johnny had ever seen since coming to Sitantal was placed on a smaller table between them together with four large cut crystal goblets. Mouth watering bouquets enticingly wafted around the *caupona* and without delaying the four diners tucked into the veritable banquet with a zest that was almost embarrassing to observe.

It was nearly two and a half hours later when the four friends rose from the divans, totally satiated and stuffed but they only stood up because the wheelwright had entered the inn and was approaching them rubbing his hands against his heavily stained leather apron and he looked decidedly perturbed.

He advised Zeo that each of the wagons had two split wheel spokes which would need replacing before they could safely continue on their journey even if it was only for a short distance and unfortunately both had differing axel hubs and so he couldn't make a swap from one wagon to the other nor did he stock spares for cargo *carrus* and would have to cut and shape the wood from scratch.

Zeo was told by the craftsman that the repair would take the rest of the afternoon and more but that he'd work late and continue again at dawn. He thought they'd be able to depart from Merusa before noon the following day.

When he explained the delay to the two non-vernacular speakers present their groans of dismay were somewhat contrived and bogus. The very idea of riding a horse for the rest of the afternoon across country wasn't something that appealed to the pair; in fact they'd quietly agreed and planned to join Euander on the wagon until their digestive systems had reduced the tension on their waistlines. Little did they know but their two native friends were also less than excited about the afternoon journey either. All of them had succumbed to the allure of gluttony and were now subject to the consequence.

After Zeo had secured rooms for the night all four emerged on the short street to be met by almost forty people waiting patiently to greet them including the villages' *praesum* who greeted them with such decorum and respect it almost verged on sycophancy but it was obvious to the guys that the crowd agreed with the chief's fervour.

It was clear to them that most of the settlements' inhabitants had been waiting all this time to meet them when they recognised a lot of faces which had been pressed against the window more than two hours ago and in a few minutes they were joined by a hoard of school children just released for the day. Heads were bowed, hands were wrung, backs were slapped and all the women and girls kissed the newcomers on the cheek, some even repeated the gestures more lustily until eventually Zeo held his hands up and called a halt to the show of affection.

It transpired that news of Zeo and his friends exploits had been borne here by the canal boatmen who plied their trade nationwide and picked up the latest gossip and news and for months now no craft had berthed at the marina without someone squeezing the latest developments from its crew and to have all three and the new member of their team come to their village was the greatest thing to ever happen here, or so the *praesum* declared.

Adam and Johnny could only be spectators within the excited throng and when word reached the mass that their four celebrity visitors would remain in the village overnight the chatter got even more excitable and animated but especially among the young women and girls who giggled and whispered to each other and almost all of them cast sidelong glances in their direction continually.

Zeo and Euander spent the rest of the afternoon entertaining the locals with selected tales of events since he'd returned to Sitantal with the *Praecipuus* and how they'd managed to defeat and confound 'Pravus' Sorus and his henchmen so far but the audience were also able to relay incidents which had happened elsewhere which he and the others were unaware of.

The village *praesum* informed the visitors that they could sleep soundly during the night, that he and the local militia would mount an all night watch around the settlement. He'd also arranged to have *musica, cantus et saltatus;* music, singing and dancing on the promenade later on to honour the occasion.

Adam had Zeo ask the innkeeper to send some leftovers to the wheelwright for Friday. The sound of music mixed with a buzz of excitement stirred the four from their quarters where they'd been resting for the past three hours and when they descended outside the inn Adam and Johnny were blown away by the gala laid on for them and everybody was robed in the most wonderful attire which Zeo told his friend was reserved for occasions of great importance. They were met with cheers of applause and heads were bowed as they were escorted to divans close to the orchestral stage where a low table had been arrayed with goblets and several decanters of wine together with dishes of cold meats, fruit, nuts and berries. The size of the assembled people had wowed them and was more than triple the number they'd met earlier and they'd assumed then that the crowd probably comprised the entire population of Merusa. It proved one thing to the visitors and that was that news travelled fast even in these remote areas and they'd also been told earlier that word had been dispatched near and far that the Temple of the Gods was again a safe destination for pilgrims.

The compact ensemble of musicians which comprised a selection of differing instruments, all string or trumpet like, some of which looked vaguely familiar to Adam and Johnny but others were completely new to them and both of them noticed that there wasn't even one percussion device in sight. This pleased Adam no end and though he'd inherited a piano in Lo Garrantraa he'd always detested them with a passion and felt that they produced only dead notes and he thought them anything but harmonious, and there were no drums either which he believed were more appropriate in a military setting.

Sweet flowing melodious sounds filled the evening air and when the miniature orchestra struck up a more brisk tempo a young man and woman appeared on a slightly raised dais and performed a sensuous and curlicue-like inspired dance similar to ballet but much more tactile and gratifying to the eye, Adam decided.

The next act to take the stage was a teenage girl and boy who sang a duet and when Adam and Johnny heard the words "*Te Amo*" they knew it was about love. Zeo whispered that the two were professing their love for each other but each singer believed that their fidelity and commitment was stronger than the other's.

As the music continued Zeo was approached by a portraitist to ask if they'd agree to be face sketched individually and when they all concurred he placed his stool and in a very short time he'd finished the charcoal images and had them append their names to each drawing. Both outsiders thought they were almost as good as black and white photographs so much so, Adam conferred briefly with Zeo and then rose and clasped the artist's hand and exclaimed *Euge!* which gained him loud applause from the entire audience and the musicians.

Later on the music pace changed again and here people paired off and danced but rarely came in contact with each other and in no time everyone was participating except for the old *patronae* and the young ladies in their care whom they kept a vigilant eye on. But this didn't stop the mentors imbibing a fair amount of the wine on offer and Adam and Johnny noticed that quite a few of those who were being chaperoned were avidly encouraging their minders to have some more.

Well into the gala all four visitors to Merusa were joined on their divans by four of the most charming young ladies in the crowd whilst their chaperones slept soundly nearby having succumbed to the allure of the vine.

As the dancing continued on the waterfront the four friends found themselves being gently coaxed away from the festivity and all of them were drawn by their partners down the short path which ended close to a fragrant pine coppice where the undergrowth was a mass of wild flowers and soft gentle ferns.

All four guys were starry-eyed and bushy-tailed when they arrived in the dining hall for *ientaculum* where they were met by the innkeeper who proudly pointed to their framed signature images and a sketch of Friday hanging in pride of place for all to see before he escorted them to the same spot near the bay window where they'd dined on the previous day. He adamantly refused any payment as did the wheelwright and blacksmith, all saying that it was an honour to be of service to them and that if they ever returned to Merusa the same would apply again.

A large crowd, almost as big as the past evening's party, were waiting at the end of the short road where the three horsemen and Euander turned east. The men and women, girls and boys, bowed, waved and cheered as the small procession passed and the four young ladies who'd taken part in the night tryst in the pine coppice fluttered their tear stained *sudariums* sad eyed but enthusiastically.

Further along the eastern road and before they would lose sight of Merusa, Zeo signalled to his companions and in unison all three riders did a perfect horse pirouette and saluted the still watching crowd whilst Euander hailed them by waving his slender whip aloft.

When Merusa was out of sight and just a pleasant memory for all of them they crossed the border into southern *Oriens* in the early afternoon where they rested and had their first coffee in more than twenty-four hours which Johnny and Adam reckoned was a milestone and a red letter moment for them and deserved to be duly noted somewhere as such. They moved after attending to the animals and just before dusk they reached the sheltered glade alongside the rambling, babbling stream where they'd made camp on their inland journey some weeks ago.

Following an early start in the morning by noon they'd reached the point where Euander encountered the irascible lady Dido who only wanted his horse and here all of them had a laugh at the memory. A few hours later they were met with genuine glee when they halted and dismounted beside the sparkling fountain in Sala village. The first thing Zeo did was to check out the reconstructed temple where he saw that a brand new brass bell now hung in its proper place. In minutes Varus, the village *praesum* appointed by Zeo on the prior visit, welcomed them and insisted they have refreshments and in a very short time a table was laid out with fresh crusty bread, cold meats and oodles of sweet *mulsum*. The elderly wrinkled lady in black whose distress had caught Zeo's attention when last here hobbled quickly across the square to meet them and when she heard that Suga Cazo and his gang had been eliminated she almost performed a whirl in delight but stopped in mid spin when she grasped the fact that the *Auguribus* had never returned to Sala and therefore must be dead she slumped to a seat and wept afresh.

While the *praesum* and Zeo sat and exchanged information Adam, Johnny and Friday wandered through the village once more as Euander prepared the horses for the road ahead.

Just like on the previous trip they made camp in a spinney they'd used in the past where Euander took first watch and towards the end of his duty a familiar perfume wafted in his direction but he didn't reach for his sword or issue a challenge to their special female agent and a good all rounder, Ailia as she approached him from the shadow of the trees. After he'd greeted her he roused the others and together they sat on a cluster of rocks inside the campsite where she told them that she had lots of news to tell them. But she waited until Zeo had read the messages from the Consul Primus and Zeor junior and as they waited Johnny brewed a full pot of coffee and when Ailia was offered a mug she accepted and uttered '*iucundus*' and continued sipping. Just then Zeo finished reading and remarked that Ailia liked the coffee taste and thought that it was interesting, and he added that before this was over most of Sitantal would be addicts to the stuff because of Johnny.

Zeo told his friends how his father had conquered vast areas of *Oriens* including Ciro City with the exception of the south of the province but a growing number of mayors and chiefs from the towns and villages in the southern regions were now flocking to the capital and pledging allegiance to his father. With obvious disappointment he told them that the one person whom he'd wanted to deal with personally, more than anybody else, Maximus had taken his own life and that Dido had fled to the Capitol. On learning of this positive development Johnny brewed another pot and all of them observed that the lady spy took the second helping with some relish though Johnny believed that she liked their company more than the coffee, or better still, maybe just him, he fantasised.

Zeo continued to quiz and debrief the girl until he felt that he'd extracted everything she'd heard and seen in her travels and when he offered her one of the sleeping bags for the night she declined saying that she must move on, that she had letters from his father and Zeor junior for Aprilis and Livia and urgent orders for General Electra which required a reply. She admitted that she was already running late having dallied too long sightseeing in Ciro City, but that it had been worth it.

They watched until she'd vanished behind the trees and when Euander declined more coffee and opted to turn in for the night Adam and Zeo remained with Johnny for the next hour discussing what they'd just learned where Zeo told them that his father planned to move on 'Pravus' Sorus in four days and wanted them to be with him. He estimated that they should reach Ciro City in about thirty-six hours where they could rest and join in the march on the Capitol.

At daylight they moved onwards and after a carefree journey through the sylvan lands of southern *Oriens* they were less than thirty miles from the provincial capital as the light began to fade. They mounted a double nigh-watch on the off chance that there could be remnants of the defeated *custodis* at large in the country-side and after an uneventful night they turned north and joined the road to Ciro City.

Though Adam and Johnny had been told by Zeo to expect a pleasing view when they reached the top of the hill they gasped in unison and Johnny whistled so loudly that a flock of tree roosting birds panicked and took to the sky in alarm.

Below in the valley nestled Ciro City in all its glory and glorious it really was to Adam's mind and it was the only city that he'd ever seen in his travels that came close to Venice in Italy but this place beat that precious gem by a long mile. It was stupendous and he was almost tempted to mimic his friend and whistle aloud. He believed he could spend the rest of his life just painting this view, over and over again, and absolutely nothing else because it was truly an artist's dream scene.

Johnny was almost as enraptured as his best mate appeared to be and though he realised that he was seeing it through less sophisticated eyes as him nonetheless he could see the beauty too.

Zeo edged his horse between them and remarked how quiet it looked since he'd last seen the place when he'd fled from there to *Extremus* and into *Terra Ferusum* on the advice of his treacherous and purportedly grandfather, Maximus.

They passed through several checkpoints en route to the Governor's Mansion without being delayed when they were told that they were expected. When they came to a halt in front of the entrance the liveried elderly retainer squinted quizzically from the door and then fussily dispatched a young aide inside the building.

Adam and Johnny had barely dismounted and were busy ogling the impressive palatial pile and gardens when the Consul Primus and Zeor junior dashed down the steps and the pair embraced Zeo and then both stepped back and scanned their S.W.A.T dressed son and brother from top to toe before the Consul dodged behind his younger son and stood rigidly in front of both *Praecipuum,* saluted and bowed and then embraced them firmly as one. This show of friendship and respect was immediately followed by a similar display from his son Zeor junior. The Consul then turned to Euander who'd remained at attention beside the wagons and horses and here he directed the retainer's aide to tend the animals and then beckoned the nervous teenager forward where they returned salutes. The leader extracted an Optio insignia from his pouch and attached the shining badge to his tunic and declared *'Bene factum!* Euander'

To have the Consul Primus *Hereditarius* recognise him by name and to confer his symbol of rank and seal of approval on him personally in the company of Zeor junior and Zeo together with the two *Praecipuum* of Sitantal, and to say to him 'Well done!' almost caused him to go weak at the knees with pride.

He only wished that his parents could see him now!

CHAPTER FORTY-THREE

When the lady Dido alighted from the coach clutching her ornate jewellery casket tightly under arm near the steps leading to the *Domus Magnus,* the attendant farrier was stabling a visiting Commander's mount and the two sentries were inside the guardroom reliving the fun from the previous night, well out of sight of the piazza. The lady was still in a foul mood having complained from early morning about the drivers handling of the coach and when he'd slowed the pace to make it less bouncy for her she'd moaned about his tardiness and the length of time it was taking to reach the Capitol, even blaming him for the checkpoint delays. She spun round and brusquely ordered the elderly female passenger to take her *sarcinae* to the Consul's apartment at once and to ensure she didn't keep her waiting.

Her temporary chaperone had developed painful jaw muscles in her effort to keep her mouth clamped shut for so long that she now felt that she was ready to explode and on the brink of losing the plot totally but she dug real deep and retained her composure until her charge had ascended the steps and had entered the building when she turned to the driver and asked if he intended to return to Ciro City right away and when he replied that he had no intention of staying here one minute longer than he had to, the aged woman mustered all her reserves and without due care dumped the baggage onto the paved sidewalk and sprightly hopped back into the coach calling out *'Abeamus!'*

The *let's go* command was barely out before the coach circled and was rapidly heading to the eastern exit from the piazza where the coach and two almost collided with a street cleaner's horse and cart as it entered the early morning and almost empty central city expanse. The cart driver's eyes lit up when he saw the abandoned pile ahead and he urged his ancient nag forward at a speed the animal hadn't achieved in years.

On duty on the first floor of the premier building the startled *factotum* didn't get a chance to announce the arrival of the lady Dido to his leader when she pushed him aside sardonically and flung the doors wide open with such a resounding crash it caused Sorus and the Commander he was conferring with to reach for their *pugios* and spring from their chairs in alarm.

Dido uttered a woeful screech and shot across the divide and launched herself tearfully on her still stunned husband-to-be while the equally shocked officer just gaped on in awe.

When Sorus had regained his wits and composure he indicated that the conference was over and the Commander hastily gathered his charts and papers and scuttled from the room showing little evidence of his lifelong military bearing.

Though 'Pravus' Sorus had been informed of the fall of *Oriens* almost two days after the disastrous event and had spent the intervening time recalling his forces from far-flung places and amassing them in the Capitol he hadn't yet heard the conclusion to the defeat and had only heard wild rumours but nothing concrete about the fate of Dido or Maximus.

He and Dido spent the rest of the morning in his private quarters where she'd raged about the loss of her entire wardrobe to the thieving chaperone and it was only when he was at the chamber door did he disclose to his lover that Aprilis had been rescued from the Arx by Zeo and his cronies but also that Puto Pollux had paid the ultimate price for his dereliction of duty for allowing it to happen, an unforgiveable deed in his mind, taking into account the fact that he had almost three hundred men guarding its only access point. And since then he'd learned that they'd escaped with the assistance of the very people they were supposed to guard against. As Dido gasped at this news and her lips began to pucker Sorus guessed that she was about to scream and throw a tantrum again or maybe worse, he closed the door firmly and headed quickly for the stairs. His pernicious streak was far from satiated and he looked forward to the evening when he'd break the news to her that Aprilis wasn't her half sister after all but had been abducted from *Terra Ferusum* a long time ago by her father and four conscripts who'd mysteriously failed to return from *Extremus* with him.

Sorus had only learnt of this while he'd waited in the anteroom at the *valetudinarium* to see Puto Pollux when a terminally ill man had told him something which had happened to him when he was a stable boy in the service of Ursus, the previous Governor of *Oriens.*

In his narrative he told the tale of being ordered to accompany Maximus and four young ensigns through *Primoris* to *Secundus* on a routine survey of the second and third regions of *Extremus.* He'd been ordered to return with their mounts in eight days hence which he'd dutifully done only to find that Commander Maximus had arrived carrying a little infant girl. There was no sign of his four companions anywhere in sight and he and Commander Maximus had returned to his villa with the four riderless horses. As he unsaddled the animals he'd heard him tell his wife Belvia that the infant was their new daughter and that the baby's name should be Aprilis. When he'd told his parents what had happened they'd insisted that he leave the capital and never return, that he could be in great danger. He'd moved to the Capitol under an assumed name but nonetheless he'd returned over the years to see his family surreptitiously when they were alive but never afterwards. He'd stressed that the only reason he was divulging this now was that he'd heard that Aprilis had perished in a fire at the Arx on the previous night and because he was near to death he believed that somebody should know the truth after so many years.

Sorus smirked maliciously where he sat behind his desk and he was already looking forward to that evening when he'd divulge this news to Dido. He was certain that she was unaware that Aprilis wasn't her half sister but a complete outsider which he was sure would make her furious to find out that she'd been duped by her father for so long and he remembered well from all their past trysts that Dido was at her very best when she was rattled about something and she'd invariably responded with unbridled energy and great passion. He fantasised that he and his *inamorata* would have a night to remember. But deep within his black soul the festering knot got tighter from the moment he'd learned that *Oriens* had been lost. And when she'd told him that her father had been preparing for *mors voluntaria* as she'd fled the capital it irked him when he felt that this defeat meant the dynamics of his grip on power had changed, big time!

Far away from there in Ciro City following *prandium* with the Consul Primus, Adam, Johnny, Zeo and the dog strolled down *Via Fons* where all the *emporia* were now open for business and a growing number of the city's population wandered around quite relaxed while others rushed about doing the things that one would normally see in any urban area, Adam observed. The Consul had been informed that the capital was now safe and that most people accepted the new circumstances they'd wakened up to the other morning and at this point Zeo explained that the schools had remained shut which would explain the squeals and high pitched chatter coming from every park they passed.

The three friends who were now attired in the native casual garb after the Consul had advised them to have their S.W.A.T gear detailed and freshened up. They would blend in with the locals more easily and then could see the city without being harassed because even here they were being spoken about as being amazing super heroes.

The three explored every aspect of the water oriented metropolis for almost six hours and on their way back to the Governor's Mansion they stopped at a colourful *taberna* where they had tankards of bitter *mulsum,* just for the road.

Zeo had taken great pride and satisfaction exploring the picture perfect surrounds of the capital with his two friends from afar when even Johnny had waxed lyrically on every-thing they viewed.

Meanwhile Euander had been seconded on the previous day by the Consul to train with a senior *Optio* to learn the various responsibilities and protocols which would be expected from an officer in his position.

It was the final day of furlough granted by the Consul to his victorious men but already preparations were under way with Zeor senior and junior gathered together with their Generals and Commanders and junior officers where they perused and studied charts and maps and inventoried supplies before they'd set off on the expected three day march to *Urbis Capitolium* the next day at first light.

'Pravus' Sorus and his *inamorata* Dido spent a highly charged and a crescendo scaling night in his apartment where the more he chided her, the more feral she became. During the sparse periods of quietude during these dark hours the few night staff on duty below stairs conferred *sotto voce* with some of them reduced to muffled giggles while others of a more reserved nature tut-tutted and shook their heads in disdain.

As the *Tempus Dico* mounted the steps outside the *Domus Magnus* to announce the new day he was momentarily distracted which, luckily, halted his progress further up the steps by an eardrum bursting screech coming from a partially open window on the second floor on the mansion ahead. The scream was instantly followed by the explosive sound of shattering glass and as he gawped upwards he was horrified to see and hear the blood-curdling screams of an almost naked blonde haired woman clutching a billowing cloth come arcing through the air from the broken window. The wailing woman landed with a sickening crunch just two steps up from where he stood rooted to the marble. The screams stopped when she hit the steps but the blood spatter reached his toecaps. For less than a couple of seconds he gazed on in shock then reached forward and folded the heavy maroon curtain across her shattered body. He turned abruptly and retraced his footsteps down the steps.

As the Time Teller exited the piazza on the north side the *Lanterna Extinctor* arrived from the south to extinguish the now redundant night lights.

For the first time in its long history, *Urbis Capitolium* went without its early morning call and in conjunction with that unique occasion the night lights remained glowing all day.

Meanwhile behind the grand facade panic had taken hold when the leader's personal *factotum* had fled for his life through its rear entrance but not before he'd given a blow-by- blow account to an edgy staff on what he'd witnessed just moments ago in his master's chamber.

The *factotum* had made his usual visit to the private apartment and while he'd been sorting things out in the anteroom the adjoining door was opened by Sorus and he was about to exit when he heard the lady Dido challenge him to return the key and her jewel box right now, that she'd seen him take them from under her head cushion when he thought she was asleep. Sorus bellowed that the treasury was virtually bare, that the annual collection of levies, tolls and tariffs were almost nonexistent and yet the costs kept rising every day because of the size of the army he'd been forced to maintain and that other channels of revenue had also dried up and now she'd have to play her part, after all, she'd promised him a coach full of treasure just a few weeks ago but had allowed the *nothus,* her so-called nephew, Zeo steal it from under her nose though she'd had a seven man protection escort at the time. The mention of Zeo's name had made her seethe afresh and she'd darted across the room to either hit Sorus or retrieve her gilded box, the *factotum* couldn't say for sure, but Sorus had remained still and when she came close he'd swung the steel box and had struck her on the temple. She'd slumped but before she'd reached the floor, Sorus had grabbed her and had charged to the window where he'd thrown her head first through the glass as she'd clutched onto the drapes in desperation.

The young man admitted that he'd raced from the chamber believing that he could be the next one to take a dive, him being the only witness to the heinous act and with these last remarks the once dependable *factotum* fled the house followed closely by all who'd heard the narration.

'Pravus' Sorus descended the stairs from his apartment in full combat gear and he wasn't at all surprised to see that the doorway to his office was unmanned and he made a mental note to have his *factotum* located and disposed off before the end of the day. The thought crossed his mind to seek out a replacement for Suga Cazo and his team as soon as he'd eliminated Zeor along with all his family and cronies. It galled him even more when he recalled that just six months ago this world was his plaything.

Though he called down the long corridor for assistance he didn't get a response and without entering his office he turned back to the stairwell and proceeded to the ground floor where he was met by one of his agents from Ciro City who confirmed that Governor Maximus had indeed committed suicide and that Zeor and his forces were preparing to march on the Capital within days.

The captain of the guard saluted and told his leader that his sentries had cleared the steps and that the attendant farrier had washed them clean whereupon Sorus reached into his pouch and handed the man a small golden bracelet and remarked that he give it to his wife or to his mistress, whomsoever deserved it the most. The confused officer stuttered his thanks as his thought process tried to collate and figure out how anybody, especially Sorus, knew of his covert dalliance when he hadn't breathed a word about it, ever!

The attendant farrier held the horse steady while the leader mounted but the handler avoided direct eye contact and though it was noted by Sorus he let it pass on this occasion but his patience might not extend into the future, he thought. More fool him Sorus thought when he'd planned to reward him for his effort on the steps with a token of jewellery. The irony of this display of largesse evaded Sorus completely where he distributed the very trinkets which Dido had sacrificed her life for and they were now being used to eradicate all evidence of how she'd died.

From the *Domus Magnus* the leader rode south to the main military barracks without escort, something he'd rarely done in the past but his mind was preoccupied with what had unfolded in his chambers earlier and he needed new space right now.

An odd thought struck him as he cantered along the street of how he'd loved Dido a lot but had never really liked her! He wondered briefly if others had ever felt the same way.

Sorus remained with his senior officers at the main barracks and in the early afternoon an agent arrived from *Oriens* and reported that Zeor's forces were preparing to march west to *Urbis Capitolium* two days from now and after learning this he ordered that new quarters be prepared for him on site, that he was moving command operations south with his new headquarter at the military base. Here he could monitor the preparations for war away from the stares of the ingrates in the Capitol. He dispatched a runner to inform the captain of the guard at *Domus Magnus* to close the house until he returned victorious after the final push to remove Zeor and his rabble army and his supporters from every corner of the country.

CHAPTER FORTY-FOUR

The Consul Primus with his sons together with Adam and Johnny and also his Generals and senior Commanders all gathered in line on the crest of the south gradient overlooking the impressive three miles long and two miles wide expanse of lush grasslands in the vale below them known as *Campus Concordia.*

Surrounded by thick forests on its eastern and western flanks the almost hallowed site was viewed as the epitome of peace and tranquillity by those who visited but that description couldn't apply now. The oblong basin which hosted along all of its perimeters countless images, effigies and statuary of heroes who'd existed in real time and others from the realms of fantasy and mythology and was the place where the Founding Members had met and had compiled the Statutes of Sitantal over two thousand years ago. The shallow vale was abuzz with regimented martial movement on a grand scale and was anything but peaceful or tranquil in appearance right now.

Two days ago when the Consul's scouts had reported that 'Pravus' Sorus had massed his forces in the extra special place the Consul was astounded and irked initially by the insensitive choice but on reflection he'd changed his mind and now thought that in fact it was a befitting location for the battle between good and evil.

Adam and Johnny remained seated in their saddles transfixed by the sight below them. The massed formations in the distance was something they'd only experienced on the big screen in the past but to witness it in real life and to know for sure that it was the real McCoy and that it definitely wasn't a setting that had been digitised, enhanced or magnified to artfully impress and blow them away was awesome and it was a sight they'd remember forever.

Every geometric shape and configuration imaginable was fluctuating and forming before their eyes as the assembled infantry and cavalry transformed and regrouped into a wholly new format time after time. Zeo steered his mount between his friends where he indicated and named each formation as it appeared in view. There was the Orb, then the Square, the Pig's head, the Wedge, the Octagon and the Testudo, an arrangement which the pair of newcomers had first encountered outside the prison in Tabo City some months ago. Zeo added that his father believed that the demonstration was deliberately staged, just for them and reckoned that 'Pravus' Sorus already knew that they'd arrived at the southern end of the battlefield designated by him. He was showing them just how powerful and organised his army was in comparison with theirs.

When Zeo rode off to join his father, Adam and Johnny dismounted and tethered their horses to a bush close by and allowed the animals to graze on the lush grass while they hunkered down near the crest and studied in detail the enemy camp below. Both agreed that they and the Consul's forces faced a formidable task ahead and they also concurred that the few gizmos they'd taken with them would need to be used selectively to make any impact on an army that looked to be almost twice the manpower as was the Consul's force.

On the previous night when they were camped in a deep, partially wooded valley miles away from where the enemy could observe them, Zeo had gathered all of their fighting men in a wide circle with his father and brother and all the senior officers together in the central space along with the cargo wagon containing the gear brought by them from *Terra Ferusum*. After explaining that what they were about to see might alarm them initially, they must realise that it wasn't necromancy or supernatural at all but was produced in another land using commonplace chemicals and such things and was virtually harmless, almost like a toy.

When the camp lanterns had been

doused or dimmed Adam and Johnny together with Euander shone the micro torches onto the trees behind which caused quite an excited buzz and debate among the gathering. The next piece of equipment introduced to them was the flamethrower which drew much louder gasps, squeals and *wows* but when Zeo lit up the night sky with a dazzling white flare the junior officers and *Optios* stationed at the back of the gathering had their work cut out to prevent a mass desertion from taking place while all the horses were corralled nearby to become accustomed to the unnatural scene.

The penultimate piece of equipment was the miniature diesel generating light tower. It had to be manhandled to the ground where Johnny set about raising the telescopic steel pole aloft and then he fiddled around with some wing nuts and buttons and the machine burst into life. He duly pressed another pad and a broad stretch of the woodlands was illuminated brighter even than daytime as the four separate light beams penetrated deeply and well beyond the outer tree line. This was met with more whoops and loud hollers of amazement. He lowered and raised the mast several times and adjusted the lamps until he'd been able to focus the beams further afield and leave the massed group around him in relative darkness which was something he'd need to achieve when the light tower would be deployed on the battlefield. Eventually he lowered the mast and with just one light beam directed on the cen-

tral area around which the men were thronged, Zeo advised that the last example of imported technology that they needed to see was the Taser Gun. He called on the two hefty looking volunteers who'd agreed earlier to be the fall guys for an equally hefty reward. Adam and Zeo aimed and fired the probes and the spectacle of the collapsing, quivering pair got an enormous but mixed response of *oohs* and *aahs* along with an unbelievable amount of giggles and raucous laughter from the now jovial crowd as they watched the two stooges writhe on the ground.
Before the soldiers dispersed large sections broke into applause and several called for an encore while others yelled that it was the best show they'd ever seen and when Zeo turned and approached the gathering in the centre he could see that the officers, which included his father and brother, were just as nonplussed and befuddled as the regular soldiers had been.

The Consul Primus' army spent the day doing manoeuvres while the engineers fortified their base camp. He and his advisers reviewed and presented the broad outline of the plans to Adam and Johnny through Zeo for the imminent attack on the enemy. All the suggestions the two *Praecipuum* made were taken up by the assembled military men with only one exception and that was merely about the size of the escort who'd protect them during the conflict and when the three friends adamantly refused to have any minders the Consul shrugged his shoulders and uttered *'Sic erit!'* So be it!

As one of only five *Optios* present in the *tententorium* Euander was totally rapt by the proceedings and when the meeting concluded the trio and Friday accompanied him to supervise the modifications being done to the four-wheel wagon they'd use in the pending assault. They watched on as the side and front panels were extended higher and hinged and almost three quarters of the roof was then covered with similar thick planking. Johnny secured the mobile lighting tower to the centre of the floor with its long telescopic pole protruding through the open space above.

The carpenters contrived several outward opening flaps on the front, rear and side panels and fitted storage boxes strategically where their gear would be visible and instantly accessible. And lastly a hinged set of broad wooden steps was attached to the rear of the wagon to deploy when in or out access was needed but could also be used as a protective barrier when raised.

When the revamped wagon was completed Adam and Johnny nodded and grinned but they were well satisfied with their improvised version of a battle tank. Zeo expressed his approval with his thumbs up and Euander could barely contain himself when he was told that he'd be the driver of the contraption.

During daylight hours numerous scouts patrolled the vast surrounds including the extensive forests with strict instructions to sound the alarm and return immediately should they spot any sudden change within the ranks of the opposing forces and the same degree of vigilance was maintained throughout the night.

Two hours before dawn the Consul's army assembled and stealthily descended from the higher ground onto the flat valley floor and moved cautiously north without being spotted until they were about three hundred yards from the Sorus encampment.

Before the enemy's *cornicen* had time to take a breather and repeat the high-pitched clarion call Euander swung the adapted four-horse wagon one hundred and eighty degrees which gave the three guys inside the walled up box their first close up glimpse of the enemy's lantern-lit tented garrison beyond.

Zeo and Adam stood at the rear of the wagon and in tandem both launched numerous flares; Bright white, red, and orange tracers shot skywards and burst directly above the campsite and even from their location the roars and shouts of terror coming from the camp in front were plainly audible and the multiple horn blasts venting from the base added to the discord.

Adam and Zeo halted the pyrotechnic extravaganza and joined Johnny where he waited patiently and peered through his night visions to monitor the progress of Zeor's infantry and cavalry and as they bore down on the camp from the gloom he could clearly see the scramble and confusion on the outskirts of the turbulent agitated compound. When they were within striking distance of the enemy he flooded the tented area with light. Immediately the main body of infantry charged into the disorganised base while the cavalry split into two separate sections with one section forking east and the second to the west. Meanwhile the Consul, who also viewed the initial infiltration through his night visions, signalled the trumpeter to alert the vanguard to disengage and return to the boundaries. Following the follow-up trumpet fanfare from the *tubicen,* his double-manned charioteers charged down the left and right flanks of the encampment smashing tents and huts indiscriminately resulting in flash fires and plumes of billowing smoke that almost neutered Johnny's artificial beams.

The speeding charioteers continued to the north end of the compound and then wheeled around and repeated the run, cutting swathes through a fresh batch of tents where *custodis* who'd managed to escape the wide careering wheels were invariably brought down by the chariots back-man's short *pili*. Consul Zeor charged his *Triarii* unit into the centre of the turmoil within the Sorus' army where they speared and hacked a broad pathway deep into the hordes of the bewildered and unprepared *custodis* where pockets of fighters responded to orders from their group leader and offered strong resistance but a sizeable proportion of enemy fighters cut and ran in every direction to escape the mayhem and carnage around them. The Consul's forces maintained the momentum onwards and the fight-back failed to halt their progress.

At dawn Johnny killed the generator and Zeo had Euander fetch the horses including his own and to leave Friday at the stables while they prepared to join the Consul Primus and while they waited he, Adam and Johnny loaded their belts, pockets and pouches with tear gas canisters and even smoke bombs though they could see that large sections of the usurpers' camp was now alight and veiled in smoke.
When they mounted their steeds they raced forward with swords in hand and into the chaotic and smouldering battle ground where they separated to minimise their target size but remained within sight of each other. All around them was evidence of wholesale death and traumatic injury and although the four had seen grim scenes before they grimaced at the macabre abattoir for man and beast they confronted. Adam almost retched at the scale and the enormity of some of the wounds that the fallen had suffered, some caused by the native weaponry exclusive to Sitantal, such as the *acus quattuor*, *iaculum* but the most repulsive lacerations were those that had been inflicted by the *globus filum*, where heads, arms and legs had been severed neatly from the *corpus*. If any of the riders witnessed unimaginable hopeless suffering he'd

dismount and administer the *coup de grâce,* certain that it was the merciful thing to do regardless whether it was a fallen soldier or horse. For almost ten minutes they carefully guided their mounts north through the debris and carnage without encountering active enemy and it was when they'd penetrated more than midway through the gory compound they spotted the solid wedge of the Consul's *Triarii* as the soldiers pushed on relentlessly some eighty feet in front of them though the clash of steel against steel had the causal effect of making the action appear to be much closer.

  Meanwhile on the right and left flanks of the battlefield the Consul's cavalry mounted sortie after sortie against the enemy' horsemen where they kept them penned in and steadily drove them further back into the camp and restricted their ability to break free and launch a counterattack. These troopers had been wrong-footed before daylight and had been unable to recover though they were by far the larger unit.

And on the northern approaches Zeor junior and his archers supported by the charioteers and several hundred infantry controlled the slope leading down on the Sorus encampment. Only the enemy deserters who'd managed to escape the charging charioteers and were unarmed and displayed the white token of surrender were spared when they were rounded up and secured with the cable ties donated to him by Johnny where already a large patch on the higher ground was littered with the trussed up prisoners of war.

On the south side Adam heard the agonised braying to his right and spotted the wounded colt between a cluster of collapsed and smouldering canvas where he instantly dismounted and weaved through the detritus and was within feet of the wounded animal when he failed to notice the pool of blood beneath the torn canvas. He lost his footing on the slippery gunge and fell backwards dropping his sword as he flailed about trying to correct his balance. Winded and embarrassed by his lapse of care he scrambled to get back on his feet before the other guys saw his ignominious blunder but he couldn't get a heel grip as he tried to gain leverage to push himself upright. As he searched about for dry ground he saw the sudden movement to one side and realised immediately he was in deep trouble when he saw the enemy markings on the tunic.

He fumbled vainly to reach a Taser gun as the *custodis* lunged forward with his blood stained *gladius* held low and when the attacker was mere feet from him he rolled to one side to avoid the blade.

Just then Friday appeared from behind and sprung with his teeth bared fully. The dog snarled and sank his fangs into the neck of the stumbling assailant and both dog and man sank to the floor with Friday's teeth still buried deep within the custodis' fleshy neck.

Adam was about to shout his appreciation and praise to his four-legged friend when he saw the tip of the blade poking through his dog's golden fur. His roar of outrage and pain echoed and transcended the battlefield din and was heard by many more than just Adam's three companions who were some distance away.

Zeo, Johnny and Euander gazed down in shock and sorrow as they witnessed their sobbing friend embrace Friday tightly in his arms, cheek by cheek; He tearfully cried out to his dying dog how sorry he was to have put him in harm's way.
Friday died just minutes later and Euander raced away and had the modified wagon brought to the edge of the battle ground where Adam gently laid the brave animal inside. He viewed his dead pet through tear-filled eyes and remembered telling him less than six months ago on Garrantraa Mountain that he should rightly be called 'Hero'

*

The bloody carnage on *Campus Concordia* continued throughout the morning and well into the afternoon and as the battlefield shrunk and the soldiers on both sides of the internecine conflict were weakening, the call went out that 'Pravus' Sorus had been captured hiding among the animal feedstuff near the remnants of his cavalry on the western flank. And as the word spread through the rank and file of the usurpers' *custodis* they began to abandon their weapons in droves and raise their empty hands and very shortly a white cloth was raised aloft by somebody in the middle of the throng.

When the resounding victory cheer echoed round the hallowed hollow the Consul Primus briefed the nearest General on what he wanted done and then rode south from the battlefield with his *Optio* and *signifer* who proudly flew the *viridis, album* and *russus* insignia even higher than before.

With his hands tied behind his back, 'Pravus' Sorus stood erect and sneered darkly when he was sentenced to death by the Consul Primus who was seated behind the long table near the southern end of *Campus Concordia* with his two sons on his right with Adam and Johnny seated to his left.

Adam had tried to keep his mind focused on the victorious and historic occasion but his thoughts had kept returning to Friday.

He'd been unaware that Johnny and Zeo had similarly struggled too.

As the condemned dictator was being led away to the scaffold he wrenched free from his escort momentarily and rushed to the table where he spat in Zeo's face.

*

In the late afternoon following the victory over 'Pravus' Sorus the Consul Primus *Hereditarius* led the small group to the northwest corner of *Campus Concordia* to the newly dug grave that would be Friday's final resting place.

Zeo had the camp carpenter construct an elegant wooden pallet earlier and now Adam, together with the three people who'd known Friday better than any other, supported the corners of the bier as they walked in step with the Consul and his elder son.

The restored leader had asserted that Friday had been a special creature and that he'd learned how he'd saved Zeo, Adam and Johnny on numerous occasions. And without this super animal there was a strong possibility that he and his entire family, but also Adam and Johnny, wouldn't be alive today but for him. He'd announced that when the country had returned to normality he'd have a monument erected in his honour equal to the grandest specimen that could be found on the perimeters of this memorable place and when the full story became known about this unique dog people would flock here in deference to him. His name and his achievements would be entered into the annals of Sitantal's history and Friday would be remembered as a true hero, forever.

At the newly dug grave the four pall bearers placed Friday to rest and before the soil was added Adam gently covered the cold body with his sweater and saluted the true friend who'd saved his life only six hours ago and though he tried his best to suppress his tears quite a few did manage to escape.

Talis est vita!

EPILOGUE

The Consul Primus *Hereditarius* had dispatched runners and messengers to the provincial capitals and large towns to deliver the news that the dictatorship had ended and that the usurper was dead. He'd also sent notes to Aprilis, Livia and *Matrona* Minula to tell them that it was safe to return home and he'd ordered General Electra to remain in *Australis* until he'd appointed new *Beneficiarius* to safeguard the Temple of the Gods. And finally he'd given orders to have *Domus Magnus* totally detailed and cleaned for his return in two days.

Before dusk the Consul officiated at the *exsequiae* rites at the many funeral pyres dotted across the headland to the south of the now tranquil vale to where the fallen from both sides of the conflict had been recovered but in contrast to this mark of respect for these fallen warriors, the body of 'Pravus' Sorus and the remains of the captured and then executed co-conspirators had been removed and disposed of deep in the depths of the forest well away from *Campus Concordia*.

Two days following the defeat of Sorus and the end of his tyranny Adam, Johnny and Euander rode alongside the Consul Primus and his two sons in triumphal procession through *Urbis Capitolium* where they were greeted by vast crowds and banner bedecked streets and buildings all the way to *Domus Magnus* where Aprilis and Livia waited at the grand entrance to the mansion, at the place where Porcia now ruled supreme as its new housekeeper to the first family.

The glittering, sumptuous banquet was the most colourful affair imaginable and Adam and Johnny were given pride of place at the top table. They received accolades and tributes which were accompanied by much table thumping and toasting from the Consul Primus, the Governor of *Australis* General Arrol, the *Pater Antistes* and other seemingly notable personages they'd never heard of before. Zeo did his best to keep them posted on what was being said but to make matters even more complex Aprilis, who had occupied her time since her release from captivity browsing the *Promptorium Parvulorum,* now believed that she was as proficient as Zeo in the English language and continually plied Adam with remarks and questions which made little sense to him at all.

On the morning following the banquet Johnny and Adam left Zeo with his father and brother together with city officials and advisers where the gathering perused the scribbled notes from the *Vipera Domina* Semele, in which she'd named the culprits who'd condemned her and her companions to a life of degradation and torture under Reptus Reptum.

The pair wandered around the imposing Capitol and though Adam had wakened feeling empty and despondent Johnny's irrepressible enthusiasm and the broad linear streets with their vast monumental buildings gradually shifted his mood to a less melancholic plane. The solid structures were interspersed with numerous *emporia* that were arrayed with the most eye-pleasing goods and produce imaginable which distracted Adam even more and when they eventually rejoined Zeo in the late afternoon he was waiting to tell them that his father was appointing him Governor of *Occidens* and his brother Zeor junior Governor of *Oriens* but the Consul had agreed that he could accompany Adam and Johnny on a tour of Sitantal before that would happen.

Three months had passed when the three friends returned to the Capitol from their country-wide tour where the Consul had Zeo ask them if they wished to remain in Sitantal or return home; the decision was for Adam and Johnny and them alone, to make.

Adam was bowled over when Johnny replied that he was now ready to depart and it took him a few seconds before he responded that he too would leave for Lo Garrantraa.

On their final night in *Urbis Capitolium* a banquet was hosted by the Consul to honour the *Praecipuum* but when the party ended and Adam and Johnny rose to go to their apartments Zeo steered them into an anteroom and away from the departing throng of guests.

He assured solemnly that the warning he was imparting to them had come directly from the Gods.

Surface Earth was on the brink of the most destructive and cruel conflict in the history of the planet and when this looming war commenced all access to Sitantal would be closed and be sealed off forever.

If they needed refuge they'd have to avail of the proposition before that time but they'd need to remember that they could never, ever, return to *Terra Ferusum* again.

VIPERA DOMINA

Printed in Great Britain
by Amazon